Revolution 2016
Take Back America

A Political Satire Thriller

Lee Boyland

and

Vista Boyland

Revolution 2016: Take Back America

Copyright © 2014 James L. and Vista E. Boyland

ISBN 978-1-62646-865-8

Published by BookLocker.com, Inc., Bradenton, Florida.

Printed in the United States of America.

This is a work of fiction. Other than events and places identified, names, characters, incidents, and places are products of the authors' imagination, or are used fictitiously. Any resemblance between actual events, locations, or persons living or dead is purely coincidental.

BookLocker.com, Inc.
First published January, 2014

First Edition

© Cover design by Lee Boyland, featuring the Revolutionary War Gadsden flag
© Authors photograph by Vista Boyland

Cataloging Data
1. Benghazi—Fiction. 2. Terrorism—Fiction. 3. Technothriller—Fiction. 4. Political Satire— Fiction. 5. International relations—Fiction. 6. FEMA Corps—Fiction. 7. Middle East—Fiction. 8. Baghdad—fiction. 9. Iran—fiction. 10. Militias—fiction. 11. Second Amendment—fiction. 12. Gun laws—fiction 13. Contemporary fiction

Novels by Lee and Vista Boyland

Revolution 2016

Clash-of-Civilizations Trilogy

The Rings of Allah

Behold, an Ashen Horse

America Reborn

OAS Series

Pirates and Cartels

http://www.LeeBoylandBooks.com

The Bill of Rights

Amendment II

A well regulated Militia,
being necessary to the security of a free State,
the right of the people to keep and bear Arms,
shall not be infringed.

Amendment IV

The right of the people to be secure in their persons,
houses, papers, and effects, against unreasonable
searches and seizures, shall not be violated, and no
Warrants shall issue, but upon probable cause,
supported by Oath and affirmation, and particularly
describing the place to be searched, and the persons or
things to be seized.

Military Officer's Oath

I, (state your name), having been appointed a (rank) in the United States (branch of service), do solemnly swear (or affirm) that I will support and defend the Constitution of the United States against all enemies, foreign and domestic; that I will bear true faith and allegiance to the same; that I take this obligation freely, without any mental reservation or purpose of evasion; and that I will well and faithfully discharge the office upon which I am about to enter. So help me God.

Military Enlisted Oath

I, (state your name), do solemnly swear (or affirm) that I will support and defend the Constitution of the United States against all enemies, foreign and domestic; that I will bear true faith and allegiance to the same; and that I will obey the orders of the President of the United States and the orders of the officers appointed over me, according to regulations and the Uniform Code of Military Justice. So help me God.

This book is dedicated to

*Ambassador Stevens, Glen Doherty, Sean Smith
and Tyrone Woods killed in Benghazi*

and

*The crew, passengers and Bart,
killed in Afghanistan on a CH-47 helicopter,
Call sign Extortion 17*

Author's Foreword

The story told in *Revolution 2016* has been rattling around in my head for several years. A story of events I was afraid could occur. In the spring of 2013 I realized it was time to write the story because events were beginning to happen. Vista and I stopped work on our second OAS series novel, and began writing this story.

We started out to write a political thriller, but as more events occurred as the story progressed, it became a satire—a political satire thriller.

The story is based upon infringement of the First and Second Amendments to our Constitution; progressive-liberals' obsession with gun control; the oath our military takes to defend the Constitution; and zero tolerance.

Court rulings and unconstitutional laws have slowly eroded freedoms guaranteed by our Constitution. Patriots have had enough and are starting to push back. Can the progressive tide be turned back? *Revolution 2016* is the story of how patriots set about doing just that.

We want to thank all of those who helped bring this story to life by proof reading, offering suggestions and providing encouragement. Special thanks to our readers, Less Merritt, Joe Oblack, Holly Vellekoop, and Michael Mullins. Any mistakes are the authors and no one else.

Lee and Vista Boyland
Near Cape Canaveral, Florida

Main Characters

U.S. Government

<u>Executive Branch</u>

Barrington "Barry" Abomba: president of the United States
John Blabberman: vice president of the United States
John Barnerman: director, Central Intelligence Agency
Victoria "Vickie" Barrett: special advisor to President Abomba
Jay Schpinmeister: White House press secretary
Gene Haggler: secretary of defense
Edison Helder: U.S. attorney general
Jerome Heinz: secretary of state
Jane Incompentado: secretary of homeland security
Colonel Virgil Savage: FEMA Corps (Blue Shirts)

<u>U.S. Congress</u>

Nellie Balogni: U.S. Congresswoman from California; Speaker
Betty Boxnutter: U.S. Senator from California
Carlos Crux: U.S. Senator from Texas
Senator Dana Finkelstein: U.S. Senator from California
Harold Realdick: U.S. Senator from Nevada; Senate President

<u>U.S. Military</u>

Major General Anthony Beck: U.S. Army, chief of staff CENTCOM

General Garry Lackiemann: U.S.AF, commander, NORTHCOM
Colonel Rebecca Collins: U.S. Army, CENTCOM
General Sampson Doughberry: U.S. Amy, commander CENTCOM
General Robert Dumpsterson: U.S. Army, chairman of the Joint Chiefs of Staff
Captain Tom Hazzard: U.S. Navy, commander SEAL Team 6
Brigadier General Charles Roberts: USMC, CENTCOM
Colonel Harold "Rocky" Rockford: U.S. Army, DELTA
Brigadier General John Ulrich: USAF, CENTCOM
Colonel Charles Vickers: U.S. Army, MP commander, Baghdad, Iraq

States

<u>Alabama</u>

Lieutenant Colonel Able: U.S. Army, National Guard
Sheriff Barringer
Robert Bowden: mayor, Mudford
Colonel Harry Callahan: Highway Patrol
Lieutenant Bale: Highway Patrol
Major General Jones: U.S. Army, adjutant general
James Todd: governor

<u>Arkansas</u>

Constance Butterworth: Tommy's teacher
Eleanor Hamm: Tommy's principal
Betty Randall: Tommy's mother
John Randall: Tommy's father
Tommy Randall: student

<u>Colorado</u>

Arthur Bartow: U.S. Army E7, retired, Colorado Militia
Orville Bartow: U.S. Army E7, retired, Colorado Militia
Colonel Bob NLN: U.S. Army (DELTA) retired, commander of Colorado
    Militia
Brian Ebert: attorney for Colorado Militia
Robert Hickengooper: governor
Sergeant Lee Jenkins: sniper, U.S. Army, retired, Colorado Militia
Pat Jenkins: Lee's wife
Jeb Justice: CBS Channel 4 reporter
Major General Clay Morrison: U.S. Army, Adjutant General
Rex: German Shepherd dog
Alphonso Zapata: attorney general

<u>Kansas</u>

Imam Ali: Muslim cleric
Mrs. Baxter: Susie's teacher
David Connors: Chairman, Shawnee School Board
Reverend Holmes: pastor
Julie Murray: Susie's mother
Susie Murray: schoolgirl
Tom Murray: Susie's father
Zackary Murray: Susie's grandfather
Harry Rogers: superintendent of Schools

Ms. Upton: Susie's principal

Oklahoma

Veronica LeGrunge: chief judge, U.S. District Court for the Western District of Oklahoma
Richard Knuckle: ACLU
Allan Sowash: CAIR

Vermont

Colonel McGill: National Guard
John Wilson: governor

Constitutionalists

Lieutenant Colonel Albert East: U.S. Army, retired; former Congressman

Race-Baiters

Tobias Dullston: Reverend, activist, National Kinetic Organization
Joseph Scoundrell: Reverend, activist, Spectrum Shove Coalition

News Media

Linda Adjetivo: Central News Network anchor
Glenn Deck: host, radio talk show and TV show
Sean Haddley: host, radio talk show and TV show
Doug Kellett: host, Radio Talk Show
Rusty Limbo: host, radio talk show and TV show
William O'Rippley: host, The O'Rippley Quotient

Islamists

Ali: Hezbollah, Chicago
Hakeem: Hezbollah, Chicago
Ibrahim: Hezbollah, Denver
Hamid Khomeini: Grand Ayatollah, Iran
Wael el-Kordi: The Egyptian
Marwan: Hezbollah, Denver
Muqtada al-Sadr: Mahdi Army
Sayeed: Hezbollah, Chicago

Prologue

The 2014 U.S. elections are a month away and Democrats plot to win control of the House and Senate. If they succeed, progressive-liberals will be free to unleash all the pent up legislation they have been trying to impose on America for decades. They will complete the transformation of America. Transform America into, into what? Yes, that is the question—*Into what?*

Election 2014: Sunset of the Great American Experiment,

A prelude chapter to *Revolution 2016* was released as a free Kindle book on Amazon, and is included as the remainder of the prologue.

The White House
Washington, DC
October 11, 2014

Victoria Barrett stood beside President Abomba in his small private office, which was actually a small, combined study-dining area, only accessible through one of the four doors in the Oval Office. Scrutinizing the other three members of the president's inner-inner circle enjoying a second round of cocktails before dinner, Barrett was mentally reviewing her master plan. *The 2014 elections are three weeks away. Tonight's the final strategy and planning session, and if we keep the Senate and win the House, this will be America's last election—a fact two of them really don't need to know.* Amused by the thought, she smiled. *Assuming a win, we have forty-six months to take control of the country. Plenty of time if we follow the Obsidians' plan, but my main problem is keeping Senator Betty Boxnutter and Representative Nellie Balogni, two important players in the plan, from giving the game plan away. Even though they don't know all the details, they both talk too much. The Obsidians are worried about maintaining secrecy, and their mastermind, a billionaire financier, is concerned about being able to control Abomba's ego. Oh, well ... that's why I get paid the big bucks,* Barrett snickered.

Edison Helder, the U.S. attorney general, who was standing close enough to hear her laugh, asked, "What's so funny, Vickie?"

Barrett gave Helder a knowing smile, "Just thinking about how much fun we'll have after we take control of the government."

"Yeah, guns first ... that'll be the ball-buster. Once we have the guns—"

"We'll own the country," the president said, finishing his AG's sentence.

"No ... no we won't," Helder responded. "We won't have the country till you replace all the four star military commanders with men or women loyal to you."

Barrett nodded, "Ed's right. So far we've replaced 198 senior officers and it's time to finish the job. CENTCOM is the key command."

"Good idea," the president said sticking out his chin. "As soon as I finish my last round of campaign speeches, the First Lady and I are leaving for Hawaii. We plan to stay there through Thanksgiving. While I'm gone, prepare a list of the commanders I need to replace, along with a list of recommended replacements. I'll give you my choices when I return."

California's Senator Dana Finkelstein approached the group in time to hear Barrett's last statement and the president's reply. "Barry, don't announce any changes before the November elections. I suggest waiting until December. Assuming we take the House and keep the Senate, replacing commanders before we introduce gun control legislation in January will shake up the military and establish your absolute authority. They won't dare object.

"We expect the Second Amendment gun-nuts to resist, and you'll need the military to suppress them."

"Yeah, you're right," the president responded, "and I have Jane Incompentado quietly staffing my police force. She says they'll be ready to enforce the new laws once they become effective in 2016."

"Oh, I didn't know she was that far along. Where's she hiding them?" Finkelstein asked.

"Dana, Homeland Security is a huge agency," Barrett answered before the president could reply, not wanting the senator to learn all her plans. "We're considering expanding the Federal Police to include a military element." There was no reason for Finkelstein to know the president's version of Iran's Republican Guard was being formed as a secret component of FEMA's Blue Shirts—something only she, Abomba and Helder needed to know.

During dinner, Senator Harry Realdick praised Barrett's idea of delaying the unpleasant provisions of The Universal Health Care Act until

January. Various provisions of the law effected different segments of the population, so Barrett's plan called for phasing in one provision at a time. After the first segment of the population was forced to accept the new regulations, the next segment would be regulated and brought to heel. The plan was designed to minimize the act's impact on upcoming elections and it appeared to be working.

Barrett steered the dinner conversation, making sure Finkelstein and Realdick didn't learn too much. Only Abomba and Helder knew about the Obsidian Group, and only Barrett knew its members' identities. The Obsidians' mastermind was obsessed with managing events and taking down small governments. Now moving into the big leagues, his next target was the United States. Establishing and controlling a world government was the Obsidians' ultimate goal.

Abomba knew the Obsidians managed his career, and as their representative, Barrett was the final authority in the White House.

After dinner, Helder, Finkelstein and Realdick departed and the president retired to his private quarters. Barrett went to her office to call Mayor Rom Cristo in Chicago to check on the status of the special voter drives—another name for illegal voters. According to Rom the teams of community organizers were almost finished recording the names on all the tombstones in every major cemetery in Illinois. Other teams around the state were transferring the tombstone names to 3 x 5 cards, and adding phony addresses. Illegal aliens could use the information on the cards to register and vote at polling places. Rom ended their conversation by saying he liked to think of voting illegals as proxies for those citizens who were no longer able to travel to polling places. As Barrett hung up, a sudden amusing thought prompted her to laugh. *Yes, Zombies would frighten voters—even if they were all Democrats.*

A call to Congresswoman Dee Dee Vasherfrau in Florida's 23rd District proved equally assuring. According to Dee Dee, similar plans were being implemented in south Florida. On Election Day, busloads of newly documented proxy voters would arrive at polling places ready to vote for Democrats. Dee Dee assured her they could expect a 150 percent voter turnout—Democrat voters of course.

Calls to other swing states resulted in similar assurances.

Barrett's last call was to the head of the Obsidians. After listening to her report, the billionaire ended the call with his usual curt command, "Make sure *nothing* goes wrong."

The Lodge at Pebble Beach
Pebble Beach, CA
Friday, October 31, 2014

President Abomba made the 32-foot putt, and then, mugging true to form for the cameras, lifted his right leg high with the knee bent and hopped around the green on his left foot yelling, "*Yeah! ... Yeah!*" like a schoolboy. Then, having finished his five-hour round of golf—one of 190 plus he'd played in the last five and a half years—he tossed his putter to his caddy and sauntered toward the lodge.

Having enjoyed a working vacation at the famous lodge for the last week, Abomba had found time—despite his busy schedule—for four more rounds of golf. After spending four days lolling round the pool, the First Lady had become bored and gone shopping in San Francisco, leaving the First Kids in the care of four Secret Service agents. With the president's huge entourage taking over the entire lodge, FLOTUS figured there was little chance of danger befalling them. Special arrangements had been made for the dog, Beau, who was to be walked three times a day, served a strictly organic diet, and kept in his own quarters. The president couldn't stand having him in the same room with him—unless, of course, photographs were being taken.

Senate President Harold Realdick, Senator Dana Finkelstein, Senator Betty Boxnutter, and future Speaker of the House Nellie Balogni were waiting to greet Abomba in the 19th Hole lounge. Vickie Barnett had been riding herd on the group, making sure they stayed on script. She was concerned about all the reporters who were skulking around. When Abomba finally strolled in they all jumped to their feet to greet him.

Completely ignoring everyone standing for him like he was royalty—for in his mind he was—the president went straight to the bar. Grabbing a *Yuengling* from an ice bucket on the counter, and jutting his chin out to assume a pose he'd copied from Benito Mussolini; he turned around and finally deigned to acknowledge the group's presence by nodding in their direction.

"Oh, Barry, after five hours on the course, you should be exhausted, but you look *wonderful*," Nellie Balogni gushed. "Thank you *so much* for campaigning for me ... and ... well really, for all of us. The voters worship you, and your efforts ensured us another victory."

Realdick, Finkelstein, and Boxnutter voiced their concurrence.

Flopping in a nearby chair and propping his feet on a coffee table, Abomba nodded. *Yeah, it's true. The voters do worship me, and well they should after all the wide screen TVs, cell phones and food stamps I've given them. As for these fawning fools—my useful idiots—I'll have to put up with them for now, even if they do annoy the First Lady.*

While it was true the president had campaigned hard for his inner group of politicos, the truth was he loved fund raising and giving speeches—especially ones where he used his teleprompter: something he depended on, even when speaking to school children. By using the electronic visual text device, he didn't have to look down at notes, could eyeball the crowd, and to his delight, strike his favorite Mussolini poses for the press. Under-informed audiences were awed by the idea he'd memorized his speeches.

Abomba had thoroughly enjoyed himself while campaigning in Las Vegas, Los Angeles, San Diego, Oakland and San Francisco. Best of all, he'd been able to squeeze in several rounds of golf at the most exclusive courses on the West Coast. Now that he was wrapping up his trip, he was beginning to feel exhausted and desperately in need of a vacation. It had been almost a month since his last one.

Sunday morning a Marine helicopter would fly him and the First Family to the Oakland International Airport, where they'd board Air Force One for the flight to Hawaii, and the president's much needed monthly vacation. The First Kids whined to their mother over leaving Beau. They wanted him to go with them. "Ask your father," the First Lady told them, "It's his call if the dog goes with us or flies solo." Disheartened when their father refused, they perked up when the president said, "Don't worry, the Secret Service'll bring him on another plane."

Once the First Family was airborne Sunday morning on Air Force One, Abomba felt positive he would be sufficiently recovered from this week's ordeal to give a rousing pre-election speech on Monday, November 3rd. Smiling to himself before falling asleep in one of the big bird's luxurious leather recliners, he gloated, *According to Rom, the election's in the bag. Now all I have to do is let Vickie run the show, and I'll reap the rewards.*

Plantation Estate on Kailua Bay
Oahu, Hawaii
Sunday afternoon, November 2, 2014

The First Lady stepped out of the limousine, looked over the palatial mansion with its manicured grounds, and finally smiled. "Barry, it's good to be back in our regular vacation house." Gesturing toward the palatial mansion where they'd been forced to vacation the previous two years, she continued, "That horrible place we had to stay the last two times was almost unbearable. Not at all up to my standards." Gesturing toward her regular vacation house, FLOTUS continued, "The owner knew we usually vacationed in Hawaii for Thanksgiving or Christmas. Yet the SOB rented *my* house to someone else. Twice! He rented it to someone else *twice*. Well this time, I called him and made it clear I wanted *my* house. I told him I'd have his guts for garters, if I didn't get *my* house this time."

"Huh, what was that you said ... 'Guts for'—what? Where'd you get that expression?" POTUS asked FLOTUS who ignored him. "Well, I guess what you said must've worked, 'cause here were are again, and everything's the way you like it—even if he did raise the rent to $28,000 per week. But, hey! Who worries about stuff like that? We aren't paying for it. *Yeah, that's true, but wait a minute. That gives me an idea. Maybe I'll have the IRS seize the mansion for our personal use ... Make it a presidential retreat, like Camp David ... Hmmm, I'll have to give that some thought.*

"I'm glad this makes you happy, Hon," he said giving the First Lady a buss on the cheek, "but tell me ... where *did* you get that expression? "

"I think it's something the people in England used to say," The First Lady replied, bestowing a rare smile on her husband. I'm not sure what it means ... heard it used in a BBC TV program. Sounded bad, so I used it. Guess it is bad, 'cause it worked," she shrugged.

"Ask Vickie, she'll know what it means. She knows everything."

"Is she coming?"

"Nah. She's minding the store. She may fly out after the election, provided we have a big win. Guess we'll probably have a bunch of guests, once the results are announced."

"*No way,*" FLOTUS hissed, her eyes flashing and her mood suddenly sullen. I don't wanna be bothered by your hangers-on. After all I've done for them, you'd think they'd leave me alone."

Deciding he was in a no-win discussion, Abomba changed the subject, "Let's go for a swim before dinner."

Early Monday morning found President Abomba standing before an array of TV cameras and reporters. His address to the nation would begin at 7 a.m., and he planned to wow the people on the eve of the election. At 6:59, a voice in Abomba's earbud began counting down, and he assumed his favorite pose. Preparing to speak, he stared into the camera's lens and waited for the red light to come on.

Across the nation, viewers saw President Abomba bathed in the morning sunlight, standing erect, with the Punchbowl National Memorial Cemetery of the Pacific providing a dramatic backdrop. Rows of white crosses, reflecting the morning sun, stretched to the northwest toward Pearl Harbor and the Pacific Ocean.

"Aloha from the beautiful island of Oahu," the president began. "Behind me is the Punchbowl, the final resting place for many of our military killed during the Pearl Harbor attack and the war in the Pacific. I can't think of a more fitting place from which to honor the heroic men and women serving in our military today.

"Tomorrow is a day when citizens exercise their most precious right—the right vote—and I call on every man and woman to do so ..."

Abomba rambled on, praising the military's sacrifices, and then, enumerating all of his successes: taking credit for killing the world's number one terrorist; and unashamedly pointing out how he'd righted the ship of state, after the previous captain nearly capsized it. More important, he boasted of how he'd rebuilt America's image in the world, stating he alone was responsible for setting the stage for international peace.

Nearing the end of his address, the president bragged about how he'd personally taken command and solved America's healthcare problems, and then began his closing remarks.

"Yet, while I have made remarkable progress, my work is not yet finished ... In order to complete ... the transformation of America ... into the nation of my vision ... I need a House and Senate ... filled with men and women ... that share my vision ... A vision of a tolerant nation ... with social justice for all.

"A nation where people can marry ... whom they choose ... Dress how they choose ... Live where they choose.

"That is my vision ... a nation ... with health care for all.

"A nation ... that will be a shining example ... for the world.

"Remember, vote tomorrow.

"Aloha."

With the exception of FOX, the major and minor networks hung on the president's every word, amplifying and enhancing his statements. Problems with the Universal Health Care Act forgotten, news anchors did everything but bow to Abomba—and that, of course, would come later.

The president spent the remainder of the day on the golf course.

Plantation Estate on Kailua Bay
Oahu, Hawaii
Tuesday afternoon, November 4, 2014

The president and his chief of staff were watching early election returns on NBC. Abomba was ecstatic. Polls in the Eastern Time Zone had just closed and the excited TV announcer was proclaiming a sweeping victory for Democrats. Exit polls in the central time zones were also projecting a Democrat sweep of the House and Senate. In Chicago Democrats were projected to win all the seats in state and federal elections. "YEEHA!" the president yelled, "Switch to FOX, I wanna listen to them cry," he told his aide, while laughing so hard tears ran down his cheeks.

FOX had declared most of the Democrat candidates in the eastern time zone winners, and the announcer was saying, "Based upon exit polls, it looks like a total Democrat sweep in Illinois and Ohio. If the trend continues, Democrats will control both the House and Senate. We're projecting Democrats taking Massachusetts, Connecticut, New Jersey, New York, Maryland, Virginia, North Carolina, Florida, Illinois, Indiana, Missouri, Michigan, and Minnesota. Maine, New Hampshire, Vermont, Pennsylvania, West Virginia, South Carolina, Georgia, Alabama, Mississippi, Louisiana, Arkansas, and Oklahoma are still too close to call, but none of them look good for Republicans.

"President Abomba's delays and changes to the Universal Health Care Act, coupled with his increases in welfare and amnesty for undocumented immigrants seem to have tipped the scales in his favor. Going into the election, the President's popularity was over sixty-seven percent and rising." Looking solemnly into the lens, the announcer said, "It looks very bad for Conservatives."

Whooping and jumping up, Abomba yelled, "I GOTTA CALL VICKIE. Looks like we've won," he added, dancing a jig around the room.

"Now I can complete the transformation of America."

"*Patriotism means to stand by the country. It does not mean to stand by the president or any other public official, save exactly to the degree in which he himself stands by the country. It is patriotic to support him insofar as he efficiently serves the country. It is unpatriotic not to oppose him to the exact extent that by inefficiency or otherwise he fails in his duty to stand by the country. In either event, it is unpatriotic not to tell the truth, whether about the president or anyone else.*"

– Theodore Roosevelt

"*As democracy is perfected, the office of the President represents, more and more closely, the inner soul of the people. On some great and glorious day, the plain folks of the land will reach their heart's desire at last and the White House will be occupied by a downright fool and complete narcissistic moron.*"

– H.L. Mencken

2014

Chapter 1

The O'Rippley Quotient
FOX Studios, New York, NY
November 10, 2014

William **O'Rippley opened his nightly show** with his usual talking points memo: a disturbing exposé on curious events in cemeteries in and around Chicago; and issues related to new federal gun control legislation.

After introducing his first guest, the show's producer, and sometimes roving reporter, Jeffrey Waters, who appeared on the split screen next to him, O'Rippley began his first segment by saying, "Welcome Jeff. In the past your roving reports have not only been enlightening, but also very entertaining. That's why I can't wait to hear how you found out about the curious happenings in Chicago's cemeteries, and what your investigation uncovered. Please tell our viewers about these miraculous headstones you discovered while on location in the Windy City."

"Well Bill, I recently started receiving numerous e-mail messages alleging voter fraud in and around Chicago during the November fourth election. One message contained several photos of headstones and suggested I should hurry to Chicago the following Sunday morning to video headstones in several cemeteries—a map showing the cemeteries' locations was attached.

"Our team arrived at the first cemetery at seven o'clock Sunday morning and was met, as you will see, with quite a spectacle," Waters said, setting up the clip viewers were about to see.

Two seconds later, after the split screen had segued to a wide-angle view of a large cemetery with row after row of headstones, O'Rippley said, "So—I don't get it Jeff … what's the big deal, where's the spectacle? All I see are headstones marked with what look like identical stickers."

"Wait for it Bill … Get a load of what the stickers say … here it comes," Jeff said, as the camera slowly zoomed in on a headstone and filled the screen with the image of a six-by-six inch, royal blue sticker. Placed just above the name of the deceased, the sticker's bright red lettering read, **'I VOTED.'**

"*What did I tell you* … was that spectacular or not?" Jeff asked, when he and O'Rippley reappeared on the split screen.

"*WHOA!* O'Rippley declared, his face morphing from surprise into a grin, "Did every sticker say the same thing?"

"Yep, they sure did, and that wasn't the end of it," Jeff said, when O'Rippley's split screen disappeared and was replaced with images of more headstones. "Here's what our cameras recorded at the second cemetery— same stickers saying the exact same thing on every headstone—just like the first cemetery.

"Now here we are entering the third cemetery. As you can see, the scene at third cemetery was a repeat of what we recorded at the first two. Since we'd encountered no resistance to our filming, we decided to press on to the fourth.

"However, as you will see, the situation there was different," Jeff said as O'Rippley's face reappeared on the split screen.

"What happened there?" O'Rippley asked.

"Apparently someone in authority got wind of what we were doing and decided to put a stop to it. Because as we were approaching the fourth cemetery's gated entrance, I noticed a patrol car parked on the side of the road. Sensing things were about to get dicey, I directed Andy, our cameraman, to start filming through the vehicle's windshield. And when we roll this next clip you'll see it was a good thing I did," he said, when the split screen showed the patrol car whipping away from the curb and stopping sideways in the middle of the street.

"If you listen carefully to the audio you can hear me instructing Andy to keep the camera on the officer and record what he says."

The viewers watched as the scene unfolded.

"Sir, I'll have to ask you to turn off your camera," the officer said, approaching the driver's side of the car and holding his hand up in front of the camera's lens. "The cemetery is closed. Please turn around and leave immediately."

"Why is the cemetery closed, officer?" Jeff asked.

"Sir, this is police business. Please turn around and leave."

"Officer, we're journalists with FOX News. Can you tell us why the cemetery is closed?" Jeff asked.

"We received a bomb threat, and we're waiting for SWAT and the Bomb Squad. Now I must insist you leave for your own safety."

"Officer, we received a report alleging voter fraud related to messages placed on some of the cemetery's headstones. Can you confirm this report?"

Now visibly angry, the police officer pointed back down the road and told the driver, "Sir, I'm ordering you to leave the area immediately. Failure to do so will result in your arrest."

The video faded, and once again Jeff and Bill appeared on the split screens. "Well, Jeff, I guess the 'I VOTED' sticker *could* be classified as a bomb ... a political bomb."

"How about an IPB, an improvised political bomb?" Jeff joked, prompting O'Rippley to join him in a hearty laugh.

Now serious, O'Rippley looked into the camera and said, "Voting headstones may be funny, but voter fraud isn't. Accusations of voter fraud are serious, especially in a national election. Charges of election fraud are sweeping the nation. Take Florida for example. Colonel Albert East was defeated in his bid to win back his old House seat. Some precincts reported voter turnout ranging from 115 percent to 182 percent." Shaking his head, O'Rippley said, "Must be the new math. I always thought 100 percent voter turnout meant every registered voter had voted. East naturally protested, and the election supervisor, a Democrat, denied his request for a recount."

Jeff shook his head. "Just like the last election."

O'Rippley agreed.

After the commercial break, O'Rippley introduced his new guest, Senator Carlos Crux, Republican, Texas. "Senator, thank you for finding time to be on my show. Let's get right to the issue. Homeland Security's purchase of 1.8 billion rounds of ammunition, and three thousand reconditioned, mine-resistant ambush-protected (MRAP) armored personnel carriers last year caused quite a fuss. Now we've learned that the department is acquiring two thousand Bradley Fighting Vehicles, several thousand SAWs, squad assault weapons—light machine guns—and is considering acquiring shoulder launched anti-tank rockets.

"What is Secretary Incompentado up to?"

"Bill, this is a troubling issue. The secretary has refused to answer questions and hasn't responded to a letter from myself and ten other senators.

"Even more troubling is the new lexicon being distributed by the White House. Veterans with any type of disability are now being referred to as potential terrorists."

O'Rippley grimaced as Crux continued, "Veterans who have defended our liberty are now being targeted. All veteran organizations are being placed on the attorney general's watch list.

"Many of our citizens now think that Senator Finkelstein's gun legislation will be the precursor to gun confiscation.

"Senator, are we about to lose our Republic?"

Senator Crux frowned and looked into the camera. "Bill, I'm afraid Senator Finkelstein's gun control legislation will pass. The President and the progressive-liberals in both houses have no respect for our Constitution and plan to totally ignore the Second Amendment. Two quotes attributed to Thomas Jefferson come to mind: 'Those who hammer their guns into plows will plow for those who do not,' and, 'When the people fear their government, there is tyranny. When the government fears the people, there is liberty.' "

Chapter 2

General Sampson Doughberry, the U.S. Army's newest four star general, gloated as he swung his short, chubby legs out of the limo and hurried toward his aircraft, a C-37 Gulfstream 550. Having just left the White House where the president had expressed his confidence in him, Doughberry had a new assignment and he was pumped.

It's gratifying to work with a President and an administration that recognizes ability and loyalty. I've worked hard to implement the President's policies. Now that he's rewarded me by appointing me commander of Central Command, I must continue to serve him by following his directives—the first of which is to assert myself, Doughberry grunted as he propelled his pudgy frame up the plane's boarding stairs. *I must immediately take command and leave no doubt that I'm the new boss.*

Nodding a greeting to his traveling companion and executive officer, Colonel Rebecca Collins, Doughberry settled back into one of the Gulfstream's luxurious leather seats and waited for the plane to take off.

"Well, m'dear we're off to Tampa," he said, cocking his baldhead to the side and grinning suggestively at Collins. "Time to take the bull by its horns and jerk those CENTCOM asshole commanders in line with the President's agenda," he postured, sitting up straight with what he deemed was a look of steely-eyed determination.

Usually quiet and observant, Collins commented, "Need I remind you Sam m'dear, they're *your* assholes now? How about a drink to celebrate?" The colonel, a fine looking woman of thirty-seven years, was not only the general's closest advisor, but also his sometimes lover.

CENTCOM
MacDill AFB
Tampa, Florida
17 December 2014

Major **General Anthony Beck, CENTCOM's chief of staff** sat brooding at his desk. He'd just been informed the new commanding general was en route from the airfield, when two brigadier generals—commanders of two subcommands—walked into his office. *Here we go again,* he sighed, assessing the overall gloomy mood of the pair. *From the perturbed looks on their faces they're no more eager to meet another new commanding officer than I am.* "Good morning gentlemen."

"Good morning, sir," Charlie Roberts and John Ulrich both replied.

"We've been through this before. You know the drill. I sent you General Doughberry's official biography, so you know what I know." Standing, he continued, "Let's go meet and greet our new boss."

Beck led them down the hall and into the commanding general's conference room, where they found two senior officers already waiting. Seated at the far end of the long conference table, with their heads together and obviously in deep conversation, Navy Captain George Hubbard, representing the 5th Fleet, and Vice Admiral Theodor Hass, CENTCOM's vice commander looked up when Beck entered.

Looks like they're as conflicted as I am over getting another new boss, Beck observed, noting each man's sour expression, as he walked the length of the table, chose a chair facing them and nodded a greeting. Both men only shook their heads and shrugged, so he directed his attention to other arriving staff members. All of whom seemed equally out of sorts and less than happy about being there.

Noticing Charlie Roberts looking longingly at the empty serving table where coffee and doughnuts were usually available, Beck suppressed the urge to smile. *That figures,* he thought. *Marines are always hungry ... or thirsty ... and John and the others are looking down the table wondering why there's no agenda.* Stifling his disgust, he gazed out the window behind the vice commander and brooded over the latest turn of events.

What a way to make a first impression. Doughberry made no effort to coordinate his arrival with me or follow any change of command protocol. Beck shook his head, *I couldn't even publish an agenda, because I had no idea what he planned to say or do. Seems to me he wanted it that way: either that or he's following the President's orders. Everyone is apprehensive over meeting yet another new CENTCOM commander—and well they should be.*

Beck frowned. *After all, any one of us could be reassigned or retired with no notice—take what happened to our last commander, General Scott, USMC. He'd only been in command six months when President Abomba sacked him. I think Scott must have known what was coming, because he asked me to accompany him when the President summoned him to present CENTCOM's final report on what Abomba referred to as, "that unfortunate Benghazi incident." Scott wanted me there as a witness, because he knew he could trust me to tell the straight of what occurred.* Beck continued frowning, remembering how the commander had stalwartly refused to use the accepted terminology by referring to the incident as "workplace violence." Instead he'd summed up his report by saying, "Well, with all due respect Mr. President, I'm of the opinion that reducing the embassy's security force by half actually invited the jihadis' attack."

"YOU ARE … are you? Well … THAT WILL BE ALL," the president had stormed, giving Scott a vindictive look. "I'll expect your letter of resignation on my desk within the hour."

It took courage for Scott to take that position—especially in light of the fact that Abomba had replaced three previous CENTCOM commanders and four International Security Assistance Force commanders over the past four and a half years."

Turning his attention to the other officers, Beck studied the worried expressions on their faces and their body language. While some attempted to appear relaxed, others were anxiously fidgeting. *They all know the score … never in the history of the United States military has a Commander in Chief changed so many four star commanders during a war.* Beck had just decided to keep that thought to himself, when CENTCOM's new commander entered the room.

Everyone stood as General Doughberry, a baldheaded, forty-four-year-old, overweight man of medium height, with a noticeable paunch and pasty complexion, walked to the empty chair at the head of the table. "I'm your new commanding officer, General Sampson Doughberry," he announced, scowling and plunking his aluminum briefcase on the table.

"Be seated," he barked, and then, making a show of taking his seat, unsnapped his briefcase, whipped out a brown leather portfolio, and set the case on the floor beside him.

So that's the way it's going to be, Beck decided, surprised by the general's less than healthy looking physique and arrogant behavior. He was, however, intrigued by the attractive female Army colonel accompanying him.

He's a real piece of work, but who's his lovely companion? Beck wondered, watching the woman pick up a chair, and after placing it a few feet behind the general, take a seat and cross her shapely legs. *Hmmm ... now there's some nice eye candy. Wonder who she is and why Doughberry hasn't introduced her. Okay, now she's taking a notebook out of her briefcase. She must be his executive officer.*

Brigadier General Charles Roberts, a Marine with three combat commands in Iraq and Afghanistan as a platoon leader, company commander, and brigade commander had also notice the woman and wondered the same thing. *Either she's his assistant or ... Oh, no—no woman that lovely would*—Roberts swallowed hard, quickly dismissing the revolting image he'd had of the colonel doing the bald headed little general. Deciding instead to concentrate on what he knew about the man, he reviewed Doughberry's undistinguished military career.

What in God's name is the President thinking? Roberts asked himself, comparing Doughberry's experience—or rather his lack there of— to the other men in the room. *According to my sources he was nothing but a staff officer who'd never held a combat command or accomplished anything noteworthy other than vigorously embracing and implementing the current administration's gays in the military policy. And what else did they say? Oh, yeah ... then he became an outspoken advocate of women in combat assignments. After that he'd attracted President Barry Abomba's attention, and his star rose like a ground based interceptor missile launched from its silo. First, Secretary of Defense Haggler deep selected him for major general, and not long after that for lieutenant general. Then, the President appointed him CENTCOM'S new commander, and the little weenie got his fourth star.*

What a farce. Every general officer and colonel in the room has more experience than this guy. Roberts caught himself before he shook his head. *He's completely lacking in command presence. There's something about him that reminds me of Looney Tunes' cartoon character, Elmer Fudd— baldhead, pudgy cheeks and nasally voice.* Roberts suppressed the urge to laugh and allowed his gaze to sweep the table. *I can tell by the mixture of blank and apprehensive expressions, they're all as perplexed as I am. But I've gotta hand it to pokerfaced Beck. He's been through this so many times he's perfected the art of disguising his emotions. Take the way he's pretending to study his notebook. Power to him, but it's this kind of bullshit that makes me wonder what the hell has happened to our country.*

Roberts, who'd just returned from Afghanistan, where things had gone from bad to worse to horrible, had been deeply disillusioned by his Commander in Chief's decision to pull troops out of the conflict. Less than 20,000 non-combat U.S. military personnel remained and they were—though no one dared admit it—prisoners in their own camps. Once troop levels fell below 50,000, President Hamid Karzai had openly expressed his hatred of America and branded the remaining troops infidels—thereby placing a target on every man and woman's back in the country. Green on blue attacks had become so common they were no longer reported. Roberts was also disturbed by the growing unrest at home. The divide between conservatives and progressive-liberals was so wide it had become a gulf. Roberts sensed the United States was a volcano preparing to erupt.

Sitting next to Roberts, and mirroring his concern over growing unrest in America, was Brigadier General John Ulrich, a graduate of the Air Force Academy and resident of Colorado Springs. Last year his state had passed draconian gun control measures, similar to the ones proposed by the senior U.S. senator from California. While gun control bills had failed in the U.S. House of Representatives, the newly elected Congress would be seated in seventeen days, giving Democrats a majority in both houses. Ulrich expected federal gun control legislation to pass and be signed into law in the coming year.

Soon after Colorado's gun control legislation passed, dire warnings about the dangers of bringing a firearm into the state were issued by several sportsmen's television programs and hunting magazines. Magpul, a Colorado manufacturer of magazines for rifles, immediately announced it was relocating to another state. HIvIZ quickly follow suit. Out-of-state hunters opted to hunt in other states, and TV programs filmed in Colorado quickly relocated to friendlier states, taking with them high paying jobs. Still the progressive-liberals demanded even stricter gun regulations. *Many gun owners are refusing to register their weapons, and the governor is threatening to send the state police to seize unregistered guns. If he does, I fear there'll be bloodshed.*

Ulrich had no doubt the ultimate goal was total gun confiscation. *If the government attempts to confiscate citizens' guns there'll be a revolution—a civil war between progressive-liberals and Constitutionalists ... Americans killing Americans—*A sickening prospect that sent a chill down the general's spine.

General Doughberry's twangy voice interrupted his thoughts.

"Gentlemen, before traveling to Tampa to take command, I met with President Abomba, Secretary of Defense Gene Haggler, and Secretary of

Homeland Security Jane Incompentado. The President and his secretaries are concerned about the increasing terrorist tendencies of right-wing groups." General Doughberry's announcement caused everyone but the vice commander to stare at him in consternation.

What the hell's this all about ... what right-wing groups is he talking about? Beck wondered, struggling to maintain a blank expression as he wrote "right-wing groups" in his notebook.

"The President expects to see domestic violence once Senator Finkelstein's three gun control bills are passed. The senator will introduce her first bill in three weeks, and identical bills will be introduced in the House by Speaker Nellie Balogni," Doughberry continued, speaking rapidly and oblivious to his staff's incredulous expressions. "I've been ordered to prepare plans to support Northern Command, NORTHCOM, and Homeland Security in putting down the expected terrorist riots.

"Secretary of Defense Haggler has directed the Army and Marine Corps to implement training programs based upon FM 3-39.40, Internment and Resettlement Operations, which as you know have provisions for controlling civil unrest.

"DHS is preparing plans to counter a possible civil war." Doughberry paused, suddenly annoyed by the looks of shock and revulsion on the faces staring at him.

"Is there a PROBLEM?" he demanded, abruptly standing and placing his hands on his hips.

Several awkward seconds passed during which no one replied. All were too flabbergasted to comment on orders they considered bordering on being illegal. Finally General Beck said, "Excuse me, sir, but what about the Posse Comitatus Act? It restricts military forces from performing domestic law enforcement duties."

Sitting down again and jerking his chair forward, Doughberry turned abruptly and scowled at Beck. "The Posse Comitatus Act became law in 1878," he sneered. "It's been amended several times and expanded since 9/11. Today it's outdated—like the Second Amendment."

A collective silent gasp went around the room.

Ignoring his staff's response, Doughberry shuffled some papers in his folder. Then leaning back in his chair and glaring around the table he continued. "Now, as to my previous statement regarding the President's concerns over civil unrest, let me review some history.

"Federal troops have been used to quell disturbances several times in the last century. President Eisenhower federalized the Arkansas National

Guard and sent troops from the 101st Airborne Division to Little Rock, Arkansas on September 24, 1957.

"President John F. Kennedy federalized the Alabama National Guard to enforce desegregation at the University of Alabama in 1963.

"More recently, Operation POWER GEYSER, a secret counterterrorism program, has a commando force of 13,000 troops—troops who've been used to protect presidents during the last three inaugurations.

"Based on POWER GEYSER, Attorney General Helder has ruled that the President can expand the force to deal with large-scale domestic terrorism, and his orders are exempted from the act.

"The AG has placed Evangelical Christians, Catholics, Mormons and Orthodox Jews on the same level with Hamas, al-Qaeda and the Ku Klux Klan.

"CENTCOM will provide the necessary men, women and equipment to support NORTHCOM and Homeland Security in maintaining order.

"Are there *anymore* questions or comments?" Doughberry concluded, standing and flipping his leather folder shut.

No one offered any objection, for all knew doing so would end their career. Standing they watched their new commander strut from the room,

My new boss is partially correct, Beck thought as he returned to his office. *Eisenhower and Kennedy were upholding the Constitution. Enforcing unconstitutional laws is a different matter.*

"This year will go down in history. For the first time, a civilized nation has full gun registration. Our streets will be safer, our police more efficient, and the world will follow our lead into the future!"

– Adolph Hitler, 1935

"Foolish liberals who are trying to read the Second Amendment out of the Constitution by claiming it's not an individual right or that it's too much of a public safety hazard don't see the danger in the big picture. They're courting disaster by encouraging others to use the same means to eliminate portions of the constitution they don't like"

– Alan Dershowitz

2015

Chapter 3

Friday, January 9, 2015
Breaking News

Central News Network's anchor Linda Adjetivo interrupted the show's usual dribble with a news alert. Wide-eyed and breathless, she excitedly reported, "We have just learned that Senator Dana Finkelstein and Congresswoman Dee Dee Vasherfrau have introduced identical gun control bills in the Senate and House of Representatives. Now we'll have the tools to end gun violence in America.

"Walt Twister will have complete details at five o'clock."

So excited she almost crossed herself and uttered *Santa Madre de Dios*, Linda blushed and caught herself just in time.

Topeka, KS
Monday, January 12, 2015

Susie Murray, wearing a black *abaya* under her heavy winter coat, stepped off her school bus, shouldered her backpack and headed up the driveway toward her house. Walking around back and entering through the laundry room door, she dropped her backpack on the floor, hung up her coat, and snickering softly to herself, pulled her matching black *niqab*, a head-cover with an eye slit, down over her face. *Mom's gonna love this,* she grinned, pushing open the kitchen's swinging door.

In the kitchen Susie's mother, Julie, was standing at the counter preparing an afterschool snack. When she heard the bus stop out front, and then someone opening the back door, she naturally assumed it was her daughter.

"Susie, is that you?" she called over her shoulder. "I made your favorite snack. Wash your hands," she said turning around holding a plate of freshly baked chocolate chip cookies. "And pour yourself a glass of mi—*YIKES!*" she screamed as the kitchen door swung open and a black-shrouded figure seemed to float into the room. *"WHAT IN HEAVEN'S NAME?"* she exclaimed, stumbling backwards and nearly spilling the cookies.

"Who-who are you ... w-what do you want? Julie asked, her voice trembling.

"*MOM ...* Susie squealed, "*IT'S ME!*" she laughed, twirling around, "Isn't this totally *awesome*?"

"*Susie, that wasn't funny. You almost scared me to death.* What in the world is that awful thing you have on ... why are you wearing it—and how can you even see to walk in it?" Julie asked, leaning over to peer at her daughter's eyes through the slit in the head covering.

"It's called an *abaya*," Susie giggled, "a dress that Muslim women wear. And this is a *niqab*," she said removing the head-cover from her face.

Biting her upper lip to calm herself, Julie placed the cookie plate on the counter, turned to face her daughter and frowned. "Susie Murray, I don't think this is the least bit amusing, and I want to know where you got that dreadful thing."

"Mrs. Baxter, my social studies teacher, gave it to me today, and I don't think it's dreadful at all. I think it's cool, and so do the other girls in my class. We all got one, because we're studying Islam. Mrs. Baxter said we must wear Muslim clothing while we're learning about the Prophet Muhammad and Allah. She's allowed us to bring them home today to show our parents. We got prayer rugs too," Susie chirped, "but we have to leave them at school, and we're going to kneel on them to pray to Allah just like Muslims. Allah is the Muslim's name for God. Don't you see how wonderfully spiritual it all is? We're even going to learn how to use prayer beads."

Feeling there was something terribly wrong about all this but not knowing what to say, Julie shook her head in disbelief. Finally she said, "Susie, take that—whatever that is—off and I'll pour you a glass of milk. You can tell me what you've learned after you've finished your snack."

Julie, an on-again, off-again churchgoer, remembered enough about her childhood Sunday School classes to know the God of the Bible clearly said, "Thou shall have no other Gods before me," and she was troubled. *I know nothing about Islam and Muslims, but I don't think this is something our daughter should be studying in school—at least not the way it's being presented. Yet Julie seems so eager to learn, so I'm not sure what, if anything, I should do about this?* she fretted, while Susie devoured four cookies and gulped down a glass of milk.

"Those cookies were great Mom," Susie said placing her empty glass in the sink.

"I'm glad you liked them. Now tell me what you learned today.

"Well, Mrs. Baxter says Islam is a beautiful peaceful religion—the only true religion and Allah is the only true God. The Prophet Muhammad founded it a long time ago, after Allah had the angel Gabriel tell him the true biblical stories. Then Muhammad recited them to his people. So, Mrs. Baxter says that means the Qur'an, which records Muhammad's recitations, is the true word of God; because, since God revealed his word directly to Muhammad, he was Allah's—God's—last prophet."

Muhammad is Allah's, God's last prophet, Julie frowned. Raised as a Baptist and instilled with the Biblical doctrine that there is no other God but *Yahweh*, Julie felt a chill run down her spine. *What's going on here?* she wondered, shocked at what she was hearing. *I've got a vague idea who Muhammad was, and I've heard the name Allah. I've even seen Muslim women wearing strange clothing on television and in Kansas City—but Islam being the true religion?*

"What else did Mrs. Baxter teach you?"

"Well," Susie continued, "She said Muhammad was a great man, a man who brought peace to Arabia, and then the whole world. Islam is the religion of peace, and following the Prophet's example is the way to paradise, heaven.

"Like I told you Mom, Muslims are very spiritual. They pray five times a day. Mom, we hardly ever pray. Islam is cool and I can't wait to learn more about it."

Smiling at her daughter, Julie Murray swallowed hard. Attempting to put a good face on something that troubled her deeply, she said, "Susie, I'm sorry I raised my voice to you earlier, but you did frighten me. I'm glad though that you're so eager to learn something new. However I think we need to share this with Dad and our pastor to hear what they have to say about it—especially your wearing that whatever-you-call-it."

"An *abaya*, Mom," Susie said, rolling her eyes and scooping up the garment. "I'd better go hang this up so it doesn't wrinkle and then get on my homework. What's for dinner?" she asked flitting out of the kitchen.

"Pizza, and it's just us. Dad won't be home till tomorrow evening."

During and after dinner Julie continued to worry about her discussion with Susie. Since Susie's Dad, Tom, was away on a business trip, she couldn't share her concerns with him, but then she remembered he'd be calling later that evening, and decided to do two things: first to ask him what he thought about their daughter learning about Islam, wearing Muslim clothing, and praying to Allah; and second to attend church the following Sunday and discuss Islam with her pastor.

As expected, Tom called at ten o'clock. After listening patiently to him recounting his successful closing of a business deal, Julie broached the subject of Susie studying Islam and coming home wearing an *abaya*.

"I have to say, Tom, she scared the *bejesus* out of me coming in the back door wearing that dreadful black thing. And then all that talk about Allah being the only true God. It gave me the willies. I really think we should go to church and ask Reverend Holmes what he thinks about all this."

"Sure, Hon, whatever you think is best. It's nice though she's so interested in learning something new," Tom muttered, not knowing what else to say, but making a mental note to ask a friend who'd served in the military in Saudi Arabia about Islam.

The following Sunday Tom and Julie stood to one side in the church vestibule waiting for Reverend Holmes to finish saying goodbye to other members who'd attended the morning service. As soon as the last person walked out the door, they approached Holmes, hoping to discuss their concerns about Susie's interest in Islam.

"Pastor, we need talk to you," Julie said softly, her eyes tearing up. "We need guidance and some answers," she continued, her voice shaking and anxiously looking around to see if anyone else was listening. "Our daughter Susie's sixth-grade social studies teacher is telling her things about Islam that are very disturbing," she said, taking a tissue out of her purse to dab her eyes.

"Her class is studying Islam, and she and the other girls are wearing an … uh, whatever you call it—some kind of long, black Muslim dress with a hood on it and an eyehole slit to look out of—at school. She wore it home the other day, and I can tell you this right now she scared the dickens out of me. Worse than that, when I asked her why she was wearing the hideous thing, she said her teacher wanted her to and that Islam is the only true religion—" Julie paused to catch her breath and stare wide-eyed at the reverend. "And, uh, this is the part that's upsetting us," she continued. "She says the teacher says that because their god is the true god—I think they call their god, Allah … isn't that right Hon?" she asked, turning to her husband for support.

"Well, I uh … yeah I think so," Tom responded with a shrug, seemingly disinterested, but actually still in the dark about the religion, because he'd failed to ask his friend about Islam.

Flustered and annoyed because Tom appeared not to share her concern over what their daughter was being taught at school, Julie gave him a hard look. Then turning back to the reverend, she said, "Anyway—*I'm upset,* and *I* want to understand what the teacher meant by telling our daughter Allah was the only true God, and He revealed His word directly to Muhammad ... to no one else. Does this mean that Christians are wrong in what we believe?

"I'm terribly confused."

Taken aback by Julie's statements, Reverend Holmes coughed nervously, attempting to formulate an answer. "Julie, some Muslims believe this to be true. It's important to remember that as Christians we must be inclusive, accommodate other religions, and above all, not be critical."

Like the Murrays, Holmes knew very little about Islam and its Prophet, but this didn't prevent him from reciting the accepted politically correct mantra. "After all, we all know Islam is the religion of peace," he added.

Tom, who was kicking himself for not having spoken to his friend, knew he was at a disadvantage. However there was something about the pastor's statement didn't make sense, so he replied, "If that's true Reverend, why are most terrorists Muslims?"

His sensitivities offended, Reverend Holmes suddenly became condescending. "Tom, only a very small percentage of Muslims commit acts of terror. Think of all the horrible things Protestants and Catholics have done down through the ages in the name of religion. The Spanish Inquisition for example. No, we mustn't repeat Islamophobes' false statements."

"Yes ... I guess you're right," Tom awkwardly replied—still not buying it, but distracted and embarrassed when Susie came bouncing up wearing her "cool" *abaya.*

"Mom, all the girls in Sunday school *loved* my *abaya*," she said twirling around. "They want one too. Mr. Anderson said he's going to invite a local imam to come and teach a lesson about Islam. Isn't that cool?"

Reverend Holmes nodded, "Yes, Susie, that sure is."

Chapter 4

Professor Doctor Wael el-Kordi, known as The Egyptian, followed Yosif up the stairs to the roof of a four-story building across the street from the walled U.S. Embassy compound. Yosif walked to the south side and said with a reverential bow of his head, "Esteemed one, behold the *kafir's* abomination."

El-Kordi remained silent, carefully observing the Great Satan's new embassy compound. Surrounded by a twelve-foot high wall, the fortress was designed to withstand a ground assault by *mujahideen*, holy warriors. Buildings were set back from the wall to prevent damage caused by a car or truck bomb detonated next to it. After several minutes, El-Kordi's lips formed what could be considered a smile. Turning to Yosif, he said, "What is the current status. How many *kafirs* are left?"

"Excellence, the American pigs have become weary of Iraq. When the embassy first opened, it employed a staff of sixteen thousand. Now there are less than six thousand, and half of them are *kafirs,* infidels. Only a hundred Marines remain. Many of the buildings are now empty."

El-Kordi slightly cocked his head sideways. "Yes, the American pigs have also run out of money, so they hired locals for security." Once again a trace of a smile appeared on his lips. "The *kafirs* are incapable of learning from their mistakes," *or perhaps they are too proud to admit them,* he surmised before continuing. "A sensible person would have learned from our assassination of their ambassador in Benghazi. We were able to place true believers in their security force, just as we have done here. Now, thanks to them, we have the exact coordinates of each building."

El-Kordi turned to gaze down at the huge 104-acre compound with twenty-one buildings on the other side of the road. It was the largest embassy compound in the world.

A key member of the Muslim Brotherhood, the *Ikhwan*, El-Kordi— The Egyptian—was an engineer and military tactician. *Not only do we have the exact coordinates, we also have the structural plans. The American's architectural firm posted them on their website, and an Ikhwan brother downloaded them before the plans were removed ... such stupidity—or was it arrogance?* "Now it is time to crush their miserable, blasphemous, billion dollar house," he said softly.

Apparently the embassy planners had given no thought to an attack by heavy military weapons when designing the U.S. Baghdad embassy. Located in the center of the city on the banks of the Tigris River, the billion dollar plus compound was actually a small town roughly the size of Vatican City in Rome. The compound's twenty-one buildings included: the embassy itself, residences for the ambassador and staff, a PX, commissary, cinema, retail and shopping stores, restaurants, and schools. The compound also had a fire station, power generation plant, water purification plant, wastewater treatment plant, and telecommunications center. In addition, for security purposes, it had a limited access, hardened structure known as the classified facility. When it opened in 2009, the facility could accommodate over 380 families. Now, greatly understaffed the compound was a sitting duck.

The Capitol Building
Washington, DC
Friday, February 13, 2015

Speaker Nellie Balogni banged her gavel to quiet the representatives. It was time to vote on House Bill 1, the sister bill to Senate Bill 3, which had passed two days prior. Both were titled, *The Comprehensive Firearms Registration and Storage Act.* The bills required all citizens to obtain a permit for each firearm possessed. A separate five-page application and a background check—estimated to cost $50—as well as proof of secure storage were required for each firearm they possessed. The bill also limited the magazine capacity for: semi-automatic rifles and pistols to six cartridges, and shotguns to three; pistols to less than 9mm; rifles to less than 5.50mm; and shotguns to smaller than 16 gauge. Assault weapons were prohibited, and a long list of rifles and carbines so designated was appended to the bill. Each registered firearm had to be stored unloaded in a weapons safe with two individual locking mechanisms. Ammunition had to be stored in a separate safe in a different room. An amendment allowing more than one firearm to be stored in the same gun safe had barely been approved. Another provision of the bill limited the use of deadly force to situations in which the person using deadly force had to have been struck by the assailant with sufficient force to draw blood. Otherwise, any person using deadly force would be charged with attempted murder or manslaughter. Failure to register firearms would be a felony with a minimum ten-year prison sentence.

"Representatives, return to your seats and record your vote," Balogni said when the din died down.

Five minutes later the vote was in and the bill passed. Two Republicans voted with the Democrats for a total of 263 yeas and 172 nays. Since both bills were identical, the combined bill would be sent to the president for his signature.

President Abomba, Attorney General Edison Helder, and DHS Secretary Jane Incompentado watched the final vote tally on a 55-inch plasma screen in the president's private office. The president smiled, raised his bottle of *Yuengling* beer and said, "Now we can begin."

Incompentado shook her head, "Not yet. Your fat doughboy general isn't ready. I think he'll need another four months to find the bathroom."

Helder snorted, "Now Jane, I'm sure that's the first place he found … or maybe it was the officer's club. However, I do agree, the fat asshole is still stumbling around."

"Good observation," the president agreed, laughing at Helder's comment. "Now, let's begin writing implementing regulations.

"Jane, how is your FEMA Corps doing?"

"Barry, we're ahead of schedule. We'll graduate our fourth class of Blue Shirts this month, giving FEMA Corps 1,200 new officers. By mingling the operating budget and personnel roster with the Corporation for National and Community Service's, it will be very difficult to determine the exact number of Blue Shirts.

"Ed has done a great job monitoring returning military from Afghanistan, Iraq and Africa, and identifying those men with the proper psychological profile for recruitment—proper for us that is," she smirked.

The attorney general smiled in response to her compliment. "Yes, some have the precise attitude we looking for."

Helder shook his head in mock resignation. "I wonder what Heinrich Himmler would think of our 'Blue Shirts?' Probably not much, but we would never have gotten away with Brown Shirts."

The president chuckled and put his feet up on his desktop, "Good work, both of you.

"We have control of the banking system, the automobile industry, and a whole bunch of support from the main stream media—they're totally behind us and doing a wonderful job of discrediting our opponents.

"Ed's enforcement of hate-crime laws has shut up most of the conservative big mouths and pastors. There are only three or four talk show hosts still causing trouble." The president scowled, "To paraphrase the Prophet—Will no one rid me of this host ... or hosts?"

The two men looked at each other and nodded. Then the president continued, "Cheered on by the west coast progressive-liberals, our Universal Healthcare program will soon begin to redistribute the nation's wealth," again the president chuckled, "What a bunch of useful idiots.

"How soon can we put the new gun confiscation law into effect?

"At least a year," Jane Incompentado answered. "We need to build up the Blue Shirts, which entails training them to operate heavy weapons and vehicles. Your new Army chief of staff is arranging for groups of Blue Shirts to train at the armor school on Bradleys. Another group is going to the infantry school. We just sent a platoon of the best to Fort Bragg for special demolition training."

"Excellent," the president said, grinning broadly as he stood.

President Clinton created AmeriCorps in 1994 to provide a wide range of public services from education to environmental clean-ups. Both Presidents Bush supported and expanded the modest program. The real expansion came with the passage of the *Edward M. Kennedy Serve America Act* of 2009, which increased the number of AmeriCorps recruits to 250,000.

Chapter 5

Susie Murray led her grandfather, Zackary Murray into her Sunday school classroom. After introducing him to Mr. Anderson, she said, "Grandfather, I'll be right back. I have to go to the ladies room," and flitted out of the room. She hadn't told her grandfather Imam Ali was going to teach her class about Islam, nor that she and her girlfriend, Betty, were planning to wear their *abaya*s and *niqab*s, however, she was certain doing so would be a wonderful surprise.

While Susie and her friend were donning their Muslim garb, Imam Ali entered the classroom and Mr. Anderson greeted him, "Ah, Imam Ali, welcome. I'd like you to meet Mr. Zackary Murray. His granddaughter, Susie, is one of our students."

Looking from Susie's teacher to the imam in astonishment, Zackary scowled and made no attempt to greet the imam.

Responding to Zackary's scowl with a curt nod, Ali intently scrutinized him. *You* haraam salle—*You bastard—you think you can give me trouble. We'll see about that. You look to be around sixty, about five-foot-ten and in good shape for your age. I'll wager you were in the military.*

Imam Ali was partially correct. Zackary Murray had retired as a Foreign Service Officer, but that was his cover. Actually he was a CIA case officer with deep State Department cover.

Immediately sensing Zackary's hostility toward the Muslim, Mr. Anderson attempted to defuse the situation. Nodding and smiling amicably, he said, "Mr. Murray ... uh, Imam Ali has been invited to tell the class about Islam ... uh, how it is similar to Christianity and Judaism. After all, we all worship the same God ... Right?"

"*Do we?*" Murray retorted, still scowling at the imam. He was about to continue when his son and daughter-in-law, Tom and Julie, entered the classroom.

Tom, who'd long suspected that his father was more than a Foreign Service officer, had never pressed for details—but now, seeing Zackary glaring at a man in Muslim clothing, wished he had. *What in God's name is this guy doing here? Oh yeah, that's right. Susie told me Mr. Anderson had invited a Muslim to speak to her class. I just didn't know it was today. It's obvious from Dad's sour expression this isn't sitting well with him. I don't remember very much about our two years in Saudi Arabia, and his other assignments to Pakistan, Iraq, and Libya were unaccompanied tours.*

"Uh—Dad, I see you've already met Susie's Sunday school teacher," Tom said, gesturing to Mr. Anderson while giving the imam a 'who're you look.'

"Ah, yes—Susie introduced us," Anderson said stepping forward, "and now I'd like you to meet Imam Ali. He's the worship leader at the local mosque, and we're overjoyed to have him here to tell us about Islam and how similar it is to Christianity. Imam Ali, this is Mr. Murray's son, Tom, and his daughter-in-law, Julie."

"Good morning," Tom said shaking the imam's offered hand, "and this is my wife, Julie."

Julie offered her hand, which the imam rudely ignored for several long seconds before reluctantly giving her outstretched hand a perfunctory shake. Julie's face flushed and Tom and Mr. Anderson stared at the imam.

What on earth is he thinking? Mr. Anderson wondered.

Incensed by the imam's rudeness, Tom was about to call him on it when Zackary stepped forward. "Julie, don't let this man intimidate you. Muslim men don't touch the hand of an inferior woman," he said, his words dripping sarcasm, "to him, you—actually all of us—are inferior *kafirs*—infidels."

While Mr. Anderson was frantically thinking what to say next, Susie and her friend Betty, both covered head to foot in their black *abaya*s and *niqab*s, bounced into the room.

"Hi everyone! Don't we look fabulous?" Susie squealed, rushing up to her parents. "I love these long black skirts and masks," she said, lifting her skirt and whirling like a dervish.

"God in heaven!" Julie gasped, mortified at her daughter's behavior.

"Holy hell!" Tom muttered, completely flummoxed by the sight of his daughter in her Muslim garb.

"What the hell!" Zackary angrily exclaimed. Outraged by the sight of two Muslim females whirling around in a Protestant church, he stood glaring at the spectacle before him.

Allah be praised for this delightful turn of events, Imam Ali smirked, realizing the girls' appearance in their black garb had unintentionally won him a small victory.

"Grandfather, isn't this cool?" Julie squealed, rushing up to Zackary and whirling around in front of him. "This is my friend, Betty."

"SUSIE! Is that you?" Zackary exclaimed, his body rigid and his fists clenched.

"Tom, what in God's name is going on?"

"I'm so sorry about this Dad, I—"

"Susan! Take off that damnable rag and throw it away," Zackary demanded.

"Now wait a minute, Dad—"

"No, Tom," Julie pleaded. "Don't be upset with your father. It's *my* fault.

"You knew about this*?* Tom asked, glaring at his wife and demanding an explanation.

"Well, uh—no not exactly. Don't you remember, I told you about Susie's social studies teacher making her class wear Muslim clothing? I never guessed she would bring her school clothes to church—"

"What do you mean by her teacher making her wear these things?" Zackary interrupted, continuing to clench and unclench his fists.

Stepping in front of her grandfather Susie removed her *niqab* and gaped at him in dismay. "Grandfather, why are you so upset? We're studying Islam in school. We wear Muslim clothing and pray to Allah on prayer rugs so we can experience the true meaning of the *ummah*—the unity of Muslims all over the world. We want to be a part of it Grandfather because, OMG ... it's *epic*—it's *totally awesome,*" she said, sighing and rolling her eyes dramatically. "We're learning about what an *awesome* man Muhammad was, and how he brought peace to his world."

"Allah be praised," Imam Ali gloated.

"WHAT? Who fed you that nonsense?" Zackary demanded, his voice the temperature of liquid nitrogen.

"W–well ... our class i–is—" Susie stuttered backing away, shaken by her normally sweet, gentle grandfather's fury. She'd never seen him angry and he was frightening her.

Swallowing hard and holding back tears, Susie sheepishly continued, "Gran'pa, we, uh ... are studying Islam in our social studies class. Mrs. Baker says Islam is the one true religion, because God, Allah, revealed His true word to Muhamm—" her voice had slowly become a whisper as she looked up and saw Zackary scowling down at her.

Zackary's expression also frightened Julie, and she moved close to her daughter. Jerking on the *abaya*, she said, "Susan, take that … that whatever-you-call it off. It's upsetting your grandfather."

Reveling in the old man's anger, Imam Ali decided to probe for its source. *Let's see what's got this old goat so riled up,* he decided, and was approaching Zackary when more class members began entering the room.

Mr. Anderson, who'd been watching the imam's reaction, began to panic. *If something isn't done, this is going to turn into an ugly scene. Tom's father isn't going to back down. Do I dare ask him to leave?* he worried, and was about to do just that when he saw Reverend Holmes enter. *Thank God the reverend's here. I'll let him handle the situation.* Catching Holmes eye, he nodded in Tom's father's direction.

What's going on? Holmes wondered. *Oh, I forgot about the Muslim cleric coming, and Anderson looks worried. Why is that visitor standing with the Murrays glaring at the imam?* Holmes wondered, turning his attention to the Muslim. On the surface the imam appeared unperturbed and wore a bland expression, but his eyes told a different story—focused as they were on Zachary, it was obvious they projected pure hatred: a realization that sent a chill down Holmes' spine.

Trying to determine who or what was responsible for the friction as he walked toward Anderson, Holmes noticed two small females garbed in Muslim attire—one bare headed and the other wearing a black covering over her head and face. Gesturing toward the black-garbed figure looking back at him through a slit in the head covering, the reverend said, "Good morning. And who have we here?"

Relieved to have an opportunity to break the tension, Anderson chimed in, "Reverend Holmes, I'd like you to meet Imam Ali. He is going to teach our class about Islam."

"Imam Ali, welcome to our house of worship. It's a pleasure to have you here. I'd forgotten you were coming today, but I'm looking forward to your presentation. After Mr. Anderson asked me about inviting you, I realized that I knew very little about your religion."

"Thank you, Reverend. I welcome the opportunity to introduce your congregation to Islam, the world's fasting growing religion," Ali replied sneering at Tom's father.

"And you are?" Holmes asked turning toward the visitor glaring at the imam.

Embarrassed by the situation, Tom quickly stepped forward. "Reverend Holmes, this is my father, Zackary Murray. I don't believe you've ever met him. He's visiting with us today ... and you know how impetuous Susie can be," Tom said, nodding at his daughter. "We were totally unaware she planned to wear Muslim dress to church—apparently to honor Imam Ali ... and frankly, well ... Dad's a bit upset."

So that's the source of the problem. Holmes concluded. "No, I don't believe I've ever met your father. Good morning, sir. I hope you're enjoying your stay, but perhaps, given the imam's presence, it's best if you discuss your displeasure with your granddaughter after church. We wouldn't want to offend—now would we?"

Tom cringed at the statement and saw his father bristle.

"Now Tom, if you'll join me, I'd like a word with you before Imam Ali begins his program," Holmes said, stepping a few feet away from Zackary and the others.

Turning his back and speaking softly so he wouldn't be heard, the reverend said, "Tom, I see nothing objectionable in Susie wearing Muslim dress to please Imam Ali, but since your father is so unreasonably upset I think it would best for him to leave."

"Excuse me!" Tom hissed, aghast by his pastor's statement and knowing full well asking his father to leave would precipitate a confrontation. "I don't think so. My father has worked in Muslim countries, and I'm anxious to hear what he has to say about the imam's presentation."

"Tom, we must be respectful of other faiths. We are an inclusive people. I do not want your father to cause a scene. I think it best for him to leave. He acts as though he's an Islamophobe."

Julie, who was curious about what the reverend was saying, had joined her husband. Holmes' statement shocked her, and she saw her husband's jaw set.

Locking eyes with Holmes, and finally seeing him for what he was, a weak-kneed, small-minded appeaser, Tom said, "Reverend, if you ask my father to leave, you're also asking my family to leave—*to leave your church.*"

Tom's statement caused Holmes to step back. Now he faced a real dilemma—lose a family, which could cause a riff in the congregation, or risk insulting the imam.

Zackary, who'd taken Susie by the arm and walked away from the imam, watched his son and daughter-in-law talking to Holmes. Seeing Tom's countenance suddenly hardened, and the reverend take a small step backwards, Zackary correctly surmised he was the subject of the conversation. Telling Susie to stay where she was, he walked over to Tom and asked, "Is there a problem?"

Knowing he had to defuse the situation, Holmes turned to Zackary and said, "Mr. Murray, Imam Ali has been invited to provide a presentation on Islam, one of the world's great religions. I am concerned that you may disrupt his presentation. I hope you can understand my concerns."

Looking at the whining minister with contempt, Zackary replied, "I have no intention of embarrassing the imam, however I will question any false statements he makes. Do you have a problem with that?"

"Uh … uh … untrue statements. I don't understand. Why would an imam make false statements?"

"Reverend, you have a lot to learn about Islam. I spent a good many years in Muslim countries and know of what I speak. Do some research. Start with the Arabic word *taqiyya*. It translates as 'deception.' If it will ease your mind our family and my granddaughter's friend will sit at the back of the classroom. You have my word there will be no further disturbance."

"Very well then. Mr. Anderson let's get on with the program."

Imam Ali, who'd been observing the discussion and hoping the heretic would be asked to leave, was annoyed to see the family taking their seats. Following Mr. Anderson to the front of the classroom, he thought about what had just transpired. *Now that he's staying, he may cause me a problem. Wish I knew more about him. I'd best choose my words carefully.* Insha'Allah, *God willing.* Ali used the Muslim's standard exhortation to avoid responsibility by declaring whatever happened was Allah's will, and thus it had to be.

Mr. Anderson began, "Good Morning class. Before we start, let's welcome our visitors. Thank you all for coming. It's so nice to see so many in attendance. As you know, we have previously learned Islam is one of the world's major religions. Instead of reading from a book about Islam, we've invited Imam Ali from our city's local mosque to tell us about his religion and how similar it is to ours.

"Please welcome Imam Ali."

Ali stood, "Thank you Mr. Anderson, and you, Reverend Holmes for providing me this opportunity to inform you about our great religion.

"Our Prophet, Muhammad, was chosen by Allah. Allah is our name for our God. You call Him by other names. Muslims believe Allah sent the angel Gabriel to reveal His true word to Muhammad, and Muhammad recited Allah's revelations to his friends and neighbors in a town called Mecca ... "

With Zackary listening intently, Ali continued his bland presentation.

Thirty minutes later Imam Ali had completed his presentation, and Mr. Anderson asked if there were any questions.

Betty, Susie's friend, who'd removed her *niqab* because she felt suffocated and was perspiring heavily in her hot *abaya*, rose to her feet. "Mr. Imam, you said Jesus was a prophet, and Muhammad was God's last prophet. Isn't Jesus the Son of God?" she asked, using a wad of tissues to wipe the sweat from her face.

Zackary looked at the young girl's flushed face and chuckled.

Ali smiled at the girl. *Such impertinence. No Muslim girl would dare ask such a question. Kafirs! One day they will be true believers or they will be slaves.* "No, that is one of the minor differences between our religions. We believe Jesus was a prophet."

"But we pray to Jesus," another boy said.

Imam Ali smiled and nodded, "Yes, I know."

"Did Muhammad ride a camel?" Another boy ask.

Ali smiled. *Ah, this is better.* "Yes, camels and horses were the only means of transportation in Muhammad's time. He rode camels and horses to bring the word of Allah to other Arabs."

After a dozen more such questions, Zackary stood and asked, "Imam Ali, is it true that Muslims consider our worship of the Holy Trinity, God the Father, Jesus His son, and the Holy Spirit idol worship?"

Ali noted the shocked expressions on the other *kafirs'* faces. *I knew he was going to be trouble.* "Yes, that is another of the minor differences in our religions. Jews also do not accept Christ as the Son of God."

"I believe that's enough for today," Anderson said, rising quickly and approaching the imam. "Your talk has been most informative, and we can't thank you enough for taking time to enlighten us about Islam. I now realize we have much to learn about your faith," he concluded, patting the imam on his back.

"You are so very welcome," the imam said, respectfully bowing his head. "It was my honor to have this opportunity to speak your class.

"In return I would also like to invite your class and the entire congregation, to attend a service at my mosque to experience for yourself our peaceful worship of Allah. Experience the peace and tranquility of true believers."

After attending the 11:00 o'clock church service, Tom and his brooding father walked out of the sanctuary. Tom was conflicted. His dad, who'd stoically sat through Holmes' non-spiritual, feel-good sermon, was still in a dark mood.

Julie and a contrite Susie, carrying her tote bag, tagged along behind. After Sunday school, Susie had removed her *abaya* and *niqab*, rolled them up and stuffed them into her bag.

Susie was worried about facing her grandfather's wrath when they got home. *I can tell from the way Gran'pa's looking at me he's still upset, and I don't understand why. I'm only doing what my teacher wants me to. What's so wrong with that?*

As the Murray family approached the church exit, they got in line with other members to bid Reverend Holmes farewell.

"I'm pleased you came to visit us, Mr. Murray. Thank you for not causing a scene," he quietly said, shaking Zackary's hand. "Your question and Imam Ali's answer surprised me. I now realize you are well versed on the subject of Islam. Perhaps, if you're so inclined, you can share some of your experiences with me during your stay here."

Zackary nodded and replied, "I'll be pleased to, but be advised you may be shocked by what I tell you."

"Oh?" Reverend Holmes responded, nonplused by Murray's remark.

Robert Johnson Elementary School
Monday afternoon, February 16, 2015

Zackary and his daughter-in-law, Julie, had been waiting in the teacher's lounge for their scheduled after school appointment with Susie's social studies teacher, Mrs. Baxter and Ms. Upton, the school's principal. To pass the time, Zackary had been reading the social studies textbook and pointing out erroneous statements and historical inconstancies to Julie. Setting the book aside when the bell signaling the last class of the day rang, Zackary and Julie sat quietly listening to the sounds in the hall of excited students eager to be on their way home.

A few minutes later when Susie, accompanied by her social studies teacher and the principal entered, both Murrays stood. After introductions and the perfunctory handshakes, Julie asked her daughter to wait in the library. Susie departed and the Murrays returned to their seats, expecting the two women to join them, but neither one made a move to do so. Instead Ms. Upton placed her hands on her hips and gave Zackary a hard look. "I understand you wish to discuss Susie's social studies class. Do you have a specific topic? We both have other meetings to attend and don't have much time," she said, cocking her head to one side.

Zackary read Upton's dismissive attitude and haughty expression, a skill he'd perfected during his many years in the field, and realized what he was up against. "Won't you at least take a seat, so we can discuss this more congenially?" he asked carefully evaluating the two women. *Baxter's in her fifties and probably tenured. No doubt she's old-school and accustomed to following her own curriculum—most likely has little to no knowledge of Islam, other than what her textbook provides. Ms. Upton, on the other hand, is in her early thirties, displays a trace of arrogance and is most likely controlling and opinionated.* His conjecture soon proved correct.

"Well, if you *insist*, but please be brief. We're very busy at this stage of the school term," Upton replied.

After both women were seated, Zackary began, "Susie has told me about her social studies class, where the students take Muslim names, wear Muslim clothing, and pray to Allah. Is this—?"

"Yes. We refer to it as immersion," Ms. Upton interrupted. *You pompous old fool; how dare you question our curriculum?* She'd taken one look at the older man and formed an immediate dislike of him. A close friend had reported the Sunday school incident, and now she was convinced she was dealing with an Islamophobe.

"I see. Does that mean that you're also going to immerse your students in Judaism and Christianity?"

Mrs. Baxter stared at the man with silver hair and piercing blue eyes. *I've wondered about that from time to time, but Ms. Upton said*—Upton's voice ended her conjecture.

"That's completely unnecessary. Our students are exposed to these religions both at home and socially," Upton answered with a superior tone.

"I see ... then surely you plan to follow up with immersion in Hinduism and Buddhism."

Upton's nostrils flared. "We have no such plans, nor does the Common Core curriculum call for immersion in those faiths."

"How about praying to God ... our God, the Judeo-Christian God. Or one of the Hindu gods?"

"*Certainly not!* Upton retorted. "That would violate separation of church and state," she smugly added, and was about to continue when she realized she'd trapped herself.

She was searching for a way out when Zackary added, "So, either Islam is not a religion, or you're giving Islam favorable treatment."

"The school board is certainly not showing favoritism to Islam," Upton snapped.

"Good. In that case logic dictates that Islam cannot be a religion.

"And, if that is indeed the school board's position, they are definitely correct."

"What?"

"Your logic isn't flawed. Islam is an ideology, a complete way of life that includes a religious component and is governed by Shariah law."

Abruptly standing, Ms. Upton scowled down at Zackary and Julie and hissed, "Mr. Murray, Mrs. Murray, thank you for sharing your concerns with us. However, your *islamophobic* fears are completely without merit. If you don't agree with my position, I suggest you take it up with the school board at their next meeting. It's at 6 p.m. on the third Wednesday of the month in the school district building."

"Without merit according *to whom,* Ms. Upton?" Zackary asked.

Ignoring Zackary's last statement, Upton whipped around, flounced toward the door and jerked it open.

"Thank you for your time," Zackary said, amused at her pique and chuckling softly at the spectacle she'd just made of herself.

"Well Julie, I think it's time for us to collect Susie and depart as well," he said standing.

"Good day to you Mrs. Baxter. I can't say it's been a pleasure," he said, and taking Julie by the arm escorted her out of the room.

Confused and conflicted, Mrs. Baxter watched the Murray's leave.

Chapter 6

Colonel Harold Rockford, commanding officer of 1st SFOD-D, commonly referred to as Delta Force, knocked on General Anthony Beck's office door.

"Come in," Beck said, looking up from a letter he was reading. "Well I'll be," he smiled, standing and extending his hand in greeting. "Rocky, this is a nice surprise. I heard you were here. It's good to see you. How are the Jill and the kids?"

"Wild as usual, sir. Jill's great, but she has her hands full," Rockford replied, shaking Beck's hand. "I'm on my way back to Bragg, but I was hoping you could spare a few minutes to discuss something?"

Rockford's expression told Beck this was not a social call. "Shut the door and grab a cup of coffee."

Rockford partially filled a mug and sat facing Beck's desk. "Tony, what do you know about the Blue Shirts? We have a platoon of them receiving special training at Fort Bragg."

Beck frowned and asked, "When did they arrive, and what special training?"

"Four days ago, and they're receiving demolition training. Apparently they already received basic EOD training at Eglin. I was told they are part of a FEMA unit, and FEMA is part of DHS. Have any idea what's going on?"

Beck sighed. *Damn, it's started.* "Rocky, FEMA Corp is part of AmeriCorps, which is part of the Corporation for National and Community Service, a government corporation. FEMA Corps was created to respond to disasters. Members are in the eighteen to twenty-four year bracket, and they do not carry weapons."

"Well, the men at Bragg are older. Most are ex-military and very proficient with infantry weapons. They're a surly lot," Rockford grimaced, "and they're rubbing the instructors the wrong way.

"If they're part of AmeriCorps, why are they bragging about being part of FEMA, and why name them FEMA Corps?"

Even though the men were old friends, Beck chose his words carefully. "Sequester has placed a severe strain on our ability to carry out our mission. General Doughberry, our new commander, arrived with orders for CENTCOM to prepare to support NORTHCOM and DHS, if domestic terrorists cause an insurrection.

"It appears that DHS is bulking up to deal with the problem."

Rockford stared at his friend in disbelief. "Sir, what domestic terrorists?"

Beck sighed, "According to our new commander: Tea Party members; veteran's organizations, such as the VFW; and discharged military personnel with recent combat experience have *all* been designated potential terrorists by the attorney general."

"Damn, what's going on? Why would any of these people cause a problem?"

Beck sighed again, "Look at it this way, Rocky. Apparently somebody thinks they might object to having their guns seized."

"Oh! Yeah, I hadn't looked at it from that perspective. I guess they might object at that. I know I sure as hell won't surrender my weapons … is that what you meant when you said CENTCOM was ordered to support DHS?"

Agitated, Rockford frowned, wondering if he had missed something. "Sir, I gotta tell you, this stinks. What about Posse Comitatus?"

General Beck's expression reflected his own frustration. "General Doughberry has informed us the attorney general has ruled that presidential orders to suppress domestic terrorism are exempt from the act.

"Sir, I'm having trouble accepting this."

Beck pursed his lips but didn't answer.

Several seconds passed while the two men stared at one another. Concluding that Beck wasn't going to comment further, Rockford stood, shook his head, and waving a dejected farewell departed without saying another word.

Pope AFB, Fayetteville, NC.
Friday 20 February 2015

Colonel Rockford entered flight operations and found Command Master Sergeant Rufus Jackson—"Roof" to his friends—waiting for him. "Thanks for meeting me, Jackson," Rockford said.

Jackson nodded, took the colonel's suitcase and replied, "No problem, sir. How's dear old MacDill?"

"About the same. More staff BS than usual. Guess the new CO likes to push paper."

Their chatter continued until the two men reached a Humvee, entered and shut the doors. Then Jackson turned to Rockford, who'd taken the front passenger seat, and asked, "Sir, is any of it true?"

Rockford glared at the dashboard before replying. "I'm 'fraid so, Roof and it may be a hell of a lot worse than we suspected."

While Rockford shared the most disturbing points of his and General Beck's discussion, Jackson's expression changed from surprise to anger.

"Damn it Rocky, I don't like this one bit. It's time for me to put in my retirement papers. I can't go along with this."

"Do you think *I can,* Roof? I thought about nothing else the entire flight home. We took an oath to defend the Constitution—"

"Against all enemies, domestic and foreign," Jackson said, finishing the colonel's sentence.

"Correct—Damn straight my friend," Rockford said, his somber expression reflecting his conviction.

"Are you suggesting we disobey a direct order to fire on American citizens—if so ordered?" Jackson asked, staring at his friend and commanding officer.

Rockford locked eyes with Jackson. "Aren't we also forbidden to obey an illegal order?"

This time Jackson said, "Correct—but sir, who decides if an order is illegal … us?"

Colonel Rockford shook his head, "Yeah, Roof … that *is* the question isn't it."

Still in a quandary, Jackson started the vehicle and drove out of the parking area toward the Delta building located deep in Fort Bragg. For several minutes the two rode in silence, until the colonel asked, "Have you received any more reports of some government agency recruiting men we suspected of abusing Afghan and Iraqi citizens?"

"Yeah, a few. Do you want me to ask around?

"Affirmative, I think you should tap into the sergeant's grapevine. Let's find out what agency's recruiting those bad boys."

For the first time, Jackson chucked. "Do ya think maybe the agency issues blue shirts?"

Rockford grunted, and then, chuckling at Roof's comment said, "Wouldn't be surprised if they do."

Neither man spoke until Jackson parked the Humvee in their headquarters' lot.

"Sergeant Major, we have some serious planning to do."

"Affirmative, sir, some careful, discrete planning."

Fort Bragg, Fayetteville, NC.
Tuesday 24 February 2015

Colonel Rockford received a call on his secure line. Caller ID showed CAPT Hazzard, the commander of Seal Team 6, located on the Joint Expeditionary Base Little Creek-Fort Story, Virginia Beach, VA. Answering, Rockford said, "Hello Tom, how goes it in Little Creek?"

"Busy. Got a few minutes to talk?"

"Sure. Sounds like you have a problem."

"Not sure. What do you know about FEMA Corps?"

Rockford sighed. "Got Blue Shirt visitors?"

"Yeah. Seems you do know about them. Thirty of them arrived with orders signed by the chairman of the Joint Chiefs. We're ordered to provide training in taking down buildings."

"Hmmm ... really? Well we've been tasked to provide demolition training—specialized training that includes setting what some idiot named IEDs. We used to call 'em booby traps."

Hazzard chuckled. "Now don't you go using politically incorrect terms. You may end up with a failing grade.

"Have any idea what's going on?"

"Maybe, and if you've got the stomach for it, I'll share what CENTCOM's new commander told his staff."

Ten minutes later when Rockford finished, Hazzard said in disgust, "Rocky, I don't like it—not one damn bit. It sounds like FEMA ... or DHS is duplicating what we do."

"Have to agree, Tom." Rockford paused to think. "Tom, I think we need to get together to plan a joint training exercise."

"Had the same thought. How about we do it on my boat, while we catch some rock fish?"

"Sounds like a plan. What about next Friday?"

"Let's do it. I'll pick you up at the airport. Bring warm clothes, it's gonna be cold."

Norfolk International Airport
9 a.m. Friday, February 27, 2015

Tom Hazzard, dressed in civilian clothes, watched the passengers on US Airways flight from Charlotte deplane. Standing when he saw his friend appear, he waved to Rocky and called out, "Ready to do some serious fishing?"

"You bet. Can't wait to smell the salt air," Rocky said, shifting his carry-on bag over to his left arm, so he could shake Hazzard's hand.

"You're looking good buddy. I see you took my advice and wore some warm civvies. Hope you've got a warm jacket in that bag you're hauling ... temperature's not bad right now but later on you're gonna need it." Hazzard said, patting Rocky on the shoulder.

The two men quickly exited the airport building and entered Hazzard's black Tahoe. "Any reason to stop by the base?"

"No. I'm on leave. Didn't want this designated an official visit."

"Good idea, let's head for the boat. I took the day off too."

After picking up a couple of lunches at Boston Market, their next stop was the bait shop where they purchased beer, several bags of ice and clams for bait. Rockford insisted on paying. Once back in the Tahoe, they headed for the Cutty Sark Marina where Hazzard's 29-foot Striper, the *Fish Finder*, was docked. Both men carried the 100-quart ice chest to the boat. Then, while Rockford returned to the SUV to get their dinner, his carry-on, and their bait; Hazzard checked out the boat; started the twin Mercury 250 outboards and prepared to cast off.

Fifteen minutes later Hazzard turned the *Fish Finder* to port and entered the main channel leading to the Chesapeake Bay. Rockford glanced at the compass, saw they were headed due north, and asked, "Want a beer?"

"Yeah, thanks. We'll clear the jetties in a few minutes and the bay bridge causeway will be off our starboard front quarter. We'll run parallel to the dual causeways and watch for gulls. The Sea Gull pier and restaurant is located on the first manmade island. It's the entrance to the first mile long tunnel under the Thimble Shoal Channel, and it surfaces at the second manmade island. From there we'll follow the causeway to the third manmade island and the entrance to the second tunnel under the Chesapeake Channel. That tunnel surfaces at the fourth manmade island. From there we'll follow the dual causeways to the dual bridges over the North Channel, where we'll start fishing. The causeways continue on to Fisherman Island and the dual Fisherman Inlet Bridges. Another short causeway connects to the eastern shore."

Rockford nodded and lifted his beer can in salute, "Sounds like a plan."

Ten minutes later Rockford watched the end of the jetty pass by as they entered the bay. It was one of those rare days that sometimes occur in February. The water was like a sheet of glass, and the air crisp with the salty smell of seaweed. Overhead, the bright sun in a cloudless sky kept the thermometer hovering around fifty degrees.

Hazzard nodded and pushed the throttles forward. The *Fish Finder* leaped onto a plane and sped across the calm bay at 32 knots. Both men remained quiet, enjoying being out on the bay. The noise from the twin outboards made talking difficult.

Approaching the North Channel bridges, Hazzard throttled back and said, "Our best bet for some good stripers—the locals call them 'rock fish'—will be near the pilings on the southern end."

"You're the captain. Are we gonna do any trolling?"

"Only as a last resort. I want to try the clams first. Soft shell crabs would be the best bait, but it's too early in the season for them. We'll anchor and drift our baits toward the pilings. Gives us plenty of time to talk."

A few sea gulls and a pelican were diving west of the bridges.

"Couldn't ask for a better day," Rockford exclaimed.

The tide was ebbing by the time Hazzard dropped anchor fifty yards west of the pilings at the southern end of the bridge. Once the anchor bit, the *Fish Finder* swung around so the stern faced the pilings. Hazzard broke out two medium sized spinning rods and secured a four-foot, seventy-pound leader with a 5/0 hook to each line. He attached a one-ounce inline sinker to one line and a half-ounce sinker to the other. "We'll try different weight sinkers until we find the fish. Let's start with the clams."

After both men had cast their weighted hooks toward the pilings and closed the bails on their spinning reels, they settled down to wait in the *Fish Finder's* comfortable chairs.

"That oughta be about the right place. Now all we have to do is sit and wait. If one of us doesn't get a bite in the next five minutes, we'll let out another ten feet of line and let the tide to carry our bait closer to the pilings. If that doesn't work, we'll reel in and add more weight," Hazzard said. "Now, tell me if you've found out anything more about the Blue Shirts?"

Rockford grimaced. "Unfortunately yes, and it's not good. Rufus put out feelers and the feedback indicates that men who like violence—have no qualms about killing civilians—are being recruited."

"Damn! My chief has gotten similar reports—Rocky, what the hell's going on?"

"Damn good question. I don't know, but I sure as hell don't like where this appears to be going."

"Yeah, it stinks."

"Looks like FEMA is preparing to turn the Blue Shirts—"

"WHOA, hold that thought," Hazzard exclaimed, as his rod suddenly bent and line peeled off the reel. Grinning at Rockford he reared back to set the hook and exclaimed, "Feels like a good one. Gotta keep him away from the pilings or he'll cut the line."

Rockford reeled in his line, got the net and stood watching Hazzard play the fish. Five minutes later he used the net to scoop up a ten-pound stripped bass, "Fine looking fish. Guess we have dinner."

"Naw, that's *my* dinner. You gotta catch yours. Now, let me change your weight to one-ounce, so you'll have something to eat."

After both men had cast their lines toward the pilings and settled back into their chairs, Rockford picked up the conversation the fish interrupted, "As I was about to say, it looks like FEMA is preparing the Blue Shirts to suppress civilian demonstrations. If gun seizing legislation is approved, there's sure to be resistance."

"When you said civilian demonstrations, did you mean civilians standing up for their Constitutional rights to own firearms?"

"Yes, and the President may order us to back up the Blue Shirts or even to take out resistance leaders."

Hazzard nodded. "The Second Amendment reads, 'A well regulated Militia, being necessary to the security of a free State, the right of the people to keep and bear Arms, shall not be infringed.' It's a one-sentence amendment, consisting of four clauses. The Constitution does not grant the Supreme Court, the Congress, nor the president the authority to change the Constitution."

"That's correct, but Article Five of the Constitution provides a method to amend the Constitution."

"So, the real question is, why hasn't an amendment to revise or repeal the Second Amendment been proposed by Congress?"

"And that, Tom, is the heart of the issue. If the Second Amendment is repealed, then gun confiscation will be legal. Otherwise, I personally believe confiscation would be illegal."

"So do I. So ... where does that leave us?"

"Not in a good place, that's for sure. I think the question becomes, would such an order be legal?"

With that troubling question hanging in the air, both rods bent and the men got busy fighting a couple of heavyweights.

"Looks like we tied into a school heading out of the bay," Hazzard called out, excitement evident in the high-pitched tone of his voice. Rockford just grunted while he watched the line peel off his reel.

"Rocky, tighten your drag or you'll lose him," Hazzard cried, tightening his.

Ten minutes later, two fifteen-pound rockfish joined the first one in the cooler and both men were shucking off their Thinsulate jackets.

"Now that was a real workout ... haven't had that much fun in a long time," Rockford said wiping sweat from his brow.

"Well, I guess you'll have fish for dinner after all," Hazzard teased. "We'll release anything else we catch."

After baiting their hooks and casting, Rockford retrieved a couple of beers and they settled down to eat their lunch and finish their discussion.

"The question was—before the fish hit—who decides if an order is legal?" Rockford began. "The correct answer would be each man or woman receiving the order, but that's an over simplification. Being right is not enough to prevent facing a court-martial. Remember what happened to Lieutenant Colonel Terry Larkin?"

"Yeah. Boy did he get shafted. As I remember the case, he wanted verification the president was a legal Commander in Chief. He requested proof Abomba was a natural born citizen, as required by Article Two of the Constitution. The military judge refused to allow him any discovery, which left him with the choice of pleading guilty in exchange for a six month sentence and dishonorable discharge, or risking a very long prison sentence."

Hazzard frowned, "Yeah, he didn't get a fair trial ... which established that the Uniform Code of Military Justice is no longer uniform or just.

"Refusing to obey an order to fire on protesting civilians would trigger the same type of *injustice*. Larkin tested the system and lost—too bad, because I personally think he was right."

"So do I. The media helped convict him by *neglecting* to mention that when our Constitution was drafted, it contained wording consistent with the accepted European definition of a 'natural born citizen,' as found in Vattel's *Law of Nations*, which reads, "Natural-born citizens, are those born in the country of parents who are citizens of that country," thereby making their offspring natural born citizens of that country. The Founding Fathers were well acquainted with the definition ... Hell, everyone was."

Rockford nodded. "I just hope we aren't forced to make such a decision. My choice will be made if—or when I'm faced with the situation."

"It won't just be a personal decision. Men and women under our command will probably follow our lead."

"I know. That's what's eating a hole in my gut."

Rockford's rod bent and his drag began screaming. Twenty seconds later Hazzard's rod bent.

Later that evening they watched FOX's 7 p.m. news and learned President Abomba had signed the Comprehensive Firearms Registration and Storage Act. The NRA was expected to file a request for a stay while a challenge suit was being drafted.

Chapter 7

Qom, Iran
Residence Grand Ayatollah Hamid Khomeini
Friday, February 27, 2015

The Muslim Brotherhood operative, known as The Egyptian, and Grand Ayatollah Hamid Khomeini sat facing one another on plush, silk cushions placed on an oversized, hand-knotted Persian carpet: one of numerous similar carpets—some locally made by Qom's renowned carpet makers—which were spread throughout the opulently decorated house. Carpets Khomeini had been obsessively collecting for years and considered priceless treasures.

Waiting quietly for a servant, who'd delivered a carafe of fragrant Arabic coffee, to pour each of them a steaming cup and depart, the grand Ayatollah began the conversation. "*Salaam*, greetings, my brother el-Kordi. Are you ready to deliver Allah's blow to squash the Great Satan's unholy compound?"

Bowing his head respectfully, The Egyptian replied, "Yes, Eminence. Praise be to Allah, we are ready. All that is required is your approval, and the *kafir's* vile compound of fornication and debauchery will be turned into rubble."

The old man stroked his long white beard and gave a slight nod of approval. "Praise Allah. My source in the American CIA has informed me that most of the remaining Marines will be ordered to depart Iraq next month, leaving approximately thirty-five to protect the Great Satan's evil embassy. Once that occurs, it will be time to deliver Allah's wrath."

"I await your command to do Allah's bidding, Eminence," el-Kordi said, bowing his head.

Iran's supreme leader nodded, "Allah be praised. Soon the *kafir* dogs will be gone from Iraq." *And then I will rule*—the thought almost made him smile.

U.S. Embassy, Baghdad, Iraq
Thursday, March 12, 2015

Ambassador Hopkins stared at the cable he'd just received from the undersecretary of state. *Now what am I going to do?* Hopkins sighed, shaking his head and stunned by the cable's message. *Having sixty Marines ordered back to Quantico will leave the embassy with the equivalent of one platoon as its main security force. Hell, I've sent several reports stating the existing Marine force was inadequate.*

Picking up his phone, Hopkins called the Marines' commander and confirmed orders for force reduction had been received. *What in God's name is State thinking? I won't have enough Marines to defend the embassy building and the classified facility;* he brooded, staring out his window at the huge, nearly deserted compound.

In a week we'll be sitting ducks—we're being abandoned just like Ambassador Stevens and those other poor souls. Now I know how they felt, because we're going to be the next Benghazi ... no this will be worse, even worse than the Iranian hostage mess—Damn, it'll probably be another Iranian mess. I can't trust the Iraqi guards, and I don't think our host government will do anything to help us. All the money and blood we poured into this miserable country has been for naught.

Deeply discouraged and anxious for the safety of everyone in the compound, Hopkins prepared a cable to the secretary of state. Describing his situation as critical, he stated that the embassy could not be adequately defended after the Marines departed. After sending the cable, he called his wife. "Martha, I think you should return to the states. I know I don't need to remind you Mary is due to deliver our first grandchild next month. You should be there early in case she needs any help with last minute details."

Golden, Colorado
Thursday afternoon, March 19, 2015

Leon Jenkins pulled under his carport, turned off the engine, and headed for the kitchen door. "Honey, I'm home."

"How was your day," his wife Pat, replied, handing him a cold Coors as he entered. I'm glad you're home early and didn't stop to have a couple with your buddies."

"Yeah, I thought about it, but I'm tired of Bob's bugging me to join the First Colorado Militia. I keep telling him I had enough military in Afghanistan. I still enjoy shooting, and I get all I need at the rifle range."

Patricia laughed, "Yes, but none of your buddies at the range will bet against you anymore. Maybe, since the militiamen don't know how good you are, you probably wouldn't have to buy a beer for months."

"Yeah, there is that to consider. Maybe I *should* join."

"Don't even think about it."

He and Pat had been carrying on like this for several weeks. He knew she didn't want him to spend his weekend in the mountains. Hell, neither did he, after serving as a sniper for eighteen months in Afghanistan's mountains and racking up eleven confirmed kills—one over a mile.

"Oh, Lee, I forgot. You got an official looking letter today from the Colorado attorney general," Pat said, giving him a quizzical look.

"Huh? From the AG, let me see it."

Flicking open his folder's blade, Lee slit the envelope and removed a single sheet of paper. Unfolding it he began reading with Pat looking over his shoulder.

"Well I'll be *damned*. The SOBs want me to provide a list of all my weapons and magazines. They've ordered me to take the list, my weapons, magazines, and proof of purchase for each weapon to the police station for inspection and registration before April 15th. And I'm ordered to surrender all magazines and weapons capable of holding more than ten bullets. Damn, they don't even know the difference between a bullet and a cartridge.

"I'll be damned if I will."

"Wait a minute Lee. Let's talk about this. Won't you get in trouble if you don't do what you're told?"

"There's nothing to talk about. Damn it, Pat, I'm not on active duty. Citizens don't have to take orders. *Fuck 'em!* I'm not making any lists, and I'm sure as hell not taking my guns in to be inspected … if I do, they might keep 'em." Lee tossed the letter on the counter. "When's dinner? I'm starved."

An hour later the Jenkins' phone rang. It was Bob.

"Get your letter?"

"Yeah, you?"

"Yeah. We're going to discuss what to do Saturday at our camp. Want to come?"

"Yeah, pick me up."
"Be ready at 0600"

Chapter 8

Baghdad, Iraq
2 a.m. Sunday, March 29, 2015

The Egyptian completed his inspection of the last Russian 2S12 120mm heavy mortar and nodded his approval. All the crews were experienced fighters who'd used mortars in Afghanistan, which was where the Egyptian acquired the six he'd located between 5.5 to 6.1 kilometers east of the American Embassy compound on the east side of the Tigris River.

Satisfied the mortar sites were ready, el-Kordi bid the crew farewell, entered his SUV and instructed his driver to proceed to the first rocket launcher site, located fifteen kilometers south of the *kafir's* embassy and the Tigris River.

Along with providing trained crews for each launcher, The Egyptian's thoughtful Muslim Brotherhood associates had assisted him in acquiring three Egyptian copies of Russian BM-21 Grad multiple rocket launchers mounted on Ural-4320 six-by-six trucks. Each launcher was capable of firing either a single 120mm rocket or a complete load of forty rockets in twenty seconds.

The Egyptian was completing his inspection of the last rocket launcher when his cell phone vibrated. Answering, he heard his forward observer's voice saying, "Praise Allah, the *kafirs* are asleep. I am on the upper equipment deck of the TV tower."

"Allah be praised. Soon I will join you."

The 205 meter TV tower, renamed the Baghdad Tower by U.S. troops, had a restaurant and observation deck at its top. Below the restaurant were three circular service decks for equipment and service personnel. The upper service deck provided a view of the entire U.S. Embassy compound. It was an excellent place from which to adjust mortar and rocket fire.

The Egyptian's driver stopped to let him out one block from the Baghdad Tower. Walking quickly to the tower and entering through an unlocked service door, el-Kordi located the elevator and took it to the upper service deck. Outwardly calm, but tingling with excitement, he stepped out onto the deck and saw his forward observer standing at the railing intently staring out into the night. Not wishing to startle him, el-Kordi approached and whispered, "*Salaam* my brother, I am here."

"*As-alam alaykum,* peace be unto you. Come and see," the man replied in hushed voice, excitedly pointing toward the partially illuminated embassy compound half a kilometer to the south. "All is quiet … Allah be praised, the evil *kafirs* are still sound asleep."

"Yes, Allah be praised, they most certainly are," el-Kordi sneered and silently rejoiced at his good fortune. "Soon the *Muezzins'* calls to prayer will echo throughout the city, greeting the dawn. Praise Allah, and when they do, Allah's mighty fist will obliterate the infidel's unholy place," he hissed, reveling in the thought of the rich rewards he'd receive tomorrow and in the afterlife.

Thirty minutes later, when the discordant sounds of the *Muezzins'* calls were at last echoing throughout the city, The Egyptian removed a cell phone from his pocket. Then moving closer to the forward observer and pressing the number one key, he speed dialed the mortar commander. When he heard the mortar commander answer from the middle site, he said, "Allah be praised, the time has come."

"Praise Allah," the commander answered.

"Fire the first ranging shot."

"Fire," the commander ordered, watching his gunner drop a WP mortar round into the mouth of the large barrel. A split second later the mortar fired, sending the 4.8 inch diameter mortar bomb on its way.

The Egyptian and his forward observer waited for the round to impact. Several seconds later they saw a white cloud of smoke with glowing streaks of fire appear inside the *kafir's* compound. The mortar bomb had impacted approximately ten meters from the east wall.

Taking the cell phone from The Egyptian, the forward observer said, "Up five-zero meters, right two-five meters. Walk the rounds west for three-zero-zero meters. Wait for the command to fire."

While the forward observer was adjusting the mortar fire, The Egyptian was speed dialing the commander of the center rocket launcher on a second cell phone. "Praise Allah. Fire the targeting rocket."

Fifteen seconds later, a single 120mm rocket left its tube and arched skyward on a parabolic trajectory toward the *kafir's* embassy compound.

The Egyptian and his observer watched the rocket explode on the north bank of the river. Taking the second phone from The Egyptian, the forward observer said, "Up two-zero-zero meters. Fire second rocket."

As soon as they saw the second rocket impact the center of the compound, The Egyptian spoke into the first cell phone, "Mortars, commence firing."

With that, five of the mortars immediately began lobbing high explosive mortar bombs, as fast as the gunners could drop them into the tubes. The remaining mortar continued firing white phosphorus shells to ensure the buildings would catch fire and further confuse the *kafirs*.

"*ALLAHU'AKBAR*," The Egyptian snarled when he saw explosive flames erupting from the mortar bombs walking across the compound.

"*PRAISE ALLAH,*" he yelled, and then, snatching the second cell phone from the observer, ordered, "*Deliver Allah's vengeance to the kafirs.*"

Thirty seconds later 118 rockets were streaking toward the American Embassy compound.

As soon as the first mortar bomb exploded, a Marine guard alerted his sergeant. "Sarge, looks like someone tossed a WP grenade over the east wall."

Both men were monitoring the surveillance cameras when the first rocket exploded at the edge of the river. "Now what?" the sergeant called out, switching from camera to camera looking for the source of the explosion. Thirty seconds later the second rocket exploded in the middle of the compound.

"WHAT THE HELL WAS THAT SARGE?" the corporal shouted.

"HOLY CRAP! WE'RE UNDER ATTACK," the sergeant exclaimed, scrambling to press the compound's alarm button and activating the imminent danger notification system, which set off alarm bells within minutes in the State Department, Department of Defense, Department of Homeland Security, the CIA, the White House, and CENTCOM; and allowed each agency to obtain live video feed of the attack reducing the entire compound to rubble. The local time was 6:29 a.m.

The explosion of the second rocket in the compound jarred the ambassador from his sleep, but left him powerless to do anything. Incoming mortar bombs and rockets were ripping the buildings apart—only the secure classified facility would survive.

The attack occurred so quickly that only a few people made it to safe locations.

As soon as the barrage lifted, Islamic fighters blew open the gates and poured into the compound, looking for hostages and information.

John Barnerman, director of the Central Intelligence Agency, was the first official notified of the attack. He received a call at 11:32 p.m. Saturday night in his Reston, Virginia home. Rising from bed, he rushed to the secure office in his basement, where he used his scrambled phone to establish contact with the Baghdad embassy compound's classified facility. Ascertaining the extent of the devastation, he ordered the destruction of classified documents and equipment. Next he called the president.

Vacationing in California, Secretary of Defense Haggler received the alert Saturday evening at 8:42 p.m. Speed dialing the president on his cell phone, Haggler heard a recorded message directing him to hold for the head of the president's Secret Service detachment.

Secretary of Homeland Security Incompentado received an 11:42 p.m. call Saturday night informing her of the alert. Deciding it wasn't her problem, she took a tranquilizer and went back to bed.

Secretary of State Heinz received his call at his home in Washington, DC at 11:44 p.m. Saturday night informing him of the alert. Wasting valuable minutes demanding three separate confirmations of the attack, Heinz finally decided to place a call requesting assistance to Iraq's president. Five hours passed before his call was accepted.

Elbo Beach Resort, Bermuda
12:48 a.m. Sunday, March 29, 2015

President Abomba was enjoying his usual end-of-month vacation—this month at Elbow Beach, one of Bermuda's five star golf resorts—when the emergency alert was received. Someone had to tell the president, and no one wanted the job. Waking the president usually resulted in a traumatic experience. Finally the head of the Secret Service detail accepted the job and softly knocked on the president's door. After knocking for the fifth time—each time louder than before—he heard the president's voice ask in an unpleasant manner, *"What'd you want?"*

"Mr. President, we've received an imminent danger notification from the Baghdad Embassy. The embassy is under attack," the agent said, his mouth close to the door.

"A what? What kind of alert?" came the muffled reply.

Repeating his message, the agent waited for the president to open the door, but he didn't. A minute later he heard the voice of the Comm Center operator in his earbud, "Tom, the DCI is on the phone for the President."

"Mr. President, you have a call from the Director of the CIA ... uh, Mr. President, this is *very* important," the agent insisted, listening at the door and hearing some movement inside the room.

"Oh, for God's sake ... all right, damn it. Put him through."

Given the urgency of the situation, the agent thought it was odd the president didn't immediately come to the door. Relieved, however, when Abomba finally agreed to take the call, the agent waited till he heard a phone ringing in the room and stepped away from the door.

Answering the special phone provided to him by the Secret Service, the president barked, "*So!* ... What the hell's so important, John?

After listening to Barnerman's report, Abomba asked, "Why are you bothering me with it? ... I don't care if it *is* like Benghazi. Get hold of Vickie and handle it. I don't wanna be bothered with this stuff. That's yours and Heinz's problem ... Yeah, Haggler too ... Now handle it, *damn it.*" The president muttered a curse as he ended the call.

CENTCOM, MacDill AFB
2331 Saturday 28 March 2015

General Beck was informed of the Baghdad embassy's imminent danger alert in his quarters, and immediately called General Doughberry's quarters.

Half drunk and exhausted from a romp with the lovely Colonel Collins, Doughberry flung her arm off his naked chest and rolled over to answer the phone.

"General Doughberry," he muttered, his voice gravely, and squinted at the alarm clock to see what time it was.

"This is General Beck, sir. We've just received an imminent danger notification from Baghdad. The embassy compound is taking heavy fire."

"Huh? Heavy fire? Our embassy in Baghdad?"

"Yes, sir."

"What's wrong?" Collins asked.

Doughberry held up his hand to stop her questions and paused to think. *What the hell am I supposed to do? Oh yeah ... now I remember.*

"Follow the damn SOP," he ordered gruffly. "Call the staff together and prepare an assessment of the situation and recommendations. Get back to me when you have something to report. I'll see you in the morning."

"Uh, sir ... we have to take immediate action. Our embassy is under attack. We have to send a relief force."

"I can't make that decision," Doughberry huffed, and Colonel Collins rolled closer to hear what was being said.

"What decision?" Collins whispered, running the palm of her left hand down Doughberry's chubby belly.

"Imminent danger alert—Baghdad ... Oh—" he gasped, as her hand slid lower and grasped his limp manhood.

Beck had heard the female voice and deduced what was going on. "Sir, you need to contact Secretary Haggler. This is a very serious situation. The SOP says to provide assistance and comply with State Department requests, but we don't have any requests."

"W–what do you ..." Doughberry gasped again, suddenly hot and forgetting who he was talking to.

"What kind of alert?" Collins whispered in his ear.

"Beck, did you say it was an imminent danger notification?"

"Yes, sir," Beck said, listening to his boss gasping. *Guess he's having a good time.* "Sir, are you all right? We, uh ... have to do something immediately."

"**Oh, FOR CHRIST SAKE, BECK!** I'm ... uh—I'll be in the office shortly. Follow the SOP, until I get directions from the Secretary."

"Yes, sir," Beck replied, realizing they were probably already deep into another Benghazi disaster. *Somebody has to do something, damn it,* he resolved, and taking a deep breath, dialed the secure number for Colonel Vickers: the senior U.S. officer in Iraq, who was located in the Green Zone in Baghdad.

"Colonel, I'm sure you know by now our embassy is under attack," Beck said.

"Yes, sir, we're aware, and the situation is dire."

"What kind of relief force can you put together?"

"Sir, only our MPs have weapons, M4 carbines. The rest of the men and women aren't armed. I'm assembling a reinforced platoon. That's all I have.

"General, we're restricted from firing on Iraqis without approval from the host government."

Colonel, use your men to relieve the embassy. Anyone inside the walls is on U.S. soil. So your orders *do not apply*. Do whatever's necessary to save American lives damn it."

"*Yes, sir.* Understood."

Forty-five minutes later, General Doughberry and Colonel Collins arrived at the headquarters building. Doughberry used his secure phone to call Secretary Haggler. "Damn it," he muttered when the call was forwarded to voice mail. *Haggler's either talking to the president or attempting to contact him,* he decided, leaving a message asking Haggler to call him.

An hour after the attack ended, the news media had the story. Breaking news bulletins were flashing on all the TV networks. "Is this another Benghazi?" the pundits were asking?

Chapter 9

Sunday morning, March 29, 2015

By five o'clock Sunday morning eastern daylight time, every U.S. and European TV network had flashing *Breaking News* banners. All were reporting variations of the attack on the American Embassy compound in Baghdad. Some networks speculated on who was responsible for the attack. CNN's Robin Read reported several thousand people were in the compound at the time of the attack. There appeared to be few American survivors. However, most of the large numbers of Iraqi citizens normally working in the compound were absent. Many, it was later learned, had left the compound Saturday afternoon.

France 24 and the BBC concentrated on the carnage and damage, and as usual, there were those like CNBC's Chris Mattersless who sought to blame America. On a morning special after the attack, Chris emphasized America had destroyed Iraq's economy in its quest for oil. Then, scowling and railing against the Bush administrations' idiotic decision to build the world's largest embassy in the heart of Baghdad, he proclaimed, "America's arrogance is responsible for the attack."

Programming for regular Sunday morning talk shows was revamped, adding "experts" to bloviate about the attack. A female representative from the State Department made the rounds, telling each show's viewers that those responsible for the attack hadn't been identified. When pressed about Iraqi response—specifically the lack thereof during the first five hours—she said the secretary of state was working with his Iraqi counterpart.

Only Chris Wallace, the host of FOX News Sunday, compared the attack to Benghazi and pressed the State Department's representative for details. When asked for a timeline on when key administration officials and the president were informed, she informed him no timeline or casualty count was available. Texas Senator Crux, who followed State's representative, accused the administration of allowing a super Benghazi to occur. "Chris, apparently President Abomba is incapable of learning from his past mistakes. On Monday I will demand an investigation."

Conversations at many churches, synagogues, VFW Posts, American Legion Halls, and on almost all military installations and aboard ships, covered a litany of complaints against the government: the lack of security provided after most of the Marine guard had been withdrawn; the deaths of those few Marines who were left to defend the embassy compound; and the inadequately armed small military police detachment in the Green Zone. All were criticizing the current rules of engagement and the liberal media's history of demeaning men and women in the military— and now Congress and the president were adding to their concerns by attempting to pass draconian gun control laws. Attitudes ranged from concern to anger, with the majority of sportsmen and veterans expressing their opposition to new and pending gun laws.

FOX Studios
Special Edition of The O'Rippley Quotient
8 p.m., Sunday, March 29, 2015

William O'Rippley's talking points memo dealt with the destruction of the U.S. Embassy compound in Baghdad. O'Rippley and the producers at FOX had spent the day preparing his special show.

"Good evening," O'Rippley said, opening the show.

"Tonight's talking points will address the heinous attack on our embassy compound in Baghdad, Iraq and the murder of Ambassador Hopkins. We'll begin by addressing the questionable decision to build a billion dollar embassy in Iraq in the first place," he continued, frowning and shaking his head. "Construction on the site began in 2005, when hopes were high for creating a western-style democracy in Iraq, which was to be America's new anchor in the Middle East—an example for all other countries.

"Well, we all know how that worked out. The question is why do all our plans in the area fail? Turkey has slowly reverted to a true Islamic state governed by Shariah law, and Iraq has fallen under the influence of Iran. Only Israel remains a true democratic nation, and President Abomba has all but abandoned Israel."

"Well, that's the subject for tonight's show. Let me welcome our first guest, Senator Crux, who joins us to share his perspective on why we've failed in our attempts to bring democracy to the Middle East. Senator, what are your thoughts?"

"Good evening, Bill. Well, your question, 'Why do we fail?' is a good place to start. Simply put, I think we fail because we view the Middle

East through western eyes. We do not understand the culture or the religion—"

"You mean Islam."

"Exactly, we do not understand Islam. Because we believe in separation of church and state, we naively assume Muslims do the same— but they *don't*. For Muslims, Islam is a complete way of life, their government and their laws, Shariah—"

"Well, I recognize that Muslims take their religion more seriously than we do. They're easily offended—"

"Yes, Bill, that's one of the problems—and that's also how they increase their power. By being constantly offended, they intimidate us by making us careful of what we say. Without realizing it, we're actually accepting their religion and form of government as superior to ours."

"I don't accept Islam as the superior religion. I—"

"Sure you do. You just don't realize it. FOX and every other network takes special care not to offend or insult Muslims. Yet, no such concern exists for Christians and Jews. Take the issue of the cross for example. Crosses have been displayed in America's public buildings since the pilgrims landed. Now they must be removed, because one or two people object." Crux paused, then continued, "Why is it similar objections are never raised against Muslim demands for prayer rooms and footbaths; or over teachers indoctrinating our youth on Islam in our public schools and colleges?"

"Now wait a minute, I disagree. I—"

"Bill, we allow Muslim students to pray during school hours, but ban the Lord's Prayer. Can you cite a single example of anyone objecting to reading from a Qur'an in a school? No, you can't. Public school textbooks have chapters devoted to Islam and a mere paragraph or two to Christianity, Judaism, and other religions. Imams and mullahs are allowed to make presentations on Islam in our schools, but God help any pastor or rabbi who does the same thing.

"Are you aware that public schools are having Muslim immersion programs? Children are being required to take Muslim names, pray to Allah, and wear Muslim clothes. Think about the liberal reaction if a Christian or Jewish immersion program was implemented."

"Well now that you mention it I agree, but time won't permit further discussion. We'll be right back after a short break."

When they returned, O'Rippley changed the subject. "Senator, tonight's main talking point is the attack on our embassy compound in Iraq. Where do you stand on this issue?"

"Bill, we should have learned from our mistakes. Benghazi was a tragic disaster caused by bungling, inexperienced senior personnel at the State Department ... and by the Secretary herself."

"My contacts tell me that all but thirty-four Marines were withdrawn the week before the attack." Crux looked into the camera and scowled. "Like Benghazi, the embassy contracted with local companies to provide guards. Our embassy in Baghdad was another inside job by jihadis."

"I've heard several terrorist groups mentioned, Senator. Do you have any information as to which one conducted the attack?"

Crux shook his head and frowned. "Bill, names mean very little. All jihadis have the same goal—dominating the West and establishing a new caliphate. No, the *important* question is who provided the funding and the planning—"

"But this time we did send support," O'Rippley interjected. "A platoon of MPs rushed to the compound to attempt a rescue."

"Yes, and now it looks like the colonel who sent them is in trouble."

"What? What do you mean by 'in trouble?'"

Crux sighed. "Bill, Secretary Heinz has already apologized to the Iraq's president for firing on Baghdad's *civilians*: civilians who were inside our embassy compound—on American soil—*killing Americans.* Can you *believe* it?" Crux asked, slamming his hand down on the table. "The colonel may be court-martialed."

O'Rippley frowned, his disgust evident. "Unfortunately ... yes, I *can* believe it.

"Do you know who attacked the compound?"

"No ... but to answer your 'Who done it?'—My money is on Iran. Now, after all the blood and treasure we have left on Iraqi soil, America's presence in Baghdad has been all but eliminated, Grand Ayatollah Hamid Khomeini will move in and dominate Iraq. He'll probably use Muqtada al-Sadr as his man. If I were to speculate, I'd say it could have been the Sadr Militia.

"Unless President Abomba takes drastic action we've lost Iraq."

Air Force One
Over the Atlantic Ocean
Sunday evening, March 29, 2015

President Abomba, in Air Force One's presidential office en route to Joint Base Andrews, slammed down the receiver on his phone. *"Damn it! Damn it! Damn it!"* he seethed. Angry, very angry, he'd just learned the extent of the damage at the Baghdad Embassy compound—the ambassador, nineteen Marines, twenty-five Army MPs, and seven hundred and thirty-one embassy staff had been killed. Worse still, over thirty embassy employees and family members were missing and assumed taken prisoner.

Who the hell allowed this to happen? What a fucking mess. My gun legislation is in the toilet. Every news network is focused on the damn embassy. Al-Jazeera is showing pictures of dead freedom fighters, implying they were killed outside the embassy compound. Glowering at one of his aides, Abomba barked, "Get Speaker Balogni on the phone."

A few minutes later, the aide announced, "Mr. President, the Speaker is on line two."

Waving the aide out of his office and indicating for him to shut the door, Abomba picked up the handset, pushed the blinking button, and said, "Nellie, I'm on my way back. What's going on?"

"Barry, this Iraqi fuck up is killing us. Even some of our dependable Representatives and Senators are asking for an investigation. Have you decided what you're going to do?"

"No. I told Heinz, Haggler and Barnerman to prepare options—wait a minute," Abomba said, suddenly having what he thought was a brilliant idea, "Hold on, Nellie, it's Bush's embassy. He built it ... yeah, that's right ... so it's *his* fault. That's the way to play it."

Speaker Balogni hesitated before replying, "Uh, Barry ... don't you think we've worn that one out?"

"Hell no! My base will jump on it," the president boasted: his face morphing into his famous egotistical expression; his chin jutted forward and up. "Yeah, they'll *love* it," he gloated, rocking back in his chair and plopping his feet up on his desktop. "Hmmm, yeah ..." he rubbed his chin, "Spin it as Bush's billion-dollar fuck up—no his *debacle* ... sounds better, don't you think?" he guffawed. "Yeah! I like it. Everybody knows how stupid Bush was. This'll prove it. Right? He wasted taxpayers' money on a billion dollar plus embassy in Iraq that's now a pile of smoking rubble. Yeah, Bush owns it, not me.

"Stress gun legislation ... yeah, that's what's really important. We gotta get more legislation passed, and we need the public's help gettin' it done. Guns gotta be taken off the streets. Our citizens, our children are being slaughtered. Pump up Finkelstein. She's good at making that argument."

"Okay, Barry. You're right. I'm on it. Getting rid of the damn guns is what's important."

The president hung up, leaned back in his custom-made executive recliner and schemed. *Damn right, confiscating the fucking guns is important. I don't want armed mobs objecting to my third term. No need for Balogni and Finkelstein to know my plans. Once the guns are in our hands, my Blue Shirts will take care of anyone who objects. Hell, I'm young enough for two or three more terms. FDR was starting his fourth term when he died.*

Golden, Colorado
Sunday, March 29, 2015

Lee answered the phone and heard his friend Bob ask, "Lee, you watchin' Bill O'Rippley?"

"Yeah. Goddamn it, Bob. What the hell is wrong with this country? Fuckin' Heinz *apologized!* Damn, we should be bombin' Baghdad ... or Iran."

"I got a call from one of my old Army buddies. Seems our *President* ain't gonna do squat ... *nada.* My buddy says the administration's gearin' up for a full court press to get our guns."

"Don't doubt it. Yeah ... good thing we've got 'em in a safe place."

"Yeah, but they've got our names on their list ... though I doubt they know what we have—so I've been thinking. When we report in to the police maybe we should just take a couple of old rifles or shotguns. What'd you think?"

"Lee scratched his head. "Hmmm ... yeah, that might work. Let's discuss it at the next meeting."

Chapter 10

Monday morning, March 30, 2015

Pundits on **MSMBC's** *Morning Coffee Show* **blamed** President George W. Bush for the attack on the Baghdad embassy. "He built it, so he owns it," Kookie Robats said, laughing so hard she knocked her reading glasses off the table. The panel agreed building the world's largest embassy in Baghdad was an insult to Muslims, and their resentment was understandable. The huge embassy compound was an affront to the Iraqi people. "If Bush hadn't built it, there wouldn't have been an attack," the host snickered. The show's five *fair-and-balanced*, progressive-liberal Democrats sat around the curved table laughing like hyenas, between comments and misstatements of the facts. Somehow dead Americans were funny, and destruction of Bush's embassy was hysterical.

CNN's coverage was similar but less strident. ABC, NBC and CBS emphasized the Bush embassy talking point, but were respectful of the dead and injured.

CENTCOM
Monday, 30 March 2015

General Doughberry hung his head as he listened to the dial tone. Secretary Haggler had chewed him out for a good ten minutes before hanging up. *Damn ... Damn that meddling SOB Beck ... ordered that dumbass colonel to send in the MPs—and the fool did; cited the standing SOP as his authority—and damn him, that bastard Beck covered his ass. Technicalities be damned ... we killed Iraqis inside the wall and the President's pissed ... pissed at ME. President Carter, said no to the plan to send Deltas over the embassy wall in Tehran to kill students guarding the hostages—and he was right—no one got killed and we got the hostages back ... even if it did take 444 days.*

"Damn Beck!" Doughberry hissed. "And damn my do-nothing vice commander, Hass," he added, slamming down the receiver and slouching back in his chair to brood; but, suddenly struck by a new idea that pleased him, he sprang forward and called out, "Colonel."

"Yes, sir," Colonel Rebecca Collins answered, rising from her desk and walking over to stand in Doughberry's open doorway.

"Issue orders for colonel, uh ... colonel what's-his-name—you know, the dick that sent the MPs to the embassy."

"Sir, do you mean Colonel Vickers?"

"Yeah, that's him. Order him to report to me tomorrow."

"General, I'm afraid that may not be possible. It would require a direct flight, and we don't have an aircraft available with that range."

Doughberry frowned. *Details ... Damn the details.* "Well, make it ASAP—Priority status. The damn fool has upset the Secretary and the President."

"Yes, sir." Collins said, entering his office and discreetly closing the door.

"Sam, don't do anything foolish," she softly said. "I think the media and citizens will welcome him as a hero."

"You really think so Becca? Haggler wants to *hang* him— figuratively of course."

"Sam, let the secretary do it. Otherwise you'll be the one ridiculed by the media. Follow orders, nothing more."

Doughberry sat rubbing his chin. *Becca's usually right. Better listen to her and wait to see how Vickers is received when he arrives.* "Good. That's what I'll do."

Colonel Collins smiled. *It's so easy to manipulate him. I should be the general. Oh well, if he doesn't fuck up, I'll get my star. Major General Beck is the one to watch. He's too quiet, and still waters run deep.*

Dover AFB
Wednesday, April 1, 2015

Television camera crews and members of the press from every major news service in the western world were on hand, waiting in and around a large airport hanger for the first C-17 Globemaster III bearing the bodies of Americans killed at the Baghdad embassy to arrive. Waiting along with the press, was a large contingent of military personnel, politicians, civilian employees, and grief stricken relatives. Still in shock, with the anguish of grief etched on their faces, relatives milled aimlessly

around. Many wept openly and muttered the same tormented refrain—
"Why, why do they hate us?"

Vice President John Blabberman, accompanied by the assistant
under-secretary of state, the chairman of the Joint Chiefs and Senator Crux,
waited in a hanger set up to receive the caskets. It looked as though the
reception ceremony was going to be a replay of the Benghazi charade—
only this one would be on steroids. Secretary of State Heinz was still in
Baghdad, attempting to appease Iraq's angry president.

Several men and women and a few reporters, who were monitoring
the tower frequency, heard the C-17 pilot's incoming transmission. "Dover
Tower, good afternoon. Angel Flight twenty-three, gear down five miles."
A few minutes later the tower responded. "Angel Flight twenty-three,
you're number one for landing. Welcome to Dover Air Force Base."

Word of Angel Flight's approach quickly spread, and all eyes turned
to the northeastern sky, where the speck of an airplane was visible. Before
long, the speck grew into a huge cargo plane, which dropped out of the sky,
settled onto the runway and taxied toward a hanger. As soon as the pilot
brought the big bird to a stop, a formation of Marines marched toward the
aircraft, flanking the path caskets would travel on the way into the hanger.
Coming to a halt near the plane's rear-loading ramp, they stood solemnly at
attention while the band played "God Bless America," and the ramp slowly
lowered to the ground.

Over the next hour, the heart-rending spectacle of Marines carrying
coffins containing men, women and children killed inside Baghdad's
American embassy was broadcast via satellite across the planet. While TV
cameramen filmed the last casket being removed from the aircraft, one
scoop-hungry newspaperman watching from the tarmac noticed a lone
Army officer following the Marines down the ramp.

Hmmm ... who can that be? Washington Times reporter Tom Rydell
wondered. *I'll bet he has a story to tell ... and I'm ready to listen,* he
decided, studying the officer and hustling through the waiting throng to
approached him. *Okay, the eagle tells me he's a colonel, his nametag says
Vickers, and his branch insignia—crossed flintlock pistols—tells me he's
with the MPs.*

"Colonel Vickers, did you come from Baghdad?" Ryder asked,
walking up to the officer.

Noticing Ryder's Washington Times press tag, Vickers mentally
shrugged at the stupidity of most reporters' questions. *Anyone with any
sense would know this was a nonstop flight from Baghdad.*

"Yes," Vickers responded with a scowl.

"You're an MP aren't you? I noticed your insignia. Are you the colonel who sent the MPs to the embassy compound?"

If he noticed it, why ask? Vickers smirked. "Yes to both your questions. Unfortunately, there was little we could do to stop the rockets and mortar rounds."

Rydell attempted to hide his growing excitement; for he knew he was getting an exclusive interview with the man many were calling a hero. "I'm Tom Rydell with the Washington Times. Can you tell me what happened?"

Vickers paused to consider his situation. He hadn't received a gag order. In fact, the only order he'd received was to report to CENTCOM's commander ASAP. *Why not make a statement? This may be my only opportunity to set the record straight.* Vickers decided and was about to respond, when a female reporter and cameraman from FOX News arrived.

Oh well, Rydell sighed, *at least I'll have the print exclusive.*

"Colonel Vickers, tell our viewers who you are and what you did to help save our embassy," FOX reporter Julie Bellmont said, moving forward to stand next to Rydell, and holding up her mike for the colonel while her cameraman began recording the interview.

Realizing this was a God-given opportunity to get his story on the record before the politicos and the PC police got into the act, Vickers responded, "My name is Colonel John Vickers. I'm the commander of the Military Police detachment in the Green Zone in Baghdad.

"I was in my office Sunday morning when the jihadis attack began. It started at dawn. One of the sentries called and reported hearing an explosion followed by two more coming from the direction of the embassy. A couple of minutes later we heard multiple explosions, and then we received the imminent danger alert from the embassy.

"I ordered my sergeant to sound the emergency recall—the emergency order for all my men and women to assemble. I told him to issue arms, ammo, and body armor, and then form up the unit. Thirty minutes later we departed for the embassy.

"Upon arrival, we saw the main gate had been breeched, and jihadi fighters were entering and leaving the compound—obviously looting. We also saw them dragging out several men and a woman.

"I gave the order to attack by squads and to engage any person with a weapon. According to our SOP, State Department and civilian guards would remain inside the embassy compound's buildings. Only uniformed Marines would be outside. This was to prevent us from engaging friendly forces." *No reason to tell them that SOP dated back to the Bush administration.*

"As soon as we approached the main gate, we came under heavy fire from AK-47s, a machine gun, and RPGs. Three of my men were killed, and I realized we were engaging a heavily armed force of company strength.

"Most of the buildings had been heavily damaged or destroyed. Many were on fire, and the area was shrouded in white smoke. From the smell, I determined it was coming from white phosphorus shells."

"Did you shoot any of the men in the compound?" Rydell asked.

Vickers stared at the young reporter with an expression that many would later describe as astonishment. "*Yes,* that *is* why we were there." Then, realizing from the reporter's blank expression he still didn't get it, Vickers continued, "The jihadis were on American soil killing Americans. *Damn right* we killed as many as we could."

"On American soil? You were in Baghdad," Rydell blurted out, obviously confused.

"Embassy grounds are considered the soil of the country represented by the embassy. Everything inside the wall was U.S. soil."

"Oh!"

Julie Bellmont, rolled her eyes at Vickers and seized the opportunity to ask, "Colonel, we've heard varying figures regarding the number killed and missing. Can you provide any specific numbers?"

"Twenty-five of my MPs were killed and five more seriously wounded. Nineteen of the embassy's thirty-nine Marines were killed—twelve more badly injured.

"Ambassador Hopkins was killed. His body was on the plane.

"When I left, the Iraqis were still recovering bodies, so I don't have an accurate count. At least 700 hundred were killed, and we don't know how many men, women and children were taken as hostages. We won't know until every body has been recovered and identified," Vickers concluded, a look of anguish on his face and his voice husky with emotion.

Both Bellmont and Rydell stared at the colonel, trying to grasp the magnitude of the disaster. Finally Rydell said, "Thank you Colonel Vickers. You and your men are national heroes."

Bellmont nodded in agreement.

Without another word, Colonel Vickers turned and walked toward flight operations. He needed a lift to MacDill AFB.

The embassy attack eclipsed federal gun legislation. Consequently, complaints about Second Amendment violations faded from news coverage, along with public awareness. However, while millions of

Muslims celebrated, America's citizens were divided in their reaction. Movealong.org, Motherhubbard.com, and similar websites posted articles criticizing former president Bush for building the embassy. After all we'd done for the Iraqi people, moderate news sites continued to wonder why jihadis still attacked us. Men and women gathering in American Legion halls and VFW posts grew angrier and more outspoken. A statement made by a retired eighty-three-year-old veteran during a TV interview summed up the general attitude among most of the veterans who'd served their country, "The remnants of the Greatest Generation are having to watch the Idiot Generation destroy what we fought to save." His comment soon hit Facebook and Twitter, where it was tweeted over and over again.

Chapter 11

The White House
Thursday morning, April 2, 2015

President Abomba was relaxing in his private study and dining area, a room only accessible through one of the Oval Offices' four doors that were so artfully concealed they appeared to be part of the wall. With his feet propped up on his desk, he was chatting on the speakerphone with Senator Dana Finkelstein about Senator Crux and his gang when Vickie Barrett, his special assistant, breezed in. Perching on Abomba's desk next to his feet, she listened to the conversation. She could tell from the high-pitched tone of Finkelstein's voice she was in a tizzy. Locking eyes with Abomba, Barrett smirked while the senator blathered on about Crux and his cronies demanding a full-scale investigation of the Baghdad incident.

"Mr. President, we absolutely cannot allow this to get out of control," Finkelstein whined, "I've talked to Harry and he agrees … says he'll never allow the investigation to go forward, and I—"

"Hi, Dana, Vickie here," Barrett said cutting Finkelstein off. "I just walked in. Let's not get our panties in a wad over Crux. I suggest we follow good old Rom's advice.

"What'd you mean?"

"Just what Rom said, Dana, 'Never let a crisis go to waste.' " Vickie grinned at Abomba.

"Everyone's focused on the Baghdad attack. Now is the perfect time to publish the first set of implementing regulations for The Comprehensive Firearms Registration and Storage Act. We've had them ready for months. All that's required is fine-tuning a few sections. I've talked to Harry too, and he's okay with the idea."

"Yeah … I like it," Abomba blurted out. "Rom always did have a whole bunch of good ideas about how to handle stuff. That's all for now, Dana. Talk to you later," the president said, turning off the speakerphone and looking at Barrett.

"Vickie, have you coordinated with Balogni?

"Yes … Nellie's going to keep attention focused on the embassy hearings. Meanwhile, we'll slip the gun regulations into the Federal Register on Friday of next week."

Abomba nodded. "Speaking of the Baghdad fuck up, how the hell did that damn colonel get on FOX? Why didn't someone put a gag on him?"

Barrett scowled, "That someone is the stupid general you put in charge of CENTCOM."

"Guess I'll have to fire him."

Barrett hopped off the desk, turned around to face the president and shook her head, "Uh uh … No, not a good idea. You've fired *way* too many generals already. Firing Doughberry would just give the rabid right more ammunition to fire at *you*."

"Oh *really?*" Abomba said, raising one eyebrow and quizzically looking up at Barrett, "Well, I'm sure you have something brilliant up your sleeve."

Barrett smiled down at her boss. "Yes, in fact I do. Did you by any chance notice Doughberry's lovely executive assistant, Colonel Rebecca Collins?"

"Abomba frowned, attempting to recall the meeting. "Yeah, now that you mention it—the good-looking brunette—what about her?"

"She's clever and opportunistic. Right now she's *his* lover ... but," Barrett chuckled, "she and I have a lot in common. She's *my* kind of woman."

Abomba laughed, and raised an eyebrow. "Ooooh … I gotcha. You mean she's *bi* ... swings both ways?"

"Uh huh, and she's quite the swinger. She's with Doughberry for one reason only—her star."

"If she can control the idiot general, I'll personally pin on her star."

Barrett started for the door, then stopped and turned to look at him. "Think I'll give her a call and set up a meeting for the weekend—" she hesitated, frowning and biting her lower lip, "but where would be a good place to meet?"

"In bed," the president said, rolling his eyes.

"Great idea. Can't think of a better place myself," Barrett winked.

"That's my girl," Abomba quipped, laughing heartily while she walked out the door.

The phone on Colonel Collins' desk rang. Glancing at the caller ID, she saw WHITE HOUSE. *Who the heck can that be?* she wondered, before answering, "Colonel Collins."

"Good morning, Rebecca, how are things at CENTCOM?"

Ah, it's Vickie, Collins smiled, for she hadn't heard Vickie Barrett's voice for several months. "Better now that I'm talking to you. Missed you."

"Missed you too, that's why I'm calling. Going to meet with the ICE folks tomorrow at Key West. A friend loaned me her condo for the weekend. I was hoping you'd join me."

Rebecca leaned back in her chair, remembering their hot weekend in San Francisco eight months ago. "Love to, but I may have a problem getting away. My boss is willy-nilly handling the embassy attack. He's ordered the MP, Colonel Vickers, to report to him, and he's scheduled to arrive today at 1300, that's one o'clock."

"Good, we're worried about him. The damn news media is turning him into a hero. Make sure Doughberry doesn't do anything stupid ... or should I say more stupid?"

So that's why she is calling. Hmmm ... looks like I might be able turn a fun weekend into a career advancement opportunity. "What do you suggest we do with him?"

Barnett chuckled, "What I'd really like to do with him isn't feasible. So I'm encouraging you to privately suggest your general give Vickers a Top Secret debriefing, and then send him back to Baghdad. Better still, bury the bastard in some remote spot."

"Good idea. I'll make that suggestion right away, and then arrange a flight to the Key West Naval Air Station. I'll e-mail you my arrival time."

"See you in Key West. I'll e-mail the address. Plan on returning Sunday afternoon."

Rebecca sat at her desk evaluating her next move. Thoughts of another weekend with the hot blonde kicked her libido into overdrive. *Now all I have to do is plant the proper idea in my doughboy,* Rebecca chuckled, *and that's so easy to do. Better get started.*

Colonel Collins knocked on General Doughberry's door, entered without waiting for permission and closed the door behind her.

"What's up, Becca?" Doughberry said, looking up from a report on his desk.

Probably you ... you horny old goat. "Sam, I've been thinking about the MP colonel. The networks news hacks are playing that damn FOX interview over and over again. Now the newspapers have picked up *The Washington Times* story. I know you're set on canning him, but doing so may cause you a problem … Uh, put you in a bad light, I mean."

"Yeah? Well, we've already talked about this."

"I know, but I've been thinking and I have an idea. Why not formally debrief him, classify the results Top Secret, and then bury the asshole in some very remote post."

"Hmmm, do you think Secretary Haggler will approve?"

"I'm sure he will."

"Why?"

Walking to a chair directly in front of Doughberry, Collins sat, casually splaying her legs and displaying the crotch of her black lace thong.

"Well, I had a call from an old friend in DC," she said, caressing her right knee with her right hand and slowly running it up her inner thigh.

"Seems the administration wants the colonel to disappear."

Doughberry's eyes glazed over for several seconds, while he fondled his manhood and ogled her lacy see-through thong. Finally shaking his head to clear his thoughts, he stuttered, "N–not a bad idea … a–any suggestions as to where to p–post him?"

"Hmmm … Africa maybe … How about Mali? I believe we have a unit there training their army. I'm sure they could use someone to help train their police force, and Colonel Vickers is the right man for the job."

Breathing heavily now, Doughberry smiled, "I like it."

"Sam, the friend I talked to in D.C. is someone I've known for years," Collins said, pulling her skirt down and breaking the spell. "She's attending a meeting with ICE in Key West this weekend, and asked if I could meet her there."

"Is she with Homeland Security?" Doughberry asked, sighing and shifting in his chair.

"Uh, no … the *White House*," Collins said with wide eyed emphasis, knowing full well the very mention of her being friends with anyone who was near the president would encourage him to let her go.

"Well, as much as I'll miss you, we wouldn't want to upset anyone at the White House. Your leave request is approved."

CENTCOM, MacDill AFB
Friday morning, 3 April 2015

General Beck observed Colonel Collins working diligently at her desk and noticed she seemed in an exceptionally good mood. Wondering what she was up to when she failed to return to her office after lunch, he decided to find out when he met with Doughberry at 1600. *I'm positive they're lovers and that she has a great deal of influence over him—more than any of his staff,* Beck was still considering the ramifications of the situation, when General Ulrich knocked on his door and called out.

"Ulrich here … got a minute?"

"Sure John, come in."

Ulrich entered, closed the door and selected a chair. "Sir, what're we going to do about the Baghdad attack? It looks like all we're doing is preparing option plans. If we're going to act we need definitive orders."

Beck sighed, "John, General Doughberry has the options we prepared. I have a meeting scheduled with him this afternoon to discuss this issue."

"Do you think he's made a decision?"

Beck pursed his lips, knowing tradition demanded he defend his boss, but also not willing to lie. "As far as I know, the answer is no. I expect he has already sent or is going to send the options plan up the chain of command to Secretary Haggler."

Ulrich took a deep breath and slowly exhaled. "And Secretary Haggler will send it back with questions and ask for more options."

Beck gave Ulrich a slight nod.

"And when Haggler's satisfied, he'll buck it up to the President, who so far has avoided making any hard decisions."

"Careful, John," Beck said, even though he knew Ulrich was correct.

"Sorry, sir. It's just that I'm beginning to think we're not going to take any meaningful action."

Beck nodded but didn't comment. Instead, he changed the subject, "How are things back home in Colorado?

Ulrich shook his head. "Not good. Got a call from one of my high school friends who owns a gun store in Fort Collins. The new gun laws have just about killed his business. Very few out-of-state hunters came this year, and several who did got into trouble. One had his guns seized. The state attorney general just sent out letters to every person who has or had a hunting license, ordering them to bring all their firearms and magazines to the local police stations for registration. My friend says resentment and anger are fermenting, and major resistance is possible."

Beck grimaced and shook his head.

"Sir, I'll not be part of using the military to suppress our citizens if they're defending their Constitutional rights."

"John, that's a bridge we don't have to cross. What you're describing is a state problem."

"Maybe, but if Homeland Security gets into the act ..." Ulrich left the rest of his statement unspoken.

Both men frowned at each other. Beck understood the ramifications of Ulrich's unfinished statement, and both knew it might be a bridge they'd have to eventually cross.

Beck's afternoon meeting with General Doughberry provided no new guidance. Just as Ulrich had speculated, the option plan had been sent to the secretary of the Army who had bucked it up to Secretary Haggler. Doughberry said he expected a request for additional options and ordered Beck to start preparing them. Toward the end of the meeting, Beck casually inquired about Colonel Collins and learned she was meeting a White House friend in Key West. Doughberry didn't know the person's name.

Returning to his office, Beck used his secure line to call Captain Hazzard. After chatting a couple of minutes about family, Hazzard filled Beck in on the Blue Shirts training. Beck commented he was unaware Blue Shirts were training with the SEALS. Hazzard responded he hoped they'd be gone before one of his men had enough of their shit and beat the hell out of one of them. Finally Beck decided it was time to ask the question he'd called about, "Tom, do you or your chief have any friends at Key West Naval Air Station?"

"I'll have to check and see. What'd you need?"

"One of our officers, an Army colonel, Rebecca Collins, arrived there this afternoon on an Air Force flight from MacDill. She's there to meet someone from the White House. It would be nice to know who."

"I'll see what I can do, sir ... anything else?"

"No, thanks."

"I'll call you when I find out."

Captain Tom Hazzard placed the receiver in its cradle and wondered what was up. Tony Beck rarely did anything without a reason. *Colonel Collins, yeah, I remember seeing her outside Doughberry's office.*

Good-looking gal. If Beck is interested in her, then I should be too. Picking up the phone he dialed Master Chief Warren Jefferson, "Chief, are any of our folks in Key West?"

"Yes, sir, a couple of retired chiefs. What do you need?

"Information. Colonel Rebecca Collins, Army, arrived at the naval air station this afternoon on a flight from MacDill. She's meeting someone, identity unknown, from the White House. It'd be nice to know the person's name, and what they're up to. This is off the books."

"I'll get right on it."

Jefferson mentally reviewed whom best to contact in Key West. Two retired chiefs and one petty officer were living there, but one name jumped out, Charles Teal, a former member of SEAL Team 6. Waking up his iPhone, Jefferson located Teal's number and pressed send. After four rings, Jefferson heard a recording, "Captain Teal Charters. We're out catching fish, so please leave a message and I'll call you when the fish are cleaned." Jefferson laughed, and when the tone sounded said, "Charlie you old war dog, this is Warren Jefferson. I'll call you this evening."

Chapter 12

Key West Naval Air Station
1523 Friday, 3 April 2015

A **young sailor standing on the tarmac was watching deplaning passengers** stepping out of a newly arrived aircraft, when he noticed a striking brunette. Dressed in civvies and carrying a small bag, the woman began slowly following the other passengers down the plane's portable staircase.

Checking the photo he was holding, he whistled softly to himself. *Oh, yeah, that's the babe I'm s'posed t' pick up.* "Now that's one hot looking colonel," he muttered, waving to get the woman's attention and walking forward to greet her at the bottom of the stairs. "Colonel Collins, I'm your driver, Petty Officer Oliver," he said saluting smartly. "May I carry you bag?"

"Yes, thank you," she said, returning his salute and handing him her bag. "I only need a ride to this address," she continued. "I'll need you to pick me up there at 1600 Sunday."

"Yes, ma'am," Oliver said, handing her a business card, "Here's my phone number. Call me if you need me during the weekend … this way to the car."

Providing a running commentary on Key West, Oliver drove out of the air station, turned west on Truman Avenue and south on Duval to the address she'd given him. *Nice digs … some rich guy must live here?* Oliver speculated, parking in front of a four-story condo facing the water in South Beach. *Wouldn't mind spending the weekend here myself,* he mused, opening the rear door and taking the colonel's hand to help her out of the car. Then reaching in the back seat to grab her bag, he asked, "Shall I carry this for you ma'am?"

"No I can take it from here, Oliver. Thanks for the ride and the travelogue," she said, walking to the front entrance. "I'll see you Sunday."

"Yes, ma'am. Hope you have an enjoyable visit."

"Oh, I plan to," she replied, waving goodbye. Then, searching the nametags beside the building residents' call buttons, she found the name

Vickie had given her, pressed it and waited for the door to click open so she could enter.

Once inside, she found herself in a typical sun-lit, Key West style elevator lobby, decorated with brightly colored Adirondack Chairs for seating and a seascape mural covering the walls.

Stepping off the elevator on the top floor, she looked left and right down a long hall and saw there were two suites. Seeing the one to her right had the door open, she smiled, walked toward it and entered a wide foyer. *I wonder what Vickie will be wearing,* she mused, closing the door and envisioning her lover's enticingly curvaceous body.

Vickie's voice greeted her from the room beyond, "Hi there. Come on in and join me in a glass of champagne."

Entering the large room, she saw Vickie standing near the bar, holding two bubbling flutes of champagne. Dressed in a short, black, spaghetti strapped, see-through negligee, a black garter belt with black stockings, and sexy, black platform pumps with ankle straps and six-inch spike heels, Vickie didn't disappoint. Her shoulder length blonde hair fell softly around her shoulders, and her bright red lipstick emphasized her pouty lips. Rebecca felt her pulse quicken as her eyes slowly traveled down Vickie's body, stopping at the blonde bush clearly visible above her sheer negligee's hemline.

When Vickie set the glasses on the bar and opened her arms, Rebecca dropped her bag and rushed into her embrace. After a long kiss, Rebecca said, "Yummm ... you look good enough to eat."

"I certainly hope so," Vickie replied, picking up the two flutes and handing one to Rebecca. "To an exciting weekend."

Rebecca drank the toast and quipped, "To a climactic weekend."

Grinning, Vickie raised her glass and said, "To a multi-climactic weekend."

"Grab your bag and follow me," Vickie said, after they'd both drained their flutes. "Our boudoir awaits," she said, effortlessly floating on the balls of her feet across the living room and leading the way into a luxurious master bedroom overlooking the ocean, "I'm sure you want to freshen up after your flight. The bathroom's in there," she added gesturing to a doorway in the large, mirrored dressing area. "I'll wait for you here, but don't take too long ... I'm anxious to get reacquainted."

Two hours later Vickie and Rebecca exited the shower, dried each other with oversized towels, and slipped on sheer, silky kaftans.

"Hungry?" Vickie asked with a sexy smile.

Rebecca shook her head, "You can't still be horny."

Vickie laughed, "I meant food, my darling girl ... are you ready for dinner?"

"You betcha. I'm hungry as a horse."

"You oughta be. That was some workout.

"I have a couple of filets. Still like yours rare?"

"Sounds wonderful. Do you have a good red?"

"Check out the wine rack and pick one."

"How about a 2005 Cahors' French Malbec?"

"Good choice, open it and let it breathe."

After dinner, they lazed on a cushioned lounge on the balcony caressing each other, kissing and enjoying the sunset. "Is the bottle empty?" Rebecca sighed, breaking their embrace to drink the last of her wine.

"Yes, let's see if there's another and open it," Vickie said rising and taking Rebecca's hand to pull her to her feet. We can catch the seven o'clock news." Then wrapping their arms around one another's waists, the lovers entered the apartment.

While Rebecca found the bottle of wine and opened it, Vickie turned on the TV and tuned it to MSNBC, where what to do about the attack on the embassy was the lead story. Flipping channels she found CNN, FOX and every other network all running the same thing—each featuring their own "expert" expounding on a different solution.

Making room for Rebecca to join her on the couch and putting her arm around her shoulders, Vickie asked, while gently stroking the nape of her lover's neck, "Did Colonel Vickers object to his new assignment?"

"No, he actually seemed relieved. I think he expected a reprimand."

"Good, the President doesn't want him making waves. Tell me, what are CENTCOM's recommendations?"

Rebecca quickly reviewed the various options prepared by the general's staff. None were good. "Vickie, we don't have any good options—short of declaring war on Iran or reinvading Iraq. Most of the staff thinks Iran was behind the attack, but they can't prove it. Some have privately suggested we could bomb Baghdad, or take out Iraq's president—"

"Well, what do you think ... what's your recommendation?"

Rebecca hesitated, unexpectedly feeling her desire rising at the sight of Vickie's voluptuous breasts and erect nipples silhouetted against the sunset. Finally, after taking a long sip of the delicious red wine, she replied, "I think Iran is the culprit, but we'll never prove it. No, I think the best solution is to let the 'experts' wear the people out and move on to other more important issues."

"Like gun control?"

Rebecca nodded, set her glass on the coffee table and reached for the hem of Vickie's kaftan.

"I think you have a bright future in our administration. If you can keep Doughberry out of trouble, I would say your star is rising," Vickie said, gasping as Rebecca's hand pushed her silky garment up and caressed the inside of her thigh.

Turning and leaning forward, Rebecca kissed Vickie's neck and slid her hand further up her lover's thigh.

Vickie felt her nipples harden. "Consider that your main duty," Vickie murmured, "Call me if you have any problems."

"General Beck may be a problem," Rebecca said, raising her head and running her tongue over Vickie's luscious lips. "Can't get a handle on him," she whispered, "He's very clever at covering his ass."

Moaning softly and using one hand to gently pull Rebecca's hand up to her blonde bush and the other to cup the back of her lover's head, Vickie kissed her hungrily.

"Let's finish the wine in bed," she said, finally pulling away and breathing heavily.

"I thought you'd never ask," Rebecca sighed.

Master Chief Warren Jefferson checked his watch, saw it read 1825, and placed a second call to Charlie Teal. This time Teal answered, "Captain Teal Charters."

"Charlie, how's the charter business going?"

"A little slow, my weekend charter cancelled. What's up? You still at Little Creek?"

Jefferson laughed, "Yep. Just checking up on you. Wondering if you'd lost your touch."

Charlie laughed, "And that means you have something for me to do."

"Uh huh, it's a favor. Need to ID someone and see what she's up to."

Jefferson repeated Hazzard's info, and Charlie agreed to perform some snooping.

"Okay, Warren, I'll call you when I've got something. Any rush?"

"Not that I know of. Thanks Bud, I owe you one."

Charlie chuckled, "More'n one, Warren. You got any travel plans?"

"No, not even an alert order."

Charlie heard Warren sigh before they hung up. *We're going to let the fuckers get by with destroying our embassy. What the hell's wrong with us? Some country's capital city should be radioactive by now. Oh well, back to Warren's problem. Both people probably arrived on government planes. That's where to start.*

Charlie Teal called a friend at the Station and learned that Petty Officer Oliver had driven the colonel to a condominium in South Beach. Writing down the address, he asked if anyone from the White House had arrived in the last few days, and learned Vickie Barrett, a gorgeous blonde, had arrived the day before on a VIP flight. Ms. Barrett was a member of the president's staff, and her driver had taken her to the same address.

Now ain't that interestin'. Key West is a full of same-sex couples. Think I'll recon their place.

Teal parked his SUV near the end of Duvall Avenue and walked down to the beach. Acting as though he was there to enjoy the sunset, he meandered along the shoreline until he was directly in front of the condo. The turning to look behind him, he glanced up at the building. The lights were on in one of the two penthouse apartments, which allowed him to see two figures, who were sitting on the balcony, rise and walk with their arms around each other into the apartment. Charlie grinned as he saw the two women's silhouettes in the doorway. *Yep, I was right. Doubt if they'll be up early.*

Joint Expeditionary Base Little Creek - Fort Story
Virginia Beach, VA
Sunday, 5 April 2015

Warren Jefferson was in his quarters reading the newspaper when the phone rang. "Master Chief Jefferson," he answered.

"Good afternoon, Warren. Your Army colonel and her girlfriend are very interesting. Colonel Collins met with a Victoria Barrett, some kind of special assistant to the President. Barrett's a good-looking blonde. The two of them spent most of their time in a penthouse apartment in South Beach. I followed them for a while on Saturday. They walked around old town holding hands and kissing. Apparently Barrett has a lot of horsepower, because they departed on a VIP aircraft for Joint Base Andrews with a stop at MacDill.

"Very interesting. Thanks."

"Tell your boss when he gets tired of catching little fish, he can come down here and I'll show him how to catch the some whoppers."

"I'll do that."

"Any alert or action orders?"

"Nope."

"Shit."

"You got that right. Thanks again for your report."

Hanging up, Jefferson called his boss.

After discussing the report with Jefferson, Hazzard placed a call to General Beck and relayed the chief's report.

Chapter 13

Senator Finkelstein gaveled the Senate Intelligence Committee to order. Surprisingly, all members were present. So immediately following preliminary announcements, Finkelstein called the first witness, who took the oath and began her testimony.

"My name is Barbara Pearson. As Deputy Assistant Secretary for International Programs in the Bureau of Diplomatic Security at the Department of State, I'm responsible for the safety and security of more than 274 diplomatic facilities."

"Madam Chairwoman," Texas Senator Carlos Crux interrupted. "I object. This committee summoned the Secretary of State to testify. Why isn't *he* here?"

"Senator Crux, although the chair did not recognize you, in answer to your question, I've been informed that Secretary of State Heinz is in Saudi Arabia. Deputy Assistant Secretary Pearson is here to provide an explanation and answer our questions."

"You may continue." Finkelstein said, giving Crux a scathing look.

For the next hour, the committee listened to Peterson's drawn-out account of the Baghdad attack that sounded similar to Charlene Lamb's 2012 testimony regarding the Benghazi attack. Actually Pearson's opening statement clearly parroted Lamb's, in that she began her comments the same way, by declaring she was there, "To have a constructive discussion with the committee about how we can best work together to prevent such tragedies in the future," and concluded by saying, "As you know, there is an on-going FBI investigation being conducted into the Baghdad attack, and we are speaking today with an incomplete picture. As a result, my answers today will also be incomplete."

Noting the similarity between Lamb and Pearson's statements, several committee members, including Crux, privately speculated State had simply provided her a template for her testimony. *Where have we heard that before?* Crux asked himself, rolling his eyes as he listened to Pearson. When the questioning finally began, he shifted restlessly in his seat. *Good God, here we go again,* he grunted, fed up with her answers. *All she's giving us is one lame excuse after another... sounds all too familiar to me ... same old same old—State blaming their failures on somebody else or some other agency. The FBI investigation is ongoing my ass. According to State, FBI investigations are interminable. Look how long it took them to investigate Benghazi. How are we supposed to have a constructive discussion when by the witness' own admission her answers are incomplete?*

Though disgusted with Pearson's excuses, Crux wisely decided the woman was just another shill for Abomba. Dwelling on her prevarications would only give the president the distraction he wanted. So instead, when he realized he was next in line for questions, he prepared to ask the one question he most wanted answered—Why the Baghdad embassy was left a defenseless sitting duck?

Having been recognized by the chairwoman, Crux began, "Ms. Pearson, I have two questions for you. To save time please answer them concurrently. First, are you aware that days before the attack, Ambassador Hopkins sent a distress cable to Secretary of State Heinz objecting to the removal of the Marines; and second, that the cable clearly requested the Marines be allowed to stay, because the embassy could not be adequately defended if they departed?"

"Senator Crux, we receive many requests from our embassies. I can examine our correspondence to see if such a request was made."

"Does that mean that you haven't already done so?"

Pearson gave the senator a contemptuous look, sighed to imply she was either dealing with a child or a fool, and then began another long, rambling reply—purposely designed to run out the clock on the senator's allotted time. Any attempts Crux made to stop her and ask other questions were thwarted by the chairwoman. Eventually Crux's time ran out, and the questioning moved on to a friendly Democrat—one who spent his time opining, bloviating, and asking softball questions.

At the end of the hearing the chair announced the committee would meet the following Tuesday to hear testimony from Secretary of Defense Haggler or his representative. Senator Crux shook his head in anger and headed for his office. On Tuesday he would learn that Colonel Vickers' testimony had been classified and the colonel was not available to testify.

Tuesday evening James Carrier, the president of the NRA, was a guest on The O'Rippley Quotient. Railing against the administration's further efforts to remove a citizen's rights to bear arms, Carrier held up a telephone-directory-size document. "Take a look at this Bill. It's Friday's *Federal Register*—" he said, turning the daily publication of proposed and final federal rules, regulations and other legal notices around so the camera could film the cover. "... and in it," Carrier continued, "are over 150 pages of new regulations implementing parts of the Comprehensive Firearms Registration and Storage Act. Provisions in the law are similar to Colorado's law, and they become effective on January 2nd. I expect more such regulations in the coming weeks."

The next day on *The Six*, FOX network's afternoon talk show, panel members devoted the entire hour to the Baghdad embassy attack. Noting that attempts to locate Colonel Vickers, the Military Police commander, had failed, Greg Gutterschpiel, writer and host of FOX late-night talk show, *Eye to Eye*, excoriated Secretary of Defense Haggler for gagging Vickers by classifying his report on the attack; and vilified White House Press Secretary Jay Schpinmeister for—in light of the president's oft-promised transparency—perpetually prevaricating to the American people. "All Schpinmeister ever says is that the FBI is investigating some incident of national importance and nothing about it can be discussed." Gutterschpiel signed off by saying, "What a dirt bag."

2nd Avenue Police Department
Durango, Colorado
7:30 a.m., Wednesday, April 15, 2015

It was the day Durango Police Sergeant Dennis Cantor had been waiting for. Raised in California, Cantor worked for the Oakland police force for three years. However, when liberal Democrats, whose political ideology Cantor admired, swept into office in Colorado, he decided to apply for the sergeant's position in Durango. Jubilant when he got the job, he moved to the town determined to put his liberal ideology into practice— and today was his chance to do just that.

Gun owners had been given one month to turn in their high capacity magazines and bring their guns into police stations for inspection and registration. April 15th was the last day to comply with the law. But so far, not one gun or magazine had been brought to his station. Aware the same was true at other Colorado police stations, Cantor expected a last day rush and was prepared. Sitting at his desk behind the front counter, sipping his coffee, he'd been waiting for over two hours for his first victim to arrive.

However the sergeant didn't wait alone. His assistant, Charlie Reddington, a newly hired young police officer, who'd cleared out a storage room where the seized weapons would be stacked, waited in the lobby. It was his job to guard the table they'd set up for citizens to place their guns on for inspection. Looking at the itemized list of required documents Cantor had taped to the wall next to the front counter, Reddington yawned. *I wonder just how many people in this town will willingly bring in their guns?* he mused, trying to stay awake. Charlie Reddington had been partying until 2 a.m. and only gotten four hours of sleep.

At 7:58 a.m., Thomas "Nighthorse" Williamson, a Native American from the Ute tribe and a decorated Vietnam veteran, entered the station with his grandson, John "Lightfoot" Williamson, age twelve. Between the two of them, they carried two shotguns—a 12 gauge pump, and a double barrel 20 gauge; and four rifles—an M1 Garand, a Winchester Model 94 lever action 30-30, a Savage .300 magnum bolt action, and young Williamson's semiautomatic .22 Marlin.

Sergeant Cantor rose when they entered and sneered. They looked like Indians and he had no use for redskins. Everyone knew they were nothing but sorry, lazy drunkards who lived on welfare.

Pointing authoritatively to the empty table, he gave the pair a sour look. "Put your guns on the table. Then bring me your paperwork," he said, cutting his eyes at Officer Reddington.

Tom Williamson had noticed the sergeant's condescending look when they entered, caught this tone, and didn't like his attitude. After placing their guns on the table, Nighthorse reached in his shirt pocket, removed a neatly printed list of his weapons with serial numbers, and approached the counter. Laying the list on the counter, he waited quietly while the sergeant scanned the document.

"Where are the bills of sales," Cantor asked.

"Sergeant Cantor," Tom said, having noticed the officer's nametag. "I've had these weapons for many years. I have no bills of sale. The Winchester and M1 belonged to my father. He used the M1 in Korea. I purchased the Savage many years ago. My father gave me the Model 60 Marlin when I was ten, and I passed it on to my grandson, John. I have no idea where dad purchased it … same thing for the shotguns."

"That so? Well, you're required to have a bill of sale for each gun," Cantor smirked.

"Well I don't have any ... *Now what?*" Williamson asked, his tone indicating he was becoming angry.

"Mr. Williamson, you were ordered to bring in all your weapons, magazines, and proof of purchase for each weapon. Since you have no magazines for the M1, and no bill of sale for each weapon, I must confiscate them."

"WHAT?"

"I'm sorry Mr. Williamson, but I'm required to by the new law."

"We'll see about that. I'm taking my guns home."

"Sir, if you attempt to remove any of those weapons," Cantor said, pointing at the table, "I'll have to arrest you ... your grandson too, if he tries to take any of them."

"Give me a receipt. I'll be back for them and—"

Cantor shook his head indicating no. "I'm not required by the new law to give receipts." High on asserting his authority, Cantor was having the time of his life. These were the first guns brought in for registration, and he expected to have a room full of them by the end of the day.

While Thomas was arguing with the policeman, John Lightfoot stood behind his grandfather tweeting on his cell phone. "Police seizing our guns. Stealing them. Don't bring in guns." A minute later he tweeted, "Police won't give receipt. Stay away from police." Within minutes, John's tweets were being forwarded across the nation. Facebook postings quickly followed, and calls to talk radio shows began clogging phone lines. Gun owners across the country had their dander up.

The warrior inside normally peace loving, agreeable, Thomas "Nighthorse" Williamson had had enough. "Well Officer Cantor, if you won't give me a receipt, I'm taking my guns with me."

"Can't let you do that," Cantor said, raising his voice. "Now leave or I'll arrest you."

Turning, Nighthorse told, his grandson, Lightfoot, in their native language to run, and then said to Cantor, "You'll have to arrest me then, and if you do, I'll charge you with theft of personal property."

Cantor had been waiting for the old man to say just that. Walking around the counter, he drew his service semiautomatic 9mm and pointed it at Williamson. "Place your hands behind your head and turn around. You're under arrest for interfering with a police operation."

Fleeing out of the station's front door, young Williamson ran to a small parking lot on the side of the building, ducked down beside a car and tweeted, "Police arrested grandfather Nighthorse." He'd just sent the tweet, when he heard a car entering the parking lot. Sneaking a peek from his hiding place, he recognized his neighbor's, Ben Abrams', SUV. "DON'T TAKE YOUR GUNS IN THERE," he shouted, running toward their vehicle. "The police'll seize 'em. My grandfather asked for a receipt and the officer arrested him."

"*What?* Tell me what happened," Abrams said.

After listening to John's quick description of what transpired in the police station, Ben "Sleeping Bear" Abrams instructed his wife to wait in the parking lot while he went inside. "I'll go in and find out what's going on. If I don't come out in fifteen minutes, go directly to the mayor."

Entering the station, Abrams noticed a young policeman standing near the rifles and shotguns lying on a table, but there was no sign of his friend Nighthorse. Seeing Sergeant Cantor standing behind the counter, Abram's approached, and said, "Sergeant, I've just been told you arrested Mr. Williamson. Is that true?"

Cantor looked at the man standing in front of the counter. *Another stinkin' Indian,* he silently scoffed, trying to remember who the man was. He'd seen him around the town, but didn't know his name. "Please show me your ID."

Abrams, a former MP officer and business owner, took an instant dislike to the arrogant sergeant. "I asked you a question. Showing you my ID isn't required unless you have a reason for such a request. Now, answer my question."

"Show me your ID now, or I'll place you under arrest too," Cantor snarled, placing his hand on his pistol.

"Then arrest me, but be prepared for a false arrest lawsuit."

Out in the parking lot, Mary Abrams was still waiting for her husband to return. When fifteen minutes passed with no word from him, she started the car and told John to get in.

"What about grandfather? I can't leave him here," John said, concern evident in his voice. "Don't worry boy. We're going to the mayor's office. I want you to tell him what happened. He won't stand for this."

Before Mayor Fernandez's secretary could object, Mary Abrams stormed through the mayor's reception area, with John Williamson following in her wake, and ripped open Fernandez's office door. Bursting in and interrupting the mayor's meeting, she stomped up to his desk and stood there fuming.

One look at the expression on Mary's face told Fernandez something was terribly wrong, "Mary, what's got you so upset. What's wrong?"

"What's wrong is your police department," she stormed. They've arrested Tom Williamson. Ben went into the station to find out what was going on. He told me to come here if he didn't come out in fifteen minutes." The mayor started to say something, but Mary held up her hand and gestured toward John. "Listen to what Tom's grandson, Lightfoot, has to say. John, tell the mayor why you and your grandfather were at the police station and what happened there."

At first John was hesitant to speak and looked anxiously from Mary to the mayor, but then Fernandez reassured him, "It's all right, John. You're not in trouble … just tell us what happened."

"My grandfather and I took our rifles and shotguns to the police station on 2nd Avenue to register them, like the letter told us to …" John continued describing in detail how he and his grandfather were treated.

When the boy finished his story, the mayor pressed the intercom and told his secretary to get the officer in charge of the 2nd Avenue police station on the line. Fernandez had been meeting with a building contractor when Mary barged in. The contractor opened his cell phone and called his foreman, "Bob, tell your men not to register their guns with the police. It appears they'll be seized if all the required paperwork isn't presented. Who the hell has receipts for guns purchased years ago? I sure don't."

"Mr. Mayor, Sergeant Cantor is on the line," a voice said through the intercom.

"Sergeant Cantor, this is Mayor Fernandez. I understand you've arrested one of our citizens and are holding another. What the hell's going on?"

"Mr. Mayor, I'm following our state attorney general's orders. The new gun registration act has—"

"Cantor, I don't give a shit about the new law, and you don't work for the AG. Release both men immediately, apologize to them, and maybe, just maybe, you and the city won't get sued."

"Mr. Mayor, I can't do that. The attorney general's instructions are clear and you cannot overrule him."

"Is that so. Well Cantor, you aren't in California any more, but I think you should strongly consider returning there."

"Also, Cantor, return Mr. Williamson's guns when you release him.

"No, Mr. Mayor, I can't do that," Cantor said hanging up.

During the conversation the mayor's voice had risen. Now he was red in the face. Not bothering with the intercom, he slammed down the receiver and shouted, "JAN, GET THE CHIEF OF POLICE ON THE LINE. I don't care where he is or what he's doing."

For several minutes, Mayor Fernandez sat glaring at the phone and muttering to himself. Then jerking up the receiver, he called the chairman of the city commissioners. As soon as the chairman answered, he growled, "Robert, are you aware our police force is seizing citizens' guns when they're brought in for registration? That liberal idiot we hired from California arrested John Williamson, when he refused to surrender his guns. Seems he was supposed to have a bill of sale for each gun. Hell, some of his guns are over fifty years old.

"And it gets worse, the idiot may have also arrested Ben Abrams ... Yes, Ben Abrams.

"I want you to call an emergency commission meeting ... Yeah that's right. Someone is going to get fired ... Good. Let me know the date and time—and yes, I do have a call in to the chief."

Fernandez was about to hang up when he noticed his other line blinking, so he pushed the button, "Mayor Fernandez"

"Mr. Mayor, Police Chief Tozzolo here, I am returning your call."

"Are you aware that idiot you hired from California arrested Ben Abrams and Tom Williamson? ... Well get over there and fix it. Someone's head's gonna roll—yours or the idiot's ... *What?* What'd you mean there's a mob gathering outside the police station? ... Men brandishing rifles and shotguns! *Damn it to hell!* I'll meet you there.

Mayor Fernandez and Chief of Police Tozzolo arrived at the 2nd Avenue police station seconds apart. Pickup trucks, SUVs, and automobiles were parked in front of the station and as far as Tozzolo could see down the street. When he saw more vehicles blocking the two side streets, he correctly assumed the station was surrounded.

Parking behind the mayor in front of the station, he observed two men with rifles slung over their shoulders, pounding on the building's front door. A growing crowd of more than twenty people—also armed—stood in a half circle behind them loudly demanding Williams and Abrams' release.

"Look at what that idiot has caused," Fernandez yelled rushing toward Tozzolo who'd gotten out of his truck. "And listen to that," the mayor said, referring the local talk radio host, whose voice could be heard coming from radios in many parked vehicles. The host was talking to angry callers who were apparently in the crowd surrounding the police station.

The mayor was about to say something else, when they saw the door to the police station open and Sergeant Cantor and another uniformed officer, whom Tozzolo recognized as young Reddington, step out. With their pump shotguns in a position known as "port arms," both men stood holding their weapons crossed diagonally over their chests and pointing to the left.

"Back away and do it now," Cantor yelled, glaring at the crowd of men and a few women who were also armed. "DISPERSE I TELL YOU," he shouted. *"This is an unlawful assembly* ... get on out of here, before I have to arrest you. As for you two who were pounding on the door, you're under arrest for disturbing the peace. Now drop the rifles, turn around, and place your hands behind you."

"That's not gonna happen," the larger of the two men replied, now holding his lever action rifle in his left hand.

Watching from behind the angry crowd, Chief Tozzolo was growing fearful of a shootout. "SERGEANT CANTOR. THIS IS YOUR CHIEF SPEAKING," Tozzolo shouted with his hands cupped to his mouth. "I'M ORDERING YOU TO STAND DOWN ... LET THOSE MEN GO AND RETURN TO THE STATION."

Shouts from the crowd, drowned out Tozzolo's orders.

"Now you're resisting a police officer ... you'd best remember this gun speaks for me," Cantor told the larger man, "If you don't drop that rifle and turn around you'll regret it," he threatened.

"Cuff him," Cantor ordered Reddington, who was standing behind him.

Frightened out of his wits, Reddington, a native of Durango, knew Mr. Dunlap—the man Cantor told him to cuff—and most of the angry men and women surrounding the building. And he had grave doubts about the legality of seizing citizens' guns. So when Cantor ordered him to cuff Mr. Dunlap, he froze, and unable to carry out what he considered an unlawful order, unconsciously released his grip on his shotgun, and lowered it with his right hand so its barrel pointed at the ground by his foot.

"Damn you, Reddington! I told you to cuff him—that's an order."

When several seconds passed and Reddington did not respond, Cantor snarled, "All right then you coward ... *I'll do it myself.*"

"DROP YOUR RIFLE," Cantor yelled, raising his shotgun to his shoulder and aiming at the man holding the rifle. "Turn around and place your hands behind your back. I'm going to count to three and then, if you don't comply, I *will* fire."

Incensed by Cantor's last statement the crowd in front of the station grew suddenly silent; and then, as if it had been practiced, came the unmistakable sounds of men and women simultaneously preparing to do battle—lever action rifles being charged, pump shotguns racked, and bolts snapping shut on rifles. Cutting his eyes at the crowd, Cantor saw at least twenty rifles and shotguns aimed at him.

"*Oh my god* ... Chief, do something!" Mayor Fernandez pleaded.

But Chief Tozzolo didn't hear him, for he was already muscling his way through the crowd toward the sergeant. "CANTOR, STAND DOWN, DAMN IT!" he yelled, grabbing the sergeant in a bear hug from behind. "Give me your shotgun and get inside."

"What ... Chief, what are you doing?"

"You idiot. Give me the damn shotgun before we all get shot. What the hell do you think you're doing?" Tozzolo demanded, turning Cantor around and ripping the shotgun out of his hands.

"Reddington, get over here. Take his service pistol and get him inside. Keep him covered until I join you."

Relieved that no one had been shot, but shaking with anger, Mayor Fernandez joined Tozzolo. "That was too close chief, but thanks to you no one got hurt ... now go on inside to see to Cantor. I need to stay here and talk to these people," he said, and waited for Tozzolo to enter the building before turning to address the crowd.

"Okay, folks I think we've all had enough excitement for today," he told the disgruntled looking group. "You need to head on home. Chief Tozzolo and I will sort this out. Tom Williamson and Ben Abrams will be released, and Tom can retrieve his guns. After that the chief and I'll figure out a way to resolve the issue of gun registration and confiscation."

Later that morning Glenn Deck picked up the Durango story on his nationally syndicated radio show. Callers reported similar incidents in other Colorado towns and cities. One caller told listeners in Colorado, "Do not take your guns in for inspection as required. If you do you'll never see them again."

Unfortunately, it was already too late for many honest men and women who'd followed the instructions in the attorney general's letter.

The expanding story continued when Rusty Limbo followed Glenn Deck. Callers from California, New York, Maryland, and Massachusetts reported questionable police gun seizures. By the time Sean Haddley was on the air, the story was huge and still growing.

At Governor Hickengooper's office in Denver, the phone lines were jammed, but he was out of the state. The same was true for the attorney general. Phones in state legislator's offices quickly overloaded. Harried staff members attempted to explain the law to angry constituents with little success. Angry men and women demanded return of their guns, not lectures and excuses.

Armed men and women began assembling near the Capitol in Denver and at other county government and police buildings.

U.S. Attorney General Helder had listened to the big three talk radio hosts—men he despised—discussing reaction to Colorado's gun laws. *For once they're being useful,* he smirked. As soon as Sean Haddley signed off, he called Jane Incompentado, "Jane, the game is afoot."

"Good. I'll alert my Blue Shirts.

Chapter 14

Golden, Colorado
8:25 a.m., Thursday, April 16, 2015

Pat Jenkins heard the doorbell chime. Opening the front door she was surprised to find two uniformed police officers staring at her.

"Good afternoon, officers. Can I help you?" she asked.

"Does Mr. Leon Jenkins live at this address?"

"Yes, he's my husband. Is he all right has something happened to him?" she asked, her voice shaking, afraid there might have been an accident.

Ignoring her question one of the policemen stepped forward. "We have information that Mr. Leon Jenkins has unregistered guns. Stand aside, we're going to search your house."

So that's what this is about, Pat realized, and standing her ground spread her arms out to bar the doorway. She didn't like the policeman's uppity attitude and was well aware of her constitutional rights. "May I see your search warrant?"

"We don't need one."

"Yes you most certainly do. Come back when you have one." Pat told them, and was stepping back to shut the door when a masked policeman dressed in black, the leader of the SWAT team stacked on the porch out of sight, swiftly pushed past the two officers, shoved her out of the way, and burst through the door.

Stunned at what was happening, Pat stood staring out the open door as more men—masked men dressed in black—ran into her house. **"WHAT THE HELL IS GOING ON?"** she screamed at the officer who'd shoved her aside.

"Sit and shut up," the masked policeman replied, pointing to a chair.

"I WILL NOT. My children are upstairs. You're going to *frighten* them."

"I told you to sit down and be quiet. NOW SIT DOWN," the officer yelled grabbing her arm and shoving her down on the chair. "Otherwise you'll be arrested. Your husband didn't register his guns as required."

"My husband *doesn't have* any guns in the house. NOW GET OUT!

"AND YOU ... STOP THAT. YOU'RE DESTROYING MY HOUSE," she yelled, jumping up and rushing up to one of the masked men yanking drawers out of her china cabinet and dumping the contents on the floor.

"Out of my way, bitch," the man snarled, backhanding her and knocking her to the floor.

"MOM! Mom, are you all right?" yelled Pat's eight-year-old son, Tommy Lee, as he and his sister raced down the stairs.

"*Mama, mama,* you're hurt," the little girl sobbed at the sight of blood trickling from her mother's mouth.

"I'll kill you for hurting my mother, Tommy screeched, launching himself at the man standing over her. His sister began screaming.

Whirling around and grabbing the boy by the scruff of his neck the SWAT team leader roughly thrust the boy into the arms of a policemen, "Put this brat in your cruiser ... the girl too. Turn them over to Family Services."

Alerted to a disturbance across the street by her barking Labrador retriever, Brutus, the Jenkins' neighbor Rachael Stack, stood staring out of her living room bay window in disbelief. Police cars and a big black SWAT unit vehicle were parked in front of the Jenkins' house.

"What's going on boy?" she asked the whining dog, as countless policemen and SWAT team officers swarmed into Pat and Lee's house. *Oh, my God, something awful is happening over there.* "I hope Pat and the children are all right?" she muttered, trembling, for she'd known the family for years and loved them.

"Oh, Brutus, they've got the children," she gasped, having heard little Lee and Jennie screaming and watching two policemen rush out the front door carrying them. "Good grief boy, they're putting them in one of the patrol cars ..." *What on earth is going on? Those poor children. I wonder where Pat is?*

"Oh no ... what have they done to her?" she gasped a minute later, when Pat, her face bloodied and in handcuffs, came wobbling out the front door supported by two policemen on either side of her. *"That does it,"* she told Brutus, "They've manhandled her into a patrol car too. You stay here boy. I'm going over there and find out what's going on," she told the whining dog.

Storming out her front door, Rachael was crossing the street when a policeman slapping a nightstick in the palm of his hand barred her way.

"What's going on here?" she demanded. "What have you done to my friend, and where are you taking her children?"

"Police business, lady. Go back to you house," the officer said.

"What *kind* of police business. I know the Jenkins. They're good people. What are you accusing them of?"

"They've got illegal guns, and we've got a report the husband may be a terrorist. He was a military sniper and that placed him on the terrorists watch list."

"Leroy Jenkins is an honorable man and a *decorated veteran.* Are you telling me that makes him a terrorist?"

"I asked you to return to your home, now I'm ordering you to," the officer said, raising the nightstick and stepping forward.

Frightened for her own safety now and so angry she was crying, Rachael rushed home to call Lee and tell him what she'd seen.

Lee Jenkins couldn't believe what he had just been told. Resisting his first impulse to rush home, he called his buddy, Bob, and repeated the neighbor's report.

"Lee, you can't go home. Head for the camp, and make sure you aren't followed. I'll have Brian Ebert check out the situation. He's a criminal attorney."

"Thanks. Better tell my boss I have to take emergency leave."

Two hours later Brian Ebert pulled his black Mercedes S63 AGM to a stop behind one of the patrol cars parked in front of the Jenkins house, got out and walked toward the front door. A uniformed policeman stopped him, "Sir, you have to leave. You're interfering with a police investigation."

Ebert handed the officer his embossed business card, "I'm Mr. and Mrs. Jenkins attorney, and I demand to see my client."

The SWAT onsite commander had seen the expensive car pull up and deduced it was probably an attorney. Walking over, he took the card from the officer's hand and read it.

"Mr. Ebert, come with me," he said.

Ebert followed the masked man through the front door and stood for several minutes staring at the living room and dining room. *Someone has completely trashed the place ... reminds me of crime scene photos I've seen from recent home invasions,* Ebert observed, shaking his head in disgust.

Furniture had been turned upside down, its upholstery slashed; family photos ripped from the walls and thrown on the floor, their frames broken and glass shattered; china and crystal from the dining room breakfront lay smashed on the floor; and the drawers of the Jenkins' desk pulled out and dumped on the floor, their personal papers strewn about the living room.

Not one item in these two rooms hasn't been savaged by these Neanderthals, Ebert grimaced, fighting not to show his anger to the masked officer standing in front of him, legs splayed apart and arms crossed.

"Who the hell trashed this house and why? Please identify yourself and show me your warrant."

Realizing he was dealing with a heavy hitter, Sergeant Brant hedged, "Mr. Ebert, as I'm sure you already know, I'm a member of SWAT and cannot identify myself."

"Fine, get a hold of your commander and tell him to get here ASAP."

Damn, another ex-military type. This guy is gonna be trouble. "Yes, sir. Give me a moment to call," the officer said, and stepping outside speed dialed his superior, Captain Regis. "Captain, we've completed a search of the premises and found no guns or ammunition. We were just wrapping things up when the Jenkins' attorney showed up. His name is Brian Ebert and he's demanding to see you."

Immediately recognizing Ebert's name, Regis cringed. He knew he had a problem. Ebert was trouble—big trouble. Known for dismembering the cases of several assistant district attorneys, Ebert was not only respected and feared by many, but also well connected. "Tell him I'm in conference with the police chief right now, but I'll be glad to meet with him if he can be in my office in a half hour. I want him out of there. As soon as he leaves, box up the evidence, including any computers, and get back to the station."

Across the street Brutus continued to sit in the bay window whining and watching the Jenkins' house. Rachael busied herself taking pictures with her iPhone and posting them on her Facebook page—complete with a description of the Nazi raid on her neighbors' house. Her posts quickly went viral across the nation.

A policewoman had been tasked with escorting Mrs. Patricia Jenkins from the holding cell in the Jefferson County Detention Center to an interview room in the main police station. Upon entering, they found the room occupied by a well dressed, handsome man seated at a table facing the door. Standing, the man, who was a complete stranger to Pat, surprised her by greeting her by name.

Not knowing what to say or do Pat nodded and smiled. Seemingly in his mid-forties, the man was tall and well built, wore a muted, pinstriped, gray suit she figured must have cost at least two grand—and apparently owned the pricey leather briefcase laying on the table before him. Suddenly struck by a wave of panic, Pat stared at the man. *Who is this guy? Maybe he's a detective who's going to force me to tell him things that would harm Lee ... maybe even beat me,* she worried, but relaxed a bit after more carefully eyeing the briefcase. *No police detective could afford a case that expensive. Who is he? Why have I been brought here? What does this man want with me?* she worried, and was grateful for the policewoman's presence. *As long as she is here—*

"Un-cuff her, then leave," the man said, interrupting Pat's thought.

Noting it was more an order than a request, Pat held her breath fearing what would come next, but nothing else was said until the door closed

"Come join me at the table, Pat," the man said, holding a legal pad in his left hand and gesturing to the chair facing him. Once she was seated, he placed the legal pad on the table in front of her and tapped it with his finger.

Looking down at the pad, Pat read the message written on it, "My name is Brian Ebert, your attorney. Act as though you know me, and call me Brian." On the next line he had written "Colorado Militia," and beneath that taped his business card to the paper.

Slowly looking up, Pat sighed with relief, and said, "Thanks for coming, Brian. The police raided our house without providing a reason and didn't have a search warrant."

"Yes, I know. My associate is drafting a request for an immediate bail hearing. I have an appointment with the assistant district attorney in an hour. With your approval, I plan to sue the city. You have a very good case."

"They *took* my children," Pat said her voice quivering and her eyes brimming with tears, "Do you know where they are?"

"No. Family Services has them, but don't worry. My associates will find them. I have the name of the social worker assigned to the case." Anticipating her next question, he said, "Your husband is safe. He's going to have to stay away until I get this in front of a judge. Trust me ... he'll be okay.

"Do not say anything unless I'm present. I'll be back for your arraignment. And don't be concerned about posting bail. It'll be taken care of."

"Now, tell me exactly what occurred. Everything, including who struck you in the face," he said, pulling out his phone and taking several pictures of her swollen split lip and black eye.

Brian Ebert knocked on Assistant County Attorney George Dumphries III's door, and without waiting for an invitation entered. "Good afternoon, George. Your guys sure stepped in it."

Dumphries was short, in his early thirties, obese, and a Harvard graduate—something he never let other attorneys forget. In short, Dumphries was an overconfident, arrogant little prick Ebert enjoyed beating in court. "Good afternoon, Brian. I understand you're representing the terrorist's wife."

"Ah … *just* what I expected from a progressive-liberal—guilty until proven guilty. Isn't that what's being taught at Harvard's Karl Marx School of Law? You know, you alumni should relocate the campus to San Francisco. That is on the *left* coast you know."

Dumphries smirked, "Insults won't win this case," he barbed back, and pointing at Ebert with his left index finger began ticking off the main points of his case. "*One,* Leroy Jenkins didn't register his guns. *Two,* Leroy Jenkins didn't turn in his high capacity magazines. *Three,* Leroy Jenkins didn't have an approved gun safe in his house. *Four,* Leroy Jenkins didn't have an approved ammunition storage safe in his house. Heard enough?"

Ebert chuckled, shook his head, and then, addressing Dumphries as if he were speaking to a child, replied, "George, let me explain the law to you. Before you charge a person with a crime, you really should first make sure a crime has been committed. Otherwise you open yourself up to all kinds of charges—say prosecutorial misconduct and malicious prosecution. Surely they covered all that at Karl Marx U."

Dumphries bristled and Ebert smiled to himself. *Good, now the little shit's pissed. Time to see what he has.* "George, admit it, you don't have a case."

"Like hell I don't. The search determined there were no gun and ammunition safes, as required by the new law."

"Do you mean your illegal, warrantless search?"

"The new law gives us authority to enter *without* a warrant."

"Are you by chance referring to the unconstitutional law Governor Hickengooper recently signed?

"That has yet to be established. I'm sure it will be codified by our Supreme Court."

Ebert shook his head. "George, it might be prudent to wait for the Supremes' decision, before charging a man and his wife with an unprovable crime."

"Who said it's un-provable?"

Ebert gave Dumphries a condescending smile. "Can't wait to see your proof." Then becoming serious, Ebert continued. "George, don't you realize you're playing with fire. Violating the Second Amendment is asking for a rebellion. The only way to legally seize guns is to repeal the Second Amendment."

Puffing up, Dumphries shot back, "The majority of our citizens in Colorado want guns taken away from our citizen."

Standing, Ebert said, "Two problems with that. First, your majority of citizens—assuming they are really a majority—can't override the Constitution. And second, your so called majority doesn't have guns."

Dumphries jumped to his feet, "Are you threatening *violence*?"

Ignoring Dumphries outburst, Ebert casually asked, "Are you going to Pat Jenkins arraignment?"

Returning to his chair, Dumphries huffed, "Yes … and I'll be requesting one million dollars bail."

Ebert didn't bother replying, just walked out the door.

The arraignment hearing was under way and the bailiff was calling the case: "Pat Jenkins, charged with violating the Colorado Gun Registration and Storage Act, and a second count of Terrorism."

Ebert and Jenkins walked forward and stood before the judge. "How do you plead?"

"Your Honor, my client pleads not guilty," Ebert said, "The police executed an illegal search of her home, found no evidence to support the charges, and removed her two children without cause.

"And, Your Honor, no evidence was presented to support the terrorism charge, nor was any evidence discovered in the illegal search.

"Therefore I move for a dismissal of all charges."

"Does the Assistant District Attorney have any evidence to support the charges?"

"Yes, your Honor. We have sworn statements that Leroy Jenkins has at least ten rifles and shotguns. Mr. Jenkins did not register any of them as required by the new law. Further, we did not find the required gun and ammunition safes in the Jenkins' house."

"How about the terrorism charge?"

"Mr. Jenkins is on the national terrorist watch list."

"Your Honor," Ebert said, "Assuming for the sake of argument that the assistant district attorney's sworn statements are true, the statements would only be true on the date they were made. Mr. Jenkins could have sold his guns or moved them to another state before the registration deadline.

"In addition, Your Honor, I am at a loss to understand how being on a watch list can be equated to actually committing a crime."

The judge contemplated the two arguments for a full minute before saying, "The motion to dismiss all charges is denied at this time. The first count stands until I hear the evidence. The terrorism count is dismissed. I will rule on the motion to dismiss the first count at the evidentiary hearing on—" the judge consulted his calendar, "On Thursday, June 25th, at two o'clock.

"Does the State have a recommendation for bail"

"Yes, your Honor. The State requests bail be set at $500,000."

Judge Parker glared down at the assistant district attorney, as if he thought the man was a fool. "Bail set at $50,000," he said. "Next case."

Chapter 15

Governors Office
Capitol Building, Denver, Colorado
Thursday morning, April 16, 2015

Governor Hickengooper's administrative assistant Miss Margaret Gofferson threw open his office door and rushed inside. "*Governor, Governor* ... President Abomba is on the phone, " she breathlessly said.

"Huh ... What? ... the *President*?" Hickengooper asked, his eyes wide with excitement.

"Uh, no ... actually it's his office. They called to say the President wants to speak with you. They're holding on line three."

Quickly lifting his handset, the governor answered, "Governor Hickengooper."

"Hold for the president of the United States," came the response.

Shaking his head, Hickengooper looked at his assistant in disbelief. Fifteen seconds later he heard the distinctive sound of the president's voice. "Governor Hickengooper ... John, if I may. I want to personally congratulate you on your state's gun laws. You are blazing the trail for the rest of the country.

"It's up to you now to set the standard; however, I understand efforts to enforce your law have met with some unfortunate resistance. You may want to consider activating your National Guard, John.

"I want to make one thing perfectly clear, John. Our gun laws *will* be enforced. I am behind you ... as is Secretary Incompentado, who stands ready to provide any support you need—*including* force.

"Thank you for calling, Mr. President. I'll do my best to set a high standard."

"I knew I could count on you."

Several seconds later, Hickengooper realized he was listening to the dial tone.

The president had hung up.

Capitol Building
Denver, Colorado
Thursday afternoon, April 16, 2015

Brian Ebert ascended the steps on the west side of the capitol. Pausing briefly to read the inscription on the fifteenth step, "One mile above sea level," Ebert chuckled, amused at the number of times the building's elevation seemed to have changed over the years. *All this fuss over distinguishing our capitol as being the only one situated a mile above sea level. After ninety-four years and three separate geodetic surveys maybe this time they got it right ... as if anybody but the engineering students at the University of Colorado gives a rat's ass. Oh, well, if the good Lord's willin' and the sea level don't keep risin' and fallin'–the third time may be the charm,* he snorted, heading on up the steps and recalling the building's history.

Modeled after the United States Capitol, the building was constructed in the 1890s. To commemorate the Colorado Gold Rush, a gold dome was added in 1908. A craftsman first inscribed the words "One mile above sea level" on fifteenth step in 1949, in order to foil vandals who repeatedly stole replicas of the original 1909 mile-high brass plaque. Twenty years later in 1969, a second step, the eighteenth, received the mile high designation, after Colorado State University engineering students discovered that the original inscription wasn't in keeping with their mile high geodetic survey. In 2003, a more accurate measurement was made using modern technology, and a new mile-high marker was installed.

Still amused by the effect sea levels had on the elevation of buildings, Ebert entered the governor's outer office and presented his card to Hickengooper's middle-aged gatekeeper, Ms. Margaret Gofferson.

"Governor Hickengooper's meeting is running over the scheduled time," Gofferson huffed, avoiding eye contact, while meticulously entering his arrival time in her daily log. After scrutinizing his card, she filled it in the correct alphabetical order in her business card holder. "Be seated. I'll inform you when he's ready to see you," the gatekeeper sniffed as she carefully return her cardholder to its precise location.

Can you say Obsessive Compulsive Disorder? Ebert thought, amused by her discourteous reception. "Thank you, I'll do just that, *Miss Maggie,*" Ebert barbed. He had noticed the absence of a wedding ring when he read her nametag, and deliberately emphasized the "Miss" to annoy her.

Persnickety old maid ... it's no wonder she's never married. She's probably been with Hicky for years—she may even be in love with him.

Seven minutes later three men walked out of the governor's office, and the gatekeeper announced that his three o'clock appointment had arrived.

"Send him in it five minutes," Hickengooper replied

The Gov needed a potty break.

Five minutes later Miss Maggie announced, "You may go in now, Mr. Ebert."

Nodding in response—he wasn't going to give her the courtesy of a thank you—Ebert rose and walked toward the governor's office.

"Good afternoon, Mr. Ebert," Hickengooper said greeting him at the door and offering his hand.

"Thank you, Governor, for finding time to meet with me."

"Yes, well, have a seat and tell me what can I do for you?" Hickengooper said, settling into a leather chair in the office's sitting area and mentally reviewing Ebert's legal career. He'd never met the man personally but knew him to be a strong supporter of Constitutional government—something Hickengooper had no respect for ... after all, times had changed. *No doubt he's here to plead some radical, right wing, red neck, gun toter's legal entanglement related to the new gun law. We'll just see about that,* he resolved.

"Governor, I'm here as a concerned citizen."

Yeah, I'm sure you are, Hickengooper thought. *Putting up with fools is part of the job.*

"As I'm sure you know, the last day for gun owners to register their guns and turn in semiautomatic weapons and certain magazines was yesterday."

Looking at Ebert with hooded eyes, Hickengooper nodded.

Ebert sensed the governor's disinterest but pressed on, "There've been a number of unfortunate incidents at police stations throughout our state. Some became, shall we say, unruly. In at least one incident, citizens came very close to firing on police who were abusing their authority—"

"Now wait a minute," Hickengooper interrupted, "There's no possible justification for citizens pointing guns at police officers,"

Ebert sighed, "Governor, the Colorado Firearms Registration and Storage Act appears to violate the Second Amendment of the Constitution.

Until the constitutionality of the act has been established, vigorous enforcement by law enforcement authorities courts disaster."

Here we go ... Just as I suspected he's here to defend that moldy, old, irrelevant document.

Leaning forward and scowling, Hickengooper emphatically stated his position, "Mr. Ebert, understand this. Failure to comply with this law will be considered an act of rebellion. *The law will be enforced.*"

Remaining steely-faced to mask his anger, Ebert continued, his hands clasped in front of him, and his voice glacial, "Mr. Governor ... I'm here today on behalf of my clients, Leroy and Patricia Jenkins who live in Golden. Yesterday, on the pretext of seizing an unknown number of unregistered guns, local police and a SWAT team entered the Jenkins' home without a search warrant. Mrs. Jenkins experienced a vicious assault at the hands of a SWAT team member; her house was ransacked, its contents smashed and destroyed; and her two children were taken from her and placed in the custody of Family Services. All of this was done without a warrant or judicial approval.

There he goes dragging up irrelevant, outmoded laws and the damn Constitution again. Hickengooper sneered.

"Governor, are you willing to risk an armed uprising by Colorado citizens? I fear it could happen, if you don't rein in the police."

Springing to his feet Hickengooper glared down at Ebert. "Mr. Ebert, is the purpose of your visit to deliver a message from insurrectionists? If so, then hear my words clearly. At the first sign of armed resistance, I *will* call up the National Guard and *put down any such rebellion.*"

"No, Governor, my mission here today is to prevent a rebellion—*not threaten one.* It would serve you well to remember what I'm about to say. Illegally entering citizens' homes, assaulting them, destroying their private property, and kidnapping their children without due process of law are the acts of a police state. If such acts are not punished, if such acts are not deemed wrong, then yes Governor, you *are* planting the seeds of rebellion.

"I sincerely pray that you will consider my words and put a stop to this madness."

"Good day, Mr. Ebert."

"Good day, Governor."

Brian Ebert met Bob at a sports bar and described his meeting with the governor.

"So, Brian, it's your opinion that Hickengooper agrees with what's going on and will not stop police raids and seizures."

Ebert nodded. "He's a progressive-liberal. Nothing will change his mind."

Bob frowned, "I prayed this wouldn't happen. It's going to get nasty. If he calls up the Guard ... will they turn on their friends and neighbors? If they disobey the governor's order ..." Bob sat staring at his beer shaking his head. "*Damn!*"

Ebert had a sudden insight, "Damn is right. I think you're on to something. The federal government is going to use Colorado as a *test case*. New federal gun control regulations are coming and what happens here will set the standard for the rest of the nation."

Bob's head snapped up, "What'd you mean?"

"I mean the federal government may send in troops to enforce the law. Hell, the Kennedys did in the 1960s to enforce civil rights laws in Arkansas."

"Yeah, but civil rights laws didn't violate the Constitution. Guess we'd better send a stronger message. By the way, did you get the name of the social worker?"

Ebert nodded.

Nationally syndicated talk radio shows
Friday morning, April 17, 2015

Glenn Deck broke the Jenkins raid story at the top of his morning radio talk show. "This morning we've confirmed a report that a SWAT unit in Golden, Colorado entered the family home of Mr. Leroy Jenkins, a decorated former Special Forces sergeant, without a search and seizure warrant. On the pretext of seizing Mr. Jenkins' allegedly illegal guns, the SWAT unit entered, over the objections of his wife, who during the subsequent illegal search was viciously assaulted and knocked to the floor by a SWAT team member. Yes folks, you heard me right. Law enforcement officers—sworn to protect Mrs. Leroy Jenkins' Constitutional rights—illegally entered her home and brutalized her ... and it gets worse folks—*much* worse.

Not only did the police arrest Mrs. Jenkins, charge her with terrorism, and take her children out the home and turn them over to Family Services, but—and this is the most egregious part—even after ripping the Jenkins house apart, the SWAT team found NO GUNS.

"Why did this happen? Because Attorney General Helder placed Sergeant Leroy Jenkins, one of Special Forces best snipers, on a terrorist watch list. A TERRORIST WATCH LIST! Can you *believe it?"*

By the time Deck's show ended, thousands of listeners had tweeted or called to report the names of other former military men and women who'd been placed on the same terrorist watch list.

Rusty Limbo, whose show followed Deck's, zeroed in on the embassy attack and the lack of information being provided by the Abomba administration. Limbo began, "Tell me this folks. Doesn't this sound like Benghazi? Today the White House issued this statement regarding the slaughter at the embassy in Iraq, 'The FBI has a team investigating the crime scene.' Oh, yeah ... they're always investigating something, but have you noticed—they never arrest anybody.

"The report goes on to say, 'So far no one knows where the shells came from.' What shells? What are they talking about? There weren't any shells to identify. Everything was blown to bits. I have a report from a reliable source that the embassy compound attackers used mortars and rockets. If true, and I think it is, then this was a planned attack by a military unit or military personnel. My source thinks the Sadr Militia was involved or actually carried out the attack. In any case, Iran's fingerprints are all over the attack.

"Folks, the facts are that hundreds of Americans were killed doing their jobs in *another* under-protected embassy. So far no one has been held responsible and there have been no arrests. And if Benghazi is an example, it will take a long time, if ever, to determine who that someone is. Even more interesting, Colonel Vickers, the man who led the MP unit that drove off the jihadis, was reassigned to a post in Mali. In other words, he's been hidden."

Later that evening Senator Crux appeared as a guest on the Sean Haddley Show. After covering much of the ground previously covered by other news commentators, Crux revealed that part of the implementing regulations for The Comprehensive Firearms Registration and Storage Act had been published in Friday's Federal Register.

"Senator, how bad are these regulations?" Haddley asked.

"Sean, in addition to banning all semiautomatic guns—rifles, pistols, shotguns, even .22 caliber rifles and pistols—any veteran who has ever had psychological counseling or has been prescribed any of a long list of medications, will be entered in the National Instant Criminal Background Check System."

"Senator, I don't understand."

"Sean, any veteran who has received counseling after being in combat, any veteran diagnosed with PTSD ... and some veterans like Sergeant Jenkins who had mandatory counseling, will *not* be allowed to own firearms."

News spread throughout the military and unrest began to grow. For the first time in the history of the United States, its military began to doubt its leadership.

Chapter 16

Arvada, Colorado
Saturday night, April 18, 2015

Captain Regis drove his Ford Expedition into his garage and triggered its power lift gate. Walking to the rear of the SUV, he reached in and grabbed his duffel bag. Having had a long day, he was glad to get home and was turning around to go into the house, when he found himself confronted by three men surrounding him in a semicircle. Their faces covered by black baklavas. Two of the men were armed with AR-15s, and the third held a pump shotgun. Instinctively reacting to the threatening situation, Regis's hand was halfway to his service pistol, when the man with the shotgun, apparently the leader, leveled it at him and growled, "*Bad idea, Regis.*"

"Do you know who I am? Robbing me will be a very bad mistake."

"We know exactly who you are, and we're not here to rob you. What we want is information. So you're going to give us your truck's fob, and we're all going to take a ride some place quiet for a nice chat."

"And if I *don't?*"

"Then you and your family will pay the price. Now, turn around, shut the tailgate, place your hands on the truck and spread your legs," the apparent leader ordered.

Fearing for his life and that of his family, Regis followed the man's orders. He had just placed his hands on the tailgate's window when the timer turned off the garage light. Now in the dark he felt his pistol being removed and one of the men expertly frisking him.

"Now get in the front passenger seat. While one of my buddies drives, my other buddy's gonna join me in the back seat. I'll have my .44 magnum revolver pointed directly at your back. Do you understand?"

Nodding he understood, Regis lowered his hands.

"Good boy—Now move it," the leader hissed, poking Regis' back with his weapon, while walking behind him to the front of the truck. "Open the front passenger door and climb in."

Regis knew a .44 magnum bullet would penetrate the seat and kill him. So he sat perfectly still while the driver backed his SUV out of the garage and headed east on route 192 into the mountains. Eventually turning onto a fire road, the driver preceded a mile or so before he pulled into a clearing and stopped.

"Get out," the leader said, jabbing the back of Regis' seat with the barrel of his revolver while opening the rear door. Seeing the other two men also pointing pistols at him, Regis opened his door and got out.

"Now kneel by the truck," the leader said.

Oh, God. He's going to blow my head off, and I have no idea why. Regis panicked watching the other men join their leader.

"Damn it, I said kneel."

"All right, all right, but at least tell me why you're going to kill me," Regis said, slumping down to his knees.

"We'll get to that, but for now we want you to tell us who gave the order for you to search the Jenkins' house?"

So that's what this is about. Taking a chance they wouldn't shoot, Regis lowered his head and shook it to indicate he wasn't going to answer.

"I'll ask you one more time nicely. After that, every refusal will result in a broken bone. So far, we're not here to punish you, but if you don't name the person responsible for the raid, you'll receive the punishment intended for the one who gave the order."

"Look ... be reasonable," Regis said, buying time in hopes of grabbing one of their weapons. "My unit was ordered to enforce the new law. The law is the law. I, uh ... w–we were just carrying out orders. What difference does it make who gave them?"

"This isn't a debating society meeting, but I'll tell you what difference it makes. The raid was *illegal*. The raid violated the Jenkins' Fourth Amendment rights, and the state gun law violates the Second Amendment. Now, answer the damn question."

I'm not dealing with criminals. These men are serious, and I've had my own doubts about the legality of the new law and my orders.

"Okay I'll tell you, but you're breaking the law by your actions. The Colorado Attorney General directed me to execute the raid."

"You received a direct order from the AG?"

"Yes, in person."

Regis didn't see the three men look at each other and nod.

"Did you question your orders?"

Regis hesitated momentarily, thinking how best to reply. "Yes, I asked myself if the law was legal."

"Not the AG?"

"No."

"Did any of your men question your orders?"

"No."

"Well, Regis, *that's* the problem. If members of an elite police unit are willing to follow illegal orders, then we have a police state."

Regis remained silent, for he'd been haunted by this very thought since receiving the order.

"Well," the leader demanded. "Did the order trouble you?"

"Yes, it did. I started to challenge it, but I knew my career would be over if I did. I–I'm not proud of my actions."

"Nor should you be."

"One more question. Who struck Mrs. Jenkins?"

"I've reprimanded the officer. His actions were uncalled for and excessive."

"His name and address … *NOW!*"

"I'll not be responsible for his death."

"We won't kill him … just administer appropriate punishment. If you don't tell us, you'll receive the punishment."

Normally I'd never rat out one of my men, but Johnson's been a problem from day one—too quick to use his hands or baton. I was told they had to restrain him to keep him from hitting the Jenkins woman's son. He needs more than a simple reprimand.

"Okay, I'll tell you. His name is Arlie Johnson. He lives at 4233 North Ford Street, in Golden."

"Good, that's all for now Regis, but understand this. Our purpose is to put a stop to this gun seizure business before the shooting starts. Up to now, no one's been killed, and we want to keep it that way. So pass this message on to your friend the AG. If another raid like the one on the Jenkins occurs, there *will* be shooting and dead police. Help us stop this from occurring.

"Now, you have a nice long walk ahead of you," the leader said helping Regis to his feet. "Your truck, with your cell phone and pistol in it, will be parked near your house. I assume you have another fob."

"Yes, I do."

"Well, good night then. Have a pleasant stroll."

Early Sunday morning, after an anonymous call tipped off the local police, officer Arlie Johnson was found severely beaten on the side of a deserted stretch of U.S. Highway 6 in the mountains. By Monday afternoon, word of his "punishment" had spread throughout local law enforcement. Some agreed Johnson's deserved his punishment. Others vowed revenge.

Aurora, Colorado
Sunday, April 19, 2015

Mr. Alfred Firla and his wife Agnes returned home from church, entered their kitchen through the garage door, and were horrified to find several heavily-armed, masked men waiting for them.

"What do you want?" Mr. Firla asked, shielding his wife with his body."

"Sit," the apparent leader said, pointing to the kitchen table.

"Better d–do as they say," Mr. Firla stuttered, and with his hands shaking, pulled out a chair for his wife.

"Good. Now, Mrs. Firla, we have a problem you can solve. It can either be a simple problem, or if you refuse to help, it can become a serious one ... serious for you that is. Do you understand?"

Not only did Mrs. Firla not understand, but she was also scared out of her wits, so she shook her head no.

"Very well Mrs. Firla. Let me help you understand. Our simple problem will remain simple, if you do exactly as I say. Do you understand *that*?"

Mrs. Firla nodded yes.

"Good. Now let me clarify the problem and its solution."

"The simple problem is that you took custody of a young boy and girl last Thursday. Do you remember them?"

"Yes. They were very frightened."

"I'm sure they were. Where did you take them?"

"I'm afraid I cannot tell you that. It's against regulations."

"Ah ... now you're turning a simple problem into a serious one," the leader said, motioning to two men who moved forward, grasped Mr. Firla's arms and began securing them to his chair with duct tape. All the men wore gloves; and, as soon as Mr. Firla was secured, one of them lit a propane torch and pointed it toward his face.

"For God's sake Agnes, tell them," Firla pleaded, "Can't you see they're *serious*?"

"Alfred, I can't just break the rules just because some brigand threatens me or you." A brain-dead bureaucrat, Mrs. Firla was incapable of making a real decision.

"Last chance to tell us, Agnes, before I order my man to inflict unbearable pain on your husband."

"AGNES, PLEASE!" Alfred screamed.

"If I do tell you … then what?" his wife blithely asked, seemingly unconcerned about her husband's fate.

"Why then it becomes a *simple* problem again. You'll simply go and get the children, and then give them to us. Afterwards, you can release your husband."

"Are these the two children who were removed from the *terrorists' house*?" Mr. Firla asked. "Are you *also* terrorists?"

"Alfred, the answer to both of your questions is *no*. The Jenkins are not terrorists—the judge has dismissed the terrorism charge. The children will be returned to their parents.

"Now, if your wife cooperates, you will spend a few uncomfortable hours in the chair and then it will be over. Once we have the children, we'll release Agnes in a remote area unharmed. Otherwise … well we hope you'll not have to find out what the alternative is."

"*I'm begging you, Agnes,* do what they want you to."

For several seconds, Mrs. Firla sat frowning, and then, sullenly sighing she said, "Oh, *all right*. I'll go with you and get the children—but I hope you realize how much trouble you're in."

"Yes, ma'am, we surely do."

Several hours later, Lee and Pat Jenkins were reunited with their children in the mountains.

As for Agnes Firla, she stumbled into a 7/11 store late Sunday afternoon and called the police.

Chapter 17

The Glen Deck Show
Monday morning, April 20, 2015

Glenn Deck's morning radio talk show featured a recorded interview with Lee and Pat Jenkins, which alerted and appalled people across nation to Colorado's police state tactics.

Attempts by progressive-liberal callers to justify the SWAT unit's actions outraged conservative listeners. One Denver area caller mentioned that the SWAT officer who struck Pat Jenkins had been found beaten on the side of a remote highway. Callers in favor of his beating were ten to one against those who were shocked by it. The program's final caller of the day declared, "I'm glad the people punished the SWAT officer, because neither the police chief nor the attorney general were going to."

Anger against the new Colorado gun law was growing, but progressive-liberals like the governor and his AG couldn't understand why. They couldn't because they had trouble accepting or understanding any point of view that differed from their own.

Governor Hickengooper and his AG scheduled a press conference on the Capitol steps for Wednesday noon. The governor's press secretary implied Hickengooper would announce increased police seizure of unregistered guns.

White House
Monday afternoon, April 20, 2015

Vickie Barrett called the president to recap the Glenn Deck Show's bombshell. "The SOB is riling up the conservatives. The damn conservatives approve of a SWAT operative being beaten for striking a suspected terrorist. I thought Helder was going to shut Deck up."

"No, Vickie. Ed is arranging for the IRS to begin auditing Rusty Limbo. He's the number one big mouth. When they find something, we'll seize Limbo's assets. We'll have to come up with another way of silencing Deck. Auditing him at the same time would cause a problem.

"Anything new with the idiot commander of CENTCOM?"

"No," Barrett replied, smiling at the thought of Rebecca. "My girlfriend has everything under control, and I plan to keep in close touch with her."

"Uh huh," the president responded in a suggestive tone.

Barrett got the innuendo and smiled again before continuing, "My friend reports that since Doughberry ordered his command to begin Internment and Resettlement Operations, training element commanders have raised a lot of questions."

"*To hell with them,*" the president groused. "Haggler ordered DOD wide training. We'll be ready for any resistance when the new regulations go into effect in January.

"Incompentado will have over 100,000 of her Blue Shirts ready to deal with any resistance. The military will be the Blue Shirt's back up.

"I'll be leaving for Palm Springs Friday afternoon. Got a golf date with Tiger."

"Have fun ... think I'll weekend in Tampa."

"Hmmm," Abomba murmured with a sly grin.

Denver, Colorado
Noon, Wednesday, April 22, 2015

Colorado's attorney general and governor stood facing the TV cameras on the west steps of the Capitol building. Hickengooper stared into the camera lens and began, "Citizens, the legislature of the great state of Colorado, following the wishes of the electorate, passed the Colorado Firearms Registration and Storage Act, which I signed into law. Many law-abiding citizens have complied with the law and turned in their guns; however, a few hardcore gun-nuts, supported by the NRA, have refused to do so. Let me make this absolutely clear. Colorado's new gun law decrees that *all* semiautomatic guns *must* be turned in, and legal guns and ammunition *must* be properly stored. I have directed Attorney General Zapata, the state's senior law enforcement official, to ensure compliance with the new law. He will now inform you of events related to his efforts in this regard."

"Thank you Governor Hickengooper," Zapata said, "It is a fact—an unfortunate fact—that a number of our citizens have chosen to disobey the new law. It is also a fact that many of our citizens did not understand that gun registration and turn-in had to occur by April 15th.

"Governor Hickengooper has offered amnesty to all citizens who register their legal guns and turn in illegal ones by April 30th. After that date, owners of illegal guns will be prosecuted.

"As part of the governor's amnesty program, citizens arrested for failure to comply with the law have been released and charges dropped.

"Now I'll take your questions. Yes Miss ... " he said, pointing to FOX News' foxy blonde reporter.

"Did the SWAT unit that raided Leroy Jenkins' house have a warrant?"

"No. I determined that a warrant was not required, because Mr. Leroy Jenkins was on the terrorists watch list, which caused me to suspect he was a terrorist."

"Was his wife also on the list?" The reporter persisted.

Zapata ignored the question and pointed to a friendly NBC reporter.

"Is it true that no guns or ammunition were found in the house?"

"Yes, Bob, that's true. The guns and ammunition had been removed."

"Have the charges against Pat Jenkins been dropped?" The reporter asked

"Yes, as part of the amnesty program."

"How about Lee Jenkins?"

"We need to interview Mr. Jenkins about the Terrorism Watch List issue." Zapata said, pointing to another man before the NBC reporter could ask another question.

"I've been told that a .22 rifle is different from a .223 rifle. Can you tell us what the difference is?" A CNN stringer asked.

Never having fired a gun and having no idea what the differences between guns were, Zapata avoided the question, "Any Semiautomatic rifle, whether it's a twenty-two, or a two-two-three, or any size, is illegal." *Who the hell cares about the differenced between guns, but I guess I'd better find out what this twenty-two stuff is all about.*

After several more questions by uninformed reporters that received equally uninformed answers, a print reporter from the Denver Post Dispatch asked, "Why and when were the Jenkins' children released by Family Services?"

It was obvious the AG didn't know the children had been released. *What idiot released them,* he wondered before replying, "I don't have the details at this time, but I'll get back to you later."

Bob, a retired Army colonel who had spent five years with Delta, and Brian Ebert laughed. "Old Zapata got caught flat-footed by that question. "I think that was the first he'd heard about the children's release," Bob said, grinning. They were seated watching TV and eating lunch at Ebert's home in the mountains west of Denver.

"Yep, Brian replied. Think I'll pass on an anonymous tip to Sean Haddley. Let the people know that justice wasn't limited to officer Johnson."

Bob raised his glass to Brian.

The new Colorado Gun Law and the Jenkins' story was the topic of discussion on The Morning Drive radio talk show hosted by Doug Kellett, in Raleigh, North Carolina. A 6:45 a.m. caller said, "My brother is in law enforcement in Denver. From what he tells me, not only did masked men administer discipline to the police officer who struck Mrs. Jenkins, but the Family Services worker assigned to the children also had what you might call a 'motivational' encounter with several masked men. After pointing out there was no basis for taking the Jenkins' children, the men convinced the woman to release the children to them. I'm happy to report the children are now with their parents."

Chapter 18

David Connors, chairman of the Shawnee County School Board, approached the boardroom's curved, modular conference table, and nodded to fellow school board members and Superintendent Harry Rogers. Taking a seat in the middle leather chair facing the room, Connors surveyed the meeting room and was surprised by the unusually large number of attendees trying to find seats. Leaning forward, he switched on his microphone, "Thank all of you for coming. I know rescheduling the meeting has inconvenienced many of you," he smiled, "But so did last week's unexpected snowstorm.

"It looks like we're going to have a full house tonight, so if you folks want to get out of here at a reasonable hour, you need to find seats quickly," he suggested, looking in dismay at the crowded room. *People are still coming in. Some of them are carrying signs of some sort, but I can't see what they say ... what the heck's going on?* he wondered, perplexed by all the hubbub and scurrying around in the big room. *If too many people want to come in, I'll have to turn some away. The room has a maximum capacity of two hundred.*

County School Superintendent Harry Rogers also noticed the inordinate number of attendees and the ruckus some of them were making. Especially a group of about fifty people, some dressed in traditional Middle Eastern garb, and others wearing Muslim Student Association T-shirts and carrying signs. Leaning over to speak to Connors, Rogers said, "Dave, I'm concerned about the number of people here tonight. What's going on?"

"I uh ... I don't know Harry, other than routine housekeeping matters and a thirty-minute presentation by Tom and Zackary Murray there's nothing on the agenda to warrant so much public interest. Unless it has something to do with the Murrays' presentation."

"Who are the Murrays and what are they speaking on?" Roger's asked.

"Tom Murray and his wife Julie are concerned about the sixth-grade Islamic immersion program at their daughter's school, Robert Johnson Elementary. Tom called me to ask permission for his father, Zackary Murray, to speak on his experience with Islam while living in the Middle East. I approved a half-hour presentation because of the agenda's short business session."

"What Islamic immersion program? Were you aware there was one? Has the board been contacted by any other concerned parents, and if so why haven't I heard about it?"

"No Harry, this was the first I'd heard about it. I can't see anything wrong with the students learning about Islam. Parents have a right to express their concerns, so I felt it was okay to permit the Murrays to speak."

"Well you're right about that, but I hope we're not going to have a disturbance over this. I noticed a large number of Muslims coming in earlier. Some of them were carrying signs and judging from the noise they're making they're obviously agitated," Rogers said, reaching for a stack of speaker request cards and looking through them. "Have you looked at these?" he asked, handing them to Connors. "Apparently several other parents are requesting to speak on the subject of Islam. If they do, you'd best keep in mind Claudia Smyth-Hampton tends to get riled up over everyone's right to religious freedom. I suggest you keep a tight rein on the meeting. If things get out of hand, I'm prepared to call the sheriff's office. Now I think you should announce the occupancy requirement and close the doors."

"Okay Harry," Connors said, banging his gavel.

"Folks, it's fifteen minutes past the time we normally begin. I'll ask you to quiet down please and take what seats are available so we may proceed with the agenda. Those who cannot find a seat will have to leave. Our occupancy permit will not allow standing room. Once the seats are filled we'll be closing the door."

The noise in the room quieted down, everyone was seated, and Connors gaveled the meeting to order. Thirty minutes later after quickly ticking off the agenda items, it was time for Connors to announce the Murrays' presentation.

"Ladies and gentlemen as you know this is the point of the meeting when we normally have public comment. Tonight we've received several request cards that indicate you wish to speak on Islam. However before we move on to public comment, we're first going to hear from our scheduled speakers, Mr. Tom Murray and his father, Mr. Zackary Murray, who will to tell us what knowledge he gleaned about Islam while living and working in the Middle East. Gentlemen, you may come forward to the podium and speak."

Superintendent Rogers noted the Muslims were grimed-faced and murmuring to one another. *They certainly are a surly acting bunch, but it looks as though one of them, the apparent leader, is trying to calm them down.*

Tom spoke first. "We wish to thank the School Board for allowing us to speak this evening. Our reason for being here should not only be of concern to every parent who has a child in the county school system, but also to every taxpayer whose money goes to pay teachers' and administrators' salaries. What I'm referring to is the fact that our daughter Susie and her sixth-grade classmates at Robert Johnson Elementary School are currently engaged in what is being called 'Islamic Immersion'—a program that requires students to dress in Muslim clothes, pray to Allah, and be instructed that because God revealed his word to Muhammad, Islam is the only true religion—something we not only find shocking but totally unacceptable." A collective gasp, along with several boos from the audience, followed Tom's last statement.

Connors, a devout Christian was stunned. He had no earthly idea children were being taught such sacrilegious nonsense in the public schools. He was about to say the same thing when board member, Claudia Smyth-Hampton bolted up from her chair and sneered.

"Why should you find that a problem Mr. Murray?"

"Well, ma'am," Tom politely said, "It's a problem for two reasons: one, because my tax dollars and those of every citizen in this county were *not intended* to be spent on teachers and administrators brain-washing our children on the merits of *one religion over another*; and two, because of what my father will tell you regarding his experiences while living and working in the Middle East. May I present Mr. Zackary Murray, who has gained extensive knowledge about Islam while living in Muslim countries governed by Shariah law."

Still standing and smirking as Zackary took the podium, Smyth-Hampton jeered, "I certainly do hope you don't plan on making an *Islamophobic* presentation, Mr. Murray."

"Ma'am, that will depend entirely upon whether you consider the *truth* Islamophobic," Zackary shot back, glaring at the haughty woman.

"We members of the board pride ourselves on being *inclusive,*" Smyth-Hampton snapped back. "We respect all other religions and cultures."

"That's enough, Claudia," Connor's interrupted. "Please *sit down* and allow Mr. Murray to continue. You're burning up his time. The clock is set back to zero Mr. Murray. You may begin."

"Thank you Mr. Chairman, but before I do, I'd like to respond to the lady's statement. First of all, ma'am, you are correct, but even though Americans are by and large inclusive, the problem is ... a great many Muslims *aren't* ... and now, if there are no further objections, I'd like to continue."

Zackary waited for the murmuring in the audience to die out and was about to speak when a student wearing a Muslim Student Association T-shirt shouted, "WE'LL ALLOW YOU TO GO ON, BUT YOU'D BETTER NOT INSULT ISLAM,"

You'll allow me will you ... we'll see about that you arrogant little prick, Zackary fumed, and ignoring the comment, began, "For those of you who didn't catch it, my name is Zackary Murray. I recently retired as a State Department Foreign Service officer. During my career, I've lived in Afghanistan, Pakistan, Jordan, Iraq, and Saudi Arabia. I've worked with Muslims. I've lived in countries governed by Islam's barbaric Shariah law that's enforced by government sanctioned religious police, the *mutaween.* I've seen Islamic authorities administer punishments, subjugate, abuse and tax those who believe in other religions—people they call *kafirs.* So I can tell you unequivocally—*Islam is neither inclusive nor tolerant.*

"Followers of Islam consider it the only true religion and believe that Muhammad, received direct messages from Allah through the angel Gabriel, who directed him to tell his followers to *fight until all say there is no God but Allah.* True adherents to Allah's dictates consider Muhammad's recitations sacred and Allah's final words to mankind.

"Shariah law, the religious rules Muslims live by, is entirely based upon Muhammad: his recitations, as they were recorded in the Qur'an; his *Sirat,* biographies of his life; and the *Hadiths*—stories of his deeds, actions and words. Muslims consider Shariah Law superior to any manmade law, including our Constitution.

"During my time in the Middle East, I watched Muslim men, women and children having their heads, hands, and feet cut off; stoned to death for infidelity; and hung for homosexuality. Even now, years later, I continue to relive these experiences over and over in my nightmares. Worst of all were the bloody canings women received for failing to wear Shariah mandated garments—those long enveloping garments called *burkas,* with eye grills covering the eyes, or *abayas* worn with *niqabs,* a head covering with nothing but an eye slit for them to see through. Suffocatingly hot, these garments cover the women from head to foot.

Zackary paused as a collective wave of grumbling, sighing and moaning swept through the room. Turning to watch the Muslims, he saw several holding up signs.

BEHEAD ALL WHO OPPOSE SHARIAH

Ignoring their silent protest, Zackary continued.

"The sadistic *mutaween,* the religious police I referred to earlier, routinely patrol the streets, malls and market places looking for Shariah violators—people who defy edicts dictated by Muhammad a thousand years ago. While in public, a Muslim woman doesn't dare look at any man other than her father, brother, or husband. Nor must she allow her ankles to show from beneath her *burka* or *abaya,* or expose her hair and face when walking in public. Otherwise she can expect to be dragged by the hair into an open space and viciously caned as an example. In more extreme instances— something I've never seen but heard of—women have been imprisoned, where they are stripped naked to the waist and lashed with a leather whip as many as ninety times. All of this for failing to honor Shariah Law, a brutal moral and religious code that dictates females wear these dehumanizing, degrading garments—cocoons that turn them into something akin to trained dogs who live to obey their masters.

"So you can imagine my outrage when my granddaughter showed up at church last Sunday morning wearing an *abaya* and *niqab.* Not to mention how disturbing it was to hear her say how *cool* she thinks it is to wear the detestable garb; how *wonderful* it is to pray five times a day to Allah; and how *totally awesome* it was to learn Islam is the *only* true religion—a fact my daughter-in-law and I confirmed with her principal and teacher."

Smyth-Hampton had heard enough. Quickly reaching forward to turn on her microphone, she interrupted Zackary, *"MR. MURRAY,"* she stormed, "I will hear no more of this … your comments are an insult to Islam."

"Claudia calm down, Mr. Murray has the floor," Connors said, "He has a right to speak. Let him finish, and then you and others can ask questions. Please proceed Mr. Murray."

Zackary nodded to the chairman. "Very well, but before I continue, I have a question for the board members. Will there be immersion programs for Judaism, Christianity, Hinduism, or Atheism?"

From the way perplexed board members were looking at one another, it was obvious none of them had ever considered such a possibility. While three of them were thinking about how to answer, Smyth-Hampton wasted no time in making her opinion known.

"Our students are well-versed in Judaism and Christianity. Hinduism is *irrelevant*, and Atheism is an individual choice. Islam is the *second* largest religion in the world, and it may soon be the *largest*. It's important for our students to learn about it."

"Ms. Smyth-Hampton, I disagree with you regarding Judaism, Christianity and Hinduism. As for Islam, I agree. All Americans should learn about Islam … learn *the truth* about Islam. Not what's being taught in your schools," Zackary responded.

"**LIAR, YOU ARE A BLASPHEMER,**" screamed an older bearded Muslim wearing an embroidered skullcap.

"**ALLAH WILL SEND YOU TO HELL!**" screamed a Muslim Student Association member sitting next to him.

"**BLASPHEMER, BLASPHEMER BURN IN HELL,**" other students around the bearded man shouted—some standing on their chairs shaking their fists, while others held up new signs.

MASSACRE BLASPHEMERS

"**ORDER! ORDER!**" Chairman Connors shouted, banging his gavel. "Anymore of that and you'll be removed from the meeting. I WILL NOT TOLERATE FURTHER INTERRUPTIONS," he stormed, which did no good, because, urged on by the bearded man, the students continued chanting and causing a disturbance.

Soon all the Muslims joined the students in the chant, "**BLASPHEMER, BLASPHEMER BURN IN HELL.**"

Ignoring Connor's call for quiet, Smyth-Hampton jumped to her feet and yelled over the chanting, "MR. MURRAY, ARE YOU IMPLYING OUR SCHOOLS AREN'T TEACHING THE TRUTH ABOUT ISLAM?"

"**BLASPHEMER, BLASPHEMER BURN IN HELL.**"

"Sit down, Claudia, you're only egging them on and forcing me to call the sheriff," Connors ordered.

"YOU THERE," Connors yelled, pointing to the bearded man who was apparently the Muslim Student Association's leader. "QUIET DOWN! Get your people under control and return to your seats right now." Connors gestured for Zackary to hold off speaking, until everyone had returned to their seats.

Once the Muslims were quiet, Zackary directed his next statement to the boards' recalcitrant member. "Yes, Ms. Smyth-Hampton, that is *exactly* what I'm saying.

"For example, your world history textbook says Muhammad brought peace to the Arabian Peninsula, which is categorically *untrue*. Muhammad waged a brutal campaign of terror to conquer the Arabian Peninsula, violently forcing Arabic tribes to convert to Islam—

"HOW DARE YOU INSULT OUR PROPHET," screamed a Muslim woman wearing a black *abaya* and *niqab* and holding up a sign.

DEATH TO ALL WHO DISRESPECT OUR PROPHET

"BLASPHEMER," a Muslim man standing next to her shouted. "KILL THE BLASPHEMER."

"BLASPHEMER MY ASS," an elderly man wearing a POW cap shouted back. "MR. MURRAY'S TELLING THE TRUTH. If you can't take it, *shut up or get out.* We're sick of your whining about religious freedom."

"YEAH, GET OUT!" several men shouted, standing and facing the group of Muslims.

"YOU RAGHEADS ATTACKED OUR EMBASSY IN BAGHDAD and killed hundreds of Americans," one yelled. *Get the hell out of here.* GO HOME! We don't want the sorry likes of you here. Go back to your stinkin' rotten country."

Once again Connors pounded his gaveled. "ORDER!" he yelled. "Everyone sit down and be quiet or I'll have all you ejected."

Zackary waited for the room to settle down, and then continued, "I wish to thank the Muslims for demonstrating their *tolerant, peaceful nature*. Now, if the rest of you would like me to continue, I'll gladly to relate some of the history of Islam and its Prophet."

Smiling when his statement triggered another round of shouting by the Muslims, Zackary looked straight Smyth-Hampton, while he waited for Connors to restore order.

"Mr. Murray, I for one want to hear what you have to tell us. Please continue," Connors said.

"Very well … history records that Muhammad, who tradition says was illiterate, was born in Mecca in 570 AD to his widowed mother who died when he was a small child. At age six, he joined his wealthy uncle's family and was taken under his wing. The uncle, a successful merchant, took young Muhammad with him on trading journeys, exposing Muhammad to other cultures. Upon reaching puberty Muhammad joined the family business as a camel driver. Intelligent, he quickly worked his way up to caravan manager. After meeting his distant, older cousin, a wealthy widow, he became her business partner and later they married.

"Camel caravans spent weeks and even months on the road, providing ample opportunity for Muhammad to be exposed to both Jewish teachings from the Torah, and scriptures from the Old and New Testaments in the Bible.

"In the year 610 AD, while meditating in a cave near Mecca at the age of forty, Muhammad claimed to have had a vision in which a bright spirit he later identified as the angel Gabriel appeared. In the vision, the bright spirit declared that Allah, the one true god, had sent him with a message for Muhammad. A message telling him to recite there was no other god but Allah, and he, Muhammad, had been chosen to recite Allah's true words: words, which all other previous prophets in the Torah and Bible had corrupted; words, which would prove Muhammad was the promised Messiah Jews and Christians had been expecting.

"Over the next twelve years, Gabriel ordered Muhammad to recite more messages from the Allah: first to his wife, who became the first Muslim; next to his tribesmen, the *Quraysh*; and then to idol worshipers at a small stone structure on the outskirts of Mecca. Enshrined in the structure's four crumbling walls, a shrine we know today as the *Ka'bah*, were 360 different stone idols, which pilgrims from tribes all over the Arabian Peninsula annually came to worship.

"During those years, only a few Meccans who heard Muhammad's recitations accepted his one god message and became followers. Thinking he was insane, most of his tribesmen simply ignored him. However, since there was no written Arabic language, listeners with any interest in his preaching either memorized his words, or, as was the case for caravan traders and pilgrims, wrote them in their own language on anything available—including their bodies—which is an important fact, because those writings eventually became Islam's holy book, the *Qur'an*.

"Needless to say Muhammad's one god message wasn't well received; for by preaching against worshiping the 360 stone idols housed in a local shrine, the Prophet was interfering with a major source of income. Pilgrims who came to Mecca paid to worship at the shrine and the coins they spent in local shops enriched Mecca's merchants. Having endured Muhammad's interfering with their income for twelve years, the *Quraysh* had enough of him. After a violent encounter in which his life was threatened, tribal leaders ran Muhammad and his small band of followers out of town."

"**BLASPHEMER, YOU LIE,**" several Muslims began screaming and holding up their signs.

"QUIET! Quiet down over there. We want to hear what Mr. Murray has to say," Connors demanded, banging his gavel.

Waiting for the Muslim agitators to settle down, Zackary turned toward them, held up his arms and said, "Call me what you will, but sometimes the truth hurts, and I speak the truth. Now, if you'll demonstrate your *tolerance,* I'll continue.

"The first twelve years of Muhammad's prophethood are known as the 'Mecca period' or Muhammad's 'peaceful period.' During this period, Muhammad recited the short, peaceful sermons I referenced earlier, which eventually became *suras,* or chapters, in the *Qur'an.*"

Zackary paused and looked at Smyth-Hampton. "My granddaughter's textbook devotes only one *sentence* to Muhammad's twelve years in Mecca, and says nothing about him and his small band fleeing for their lives north to *Yathrib*—a thriving, prosperous town later renamed Medina. Nor does it mention the Jews refused to accept him as the messiah they were waiting for. In a couple of years, Muhammad became short of funds and began robbing his tribe's caravans. This is important because once it became known he and his followers obtained booty from their raids, the ranks of his followers grew from a few hundred to ten thousand.

"Distribution of the booty was solved by a message delivered by Gabriel. Allah and his Messenger would keep one-fifth, twenty percent."

"BLASPHEMER! YOU LIE!" the Muslims shouted, and then began chanting and stomping their feet—a typical tactic Muslim Student Associations engaged in to shut down a speaker they didn't like, "**DEATH TO THE BLASPHEMER. ALLAH IS THE ONLY GOD AND MUHAMMAD IS HIS PROPHET.**"

Finally having had enough, a group of about thirty Christian and Jewish men stood and began moving toward the chanting Muslims.

"THAT DOES IT, DAVE, I'M CALLING THE SHERIFF," the superintendent stormed into his open microphone. "I want to hear what this man is saying, but those people are getting out of hand."

"Do it," Dave said, putting his hand over his mike. "It won't hurt to have the deputies come in to put on a show of force," he added, leaning forward and removing his hand covering the mike, he shouted, "QUIET! "Quiet down, or I'll have all of you ejected."

Certain a riot was about to break out, four school board members sat in stunned silence holding their breath. The fifth, Smyth-Hampton, shook her finger at Connors and stormed, "MR. CHAIRMAN, I DEMAND THAT YOU PUT A STOP TO THIS ... this—*islamophobic* rant immediately. These poor

Muslims have had enough verbal abuse for one evening. I don't blame them one bit for being upset."

"Maybe you should shut the meeting down," one board member meekly suggested to Connors.

"I don't think so … calm down." Superintendent Rogers said. "From the looks of things the Muslims have quieted down after they heard me say I'm calling the sheriff. Those who confronted them have returned to their seats. So let's move along, I want to hear the rest of what Murray has to say."

"So, do I," Connors agreed, "Mr. Murray, because of all the interruptions, we're extending your time. Please continue."

Zackary nodded and began, "According to the sacred *Hadiths*, no sooner had Muhammad arrived in Medina, than he began declaring his prophethood and preaching his one god Allah sermon to the three Jewish tribes living there. Declaring the one true god Allah had sent him, as his last Prophet and Messiah, he said his recitations were meant to correct the corrupted messages in previous prophets' statements written in the Torah and the Bible's Old and New Testaments. When the Jews flatly refused to listen to his claims, because he didn't fit the Torah's criteria for a prophet, he became furious. Deciding to expel the most contentious tribe, he ordered his band to raid the Jews homes and drive them out, which they did. Later he laid siege to the second Jewish tribe and forced them to flee. In both cases, Muhammad allowed the Jews to leave taking what they could carry. Muhammad wisely decided—knowing his men's loyalty depended on the booty—to keep only a fifth for himself along with the Jew's land.

"In the meantime, the leaders of Mohammad's tribe in Mecca got tired of his murderous gang robbing their caravans and sent a small company-sized unit to stop the raids, but Muhammad defeated them. Several more battles with the Meccans occurred, culminating in the last major one, the Battle of the Trench: so named, because when spies reported a large Meccan army was coming, Muhammad ordered a defensive trench dug around Medina. The trench proved to be unbreachable and eventually the Meccans ran out of food and water and went home.

"While the Battle of the Trench raged, Muhammad learned of a pact between the Meccans and leaders of the remaining Jewish tribe, who had agreed to aid the Meccans in their siege. Angry with the Jews and at the same time fearful of them, he ordered all the Jewish men and pubescent boys lined up around the trench and watched while they were beheaded. Records of the number killed vary from 700 to 1,000. Once the slaughter was over, Muhammad declared all the women and children were 'people of the right hand,' slaves. Many were sold, but not before Muhammad's brigands had selected the best of the women for concubines, including young girls who had reached puberty—some as young as nine years old."

Pausing to look at the Muslims when an angry murmur swept through the audience, Zackary caught sight of several of the sheriff's deputies entering and taking up positions at the rear of the room. Watching Connors, Zackary waited until he saw him nod before continuing.

"After the Battle of the Trench, Muhammad and his jihadis, holy warriors, swept across the Arabian Peninsula terrorizing the inhabitants, tearing down their pagan idols' shrines and killing anyone who refused to accept Muhammad's prophethood and his one true god religion—Islam. Further details of Muhammad's savage subjugation would take more time than I've been allotted. Suffice it to say that by the time Muhammad died in 632 AD, the illiterate, one time camel driver and caravan manager had created a religious ideology that not only drove his mighty army of holy warriors to conquer Arabia, but also altered the progress of civilization for centuries to come.

"As for the Islamic holy books Muslims live by. The *Qur'an,* Muhammad's recitations from Allah, were compiled twenty years after his death. The *Hadiths,* records of his words and deeds during his lifetime, were added to and embellished for centuries. It wasn't until 812 AD, 180 years after his death, that Islamic scholars began authenticating and compiling them. Other scholars created the *Sirat Rasul Allah,* Muhammad's biographies. The first one was completed 200 years after his death.

"I'll conclude by paraphrasing what acclaimed Muslim researcher and author, Robert Spencer has written in his excellent, thought-provoking book, *The Truth About Muhammad*: Muhammad's god, Allah, is an angry god; Allah's Islam is based on the will of an angry god who demands total submission; and finally, Allah's so-called Prophet was nothing more than a bandit, slaver, murderer, warlord, and a pedophile by today's standards. A man who ordered his followers in his final address in March 632 AD—and I quote here, 'To fight all men until all say there is no God but Allah.' "

"**YOU BASTARD, YOU F'ING LYING BASTARD,**" screamed the furious bearded Muslim Student Association leader, taking his shoe off and holding it up in the air."

"**YOU'RE THE F'ING LYING BASTARDS,** screamed a man wearing a Desert Storm T-shirt. "ALL YOU RAGHEADS practice *Taqiyya*—deception— to deliberately conceal your scheming, murdering agenda. I know, 'cause I lived among you and lost my arm serving my country," he continued, with his prosthetic arm held high. "I've had it with all this political correctness crap. **I'LL BLASPHEME MUHAMMAD** if I want to. That's my right as an American."

"**YOU DARE TO DISRESPECT OUR PROPHET?**" One of the students screamed, also taking off his shoe. "**KILL THE BLASPHEMER!**"

Knowing what was coming, for he'd seen angry Muslims throwing shoes before, Zackary was turning to warn Connors, when Ms. Smyth-Hampton pointed to him and shouted, "NOW SEE WHAT YOU'VE DONE. YOU'VE MADE THEM HATE US. YOU ... YOU ISLAMOPHOBE!"

"SHUT THE HELL UP, LADY," the T-shirted man yelled. If they don't like it here they can get out of America ... go live in a country where peoples' heads are cut off for saying what they think. We're not gonna live with the likes of them and their stupid-assed religion. While I served in the Army, I had to put up with the military's pukin', yellow-bellied counterinsurgency initiative, COIN, to 'win the hearts and minds' of them ragheads. I came home minus an arm, and we lost over 2,000 men trying to win them hearts or minds. So I'm here to tell you high and mighty school board members that you'd better not try to brainwash my kids 'bout how peaceful Islam is' ... cause I know differ'nt."

"**HOOHA!**" shouted several men around him wearing similar T-shirts.

"*ALLAHU'AKBAR*! **MAY ALLAH SEND ALL YOU KAFIRS TO HELL AND BURN YOUR SOULS FOR ETERNITY,**" the bearded Muslim screamed, hurling his shoe at Zackary and inciting the others to join him. A barrage of shoes followed, aimed both at Zackary and the school board members on the raised platform.

Before the sheriff's deputies could react the entire room was in an uproar. While the Muslims continued throwing shoes, every able-bodied, non-Muslim male began snatching up shoes to use as clubs. Clambering over the chairs men on both sides went at each other. Even the women got into the act, scratching one another's faces, pulling one another's hair, a few falling to the floor in a vicious struggle. While the sheriff's deputies attempted to restore order, two people were trampled, and a several sustained serious injuries.

A survivor of previous shoe barrages, Zackary dodged the flying missiles, but the board members were caught totally unaware. Two fell out of their chairs trying to avoid being hit, while a third wisely ducked under the conference table with Connors and Rogers.

Oblivious to the danger, Claudia Smyth-Hampton's only thought was for the Muslims. So instead of hunkering down, she climbed on top of the conference table and stood screaming at the sheriff's deputies, "**STOP**

THEM! STOP THEM, I tell you. Don't let them hurt those poor peaceful Muslims."

"YOU ... YOU'RE RESPONSIBLE FOR THIS," she raged at Zackary, and was about to jump off the table and go after him, when a heavy boot slammed into the bridge of her nose. **"ARRRGH!"** she screeched, clutching her bleeding nose with both hands, and then, losing her balance, tumbled to the floor in a disheveled heap at Zackary's feet.

"Ooooh ... why have they hurt me?" she groaned, trying to staunch the blood streaming from her nose. *"Help me,"* she pleaded, reaching up to Zackary and struggling to sit upright.

"GET OUT OF MY WAY KAFIR BITCH," a burly Muslim student yelled, kicking her in the side and pulling back his fist to punch Zackary.

"I wouldn't do that if I were you, son," warned Zackary, a black belt with years of training.

Snarling as he lunged, the student threw a vicious punch aimed at Zackary's face, but the old *kafir* surprised him. By expertly deflecting the blow with a left forearm block and following through with a right hand palm strike to the base of his nose, Zackary laid the punk on the floor next to Smyth-Hampton. Slumped over with blood streaming from his nose, the student squinted at the woman beside him and grunted in pain.

"Won't somebody please help me?" Smyth-Hampton moaned, clawing at Zackary's pant leg.

"Ask your peaceful Muslim there—maybe he'll help you," Zackary replied, amused at seeing them sitting side by side with bloody noses.

"That was quite a punch Dad," Tom said, rushing to his father's side. "Let's get out of here before you have to hurt anybody else."

"Yeah, son, you're right ... I believe I've had more than enough of this peaceful riot," Zachary laughed, and rushing after Tom followed him out a side door marked "Exit."

Additional deputies were required to end the riot. Several men and women were arrested, and over twenty people taken to area hospitals. Tweets, followed by Facebook postings, and a graphic YouTube video spread the story.

Early the next morning local and national TV and print news carried the story, complete with cell phone pictures of the melee. Glenn Deck spent most of the first hour of his radio program discussing the school board riot and Islam. "Are your children being fed a pack of untruths by their schools?" he asked the listeners. "Are your children being immersed in a violent ideology?" Slowly the topic of discussion morphed to the lack of progress in the investigation of the Baghdad embassy attack and to questions as to why no one had been arrested.

Rusty Limbo expounded on the embassy's lack of security, calling it a super Benghazi, and sarcastically ending his show by quoting former Secretary of State Clinton, "What difference, at this point, does it make?"

Sean Haddley picked up the baton on his talk show, and the Baghdad embassy story flowed to the evening TV talk shows, where ABC, NBC and CBS hosts finally began asking questions.

President Abomba watched part of The O'Rippley Quotient and ground his teeth.

The following morning, the phones of school board members, school superintendants and principals lit up all across the nation. Already angry over the Baghdad embassy attack and slaughter, the American people, were furious with their school boards. The absurd answers angry parents were getting only added fuel to the fire. In a number of states, parents stormed into schools, grabbed history textbooks and berated principals and teachers. In several instances they ripped textbooks apart, piled the remains up and burned them in front of the schools.

Next to be called and questioned were church leaders, pastors, priests and rabbis. Church and synagogue members wanted to know why their spiritual leaders hadn't told them the truth about Muhammad and his false religion. Why hadn't they explained the reason Muslims hated Christians and Jews?

The answers callers received quickly revealed, most religious leaders were woefully ignorant about Islam. Platitudes were no longer acceptable.

Slowly the anger began shifting to the current administration and its attempt to ban guns.

Chapter 19

Attorney General Zapata was chairing a conference call with the chief of the Colorado State Patrol and the state's police chiefs. Sheriffs were elected by county and weren't under the AG's authority. In fact, the sheriff's organization had filed a legal challenge to the earlier 2012 gun law, which was working its way thorough the courts. In compliance with the new law, a number of citizens across the state had brought their firearms in for inspection and registration. Seizure of semiautomatic .22 rifles and shotguns had resulted in several confrontations and arrests. In some localities citizen protests in front of police stations had become unruly, resulting in more arrests. Citizen outrage was growing, yet the AG and governor appeared unconcerned. Governor Hickengooper's amnesty program had expired on Saturday and enforcement would begin today.

"I want to make my orders absolutely clear," Zapata said. "This new law authorizes your police officers to go door-to-door in search of unregistered or illegal guns and illegal magazines. If one of your officers experiences any suspicious behavior by a citizen or any attempt to dodge answers—search the house.

"If illegal items *are* found, arrest everyone in the house.

"If guns are *not* stored in a safe with two locks, arrest everyone in the house.

"If ammunition is *not* stored in a separate safe with two locks, arrest everyone in the house.

"Are there any questions?"

After several seconds of silence, Durango's police chief commented, "Mr. Attorney General, following your instructions will probably result in armed citizen resistance. We almost had a shootout at one of our police stations when one of my officers attempted something similar to your instructions. The city council ordered the mayor to fire the officer."

Another police chief agreed. "Mr. Attorney General, your orders can spark an uprising. Do you expect our police to fire on our citizens?"

"Chief, if citizens fire on your police, I expect you to use all available force to put down any resistance. *Is that clear?*"

"Your instructions are clear. What isn't clear is whether our police should fire on citizens protecting their Constitutional rights to own guns."

"I can't believe you said that," the AG said.

"Well, *I believe* it," an unidentified chief interjected. A number of participants in the call agreed, saying, "So do I."

Undeterred, Zapata continued. "The governor will call up the National Guard if there's any indication of a rebellion. The guard will put a quick end to any resistance."

Zapata waited to see if there were any more comments. Hearing none he ended the call, "All right—begin enforcing of our new gun law."

Mable had been watching two police officers get out of a patrol car parked at the end of her block on the opposite of the street from her house. While one officer walked across the street and up to the front door of the first house on the opposite side, the other walked toward her side. Mable, one of the neighborhood's busy-bodies, couldn't see what the officer on her side was doing, so she'd watched the other officer as he knocked on the Sawyer's front door. Jenny Sawyer opened her door and was speaking with the officer, when he suddenly pushed her aside and burst into the house. "What the heck?" Mable gasped.

Aghast at what she'd seen and curious about what was going on, Mable, immediately picked up her cell phone and speed dialed her partner in meddling, Betty, who lived in the middle of the block on Mable's side of the street.

"Betty, there's a patrol car parked at your end of the block. Two police officers got out, and I just saw one of them burst into Jenny's house. You're closer than I am, check it out. Can you see what's happening?"

"I've gotta go to the front window. I'll call you back if I see anything," Betty said.

Quickly retrieving her binoculars, Mable settled down to watch Jenny's house, while she waited for Betty's call and speculated on what terrible thing Jenny must have done. Ten minutes later, Mable blinked in surprise and readjusted her binoculars; for coming out the front door was the police officer with a handcuffed Jenny in tow.

"What in the world's going on?" Mable muttered and was reaching for her cell phone when it rang. Too occupied to check caller ID and assuming it was Betty, she asked, "Did you see that?" and was surprised to hear Betty ask the same thing.

"Yes," they both said simultaneously.

"Oh, for heaven's sakes," Mable said, annoyed they were repeating one another. "What do you think Jenny's done to get arrested? Could she be doing drugs?" she asked, still squinting through her binoculars.

"I don't know, but he's putting her in the back seat of his patrol car, and—Oh, my God, Mable look ... that other officer's leading little Shirley Robertson to the car. She's handcuffed too, and he's putting her in with Jenny. Mable, what'd you thinks' goin' on—could they both be doing drugs?"

"I don't know, but I'm not wasting another minute sitting here. I'm going out there and get to the bottom of this."

"Wait for me. I'm going with you."

Betty and Mable were marching down the sidewalk toward the patrol car, when they saw the officer who'd arrested Shirley carry a shotgun and three boxes of shells out of her house and place them in the patrol car's trunk.

Stopping on the sidewalk a little way off from the car, Mable called out to the policeman, "Yoo-hoo! Officer ... what is going on? Why are Mrs. Robertson and Mrs. Sawyer being arrested?"

"Ladies, this is police business. Please return to your home. One of us will be visiting you shortly."

"Well I never," Mable exclaimed. "Officer, why are you knocking on our doors?"

"You have to have a *reason* to enter a private residence," Betty added. "We *demand* to know what's going on."

Officer Chang looked at the two women and hesitated. He was ashamed of what he'd been ordered to do and didn't want to explain, but to be polite he said, "Ladies, the police department is enforcing the new gun law. Any person not in compliance will be arrested. I'm just following orders." Chang listened to his own words and felt ashamed. *I don't agree with any of this. Seems illegal to me, but the AG ordered it.* Chang sighed, and walking past the women headed up the sidewalk to the next house.

"No one's home—they both work," Mable called out to Chang's back.

Motioning for Betty to follow her and keeping an eye on Chang, as he approached another house, Mable hurried toward the patrol car.

"Shirley, it's me Mable," she said, leaning down and speaking through the window, "Why were you arrested?"

"Mable, my husband had locked his shotgun in a closet. We can't afford to purchase two safes to meet the new law. We can't spend over three thousand dollars to store a shotgun and a few boxes of shells. It's the same with Jenny. Please call our husbands and tell them what's going on."

"You can count on us. We most certainly will," busybody Betty replied.

Similar scenes were playing out throughout the Denver area. The police quickly ran out of room for all the arrested citizens: most of whom were women, which created the problem of school children returning to empty homes. By early afternoon Family Services was reporting they had no way of handling the surge of children placed in their care.

Tom Robertson and his father arrived as Officer Chang was escorting Mildred Michaels to his patrol car. Chang watched a pickup truck skid to a stop behind his car and two angry men jump out. Stomping toward him in an extremely hostile manner, the younger of the two snarled, "My name is Tom Robertson and this is my father. What the hell are you doing?" Tom demanded. "Let Mrs. Michaels go, this instant, and then release my wife and the women in your car and return our guns—and you'd damn well better be quick about it."

Noticing the older man moving to his left side, Chang realized a confrontation was brewing. Just then two more automobiles arrived, screeched to a stop in the middle of the street and four more obviously angry men got out.

Officer Taylor watched the menacing looking men moving toward his partner and quickly crossed the street to join him. On the way he called for backup and learned there was none available. Realizing they were out numbered and on their own, Taylor rushed to Chang's side and warily watched the angry husbands and brothers quickly surrounding them. Looking at one another the two officers knew they were in trouble.

"What are you waiting for?" Tom asked, glaring at Chang. "I told you to release the women in that car and return our guns. "If you don't do as you're told, you're gonna get hurt."

Reacting to the threat, Taylor who'd made a movement to place his hand on his holstered service pistol, suddenly felt a knife at his throat. "Son, if you draw your weapon you're going to have to fire it," an older gravelly-voiced man growled in his ear—his hot breath raising the hair on

Taylor's nape. "And if you fire it," the voice continued, "you'll have declared open season on every man and woman who's wearing a police uniform in this state. Now release the women, give us our guns, and then get the hell out of here while you still can. Oh, one more thing ... tell your boss hunting season will open tomorrow if all the other men and women that are currently being held aren't released by dawn."

"And all the guns and ammo that's been confiscated better be returned too," another man added.

After helping the women out of the patrol car, Chang used his keys to uncuff them and he and Officer Taylor got in. "Whew ... that was a close one," Chang muttered, as they drove away. Worried about what they'd have to report when they reached the station, they were surprised to learn other officers had similar stories.

By late afternoon, hundreds of angry citizens were gathering outside multiple police stations around the state. Jails were overflowing with frantic parents, and neighbors were caring for numerous terrified children. Finally after receiving a call from the chief justice of the state Supreme Court, Governor Hickengooper was forced to order the arrested men and women released. There was no other choice, because it was impossible to hold that many people, especially when so many children needed their parents. Governor Hickengooper and Attorney General Zapata were learning about unintended consequences. One of several lessons they'd soon be learning.

That night an epidemic of Blue Flu swept through Colorado's police and state patrol, and by the next morning duty rosters were down by eighty percent. A few units were sent to execute house searches, and within minutes of their arrivals, an unarmed man approached each unit and told them to leave. When police refused, the man pointed to a group of men armed with rifles—rifles aimed at their patrol cars. The police units departed and no shots were fired.

Governor Hickengooper was furious and activated the National Guard.

Tuesday, May 5, 2015

Hickengooper and Zapata were meeting with Major General Morrison, the state's adjutant general and commander of the Colorado National Guard and Colonel Scott, chief of the Colorado State Patrol. Morrison and Scott had spent over an hour attempting to convince the governor and AG that enforcement was a bad idea and they needed to back off.

Finally Zapata had enough of their bitching. Clinching his jaw and glaring at the two men, he snarled, "We *need* to make an example. By keeping up the house-to-house searches we'll eventually get armed resistance. Then we'll use SWAT units to crush resistors. That'll send a message the rest of the Second Amendment nuts will understand."

Yes, it certainly will, but it may not be the message you intended. General Morrison thought as he and Scott departed. Though they didn't say it both men knew big trouble lay ahead.

Determined to set an example, Zapata quietly ordered his staff to begin combing through gun records, looking for a gun owner who would resist with force. Four names surfaced and were on the short list. Two brothers, Orville and Arthur Bartow, were circled at the top of the list, with "Rednecks" penciled in next to their names.

After evaluating all the names and locations, Zapata selected the Bartows because they lived in a house on a remote lot. The house could be easily surrounded and there was little chance for collateral damage—best of all it provided ample space for TV trucks. *They're the perfect target*, Zapata decided. *First I'll order Captain Regis' to back up Golden's Police with his SWAT unit, and then have a staff member tip off the press.*

Chapter 20

Golden, Colorado
Wednesday, May 6, 2015

Suspecting he was being used, Captain Regis personally reconnoitered the Bartow brother's one story log cabin style house. Set back off a rural road on five acres in a remote area northeast of Golden, the house appeared decades old, but was well built and maintained, with a detached shed located a few yards distant. Modern housing developments were creeping toward the area, but the surrounding trees and brush made the location appear remote. There were no shrubs or trees near the house, making surreptitious approach difficult and affording good fields of fire for those in the house. After returning to his unit, Regis prepared an assault plan and sent it to the AG, who was so pleased with it he scheduled the raid for the next morning. Intent on furthering his own political ambitions by having his name publicized in connection with enforcement of the new gun law, he cunningly arranged to have the time and location of the raid leaked to local TV stations.

As dawn broke the following morning, the SWAT unit took up concealed positions inside the brush and trees surrounding the Bartow brothers' home. No action was expected before eight o'clock—the time a Golden police officer would arrive and knock on the brother's door.

Inside the house, Orville woke to the sound of Rex, the Bartows' German Shepherd, growling. "What's the matter boy?" Orville asked getting out of bed and looking out his bedroom window. "Don't see anything out there boy, must be some rascally critter you're hearing. Let's go outside and see," he told Rex, getting up to follow his usual routine of letting the dog out to take care of his business; but rather than eagerly running out as he normally would, Rex hesitated at the threshold. Then, growling and sniffing the air with his head held high and ears pointing forward, he trotted a good distance out in the yard and stopped to stare at the tree line.

Seeing Rex's hackles up and hearing his continued growling, Orville stepped out in the yard to see what had him so upset. After carefully looking around, he assured the dog, "It's okay, boy ... nothing out there. Now come on back and do your business, so I can go in and fix us breakfast."

Rex returned for a pat on the head, did what was expected of him, and obediently followed Orville back into the house. Once inside however, he continued softly growling and uneasily pacing back and forth.

"What's got Rex so upset?" Arthur asked, yawning as he came out of his bedroom to join his brother,

"Don't know ... been acting that way ever since I got up. I fed him but he won't eat," Orville said, gesturing to a full bowl of dry dog food on the floor by the refrigerator. "I checked around outside but didn't see nothin'. I reckon it's a coon ... coffee's ready, grab a cup and turn on the TV. The seven-thirty news ought'a be on in a couple of minutes." Both watched the local news channel until the top of the hour.

While the unsuspecting brothers finished their breakfast and watched the eight o'clock local news, Officer Perry, a rookie with three months on the force, was driving up the secondary road toward their property. Stopping his patrol car at the entrance to their driveway, he got out to open the gate.

"I've heard enough ... think I'll go outside and work on the lawnmower. It's been running rough. I'll take Rex with me. He's still restless," Arthur said, opening the front door. *"Whoa boy! ...* Best wait a minute," he said, grabbing the big Shepherd's collar, when he saw a patrol car driving up their 150-yard gravel driveway. "Got a visitor Orville—police," he said, closing the door and trying to calm Rex's barking, while they waited to see what the police wanted.

Officer Perry got out of his patrol car, walked to the front door and knocked. The sound of Rex's fierce growl from the other side of the door caused him to back up.

"Quiet, Rex," Perry heard a man say.

Opening the door a crack, Orville asked, "What'd you want, officer?"

Perry was nervous and the growling dog didn't help. This was his first solo assignment, and he wanted to prove himself. "Mr. Bartow, would you please step outside without your dog, uh ... so we can talk?"

Orville stepped out, closed the door behind him and asked, "What's this about officer?"

"Sir, are you aware of Colorado's new gun and ammunition regulation laws?" Perry asked holding up a copy of the law.

Orville nodded yes.

"I'm here to inspect your house for guns. Our records show no guns have been registered at this address; however, our records also show you've purchased ammunition in several calibers and shotgun shells.

"Do you still have these guns? If not, I must see your transfer or sale records."

"Let me see your warrant. After I inspect it, I'll call my lawyer. If he approves, you can come in."

"Mr. Bartow, no warrant is required." Officer Perry had been taught about search warrants, but his sergeant had assured him none was required in the new gun law. It never occurred to him to wonder why.

"Well, no warrant—*no inspection.* Come back when you've got one," Orville said, shrugging as he turned, and opening the door, entered and closed it; leaving Perry holding his copy of the new law and listening to the snarling dog on the other side of the door.

Now what do I do? Perry wondered, suddenly aware of a cramp in his stomach. *Guess I'd better call this in,* he decided, returning to his car to report Mr. Orville Bartow's refusal to allow him entry.

The dispatcher told him to wait for backup.

Orville and Arthur watched the young officer return to his car and use the radio. When he didn't leave their property they became suspicious. Since both brothers belonged to the Colorado Militia, they'd participated in a plan to handle forced inspections. Using their phone, which Arthur assumed was tapped, he followed the plan and dialed the number of a pay phone in a local diner to call Tom.

"Hey Buddy, we can't make lunch. Something's come up," Arthur said.

Tom laughed, "What's the matter, more coons in your shed?"

"Naw, this time it's a skunk. Think there's a family of 'em in the woods."

"Good luck with that," Tom said, hanging up. His next call was to Bob.

Hunkered down in the woods near the fence line, Captain Regis was watching the brothers' house through binoculars, when he heard vehicles approaching. Looking back down the road, he saw two TV vans pull to a stop behind the police department's command trailer. Regis had positioned the trailer so it wasn't visible from the house. *I wonder who tipped off the press,* he thought, walking past an ambulance and the command trailer to the lead TV van.

Addressing Regis from his open window, the driver said, "We understand you're going to raid a house to seize guns."

Damn, Zapata set this up, and this isn't going to end well. "We may have to take down the house, but first we have to give them a chance to comply. Come with me."

Regis motioned to the driver in the second van to join them and started back toward the gate. Pointing to a place on the gravel road, he said, "You can set up here. Try not to attract too much attention. The police officer in the car near the house was refused entry. He's waiting for orders.

"I'm going to talk to the men in the house to see if I can resolve the problem."

"What happens if you can't?" asked a reporter who'd followed the vans' drivers.

"Then SWAT will assault the house and you'll have a story. Use your long lens to get the action, if there is any. Don't under any circumstances go closer than this spot right here."

Regis turned and walked back to the command trailer.

It was time to call the Bartow's. Entering the command trailer, Regis ordered the officer manning communications to call the house, and then, picking up a receiver, stood listening for one of the brothers to answer.

On the fourth ring, Arthur did, "Hello," he said, wondering if it was one of his militia buddies.

"Mr. Bartow, this is Captain Regis, Denver police. We have reports that you and your brother have illegal and unregistered firearms. If you have registered your firearms, now would be a good time to tell me. Otherwise, we're going to search your house for illegal weapons and ammunition."

"Captain, when you send the young officer up with a search warrant, I'll call my attorney. If my attorney says the warrant is valid, you can search all you want. Otherwise *do not* come on our property."

Regis sighed … *Damn, he's going to test us. I don't want this to go down with TV cameras broadcasting the action … Oh my god, that's exactly what Zapata wants, a demonstration of power with TV coverage. Zapata deliberately picked a hard case for the TV networks to cover, that's why they're here. Damn, I'll end up being the bad guy and take a fall if this raid goes south. Better think this through.* "Mr. Bartow, let's talk about this. I'm going to come to your door."

"Suit yourself."

Regis told his men to relax, and then walked up the driveway past Officer Perry in the patrol car and knocked on the front door. He could hear a dog growling inside. "Mr. Bartow, please leash your dog, and then open the door."

A few seconds later the door opened, and the man standing there said, "Come in, I'm Arthur Bartow and this is my brother, Orville."

Offering his hand, Regis said, "Nice to meet both of you, I'm Captain Regis. I want to resolve this problem of your guns in a peaceable manner. I don't want either of you or any of my men to get hurt."

"Think we can all agree on that," Orville replied. "As soon as our lawyer reviews your search warrant, you're welcome to search our house."

Regis knew talk wasn't going to work, but he had to try. "Orville ... Arthur, I have a SWAT unit ready to force entry. If you resist, one or both of you may be injured or killed. I don't want that to happen."

"Well, seems to us you've forgotten about your oath to uphold the law. Forcing entry without a warrant is illegal," Arthur said.

"I have my orders."

"So did the Nazis ... however, as history recalls, we hung several of them for following *their* orders. Your orders are illegal without a court issued search warrant," Orville added.

Regis realized he wasn't dealing with rednecks and knew they were right. *Well, I guess it's shit or get off the pot time. I'm not going to be responsible for either of these men's death nor the death of any of my men.* Standing, he said, "Thank you for your time. I'll report your position to my boss."

Stopping at the police cruiser, Regis told the young officer to leave, and then walked briskly back to the command trailer. *Those men are never going to peacefully relinquish their guns. They'll fight to the death to defend their property and I can't blame them.*

Once inside the command trailer, Regis called the chief, "Sir, I just left the Bartows' house, and I regret to report I was unable to convince them to comply with the new gun law. They refuse to allow a search of their property without a warrant approved by their lawyer."

"Regis, I don't give a damn what they say. I'll hear no more of it. You *will* follow my orders and storm the house."

"No, Chief, I *won't*. I consider these orders illegal, and I *will not* be responsible for what I'm certain will turn into a bloody shootout."

"Very well, you're relieved. Sergeant Reed is in command. Put him on and then report to me back here at the station."

"Yes, Chief," Regis replied and handing the phone to Sergeant Reed said, "It's your show now, Reed. Chief wants to talk to you."

"Chief, this is Sergeant Reed."

"Sergeant Reed, you're now in command of SWAT operations. Execute the orders to search the house and arrest the occupants if guns or ammunition are found.

"If they resist make an example of them."

"Yes, Chief," Reed replied, smiling as he watched Regis get into his SUV and drive away.

Reporters from KCNC Channel 4 and KDRV Channel 31 had also been watching and seen Regis return from the house and enter the command trailer. Now they wondered about his departure. The CNBC reporter, who'd acquired the listed phone number for the house, called it. When Arthur answered he said, "I'm Jeb Justice, CBS Channel 4 News. Can you tell me what the police want?"

"Yes, they want to search our house for guns and ammunition. They don't have a search warrant and we're not gonna allow them to enter without one. If they do they're violating the Second and Forth Amendments of the Constitution."

"Can I quote you, Mr. Bartow?"

"Sure thing, as long as you include my references to the Constitution."

"If they force entry, will you and your brother resist?"

"Yes. We'll defend our property from illegal invasion. Now I have to go." Arthur hung up. It was time to prepare for the coming assault.

Jeb Justice called his station and told them to be ready to go live from his location.

Orville opened the closet door and removed two M1 Garand rifles with 4X scopes. The rifles were zeroed at 100 yards. Arthur opened an ammo box and removed twenty, eight round stripper clips holding 30-06 cartridges with black tips, and then loaded both rifles.

Orville used a pole with a hook to close the heavy wood shutter on a side window, and then secured it with two metal throw bolts. He repeated the process until all windows were sealed. The shutters were reinforced and had cross-shaped firing ports. The walls of the house were thick and would stop any bullet below a .50 caliber—something the police didn't know. Another thing the police didn't know was that both men had served in the U.S. Army Corps of Engineers, had experienced combat, and had been trained in explosives and mines.

The telephone rang and Arthur answered. "This is Sergeant Reed. Come out with your hands clasped behind your head."

"Why should we do that? Do you have an arrest warrant for either of us? If you do, you can present it, and then make your arrest."

Reed was a hardass, and he was enjoying his job. "This is the last time I'm going to tell you, come out with your hands clasped behind your head."

With his attention focused on the house, Reed hadn't realized reporters from both local TV stations were videoing him and recording his words.

"If you don't have a warrant, don't step on our property. If any of you do, we'll consider it trespassing and call the police."

"WE ARE THE POLICE, " Reed shouted.

"Why did you say that?" the reporter from FOX asked.

Reed turned around, glared at the reporter and saw he was being recorded, and ordered, "Leave the area immediately. GET OUT OF HERE."

The policeman's a hothead, the reporter realized. *This has all the makings of a great story.* "Sorry, but you can't order the press to leave."

Reed reconsidered. *Yeah, it's gonna be a big story, and I'll be the star.* "All right ... but stay back. Looks like they're gonna resist. There may be shooting."

The FOX reporter called his station and alerted them to be ready to go live.

The phone in the house rang and when Arthur answered he heard Bob's voice, "How's it going?"

"Looks like a storm's coming."

"How soon?"

"Any time now. A SWAT operator, named Regis, paid us a visit. Said he didn't want any trouble. Looked like the told the Golden police officer to leave. Later a Sergeant Reed called and drew the line. Expect them to cross it any time now."

"We have a couple storm chasers nearby."

"Good, looks like a tornado's gonna to touch down."

The call was recorded in the command trailer and a trace showed it came from a burner phone.

Full of himself, Sergeant Reed donned the remainder of his combat gear. Leaving the trailer, he strutted to the edge of the property line. Using his command net, he ordered his men to fire tear gas grenades through the window of the house. Reed expected the rounds to penetrate the shutters.

Peering through a firing port with a monocular scope, Orville saw four men carrying grenade launchers cross their property line and head toward the house. "Here comes the tear gas."

Chapter 21

Alerted by on site reporters, both local TV channels went live with "breaking news" banners. Soon the national networks would pick up their coverage.

Approaching the Bartows' house from the wooded area along the side of their property, SWAT Operative Smith stopped thirty yards from the house. Taking aim at the nearest window, he fired his TLG-6 pump action, six shot 40mm grenade launcher. The CS grenade impacted near the top of the shutter and bounced back—as did the next five. When the other operatives' CS grenades also bounced off, Smith reported, "Grenades won't penetrate the shutters."

Reed had watched the grenades bounce off, but undeterred, he ordered, "Fire more CS grenades close to the house and then withdraw. The gas will get inside."

As soon as the grenades were launched, Orville and Arthur had donned M14 gas masks and placed a homemade mask on Rex.

Reed anxiously watched the house waiting for the brothers to come out, but they didn't. Angry and frustrated, he called the house but no one answered—talking on a phone with a M14 gas mask on is next to impossible. With the TV cameras pointed at him, Reed knew he had to do something. CS wasn't working so that left a full assault, which he immediately ordered.

When the CS barrage stopped, Orville and Arthur peered through the shutter's firing ports and saw the SWAT operatives dressed in full combat gear and carrying Sig 556 rifles emerge from the woods. Seeing the men advancing toward the house, the brothers rightly assumed Reed had ordered an all out siege. Technically the CS grenades counted as the first shot, but neither brother wanted to be the first to fire. Now they had no choice, so Orville decided to wound one of their attackers. Placing the crosshairs on one of the SWAT operative's thigh, he applied pressure to the trigger until the M1 fired. Recovering from the recoil, he watched the SWAT operative spin around, grab his right thigh and fall.

The armor penetrating .30 caliber bullet had passed through his body armor like it was cardboard and exited the back of his thigh.

The advancing SWAT riflemen opened fire with their Sig 556s.

"They're still coming," Orville reported.

"Damn! No choice now. Fire for effect," Arthur said, and they proceeded to drop three more SWAT officers.

Reed watched his first man fall and thought the bullet had somehow found a weak spot in the man's body armor—but when three more men fell and two didn't move, he exclaimed, "Damn it! They have armor piercing bullets." Keying his mike he ordered, "Withdraw."

Following Reed's order, his men carried the first wounded operative back to the ambulance in front of the command trailer. A quick inspection of his body armor revealed a clean bullet hole through the armor. Reed commented it looked like a .30 caliber hole. The medic treated the wounded man and the senior EMT called for more ambulances.

Governor Hickengooper and his AG, along with a major portion of Americans, were watching CBS and FOX and heard Jeb Justice, the local CBS reporter, say the men in the house had agreed to allow a search, when a proper warrant was presented. Squirming in his chair, Hickengooper began to worry about public opinion. *Oh my God, men have been shot. Maybe I've gone to far to fast.*

Zapata, having no such concerns, was fuming. Using his cell phone, he called Reed. "What the hell's going on?"

Realizing he was in over his head, and in charge of a disaster, Reed hesitantly replied, "Sir, the house is fortified, and they're using armor piercing ammunition. One of my men is wounded. Three more are down and may be dead or seriously wounded."

"Send in your armored vehicle and *end this* ... Make an example of them. Blow the hell out of the place."

By now Reed had figured out two things: first, the reason his captain had left; and second, he was now the scapegoat. "Yes, sir. The vehicle's on its way here."

Zapata shook his head and was about to lambast the stupid officer for failing to have the armored vehicle there, when he remembered, *Oh, hell ... it was that fool Regis who planned the raid,* and ended the call.

Shaken by his wounded and possibly dead men, and Zapata hanging up on him, Reed jumped when the phone in the command trailer rang.

"Command trailer, Officer—" the communication's officer answered, but before he could give his name, he heard the caller say, "Tell your boss he can come on the property and recover your men. No weapons."

"Who's calling?" the officer asked, but all he heard in response was the dial tone.

"What ... Who was that?" Reed asked, gaping at the officer and fearing it was Zapata calling back.

"One of the Bartows ... sounded like Arthur ... says we can come on property and retrieve the downed operatives. He also said no guns."

"Thank God. Call for more ambulances," Reed said, relieved it wasn't Zapata, and glad to be able to recover the downed men. Then quickly contacting his uniformed police at the gate, he ordered them to remove their service pistols and escort the two remaining EMTs to the three wounded men.

A few minutes later the first ambulance summoned by the EMT arrived, drove up the driveway and across the yard to the closest SWAT operative lying on the ground. He was alive. One of the EMTs began treating him, and the other went to evaluate the remaining two wounded men. One was dead and the other had a serious wound.

Two more TV vans and four ambulances arrived, and Reed sent two ambulances to collect the wounded and dead SWAT officers.

Half an hour later the armored SWAT vehicle arrived on a flat bed truck. Orville used a telescope to examine the strange looking vehicle. "Looks like some type of tracked, armored bobcat. Has T.R.A.C. painted on its side."

"Let me see," Arthur said, taking the telescope from Orville. "Yeah, it's an armored-up M series Bobcat. Heard about them. Looks like it has an armored shield with a door mounted on the front. Probably holds three men. Cab's most likely armored too."

"Will our armor piercing bullets penetrate it?"

"Looks like we're gonna find out."

◆ ◆ ◆

The Colorado Militia had acquired several thousand rounds of WWII M2 (AP) armor piercing black tipped ammunition for M1 Garand rifles. Like several other militia members, Orville and Arthur had pulled the bullets, emptied the old propellant, pushed out the primers, and reloaded the cartridge cases with modern primers and powder. The bullets had a tungsten core surrounded by lead, and were jacketed with gilding metal. Originally rated to penetrate .35 inches into a 7/8-inch homogenous armor plate at 100 yards, the reloaded rounds would do better.

◆ ◆ ◆

With all the publicity about the assault on the Bartow brother's, word spread rapidly. Many across the nation sat glued to TV screens, watching police unload what looked like a modified tracked bobcat. Exactly what was the ominous looking vehicle, they wondered, and how would it be used to take down two men defending their right to bear arms?

CBS videoed the unloading of the vehicle. Seeking answers for their viewers, Justice and his cameraman approached Reed.

"Officer Reed our viewers are curious about this vehicle. Can you tell us what it is and exactly how you intend to use it to bring down the Bartow brothers?"

Eager for the spotlight, Reed grinned and strutted over to what looked like some sort of modified tracked vehicle. "What you see here is an armored vehicle called a T.R.A.C.," he said, spelling out the four letters, "which is actually an acronym for a Tactical Response Armored Car. The black assault platform, with rounded sides that's mounted on the front, is also armor plated and has ballistic glass windows. It will carry three SWAT operatives up to the front door of the house." Reed pointed to the access door on front of the shield, "See this access door. When the T.R.A.C. reaches the entrance to the house, operatives will open this door and break through the Bartows' front door. Using the T.R.A.C. as a shield, other SWAT operatives will follow along and enter the house through the door in the armored shield."

"Do you think this much fire power is really necessary? Isn't it overkill? After all, you're dealing with two men who are defending their property and their constitutional rights."

"Absolutely not. Colorado's new gun law demands these men turn over their unauthorized weapons. The Bartow brothers have not only refused to do so, they've also used armor piercing bullets to kill one of my SWAT operatives and wound three others. My orders are to use whatever resources our department has to protect the lives of our police."

Twenty minutes later the T.R.A.C., with three SWAT operatives standing on the assault platform behind the shield, started up the driveway. Orville watched and waited until the strange looking assault vehicle was seventy yards from the house. Looking through his scope, he saw a masked face peering through a small rectangular ballistic glass window on the front of the black shield. Estimating the man's size, he centered the scope's crosshairs above where he thought the man's shoulder would be and fired. Traveling at 2,851 feet per second, the M2 AP bullet struck the hardened steel shield, stripping away the outer lead jacket as the tungsten core passed through the armored shield, and creating a deep dent when it impacted the front of the T.R.A.C.

When the startled driver heard the bullet core impact his shielded cab, he stomped the breaks, throwing the man behind the ballistic glass window forward.

"STOP!" the man behind the shield yelled. "A bullet just penetrated the shield."

Everyone on the command net—including Reed who was now a nervous wreck—heard him. "WITHDRAW! WITHDRAW!" Reed yelled into his mike. "Get the hell out of there!"

Hickengooper and Zapata had watched the T.R.A.C. assault on their TV, seen the vehicle start up the driveway, and gleefully waited for SWAT to take out the rebels. *Now we'll see how tough those redneck assholes are,* Zapata silently crowed, certain he'd get the glory for wiping out what he called "those stubborn, gun-toting terrorists."

But when the T.R.A.C. suddenly stopped, and then began rapidly backing down the driveway, Zapata exploded. "Damn it—now what?" he snarled, punching the speed dial button for Reed. "WHAT THE HELL JUST HAPPENED?" he yelled when the sergeant answered.

"Sir, a bullet passed through the armored assault shield and dented the cab."

"WHAT? I was told the shield would stop a rifle bullet."

"Yes, sir, it will—a normal bullet—but apparently the Bartows have armor piercing bullets that can pierce the T.R.A.C.'s armor. I ordered SWAT to withdraw before anyone else got shot," Reed responded, and was about to explain further, when another phone in the trailer rang.

"Sergeant, it's a call from the house," the communication officer said.

"Sir, I have a call from the house. I'd better take it," Reed told Zapata.

"I'll hold while you talk to them. Let me know what they want."

Taking the receiver, Reed answered, "Sergeant Reed."

"Did I miss the man on the vehicle? Didn't want to hit him."

Reed frowned, "You didn't want to hit him?"

"That's right. I shot the first man in the leg. If your men hadn't continued firing at us, no one else would have been shot. Anyone get killed?"

"Yeah, one is dead, and two have serious wounds."

"Sorry to hear that. Didn't want a fight. Still don't."

"Unless you surrender, we're going to kill you."

"You probably will, but how many men are you prepared to lose? Think about it. We suggest you discuss this with your boss. We aren't going anywhere."

When the line went dead, Reed picked up the other phone and repeated the conversation to Zapata, who was finally beginning to realize he had a tiger by the tail—the men in that house were well versed in the art of war. CBS and FOX reporters who were in the trailer overheard Reed's explanation of the circumstances, and both left the trailer as soon as Reed completed his call.

While the FOX reporter was calling his station to report, Jeb Justice, called the house. "Mr. Bartow, what's going on? Why did you call Sergeant Reed?"

"I called to see if I missed the man on the vehicle. Didn't want to hit him."

"I don't understand."

"There was a man riding behind some kind of black shield on the front of the vehicle. I shot a hole in the shield above his shoulder. Just wanted to make sure I didn't hit him. Enough men have been shot. Don't want to shoot any more unless I have too."

Justice was totally confused. "Mr. Bartow, did I understand you correctly? You said you shot a bullet through the armored shield?"

"Yes."

"H–how could you do that?"

"Don't know much about guns, do you? We have armor piercing bullets, World War II armor piercing bullets. Government made millions of them for the M1 Garand. The Germans had light armored trucks and our men needed ammunition that would penetrate them."

"Oh. That's how you shot the SWAT men wearing their bullet proof gear."

"Yeah, that's how. Now, will you tell your viewers we did nothing wrong. The crazy law the lefties passed is *unconstitutional.* Tell them it should *not* be enforced until all the legal challenges work their way through all the courts."

Justice, who had focused on the "millions of rounds of armor piercing ammunition," was only half hearing what Arthur was saying, responded, "Yeah, I will."

"Thanks," Arthur said and hung up.

Positioning himself so the house was behind him, Justice began his live report. "I've just spoken with one of the Bartow brothers. He told me they have World War II armor piercing ammunition for M1 Garand rifles— millions of rounds. These bullets will penetrate the battle armor SWAT uses. He also said their bullets would penetrate the armor on the police vehicle. Let's see if they did."

Walking over to the T.R.A.C.'s black shield, Justice pointed to the bullet hole and said, "Sure enough, there's a bullet hole in the shield to the right of the window. Look at this," he continued, sticking a drinking straw through the hole, demonstrated how the bullet passed completely through the shield. "As you can see, the bullet did pass completely through the shield. Mr. Bartow told me he deliberately shot high in order to miss the man. Said he didn't want to shoot any more police. He never wanted to shoot any police. He said he intentionally shot the first man in the leg so as not to kill him."

Looking into the camera, Justice concluded, "Mr. Bartow said the new law is being challenged in the courts and should not be enforced until the courts have rule on its constitutionality." Justice frowned and added, "Makes good sense to me."

Bob had watched what had so far been a one-sided battle play out from a distance. *What a mess. No way out for Orville and Arthur. They've drawn a line in the sand—a red line. Damn. Wonder if General Clay Morrison'll send in the Guard?*

Still glued to the TV in the governor's office, Zapata watched the newscast and brooded. *I'll crush those two redneck SOBs ... make an* *example of them yet.* Turning to Hickengooper he said, "Governor, it's time to turn this over to the National Guard."

Jane Incompentado had also been watching. *If these Second Amendment nuts win, we'll have trouble enforcing the national law*, she fretted, but once it occurred to her the situation was tailor-made for her Blue Shirts she was ecstatic. After getting the president's approval she called Governor Hickengooper to restate her offer, and then issued orders to her Blue Shirts.

Thirty minutes later, General Morrison, who'd also been keeping abreast of the Bartow debacle, received the call he'd been expecting. "Good afternoon Governor."

"General, have you been keeping up with events at the Bartows' house?" Hickengooper asked.

"Yes, Governor. I have an observer there. Seems like SWAT has a problem."

"Yes, I agree. That's why I'm calling. I want you to take over and destroy those anarchists. Do whatever's necessary."

"Governor, I'm not sure they *are* anarchists. I've received several reports that the Bartow brothers *will allow* a search, as soon as a search warrant has been issued and presented to their lawyer. That seems like a reasonable request to me."

Hickengooper felt his anger rising. "General, they've shot four policemen, killing one of them. I want them—" the governor paused, and then blurted out, "I want them DEAD."

Sure you do, the general grimaced. *If they win ... you lose, and your ridiculous, unconstitutional gun law will be repealed. The bottom line is, I have no intention of becoming your executioner.* "Governor, I'll go to the house and attempt to talk them down, but ... I *will not* order an assault. It's my belief the courts will find your attempt to search their house without court approval illegal, and—if I or my men kill them—we can be found guilty of manslaughter."

"Are you telling me you won't obey my order?"

"Governor, as I *just* explained, I cannot be certain your order is *legal*. So, yes, I'm refusing to attack the house and kill men who only seem guilty of protecting their rights under the Constitution.

"I'll submit my resignation today."

Hickengooper was about to say "good," but, after considering how it would play in the media, stifled his anger and sarcastically said, "Very well then, General Morrison. I'll inform you of my decision regarding your resignation in the next couple of days."

Obviously out of sorts, a scowling Attorney General Zapata held a press conference on the steps of the Capitol at four o'clock. Glaring at a large mixed crowd of veterans, gun owners, anti-gun law supporters and five TV cameras he said, "Citizens of Colorado, we have an insurrection on our hands. The crazy gun-nuts are shooting and killing our police. THIS IS WAR."

"BEFORE ATTACKING THE BARTOW BROTHER'S HOUSE—DID YOU SERVE A WARRANT … ?" shouted a reporter in the crowd.

Ignoring the question, Zapata continued ranting. "Colorado has a new law—the Colorado Gun Registration and Storage Act. As chief law enforcement officer of this state, it's my duty to enforce this law.

"This resistance began when a man named Leroy Jenkins defied the new gun law. A trained killer on the Homeland Security terrorist watch list, Jenkins is armed and considered extremely dangerous. As such, I'm issuing a warrant for his arrest—"

"ARE YOU … YOU SON OF A BITCH … calling a decorated Army sniper a terrorist?" screamed one of several angry men wearing veterans' insignia, emblems and regalia.

"YOU AND YOUR LIBERAL PALS ARE THE REAL TERRORISTS," another screamed.

"WHAT HAPPENED TO THE CONSTITUTION," still another screamed, throwing an egg at the Zapata and prompting security to hustle the AG into the building.

"GO HOME YOU DUMB OLD FOOLS," a young anti-gun supporter screamed holding up his **STOP GUN VIOLENCE** sign; and that was all it took to set off a riot between gun owners, vets and gun-law supporters. As TV cameramen on the scene recorded the advance of the riot squad, a FOX News local reporter summed up the mêlée with the following comment. "Judging from the battle these vets are putting up, it looks as though they're disproving WWII General MacArthur's saying about old soldiers. These old fellows sure aren't fading away. They're fighting mad in defense of our Constitution."

As veterans and active duty military men and women watched across the globe, their smoldering anger grew. "It's not enough for American men and women to give their lives for our country abroad. Now you want to take away our right to defend ourselves on our own soil," was the hue and cry reverberating across the country and on military bases around the world.

Uneasy gun owners with no military background watched with equal disquiet and increased determination to defend their rights. "WE'RE *NOT* GIVING UP OUR GUNS WITHOUT A FIGHT," became their battle cry. Colorado was trampling on the Second and Fourth Amendments. Was this, they wondered, a prelude to federal action when the new gun laws came into effect in January? Zapata had ordered the Bartow brothers removed from their home. They'd resisted, and the nation had watched the resulting altercation with mixed emotions—a historic event had occurred that would later be called the beginning of the revolution.

Night was falling and Sergeant Reed was still waiting for orders. Reporters, many who'd been hanging around since dawn waiting for a scoop, decided nothing else was going to happen until the morning and left. Told to do nothing until he received orders directly from the chief, Reed's was worried. *What's going on? Why hasn't the chief called ... am I gonna be sacked because of the dead and injured,* he wondered. What Reed didn't know was that the chief was doing everything he could to distance himself from the situation—a situation that had little chance of ending well.

Deep in the mountains west of Denver, Lee Jenkins watched Attorney General Zapata's news conference and the resulting riot. "That SOB just put a death sentence on me," he muttered, cutting his eyes at Pat, who along with several men nodded in agreement.

"Well," he concluded, his jaw rigid and voice cold as ice. "Death sentences work both ways."

Chapter 22

Sergeant Reed watched a black sedan approach the command trailer and pull to a stop. The driver, wearing a camouflage uniform got out and opened the rear door for a tall man wearing the same uniform to exit and walk toward the trailer. Stepping outside to greet the tall men, Reed noted the name Morrison and several military insignias on the man's blouse; but, since he'd never been in the military, the badges meant nothing to him. However, he did know the two black stars on his uniform indicated he was a general. Offering the general his hand, Reed said, "Good morning General Morrison. What can I do for you?"

"Good morning, Sergeant Reed. I'm here in my capacity as adjutant general to evaluate the situation and talk to the men in the house. Can you contact them from the trailer?"

"Yes, we can. Come in and I'll have one of my men place the call. So far, talking to them hasn't produced any results."

General Morrison followed Reed into the trailer, and while he waited for the call to go through recalled what he'd read in Arthur and Orville's 201 files. Both Bartow brothers had served with distinction in the U.S. Army Corps of Engineers and retired as E7s. Their records recorded extensive combat experience in Iraq. They'd both received Purple Hearts, and Orville had been awarded a Bronze Star. Their specialty skills included demolition and mines.

A formable pair, Morrison decided, and again wondered why authorities had selected these particular men for gun confiscation? A question he and his driver, Master Sergeant Allen, had discussed on their way to the brother's house. *Hmmm ... Allen also thinks it's odd since the brothers have no police records. Said the only reason that made sense to him was their membership in the Colorado Militia. Perhaps that's why the AG selected them. Zapata wants to make an example.*

Morrison had just concluded Wood's was probably correct when Reed's voice interrupted his thoughts.

"General, I have Orville Bartow on the phone."

Morrison thanked Reed and took the phone. "Good morning Sergeant Bartow, I'm General Morrison, commander of Colorado's Army National Guard."

"Good morning, sir. What can I do for you?"

"I'd like to meet with you and Arthur personally and talk to you. I'm in the command trailer down the road from you house."

"General, it would be an honor to speak with you. When do you want to come?"

"Now, if that's acceptable."

"Yes, sir. We'll be waiting for you."

Reed followed the general out of the trailer and pointed up the road. "The road ends at their driveway. Would you like for me to accompany you?"

Master Sergeant Woods who was standing near by shot his boss a questioning look, which the general caught, and then smiling pleasantly replied, "Thank you Reed, but that won't be necessary. I'll go by myself. While I'm gone why don't you brief Master Sergeant Woods on recent events and your plans?" *Woods has forgotten more about combat than this jerk will ever know.*

Without waiting for a response, Morrison turned and walked toward the entrance to the Bartows' property. Crews setting up the four TV vans paid no attention to him as he walked past them.

Watching the driveway through a gun port, Arthur saw a tall man dressed in the new sand-brown-desert ACU, Army Combat Uniform, walking up the driveway. "The general's walking … bet he's infantry."

"Good," Oliver grunted, "That means he's a real soldier, not a desk jockey."

Arthur opened the door and quickly read the rank insignia and badges on Morrison's uniform: two black stars that made him a major general; the Kentucky Rifle; the master parachutist badge with four combat jump stars; and the Special Forces tab on his left shoulder. All of which confirmed Arthur's speculation—the general was a combat infantry officer who'd been there and done that.

"Good morning, General. Please come in."

Morrison noted that both men were standing at attention, so he said, "Thank you for receiving me. Can we be seated and keep this informal."

"Yes, sir," Arthur replied and pointed to the kitchen table.

Morrison was taking a seat when Rex began growling from behind Orville's closed bedroom door. Morrison looked at the door and said, "I didn't know you had a dog. Did the CS bother him?"

Orville shook his head, "No, sir. We made him a gas mask."

Morrison chucked. "I like dogs. Let him out."

"Yes, sir," Arthur said, going to open door. "It's all right, boy, be good and come meet our visitor," he told the dog, taking hold of his collar and directing him toward the kitchen.

Walking slowly forward, Rex, his ears up and carrying his tail low, stopped for a second or two to study the stranger. "Easy boy," Arthur said, when the dog started moving closer to Morrison to sniff his pant leg and the hand the general lowered for inspection. Then slowly wagging his tail and nuzzling the visitor's hand, the big dog sat down next to Morrison to enjoy having his head and ears rubbed.

"Well I'll be damned," Arthur said. "Rex hardly ever warms up to a stranger. Seems he trusts you, General, and that's good enough for me."

Orville nodded his agreement.

Continuing to rub Rex's head while addressing the brothers, General Morrison said, "I'm very much afraid you fellows have gotten yourselves into an extremely bad situation. Both the Attorney General and the Governor want your heads.

"I've been ordered to end this standoff, and I'm of a mind that the best way to do so is for both of you walk out of here with me."

Orville and Arthur looked at each other. Each shook their head and Arthur answered, "No, sir ... sorry, but we can't do that. If we back down now we're admitting the Constitution no longer has any value."

"If the Second and Fourth Amendments can be ignored, then the entire Constitution can be ignored," Orville added.

Morrison knew they were correct and sighed, "Personally, I agree with you. I've told the governor I will not order an attack. I also offered him my resignation, but so far he hasn't accepted it. Though I have no doubt if he does, he'll appoint who *will* order an attack, and you'll probably be killed."

"Yes, sir, we understand. Thank you for honoring your oath and for leveling with us," Orville said, standing.

"I admire both of you for your courage and patriotism. I've done all I can," Morrison said, standing and offering his hand to each man.

"There is one more thing you can do for us," Arthur said.

"If I can, I will."

Arthur looked at his brother, and then at Rex, who stood looking apprehensively from one of them to the other. Orville nodded and Arthur continued, "Sir, you're correct—we probably won't survive."

Morrison nodded.

"Sir, Rex has obviously taken to you," Arthur said, tears welling in his eyes. "Will you take him with you and keep him as your own?"

Arthur's request shook Morrison to the core—he knew what it meant. Looking down at the dog, he saw Rex's drooped ears and tail and knew the animal sensed the tension and was distressed. In the end, it the soulful look in Rex's eyes that decided Morrison's answer—he couldn't say no. *Why not? Their request clearly indicates they plan on fighting to the death.* After studying the dog, Morrison looked up and said, "It will be my honor to take Rex."

"Thank you, sir," Arthur said taking a leash from a peg and attaching it to Rex's collar. "We feed him Purina Dog Chow twice a day. He's had all his shots and his records are at the Golden Animal Hospital."

Then squatting with Orville to love Rex goodbye, Arthur held the dog's head in his hands and looked in his eyes. "Be a good boy. Go with General Morrison and do what he says. He's gonna take good care of you," he said patting Rex on the head as he rose and handed the leash to the general. Rex seemed to sense what was happening and whined when Orville open the door.

Touched by the finality of the scene, Morrison walked out without saying another word. There was nothing left to say.

TV cameras set up on the road were looking for a target. They found one when a tall man came out of the house leading a large German Shepherd and started walking down the driveway.

The world watched the man and wondered why the dog kept looking back at the house.

A few, including Bob and Lee Jenkins, understood the significance of the dog and its behavior.

Jeb Justice and his cameraman were waiting for the general at the gate. Justice, who'd met Master Sergeant Woods, knew who the general was and why he had gone to the house. As Morrison and Rex approached the gate Justice asked, "General, are they going to surrender?"

"No. Until a valid search warrant is served, they will not allow the police to search their house. I believe that is their right granted by the Fourth Amendment of the Constitution."

Justice had taken time to read the first four amendments and was beginning to understand the issue. "General, I understand you're the commander of the Colorado National Guard." Morrison nodded and Justice continued, "Are you going to use the National Guard to attack the house?"

Morrison stared at the reporter for several seconds before answering, "It's up to the Governor to order the National Guard to take part in this operation. I'm here to access the situation."

Justice was about to ask another question when the general squatted down and put his arm around the dog. Justice had noticed the dog, but paid no attention to him. Now he and his viewers saw the animal looking at the house and whining. "Why is your dog whining, general?"

Morrison looked up and viewers saw a battled hardened man with tears in his eyes looking at them. "He isn't my dog. Rex belongs to the Bartow brothers. They asked me to take him."

The camera switched back to Jeb Justice who blurted out, "Why?" and then, feeling like a fool, he understood and blurted out, "Oh … because they may be killed."

Morrison stood and led Rex down the road.

Brian Ebert entered the Colorado Supreme Court building and presented his request to the Chief Justice's clerk for an emergency injunction to halt enforcement of the Colorado Gun Registration and Storage Act. "Please tell the Chief Justice the reckless enforcement of this act is going to result in bloodshed. The Constitutionality of the act must be determined or the people will revolt."

The clerk sighed, knowing the Chief Justice didn't interfere with lower courts.

General Morrison met with the AG and governor at noon and reported on his meeting. "Governor, Arthur and Orville Bartow have no police record. They're decorated veterans, and—as far as I'm concerned— have every right to own guns. Personally, I consider your law a violation of the Constitution."

"Are you saying you *will not* attack the house," Zapata asked, glaring at the general.

"I have already informed Governor Hickengooper of my position and tendered my resignation."

Zapata looked at Hickengooper, and said, "I suggest you accept his resignation and then appoint a general *who can* follow orders."

Hickengooper stood, and said, "General, thank you for attempting to solve the problem. I'll let you know my decision regarding your resignation by the end of the day."

Morrison replied, "Very well, Governor," and departed.

Red in the face and huffing, Zapata was clearly upset. "Why didn't you fire him?"

Hickengooper suppressed a smile, "Because I have a better option."

Clearly surprised by the governor's comment, the AG asked, "What other option?"

This time Hickengooper smiled, enjoying demonstrating his superior knowledge and power. "Homeland Security's sending me a unit to take down the house."

"Oh."

Hickengooper smiled again.

General Morrison and Rex were scheduled to appear as guests on the Sean Haddley Show. Already a local symbol of the resistance, the German Shepherd was fast gaining star status. Rex and the general were in the KDVR studios in Denver, waiting to appear on Haddley's program. It had taken Rex an hour to adjust to the lights and noise of the studio, and now he calmly sat beside the general, watching the activity around them with interest. When a voice in Morrison's earbud began speaking, the dog looked up at the general's ear. Cocking his head to the side, he listened as the voice told Morrison they'd be on camera in ten seconds and began counting down. As soon as the voice said zero, a red light on the center camera came on, and Sean appeared on a large monitor off camera in front of them.

Morrison had his hand on Rex's head and the dog looked into the lens like a pro.

Arthur and Orville watched Haddley's show with pride. "Can you believe it Arthur, our dog is on national TV," Orville exclaimed.

Millions of viewers were also watching Rex, as Sean began to recount the Bartows' story. Whenever Morrison mentioned Arthur or Orville, Rex would look around and whine. By the end of the program Rex and the Bartow brothers were American gun owners' heroes and Rex became the symbol of the Second Amendment movement. His photograph would soon adorn the covers of several magazines and appear on thousands of posters.

In the meantime, in another part of Golden, while Haddley interviewed General Morrison and Rex, a convoy including several chartered busses, and tractor trailers hauling armored HMMWVs, mounting heavy machine guns, arrived and bivouacked for the night at an abandoned strip mall.

FEMA's Blue Shirts had arrived.

Chapter 23

Attorney **General Zapata heaved himself out of his Lexus 460** and plodded toward the command trailer. Surprised to see him, Sergeant Reed popped out of his chair and greeted him as he entered. "Mr. Attorney General, I didn't know you were coming," and then, not knowing what else to say, added, "May I get you a cup of coffee?"

Jeb Justice, who was sitting with his back to the door, heard Reed's greeting when Zapata entered. Not wanting Zapata to know he was there, Justice decided to remain still and listen. Looking at Reed as though he smelled something offensive, Zapata shook his head, indicating no to the coffee offer, and snapped, "*You're no longer in charge.* At the Governor's request, the Department of Homeland Security is sending a FEMA unit to take charge of this disaster. They'll arrive shortly. As soon as they do, you and your men may leave … or stay if you like and learn how it *should* be done. Either way, the command trailer *stays.*"

Oh boy, do I have a scoop, Justice gloated, slowly standing and working his way unobserved out the trailer's rear door. Once outside, he called his station, told them a story with national implications was breaking at the Bartow's, and then hurried off to his van. "Come with me," he yelled to his cameraman, "A unit from Homeland Security is on the way."

Alerted by Channel 4's breaking news banner flashing on their screens, Colorado's viewers watched crystal-clear, high definition video, shot from the station's helicopter, of a convoy of five military vehicles rolling along a gravel road.

Technicians monitoring competing channels quickly alerted their bosses and soon three more helicopters were on the way.

Channel 4's excited news anchor, Brett Bear, began describing the scene as the helicopter's camera zoomed in on what some viewers recognized as HMMWVs—High Mobility Multipurpose Wheeled Vehicles—commonly known as the 'Humvees,' mounting heavy machine guns. "What you're seeing is a convoy of Homeland Security Vehicles heading for the Bartow house standoff. It looks as though local authorities, attempting to enforce our new gun control law, have decided to bring in the big guns to rout the brothers out of their home and take possession of their weapons. Let's go live to Jeb Justice, our on-the-scene reporter.

"Jeb, can you tell us what's going on at your location?" Brett asked, when transmission switched to the Jeb's cameraman at the remote location.

"Yes, Brett, I can," Jeb said focusing on the camera lens. "I am presently standing on the gravel road leading to the Bartows' house. Behind me is Golden Police Department's command trailer, where Attorney General Zapata arrived a short time ago to inform Sergeant Reed he was relieved from command, because the Golden police are no longer in charge. Even so, he made it absolutely clear the police command trailer would stay. According to the attorney general, the governor had requested that Homeland Security assume control, and the department was sending in a FEMA unit to resolve the situation. A convoy of heavily armed FEMA vehicles is coming up the road as I speak," Jeb said, while his cameraman panned to capture the lead Humvee's approach and follow it until it came to a halt several yards away. As soon the lead vehicle stopped, a burly man wearing blue camouflage BDUs got out and looked around as though expecting someone to welcome him.

When the camera zoomed in on the man, the news anchor, Bret, said, "Jeb, that man appears to be leading the convoy. Is he wearing a UN military uniform? I know the governor has proclaimed his determination to enforce the new state gun law, but why has he called in UN troops?"

"No, Brett. Although the uniform resembles those worn by UN forces they *are not* UN troops," Jeb replied as his cameraman zoomed in on the lead vehicle's side. "Look at the Humvee's identification markings painted on the door. It reads, "Department of Homeland Security, FEMA Corps.

"As you can see, the men in this convoy are Homeland Security FEMA Corps Troops. And, as I reported earlier, according to Attorney General Zapata, they are here at the Governor's request."

"So the man who got out of the lead Humvee is a FEMA Corps officer. Did the Attorney General mention his name?"

"No, Brett, but stay with me because I believe the Attorney General is still in the trailer. If he is, I'm going to attempt to find out who the man is, and what his orders are with respect to assaulting the Bartows' house."

Having grown tired of waiting for someone to greet him, Colonel Savage, the commander of the FEMA Corps unit, started walking toward what he assumed was the police command trailer he'd been told about. However, having seen the Channel 4 cameraman and a man he thought was a reporter heading toward the trailer's steps, Savage decided to hold back. The last thing he wanted was a confrontation with a nosy reporter.

Zapata, who'd seen the Humvees arrival on the command center's surveillance screen, watched as Savage got out and walked toward the trailer. Opening the trailer door, the AG was about to descend the steps when he noticed Justice and his cameraman. Mugging for the camera, he'd just reached the ground when Justice rushed up and stuck a microphone in his face.

Colonel Savage scowled at the reporter's behavior and almost said something, but decided not to interfere and simply watch the exchange.

Zapata also resented having the microphone stuck in his face, but swallowed his bile and smiled at the rude reporter. A true politician, he recognized the Channel 4 reporter from an earlier press conference and couldn't pass up taking advantage of free publicity, so he stopped at the foot of the stairs and said, "Good morning Mr. Justice."

"Good morning Mr. Attorney General. I wasn't aware Homeland Security had military personnel. Where did these men come from, and who is their leader?"

"I'll be glad to give you an interview later, but now isn't the appropriate time. The gentleman in question is Colonel Savage, commander of the FEMA Corps troops, who are here to put an end to the standoff. Though you may not be a party to my discussion with the colonel—it wouldn't do for the Bartows to hear the colonel's plans—you may however video our exchange from a distance," Zapata said, nodding a greeting to the man standing a several feet away.

"Colonel Savage, I'm Attorney General Alphonso Zapata," viewers heard Zapata call out to Savage as he walked toward him.

Zapata sized up the large, thick-necked FEMA commander, but had no way of knowing Savage was a former U.S. Army infantry major who had been forced to resign his commission and given a general discharge for brutality to his men and civilians. A record that should have prevented him from obtaining a position with DHS, but instead made him just the kind of man the up-to-now secret component of FEMA Corps was looking for.

Keep the video rolling, Justice signed to his cameraman, spinning his hand in a circle and then tapping his chest, which indicated the cameraman should pan around to him, "As you can see, Brett," Jeb said focusing on the camera lens, "the Attorney General is discussing plans to bring the Bartow brother's to justice. We're going to stand by here on location to cover new developments in this tense gun confiscation standoff and will alert you when they occur. Now back to you Brett in the studio."

"Stay here and keep filming, while I try to get close enough to hear what they're planning," Justice told the cameraman. Then, easing forward to where the two men stood facing away from him, he edged up close enough behind Zapata to listen and take notes.

There's something about this Savage guy that gives me the creeps, he thought, recalling the chilling look the colonel gave him and his cameraman when he realized they were videoing him. A look Justice had seen in several men's eyes while imbedded in three U.S. Army combat units in Afghanistan—the look of men who enjoyed war too much—men who'd discovered they liked killing. The kind of men the Army didn't want and made every effort to get rid of.

"Mr. Attorney General, I have orders to take down a house containing terrorists. I understand they've fired on your police and have armor piercing ammunition," Justice overheard Savage say. *Terrorists ... since when are citizens who are defending their Constitutional rights terrorists?* Justice grimaced, writing the word "terrorist," in his notebook.

"That appears to be correct. Three SWAT operatives have been wounded and one killed. The governor and I want you to make an example of these insurrectionists—these men you called terrorists," Zapata said.

Make an example of those men who're just trying to defend their rights? I don't like the sound of this, Justice frowned and scribbled, "Make an example of."

"Yes, sir," Savage said, "I came prepared to do just that. I have five armored vehicles with M2 machine guns that can rip their house apart."

Those poor bastards don't stand a chance against that kind of firepower, Justice sighed, writing the words "Rip the house apart," and underlining them. *That confirms it ... Now I know for sure ... there's no two ways about it—that guy Savage is a killer. God help those two men.*

"Now, with your permission, Mr. Attorney General I want to recon the area."

"Certainly, I'll be in the command trailer.

"REED," Zapata, yelled to the police sergeant, who'd been chatting it up with the lead Humvee's driver, "GET OVER HERE! Show the colonel the way to the Bartow's."

Savage signaled his sergeants in the other Humvees to follow, and he and Reed headed toward the entrance to the Bartow's property.

Viewer reaction to the appearance of Homeland Security at the Bartow brother's house was mixed. While a few bleeding hearts hoped the excessive show of force would end the standoff; the majority was shocked to see DHS was deploying a heavily armed, uniformed military force—a force that was preparing to use armored vehicles mounting heavy machine guns against private citizens. It was obvious the two brothers were going to be slaughtered as an example.

"Intimidation," many viewers muttered, followed by, "We *will not* be intimidated."

Savage and his five sergeants had completed their recon and were returning to the command trailer, when they noticed a long line of pickup trucks, SUVs and sedans pulling to a stop behind the DHS convoy blocking the road. "What the hell?" Savage muttered.

In a matter of minutes, as many as a hundred men and a few women had exited their vehicles, scrambled around the convoy of Humvees and assembled in the middle of the road. Then shouting epithets and shaking their fists they rushed up the road and converged on Savage, his men and Reed.

"I don't like the looks of this," Savage told his sergeants, placing his hand on his side arm. "Reed, this is your problem. Get rid of these protesters."

"No, sir ... afraid I can't do that. The Attorney General has relieved me of my authority."

"*Damn,*" Savage snarled, and looking at his men, ordered, "Return to your Humvees and await my orders."

"Come with me, Reed," Savage snarled, stomping up the command trailer's steps and bursting inside.

"Mr. Attorney General, you need to have Reed get rid of those civilians."

Startled by the colonel's abrupt entrance, Zapata started to say "what civilians," but decided instead to open the command center's door and see what was going on. As soon as he stepped on the threshold, reporters, TV cameras, and the growing crowd of angry protesters confronted him.

"MR. ATTORNEY GENERAL," the FOX reporter shouted, "Why is Homeland Security here?

"YEAH ... and why do they have military vehicles with machine guns?" another reporter yelled.

"Why isn't the National Guard here?" a third asked, followed by a volley of shouted questions from the protesters.

Standing behind Zapata and watching the inquisition over his shoulder, Savage leaned forward and murmured in the AG's ear, "Have the local police clear the area ... make it a matter of public safety."

Zapata nodded and shouted over the bedlam, "CALM DOWN FOLKS! For your own safety I insist that you disburse. This is a police matter and in the interest of public safety you *must* go home."

The crowd quieted and Zapata thought he had gained control until an eager beaver reporter, who'd just arrived shouted, "DOES HOMELAND SECURITY HAVE A SEARCH WARRANT?"

The question ignited aggressive members of the crowd who began shouting questions.

"GO HOME!" Zapata shouted back, "This is the last time I'm going to tell you." Then throwing up his hands in disgust, he whirled around, entered the trailer, and slammed the door behind him.

"REED!" He snarled, "Get out there with your men ... do whatever it takes to clear the area. I will not tolerate this kind of civil unrest."

"I'll do what I can sir, but when you relieved me, I sent most of my men home," Reed replied, exiting the trailer.

Twenty minutes later Savage, who was standing on the trailer steps with Zapata watching Reed's pitiful attempt to get the protesters under control, had had enough. Sneering, he said, "Mr. Attorney General, I'm going to carry out my orders. You'd better get Reed some backup so he can keep these people from following my vehicles."

Storming down the steps and grabbing Reed by the arm, Savage snarled, "I'm heading for the Bartow's. If you don't keep these civilians from following us, you'll be responsible for the consequences.

"Now get these people out of my way."

Shoving Reed aside, Savage shouldered his way through the throng and jumped into the lead Humvee. "GO, GO, GO!" he yelled at his driver, and then keying his mike ordered the other Humvee drivers, "Follow me ... Run over the SOBs." Sneering, Savage cursed the civilians as his driver gunned the Humvee and charged toward the crowd standing in the road.

Panicked by the sight of the huge Humvees leaping forward, Reed and the civilians scattered like a covey of quail as the vehicles roared toward them. Watching the civilians regroup and follow the convoy, Reed came to a decision. *There's no way in hell to stop these people from going after that mad man. Attorney General Zapata's orders be damned. As soon as I can get what's left of my men together, we're outta here.*

As soon as the convoy had moved out, cameras on four network helicopters hovering over the action switched to cameras mounted on TV vans positioned near the gate. Viewers watching the big Humvees advance held their breath. All were anticipating what they sensed was going to be a bloodbath. There was no way those Bartow brothers could survive such an assault.

The convoy had almost arrived at the Bartow's gate when Savage received word from the trailing Humvee that the civilians were following. *"Damn them to hell,"* he hissed, and going ballistic keyed his mike. "HALT!" he yelled, "all units hold your position until I return. None of you move without my command. I'm going to put a stop to these civilian protesters once and for all.

"Driver, turn around and drive back toward the belligerent bastards."

"Gunner, when I give the signal, aim your M2 at the ground in front of those assholes. Do not fire … unless I give the order."

A few seconds later, when they were a few yards from the advancing protesters, Savage ordered, "Stop."

Climbing out of the Humvee and facing the protesters, Savage cupped his hands to his mouth and shouted, "YOU ARE ORDERED TO TURN AROUND AND LEAVE. THIS IS A HOMELAND SECURITY OPERATION. LEAVE … LEAVE FOR YOU OWN SAFETY."

"HELL NO," a red-faced man shouted. "You're getting ready to murder the two men in that house. We demand to see your warrant." Others joined in, shouting their agreement.

Out of breath from rushing to get ahead of the protesters, Justice and his cameraman arrived just in time to video an elderly man confronting Savage, demanding, "Who the hell *are* you, Sonny? I'm a retired vet and I don't recognize your uniform."

"I am Colonel Maxwell Savage. My troops and I are members of FEMA Corps, part of Homeland Security. Now, do as I say and leave or—"

"You don't give me or any of us orders, *Sonny,*" the old fellow interrupted. "This ain't Nazi Germany."

"You don't want to cooperate, you rebellious sons-a-bitches. THEN SUFFER THE CONSEQUENCES," Savage shouted, abruptly raising his left arm and turning to point to the Humvee's gunner. "See how you like this," he jeered, turning back toward the protesters and dramatically pointing to the ground in front of them. Glaring at the defiant old man who'd taunted him, Savage fully expecting him to cower along with others in the crowd when the big M2 .50 caliber machine gun swung around toward them. But, rather than cringing in fear, the citizens grew angrier and became even more aggressive, shouting insults and demands, and daring him to fire.

Savage sneered. *They think I'm bluffing. Well, if that's what they think, they are in for a big surprise. They're forcing me to shoot. Let 'em keep it up and I'll have sufficient justification to fire.*

Glued to his TV screen tuned to Channel 4, Governor Hickengooper squeezed the arms of his chair and exclaimed, "OH MY GOD! This is getting out of control." Picking up his cell phone he speed dialed Zapata. When the AG answered, the governor shouted, "DO YOU KNOW WHAT'S GOING ON? That damn fool from Homeland Security just pointed a machine gun at a group of our citizens. STOP HIM before the situation gets completely out of control. Damn it, more people are arriving."

Zapata who was still inside the command trailer had no idea what was going on, for no one had thought to turn on the TV. "How do you know?" he asked, suddenly panicking.

"I'M WATCHING TV ... and your little circus is performing on all the channels. Now, go *stop* that crazy fool. The entire nation is watching, and it looks like half of Golden is out there protesting. The public is turning against us."

"I'm on it, Governor," Alfonso Zapata said, and heaving the substantial abdominal girth he'd acquired during years of chair warming, hurried out of command trailer. Then, quickly looking around, "Alfonso the Fat"—the disparaging nickname political opponents used to compare the AG to Alfonso II, an obese 13th century Portuguese King—took off in a "waddle-trot" up the road toward the Bartow's gate.

Finally reaching the unruly throng standing in front of the Humvee, Zapata was so out of breath he could barely speak. Gasping for air, he pushed his way through the shouting crowd until at last he reached Colonel Savage, who was standing with his right hand on his sidearm, spread-legged in front of his vehicle. Squinting, first at the colonel and then at the top of the Humvee, Zapata gaped in disbelief at the very large machine gun pointing down at him. "W–hat's ... g–going ... on?" he finally managed to wheeze between gasps.

Sneering at the panting, rotund little man, Savage sarcastically taunted, *"What's going on*? I'm *carrying out* my orders, *Mister* Attorney General—this is *now* a federal matter. I have told these civilians to leave, and I am now going to enforce my order."

Savage's reply flabbergasted the AG. *"Like hell you will,"* Zapata managed to growl, despite his breathless state. "I–I'm ordering you to go to the Bartow's gate, and ... and do your job," he gasped, "I–I'll deal with these people."

Looking at the protesters who were suddenly deathly quiet, Savage noticed the TV camera pointed at them and hesitated. *It won't do to have this scene recorded.* "Damn TV and damn reporters," he muttered, and turning on his heel got in his Humvee.

Like the governor, the Bartow brothers were also watching TV. Electrical service to the house had been cut, and their diesel generator was supplying power. They'd been switching channels in an effort to obtain a tactical perspective. Of particular interest to them were the live news alerts Channel 4 had been broadcasting directly from the scene outside the police department's command trailer and from cameras on the road leading to their property. They'd seen the Department of Homeland Security convoy of Humvees arrive and heard the exchange between Attorney General Zapata and Colonel Savage.

They'd also watched with concern the confrontation between the colonel and a crowd of civilians loudly protesting the presence of federal troops to enforce a state law—a law the angry people were screaming was unconstitutional. When the crowd refused to disperse and followed the advancing Humvees toward their gate, both Bartow brothers became deeply concerned. While they were prepared to die for their convictions, neither brother wanted to see other people injured or killed defending the their right to do so.

"That guy Savage is a hothead. He's not gonna put up with being harassed," Orville said, "Look, the convoy has stopped at our gate, but for some reason Savage's lead vehicle is turning around. I think he's going back after the protesters. Damn it, Arthur, his Humvee has stopped and he's getting out to confront those people again ... and this time it looks as though he means business, because the gunner's lowering the M2. *Oh, my God,* Arthur, he's going to mow them down ... " Orville gasped, jumping up from his chair.

"No ... hold on—*Look,* there's the attorney general," Arthur said as they watched the paunchy little man push his way through the crowd and stumble up to Savage. "Can't make out what he said, but the gun's being raised."

"Yeah, it looks like the attorney general stopped a massacre ... just in time too," Orville commented, "and from the looks of it, the colonel's hoppin' mad. He's getting back in the Humvee, Arthur ... and it's turning around ... coming our way."

"Yep, and you can bet he's not coming for a chat and a cup of Joe. He's gonna come in shootin'."

"Yeah, and those .50 cals can shoot right through our shutters and the walls," Orville agreed.

Arthur opened a trap door in the floor, and the brothers and Rex scurried down the stairs into the basement. While Arthur turned on a TV, Orville booted up an old computer connected to four cams mounted under the eves of the roof—cams that would allow them to see all four approaches to the house. Orville selected the cam facing the driveway.

As soon as the TV was on, Arthur went to the east wall where a pipe, with four sets of cables hanging out, protruded through the cement wall. Taking hold of the cable tagged No. 1, Orville untwisted the pair of wires, and connected them to a 12-volt battery and announced, "Front mines hot."

On his way back to join the convoy, Savage received a message from his men that a large group of men and women had reached the gate and formed a line with their arms locked together, effectively blocking the Humvee's path.

"I'm going to kill *every last one* of those belligerent bastards!" Savage hissed, his blood boiling. "Driver, pull up in front of the assholes. When his Humvee was twenty feet from the line of men and women, he ordered, "STOP!"

Jumping out of his Humvee, Savage drew his side arm and ran toward the protesters, screaming, **"GET THE HELL OUT OF MY WAY."**

"NAZI ... MURDERER ... STORM TROOPER," the people taunted, drowning out his words.

Now completely out of control, Savage's true personality surfaced. "MOVE or you'll regret it," he yelled, waving his pistol.

But instead of creating fear, he created defiance.

Glaring, Savage evaluated his options, *Damn these weak-kneed civilians. Well, I am the law now, and I'll restore order. I always wanted to mow down weaklings and this is a perfect opportunity.* "PREPARE TO FIRE," he yelled to his gunner, Trayvon Thomas.

Trayvon, who had no real military experience, grinned from ear to ear. He flat-out hated white people and was always saying "they were holdin' him down." So ever since FEMA'd trained him to fire the big gun, he'd fantasized about using it to, "blow dem white cracker mo-fo'ers away." To Trayvon his M2 was the "biggest, badasstest, bestest thing" that ever happened to him. In fact, prior to joining FEMA Corps to escape a jail sentence, he'd been a Chicago gangbanger who'd never handled anything larger than a 9 mil. *Now dey's trained me to fire dis here mo-fo'in big gun, I'm gonna do dem mo-fo'in honky crackers,* he snickered as he aimed his M2 at the line of defenseless people.

"FIRE ON MY COMMAND," Savage shouted.

Turning to the protesters he screamed, **"THIS IS YOUR LAST WARNING. LEAVE!"**

His answer was more shouts.

"PREPARE TO FIRE."

The shouts continued.

Chapter 24

Observation point overlooking the Bartow house
Late morning, Saturday, May 9, 2015

Lee Jenkins, who'd backpacked into the mountains the previous night, had located an advantageous spot from which to observe the Bartow house and the road leading up to it. Up since the crack of dawn, he'd been using his CounterSniper Optics 4-50X 'Crusader' Tactical Scope to watch the action below. He'd seen the convoy of five Humvees mounting the M2 Browning .50 caliber machine guns arrive and stop in the middle of the road near the command trailer. Expecting the men in the vehicles to be National Guard, he was stunned when the apparent commander of the convoy got out of the lead Humvee wearing a blue camouflage BDU uniform similar to that worn by UN troops.

What the hell? Why is the UN involved in this local law enforcement issue? he'd asked himself. As the morning wore on his curiosity grew. Continuing to use his scope, he'd observed the carloads of protesters arrive: and, thanks to his earbuds connected to a small AM/FM radio, he'd listened to the conversation between a talk show host and two protesters calling on cell phones. Both callers reported the Humvees were from Homeland Security, and the men were FEMA Corps. The second caller said their commander was Colonel Savage, and neither Savage nor the handful of police who were there could make the protesters leave. He added that as far as he knew, the attorney general was in the police trailer.

Jenkins lay on his sleeping bag, pondering the information. *What's that fat little shit Zapata doing out here? Why is Homeland Security here—and what is FEMA Corps, and where did it come from?* He was searching for answers, when he noticed a disturbance in the crowd of protesters. Checking it out with his scope, he saw the colonel push his way toward the lead Humvee and climb in. Seconds later, apparently with no warning, the colonel's Humvee, followed by the other four, sped toward the protesters, causing them to scatter and leaving one man hopping around on one foot.

"You SOB," Jenkins muttered, continuing to watch the column of five Humvees move out toward the Bartow's gate, and the protesters, apparently unscathed, regroup and follow. *Now what's the bastard doing?* He wondered, alarmed when the column suddenly stopped and the colonel's lead Humvee turned around and sped back toward the people. Angrily watching Savage confront the people and signal his Humvee's gunner to point his gun at them, Jenkins was relieved when the attorney general intervened. However, when Savage got in his Humvee and returned to the head of the column and confronted the protesters who'd locked arms in front of the gate, Jenkins knew he had to do something.

"Damn," Jenkins grunted. *Things are going south fast.* Rolling over, he picked up his Sako TRG-42 .338 rifle, with a 27-inch 1:10 twist barrel lying on top of its case and mounted his scope. Using his jacket as a pad, he positioned the rifle on a rock so it was supported by both the rock and its bi-pod. Setting the scope at 20x, he adjusted his position until the scope showed the men and women at the gate. It was apparent things were getting out of control. Rolling to his left, he used his Nikon laser ranger finder to determine the range. The reading showed 4,252 feet to the Humvee. Adjusting the setting on his scope and assuming a prone position, he zoomed in at 35x, and watched the colonel and gunner on the Humvee, while listening intently to the talk show.

When he heard a third caller tell the host, "The colonel just said, 'Prepare to fire,' " Jenkins knew he had to act. Clenching his teeth he grasped the bolt handle, pulled it back and then drove it forward, inserting a hand-loaded cartridge into the rifle's chamber. Zooming to full magnification, he centered his cross hairs on the gunner whose evil smile clearly indicated he was itching to kill. *"Damn it ... I'd hoped it wouldn't come to this,"* he hissed, watching Trayvon place his thumbs near the V-shaped butterfly trigger. *Yep, he's going to fire.*

Placing his finger on the rifle's trigger, Jenkins' training took over and he zoned in on his target—Trayvon's sadistic face became his whole world. Now only the man behind the M2 machine gun existed.

Colonel Savage was beyond furious. Facing the line of civilians, he shouted, "I'M GOING TO COUNT TO THREE. If you don't move I'll order my gunner to fire."

Listening intently to his radio, Jenkins heard a caller say, "He's counting ... preparing to fire." As soon as the man said "one" Jenkins began applying pressure on the trigger until the heavy Sako recoiled, sending a HSM 250grain Sierra Match King bullet toward Trayvon at a speed in excess of 2,900 feet per second. By the time Jenkins heard the man on the radio say, "two," he had reacquired his target, and the heavy bullet was halfway there.

Glaring at the line of civilians, Savage was about to say "three," when he heard a sound he hadn't heard for several years—the sound of a heavy bullet striking a human body at supersonic speed. Most of the men and women facing him were looking at the gunner who was grinning down at them over his gun. A few had just realized he really was going to fire. When the heavy bullet impacted his face just below his nose—effectively exploding his head and decapitating him—many were traumatized. Several women screamed and one fainted.

Zapata was begging Savage to stop when the gunner's head exploded, and that was all it took to send the armchair warrior to his knees, puking his guts out.

Assuming the shot had come from the house, Savage quickly keyed his mike and yelled, "UNITS TWO AND THREE—PLACE FIRE ON THE HOUSE.

"ATTACK ... GO, GO, GO! MOW THE BASTARDS DOWN," he screamed as he watched the first two Humvees facing the line of protesters speed forward, scattering the civilians and bursting through gate.

While Humvee number two charged up the driveway, Humvee number three turned onto the lawn and headed toward the house—both Humvee gunners raked the house with .50 caliber bullets. Humvee two, several yards ahead of Humvee three, reached a point fifty-yards from the house. Weighing considerably more than a pickup truck or medium SUV, number two's right front wheel caused the thin steel plate, buried several inches below the driveway's surface, to collapse onto the bottom plate—in effect closing an electrical switch, sending electrons flowing from the battery to a blasting cap, and detonating the case of 90 percent dynamite buried below the driveway. The explosive force, directed upward by the hard ground into the Humvee's undercarriage, lifted the heavy vehicle into the air, breaking it in two and tossing it, along with a number of bloodied dismembered bodies, across the lawn.

Stunned by the sudden explosion, Humvee number three's driver stomped the brakes and managed to stop a couple of feet short of another pressure plate trigger. Having gained experience with IEDs in Afghanistan, the frightened driver slowly backed his vehicle toward the gate.

Wiping his mouth on his shirtsleeve and gaping in disbelief, Zapata required several seconds to process what he'd just seen. Suddenly aware that he was watching his plans literally going up in flames, he snapped and began screaming like a madman, "KILL THEM ... KILL THE BASTARDS ... KILL THE BLOODY BARTOWS."

As fate would have it, a TV cameraman, standing near the gate filming the burning Humvee, heard Zapata's ravings and quickly turned his camera on the hysterical AG. Several protesters, who'd also witnessed the madman's outburst, quickly called local radio stations to report what Zapata was screaming.

Still watching through his scope, Jenkins frowned when he heard the first radio caller's report from the scene, and zooming out to 35X located Zapata. Zooming back to 50X, he centered his cross hairs on the man who'd caused him so much trouble by accusing him and his wife of being terrorists: a man who'd placed a death sentence on him. Then, with a myriad of sensations assailing him, an old rhyme popped into his head—*In for a penny in for a pound ... Why not?* he asked himself and worked the bolt to chamber another cartridge. Centering the crosshairs on Zapata's chest, Jenkins slowly squeezed the trigger.

Savage had just turned to look at the attorney general when the Sierra Match King bullet impacted the fat little man's chest. Like the first shot, Savage heard no report. This time he realized it was a sniper and dove behind a Humvee.

Keeping low and staying behind cover, Lee Jenkins broke down his rifle, policed his brass, and quietly withdrew to a thicket a mile distant. He would wait for dark to exfiltrate.

Shaking his head in disbelief, Governor Hickengooper realized he was in serious trouble. Reaching for the phone he called General Morrison. "Have you been watching?

"Yes, Governor. I'm watching."

"Please go and take charge. The Homeland Security bunch has started a war."

"Yes, Governor, I'll do so, but I *will not* attempt to take the brothers into custody. As far as I'm concerned, they were defending their home."

"I'll tell Attorney General Zapata to prepare charges."

"Governor, you'll have to appoint a new attorney general. Zapata has been killed."

"*Oh my God.* When? How?"

"As far as I can tell, a sniper shot him from a great distance. The same sniper, I believe, who also shot—actually shot first—a FEMA gunner preparing to fire a heavy machine gun at a line of citizens."

"Oh my God!"

An hour later General Morrison, leading a convoy of National Guard Humvees, arrived. Colonel Savage saw the general approaching, walked out of the command trailer, and saluted. Morrison returned his salute and barked, "*Colonel,* you have exactly thirty minutes to pack up and leave. I want you and your men *out* of Colorado by this time tomorrow."

"General, I can't do that. I am here under orders from the Secretary of Homeland Security."

"Colonel, or should I say *major,* if you are in my state twenty-five hours from now—I will personally shoot you." Morrison turned and walked toward the trailer, leaving Savage staring at his back.

Inwardly seething from the general's insult, Savage was walking toward his remaining FEMA Humvees when he noticed a National Guard master sergeant, standing off to the side cradling an M16 and smiling at him—and it wasn't a pleasant smile. Deciding he'd had more than enough trouble for one day, Savage told his men to pack up.

Still keeping a sharp eye on Savage, Master Sergeant Woods watched the four Homeland Security Humvees drive down the road, and this time smiled a genuine smile. Then, recalling an old expression his mother liked to use, he muttered "Good riddance to bad garbage," and laughed heartily.

Once inside the command trailer General Morrison called the Bartows. "Hello, this is General Morrison. You fellows okay in there?" he asked.

"Orville here ... yes, sir—thank you for asking,"

"Well Orville, you and Arthur have sure made a hell of a mess. No one knows what to do with you ... but I'm in charge now and until you hear otherwise from me, consider you and your brother under house arrest. Unload and store your weapons and you can come out into your yard. Do I have both your words that you will remain on your property?"

"Yes, sir."

"Yes sir," Arthur said, standing close to Orville, so he could hear the general.

"If you need anything, signal the guard posted at your gate. He'll take care of your request. Now ... try not to blow anything else up."

"Yes, sir," both brothers said in unison.

Secretary Incompentado and the president had also watched the fiasco in Golden on TV and neither one was amused.

The shootout at the 'Bartow Corral,' as the media had dubbed it, was the hot topic on all evening news programs, and would be for the next several days. Three Sunday morning news shows invited the secretary of homeland security to appear, but she declined. No one from DHS was available, and DHS's spokespersons deflected questions about the paramilitary FEMA unit—implying it was a special unit created to evaluate response options. The same spokespersons pooh-poohed the idea that FEMA Corps was the president's police force, the one he'd mentioned during his first campaign.

The question of whether the Bartow brothers had a right to defend themselves was grist for radio and TV talk show mills across the nation. Whereas some callers thought they'd murdered police and Homeland Security personnel; the majority thought the brothers had a right to defend their property and home against illegal search and seizure.

"Is this a sample of what's going to occur in January?" O'Rippley asked his viewers.

Two days later the Chief Justice of the Colorado Supreme Court issued a ruling staying enforcement of the Gun Registration and Storage Act—a victory for gun owners and a downer for gun-law enforcement advocates.

Later that same day, Hickengooper's aide entered his office and found the governor seated at his desk—head in hands—muttering, *"Oh my god ... Oh my god."*

"Uh, Governor, I didn't understand what you said."

Looking up, Hickengooper whined, *"Nothing—I said nothing ...* come back later."

As soon as the aide left, the governor lowered his head and muttered, "Oh my god," but then realizing he didn't believe in God, shook his head, sighed, and muttered, "Oh my god."

Chapter 25

Capitol Building
Denver Colorado
Monday, May 11, 2015

General **Morrison was hurrying through the rotunda** on the way to his office. He was almost to the exit when, much to his annoyance, he heard Representative Naomi Goldberg distinctive scratchy voice.

"Woo-hoo! General Morrison … hold up a moment."

God give me patience ... what does that woman want now? It's always something with her. I don't have time for this, Morrison thought, turning to face her and bracing himself for another one of her rants. "Madam Speaker, what can I do for you?"

"General, what do you intend to do about those terrorists in Golden?" Goldberg demanded, looking up at him with her arms crossed.

"Madam Speaker, I'm unaware of any terrorists in Golden. To whom are you referring?"

"Wh—What terrorists am I referring to? Have you lost your mind? You were there!" Goldberg spat.

General Morrison, who'd long since lost patience with idiotic progressive-liberals, looked down in disgust at the dumpy, frizzy-haired, arrogant woman. "Madam Speaker, dare I assume you are referring to Arthur and Orville Bartow, the two patriots who were defending their Constitutional right to bare arms and defend their property."

"Who *else* could I be referring to, General?"

"Who else? Perhaps the FEMA Corps men in the blue uniforms … they're one possibility. Are you aware their commander ordered his machine gunner to point his gun at civilians? Actually he gave the order twice, and the second time he was about to order him to fire when a sniper blew the gunner's head off."

"You *can't* be serious. Those men were from Homeland Security. How *dare* you accuse them?"

"I dare because it's true. FOX has been showing video clips of FEMA corps' attack. And a local radio talk show has a recording of a man calling from the scene repeating the commander's order to fire on the count of three. The caller said the commander had said 'two' and was about to say 'three' when the gunner was shot. Glenn Deck and O'Rippley have been talking about it on their shows. Tonight Sean Haddley will be rebroadcasting the taped message from the sniper he received during his afternoon radio show."

"I *don't* watch FOX, and I *certainly* don't listen to those bigots on the radio."

"Perhaps, Madame Speaker, that explains your problem—the reason you and your progressive-liberal cohorts pass laws that violate the Constitution."

"I assume, *General,* you are referring to our new gun laws. Well, get ready for more, because next we're going to ban *all* guns."

Shaking his head, Morrison stood looking down, studying Goldberg's pompous, prune-shaped face as she glared up at him. Trying to decide how to penetrate her know-it-all mindset, Morrison pondered what—if anything—to say. *Like all Socialist leaning ideologues she's positive she has all the answers, but she never takes time to analyze anything ... this is probably a waste of time, but I'll try once more to make her listen to reason,* he decided, sighing and giving her a stern look.

"Madam Speaker, with all due respect, your current law is forcing citizens to defend their Constitutional rights with force. Thomas Jefferson predicted the time would come when guns would be needed to control a tyrannical government. I'm beginning to understand his reasoning.

"Our overzealous *former* attorney general's unconstitutional, illegal enforcement has sparked armed resistance. Blood has been spilled. If you and your colleagues persist you will cause an uprising."

"General, it's *my* job to pass the laws and *yours* to enforce them," Goldberg snapped, poking her finger in the general's chest.

"No, Madam Speaker, it's *not,*" Morrison said, stepping back from her. "I've submitted my letter of resignation to Governor Hickengooper, and he's considering whether he will accept it.

"One SWAT operator has been killed and three more wounded while following the AG's orders. In fact the AG was videoed screaming 'Kill the Bartows,' when the FEMA Corps unit attacked the brother's home. FEMA lost seven—no eight men.

"Zapata issued orders to search citizen's homes without warrants. When SWAT attempted to force a search of the Bartow brothers' home without a warrant, they were shot. Before any further action concerning the brothers is taken, it must be determined if they were legally defending their property—"

"General, the governor will appoint a new attorney general, and he *too* will enforce the gun laws."

"Madam Speaker, some unknown citizen, who refused to have his or her constitutional rights trampled on, killed the last attorney general during the Bartow attack. Zapata found out he wasn't bullet proof. Now, my question to you is ... Do you think *you* are?

"Good day, madam," Morrison said, and turning on his heel marched toward the exit.

Speechless and shaken by Morrison's final words, Goldberg stood staring at the general's back. "Bullet proof ..." she muttered, a cold chill running down her spine. It had never occurred to her that anyone would actually want to shoot her.

U.S. Capitol Building
Washington, DC
Thursday, May 14, 2015

The Senate Homeland Security and Governmental Affairs Committee began its hearing on the "Golden Event" at ten o'clock. Minority members were demanding information on FEMA Corps and Blue Shirts. President Abomba had exercised executive privilege, forbidding Secretary Incompentado from appearing. The only DHS witness, Marvin Witless, associate assistant director of compliance in the DHS privacy office, the protective service arm of the associate assistant deputy secretary, to the assistant deputy secretary, to the deputy secretary of Homeland Security had just been sworn in and made his opening statement—remarks that clearly set the hearing's tone.

Expounding vigorously on his overriding concern—the privacy of DHS employees—when minority members asked about FEMA Corps, Witless testified he had no knowledge FEMA Corps even existed, nor that the Golden Event ever occurred. When questioned about Blue Shirts, Witless again professed ignorance.

With Witless the only witness, the hearings dragged on for two boring days. At the end of the second day, after obtaining no relevant information, the majority party closed the hearing, hoping they had ended the issue and buried the Blue Shirt problem. The national media followed the committee's lead—at least they tried to.

While gun owners and Second Amendment groups continued to demand answers about FEMA Corps' involvement in the "Golden Event," progressive-liberal gun control advocates faced a conundrum. Many voting Democrats, especially union members, were hunters and shooters—men and women who had no intention of giving up their guns, and were letting their senators and representatives know it.

Even so, the administration held to the position that federal gun laws were the law of the land, and the president would veto any bill that attempted to change or repeal them. Realizing the clock was ticking and new regulations—some still to be published—would go into effect on January 2nd, gun and ammunition buyers across the nation began a second wave of purchases. By the end of May the shelves in most gun stores were bare. It was apparent to everyone but far left progressive-liberals that guns weren't being purchased so they could be turned in the following year. Desperate to shift the spotlight from guns and FEMA Corps, the Democrat's leadership focused attention on the Baghdad embassy massacre.

Perhaps that wasn't such a good idea.

The national media began dredging up details of the Baghdad attack. Calls from reporters flooded telephone lines at the White House, State Department, Department of Defense, AFRICOM and CENTCOM. Damage control teams fought the onslaught, and as usually occurs when the government is in panic mode, contradictory statements were made and whistle blowers began surfacing.

CENTCOM, MacDill AFB
Monday 1 June 2015

General Doughberry swaggered down the hall on his way to chair his senior staff meeting—something he did every Monday morning. Breezing into his executive conference room, he mumbled, "Good morning," jerked out his chair and without looking at his men sat down.

"Good morning, sir," everyone responded, including Colonel Collins, who now sat ready to take notes at the table on Doughberry's right.

General Beck, who sat next to her, opened the meeting. After spending fifteen minutes addressing routine agenda items, he reached the hot button topic, the numerous requests for statements and interviews regarding the Baghdad embassy attack. "Based on the increasing number of interview requests from the media, I don't think we can keep stonewalling. We need to hold a press briefing."

Leaning forward in his seat, Doughberry nodded in agreement. After listening to Beck's assessment, he'd decided the general was correct. "Lewis, set up a press briefing," he said, addressing the public affairs officer, an Army colonel, "I'll make a statement and answer questions."

Oops, not a good idea, Collins inwardly winced and struggled to maintain a pleasant expression.

General Beck, also struggled to remain expressionless, but contrary to Collins, he thought it was a great decision. *My boss is clueless as to what he's in for. He'll probably let the cat out of the bag, which may be a good thing—the public needs to know the truth.*

"Are there any other questions or topics we should know about," Doughberry asked, preparing to end the meeting.

"Yes, sir," Brigadier General Uric said. "I've received a ton of e-mails from friends in my home state—some describing the attempted take down of the Bartow's house in Golden; however, most are asking about DHS and FEMA Corps. In particular they're questioning who the paramilitary men in blue combat uniforms were.

"Does anyone know who they are, and why they attacked a private citizens' home with heavy machine guns?"

FEMA Corps? Blue uniforms? What the hell is John talking about? Doughberry wondered. "Does anyone know anything about this?" he asked, oblivious to the incredulous expression on the faces around the table.

Where the hell has he been the last few days? Beck wondered, providing others a chance to answer. When no one did, he explained, "Well … yes sir. FEMA Corps' Blue Shirts—that's the name our military has been using for them—appear to be a paramilitary component of DHS. Following orders issued from the Secretary of the Army and sometimes from the Secretary of Defense, Blue Shirts have been receiving training at Fort Bragg, Little Creek, Fort Knox and Fort Benning.

"I've been receiving disturbing reports about them," Brigadier Roberts added. "Seems most Blue Shirts have an attitude problem. They've been involved in numerous bloody fights, and I'm aware of at least one instance where an instructor struck a Blue Shirt for insubordination,"

"Apparently they are a particularly brutal group," Beck added. "Take for example the way that Blue Shirt officer in charge of the attack on the Bartows conducted himself. On two occasions he was videoed on the verge or ordering a machine-gunner to fire an M2 at a line of civilians. If he had, the public would have viewed body parts flying in all directions in real time.

Doughberry frowned, "This is unacceptable. I must speak with the Chairman."

And I'd better call Clay Morrison and get the straight scoop on what happened, Beck decided.

As soon as the meeting ended, Rebecca Collins scurried off to call her gal pal, Vickie Barrett—only to discover Barrett was in Europe, and so she left a message.

Beck also made a beeline for his phone and had a long conversation with General Morrison. When it ended he sat staring at the wall, analyzing the situation from several angles. *It's worse than I thought ... Damn. The Blue Shirts are thugs, no other way to describe them. What the hell is our Commander in Chief up to?* Brooding and biting his lower lip, he was about to stand, when a thought occurred to him. *There's no doubt POTUS has an agenda, but I'm beginning to suspect he has no grasp of the real situation. Once force is used to seize guns, people are going to die—lots of people ... civilians and police. Happenings in Colorado have clearly demonstrated that. Yet ideologues refuse to accept anything that contradicts their belief the Constitution is outdated. They think passing laws gives them the authority to override the Constitution and seize guns. It sounds so simple until they attempt to implement their agenda. They fail to realize, actually refuse to accept, the majority of Americans still revere their Constitution and will fight to keep it.*

Progressive-liberals refuse to learn from their mistakes. After pulling our troops out of Iraq and Afghanistan, the Baghdad embassy attack caught them with their pants down—something that never should have happened after Benghazi, and that's one more consequence of their idealistic thinking. The President's a perfect example. To his way of thinking, if he says the war is over, the war is over ... despite the fact that terrorists are still killing our people around the world." I don't think what happened in Baghdad is the end of it. Something else is coming and no one is preparing for it. Damn! General Beck sighed, and shaking his head decided to go home and make some calls on his burner cell phone. He no longer trusted his own people.

Chapter 26

Colonel James Lewis addressed the group of reporters, "General Doughberry will make a statement regarding the attack on our Baghdad embassy, followed by a brief question and answer session."

General Doughberry walked to the podium and began his canned remarks before the large crowd of clamoring reporters. "Good morning and thank you for coming. As you know, we are still gathering information pertaining to the tragic events in Bagdad. According to our latest report, a well-planned and coordinated attack on our Baghdad embassy compound began at dawn. The Marine guard and State Department diplomatic security personnel followed SOPs and sounded the imminent danger alert. CENTCOM received the alert three minutes after the attack began and deployed the only available force, a reinforced platoon of Military Police. The MPs attempted to relieve the embassy but encountered a superior force of insurgents. Even so, they were able to rescue over eighty Americans. I have a team in Baghdad accessing the damage. Now I'll take your questions."

"WERE THE ATTACKERS ISLAMISTS?" a reporter shouted from the back of the crowd.

"Islamists is an overly broad term."

"I UNDERSTAND THE ENTIRE COMPOUND WAS DESTROYED. IS THAT TRUE?" another shouted.

"The compound suffered severe damage. As I said, my team is there assessing the extent of the damage."

"*Will the embassy be rebuilt?*" the FOX News reporter asked.

"That's a question for the President and Secretary of State."

"*Did you have intelligence that an attack was coming?*" a Breitbart News reporter asked.

"We had the usual reports of insurgents—nothing specific," Doughberry said, sounding dismissive and looking away.

"BUT, SIR ..." Breitbart's reporter yelled, raising his arm and waving to get the general's attention, "A follow-up on that, if you would sir—I understand the Ambassador had requested additional security and protested when most of his Marine guard was brought home. Can you confirm this?"

Huffing and red in the face, Doughberry was visibly irritated. "*No ...* I told you—we're just beginning the investigation," he snapped, but suddenly aware of the astonished look on the reporters' faces, he paused to control his temper. "That is a question for the State Department," he responded in a calmer tone.

"Maybe so, but were you aware of the Ambassador's request?" a reporter from CBS asked.

"My staff would have received copies of his requests, but they were information copies. CENTCOM is not directly responsible for embassy security." Doughberry looked at his watch, clearly signaling he was preparing to leave.

"WHERE IS COLONEL VICKERS? I, WE, WANT TO INTERVIEW HIM," a reporter from ABC shouted.

Ignoring the question, Doughberry turned to leave.

"WHERE IS COLONEL VICKERS?" a chorus of reporters began shouting as Doughberry retreated from the stage.

Coverage of CENTCOM's press briefing by major TV networks was decidedly unfavorable. Almost every major TV networks' evening news anchor implied the Baghdad embassy attack was another intelligence failure. "Would there be more attacks?" they asked.

President Abomba and Secretary of State Heinz were not pleased.

General Beck decided to visit Little Creek and Fort Bragg.

A growing number of citizens across the country began openly declaring their discontent with the government's infringement on their constitutional rights. Things were out of control and the news media was bouncing from anti-gun control demonstrations, to voter fraud, to the Baghdad embassy attack, and now to a major intelligence failure. An undercurrent of frustration was fomenting anger, and the nation's mood was turning ugly. Unlike Europeans, angry Americans have a strong tendency to act. All they needed was a target.

Dearborn, MI
5:35 p.m., Thursday, June 11, 2015

Jamal looked up from his workbench, as the back door to their small, East Dearborn house opened, and his partner Hakeem entered carrying a large box.

"This is all of them, Jamal," Hakeem said, setting the box on Jamal's bench and opening the box lid to reveal its contents—a full array of various sized plastic bottles and jugs, some resembling large vitamin bottles. "There's more than enough here to complete the bombs."

"Excellent my brother, *Allah be praised,*" Jamal said standing and patting Hakeem on the back. "I have completed the first one. Now that you have arrived, I can finish the second one, and … if Ali is able to obtain another pressure cooker, I can complete the third one tomorrow. That means we will have sufficient time to take them to Chicago. Now let's see what you have brought me."

Jamal, who'd received training in explosives and bomb making in Iran, eagerly began removing the various one-pound containers of gun power from the box. He was especially pleased when he saw a five-pound container of Accurate No. 2, and a four-pound container of True Blue pistol powder.

"Perfect, just what I needed for the third bomb," he said grinning at Hakeem. "Our leader has done well for us," he said, referring to their cell leader, Sayeed. Planning well in advance, Sayeed had arranged for believers scattered throughout Michigan to systematically purchase single containers of gunpowder from different gun stores throughout the state— gunpowder that shooting enthusiasts routinely used to handload cartridges. The type of powder purchased varied, so as not to create a suspicious pattern. Hakeem's job was to collect the containers and bring them to Jamal. With this delivery he had completed his task.

Hakeem was excited. He was finally going to participate in *jihad*, become a *mujahedeen*—a holy warrior. "Jamal, how big will the explosion be? How many *kafirs* will it kill?"

"The explosion will be large, but not as large as it would be if we had plastic explosives. There is never any way to predict the number who will be killed and wounded."

"Why would plastic explosive be better?"

Jamal smiled. " 'Hakeem the Curious' … that should be your name. I will try to explain. It has to do with how fast the reaction takes place.

Powder like we have here and high explosives decompose and release energy. Both will burn if spread out on the ground. Let me show you."

Jamal picked up a gunpowder container he'd almost emptied into the bomb he was constructing and poured a small amount on paper towel. Then picking up the paper towel, he carried it out of the house and set it down on the screened-in back porch. Opening a matchbook and striking a match, he said, "Watch the powder on the towel and see what happens when I drop the match on it." As soon as the burning match landed on the powder, it produced a flash and a thin cloud of smoke in less than a second.

"The flash and smoke were produced by the burning powder. If that small amount of powder had been contained, you would have heard a bang like a firecracker," Jamal explained.

Hakeem frowned and shook his head, indicating he did not understand.

"You know what a pistol cartridge is." Hakeem nodded. "Good. The powder is in the cartridge case. If the cartridge is placed in a fire, heat will cause the powder to ignite, producing hot gases and pressure. Pressure causes the brass case to expand. When that happens the bullet will fly in one direction and the case will fly in the opposite direction, producing a sound like a large firecracker."

Still frowning and attempting to visualize the event, Hakeem nodded.

"However, if the cartridge is placed in a pistol chamber, the brass case cannot expand. The decomposition rate of the powder is determined by pressure and temperature. So, when the pistol is fired and the powder ignited, the temperature and pressure inside the cartridge increases very quickly, and the only thing that can move is the bullet. The reaction happens so quickly it seems instantaneous."

Hakeem thought about what Jamal had said, and then commented, "Oh ... now I understand. The pressure cooker contains the powder, allowing the pressure to increase until the container flies apart."

Jamal nodded. "You understand the concept. High explosives are different. It requires a shock to start the decomposition reaction. Once started, the reaction is so fast there is no time for pressure to build up. When an explosive detonates, it produces a shock wave that shatters. If the explosive is in a metal shell, an artillery projectile for example, the shock wave shatters the metal container and propels the pieces of metal away at speeds greater than a rifle bullet."

Hakeem stood, continuing to analyze what Jamal had said as he followed him back to the workbench.

Jamal smiled as he picked up a one-pound container of Hodgdon rifle powder and opened it. Then taking care to grasp the body of the eight-quart Presto stainless steel pressure cooker with his left hand—to prevent a static charge from igniting the powder—he carefully emptied part of the powder into the pot. Still holding onto the pot, he slowly added a handful of roofing nails, followed by the remainder of the powder and more nails. By then the pot was nearly full of a combined mixture of nails, and rifle, pistol and shotgun powders. When the last of the finely milled, grayish powder had been poured into the pot, Jamal said, "That is enough. Time to install the squib. Hakeem, hand me the pressure cooker's lid."

Grasping the lid with one hand, and a pair of wires from the squib— their bare ends twisted together—with the other, Jamal threaded the wires through the relief valve hole in the cooker's lid, and then carefully pushed the squib into the gunpowder. After making sure there was no powder on the rim, Jamal placed the lid on the pot and closed the clamp, locking the two together. Pointing to the wires protruding through the lid's hole, he said, "I will connect them to the cell phone timer when we reach Chicago."

The sour expression on Jamal's face reflected his disappointment, when Ali arrived the next afternoon with a small six-quart Presto stainless steel pressure cooker.

"Forgive me my brother," Ali said, fearing Jamal's anger and hanging his head. "I know you wanted a larger pot," he continued, setting the pot on the workbench, "but I searched everywhere, and this was the only small stainless steel pot I could find. The only other choice was a thirty-quart, and it was far too big for a backpack. All the rest were aluminum."

While Jamal continued staring at the pot with an unhappy expression, Ali, not knowing what to expect, stood off the side looking down at the floor. When Jamal finally spoke it wasn't the rebuke Ali expected. Instead, Ali was relieved when Jamal said his concern was how to get the task done using what they had to work with, "I will have to remove the handles. It is small but it will have to do. *Insha'Allah*, as Allah wills.

"Ali, make yourself useful and hold the pot while I saw off the handles," Jamal said, turning the pot on its side. Then, using a hacksaw, he cut the two-part handle off close to the body.

"Now watch and learn while I finish preparing the pot," he continued, reaching for a five-pound container of Accurate No. 2 powder and removing its lid.

"To avoid creating a spark I must carefully pour all of this powder into the pot … a small portion at a time, adding nails as I do. On top of this layer of powder and nails, I will empty the contents of this four-pound container of True Blue pistol powder mixed along with more nails. Now, as you can see, I have room for just a little more powder. So I will top it off with this," he said, opening a one-pound container of Winchester WST. Last of all I will install the squib. Hakeem, hold the lid while I insert the wires."

Ali watched wide-eyed as Jamal inserted the squib's wires through the cooker's top, and then carefully pushed the squib into the mix of powder and nails. Satisfied, he placed the lid on the pot. "… and *that,* my brother," he said locking the lid to the pot, "is how you make a pressure cooker bomb."

"Now we are ready to deliver Allah's special gifts to the *kafirs.* Hurry, Hakeem, get the backpacks."

With Ali still watching in wonderment, Hakeem held each backpack open as Jamal wrapped each pressure cooker in an extra-large T-shirt and slowly eased it into the bag. Next he placed a cell phone with a pair of protruding wires in a side pocket of each backpack. "We're almost finished here. Tomorrow morning each of us will separately drive one of the backpacks to the house in Chicago. Ali will leave at six o'clock. Hakeem will follow at nine o'clock, and I will depart at noon. Ali, you must call me every two hours and give me a traffic report. Hakeem, do the same. If you don't call, it will mean you have encountered a problem, and the rest of us will have to assume the worst.

"Once we have delivered the backpacks to their hiding places, we will spend a few days determining the best places to leave them when the time comes.

"Ali, get rid of these empty containers," Jamal said, gesturing to the empty gunpowder containers, and then to a large garbage can, lined with a green plastic bag, that sat next to the bench. "We don't want to leave anything in this house that can tie us with the bombs.

"Now, let us go to the Islamic Centre of America for evening prayers. It will be our last opportunity to go."

The Islamic Centre of America, located in Dearborn, is one the largest mosques and the oldest Shi'a mosque in America.

Qom, Iran
June 17, 2015

Grand Ayatollah Hamid Khomeini, once again in his opulent residence, was deep in conference with another of the pawns on his chessboard of world domination—the young firebrand, Muqtada al-Sadr.

◆ ◆ ◆

A product of the Second Gulf War, al-Sadr became the leader, in the spring of 2003, of some 500 Islamic students—a ragtag militia—in the Sadr City district of Baghdad, which was once know as Saddam City. His ragtag militia grew, and in June of that year al-Sadr named it the Mahdi Army, an Iraqi paramilitary group, which continued to expand and develop under his leadership. By April of 2004, he commanded over 10,000 fighters. On Friday April 2, 2004, al-Sadr preached a fire and brimstone sermon that ignited a major uprising. Assuming a leadership role, al-Sadr continued to increase his power and became a thorn in the Multinational Force Iraq Coalition's side. After many battles, the Mahdi Army was pushed back to Basra, and Prime Minister Maliki ordered a March 2008 attack to defeat al-Sadr's army. Al-Sadr retreated to Iran and remained there until most of the U.S. military had departed. He resurfaced in Iraq as a politico in 2011 and was elected to Parliament.

◆ ◆ ◆

Both Khomeini and al-Sadr wore black turbans to indicate they were descendants of the Prophet Muhammad—men who were, according to tradition, revered and unquestionably obeyed. "The time has come for you to become Iraq's leader; time to cast out the remaining dogs belonging to the Great Satan; time to begin the Iraqi peoples' conversion to the Islamic Republic of Iraq; time for Iraq to be governed by Shariah law," Khomeini declared.

"Allah be praised. Eminence, your plan must have been inspired by Allah. Truly Allah must be guiding your deft hand. How else could your servant el-Kordi, The Egyptian, have obtained such success?"

The old man's lips hinted at a trace of a smile, as he stroked his long white beard. *Yes, my plan was truly inspired. Soon, you will be my servant in Baghdad. Once Iraq is mine, I can grasp the home of my enemy, Saudi Arabia.*

Khomeini watched al-Sadr's eyes and reveled in the fanatical fire he saw burning there. *My young tool has grown and matured, but praise Allah, he still has the spirit of a mujahedeen leader. He is ready for his next task.* "President Abomba, the Great Satan's leader, is an arrogant, indecisive, weak man concerned only with himself. He has plans to become a shah, the ruler of his abominable country. He is the product of his socialist education and surrounds himself with idealistic progressive-liberals who believe their ideas are the only answer. He will continue to appease Muslims and weaken his army, while he builds a paramilitary police force loyal only to him."

"It appears he's doing our work for us," al-Sadr observed, snickering. "Truly, Allah is the best schemer."

"Yes, Abomba and American presidents before him have appeased us in hopes of achieving peace. Allah has guided *them* to do his work. The number of believers in The Great Satan grows, just as it continues to grow in Europe and England. Allah willing, our population jihad will continue uninterrupted, and true believers will be able to convert these *kafir* countries to Islam without the sword, but that will take time.

"Today it is time to continue performing the tasks Allah has given us.

"Raise up your Mahdi Army and seize the government. Allah's slaves require a strong master. Saddam was strong, but he had lost his faith and Allah allowed the Bush devils to destroy him. Your faith is strong and Allah will guide you.

"Return to Iraq and restore the true faith, implement Shariah law. Drive the Great Satan's remaining dogs into the sea."

Bowing to the Grand Ayatollah, al-Sadr said, "It will be as Allah commands."

Chapter 27
May 2015

While the international news continued to focus on Baghdad, America's media kept up a steady stream of alerts and stories related to gun control laws. Of particular interest to Colorado residents was the report that the state's newly appointed attorney general had announced an end to searches for guns in private homes. No further enforcement would be undertaken, until higher courts ruled on the constitutionality of Colorado's gun laws.

As expected, progressive-liberals were unhappy, but the threat of another round of recall elections calmed most of them. The Golden Event—specifically what to do about the Bartow brothers—was still a problem in search of a solution. In the aftermath of the siege on their property—thanks to General Morrison's intervention—the brothers had surrendered to the local sheriff and been charged with setting off an explosive device without a permit. A day or so later they'd been released on a $10,000 bond each and returned to what was left of their bullet-riddled house. General Morrison was waiting there with Rex to greet them and enjoyed watching the joyful reunion—complete with lots of yipping and licking. The issue of whether the brothers were defending their property from an illegal search or guilty of second-degree murder had yet to be decided.

South Side Chicago, IL
Sunday morning, June 14, 2015

Jamal, Ali, and Hakeem returned from morning prayers and found their Hezbollah controller, Sayeed, waiting for them in their safe house. "My brothers, Allah has smiled upon you," Sayeed said. "The time and place has been set. We will strike Allah's blow in the center of the Great Satan's land. Strike the blow on the day this unholy abomination was created. We will strike the night of July 4th."

"Praise Allah, we are ready," Jamal said.

"*Allahu Akbar*," Ali and Hakeem said in unison.

Sayeed—of course that wasn't his real name—led them into the kitchen and poured each a cup of tea. "Now, let me tell you about your targets. Each one will have a concentrated group of *kafirs*. Ballparks were not chosen because their extra security makes planting bombs too risky. Every person entering must pass through gates where their bodies and possessions are inspected.

"Evening fireworks displays along the lake are the most inviting targets. Thus they are your targets. Backpacks are common, and once the fireworks display begins no one will notice you leaving yours."

"Praise Allah," Hakeem exclaimed. "Now I will be a true Islamic warrior, a mujahedeen."

Sayeed smiled and nodded at the boy. "Yes, my brother, you will become a *mujahedeen*. This will be your first jihad, and your target is one of the cruise boats taking *kafirs* out on the lake to view the fireworks. We have arranged for you to start work on a boat tomorrow as an assistant waiter and kitchen helper. This will give you the opportunity to select the best place to leave Allah's gift. I suggest the top deck, for that is where most of the *kafirs* will gather to watch the fireworks. Once you have placed the device, go to the back of the boat on the lower deck. You will be safe there.

"One of our brothers works on the pier where the boat is moored. Starting tomorrow, he will drive you to the dock and bring you back. Expect to leave here at eight o'clock tomorrow morning. The boat will make two—uh ... how do they say it—trips? Ah, yes—will sail twice a day."

"I am ready to carry out Allah's will," Hakeem said, beaming with pride.

Sayeed gave a slight bow and continued, "While Hakeem is learning how to be a sailor, we will scout the Navy Pier, Montrose Beach, and the place known as the 63rd Street Beach, and decide which two of these sites will receive Allah's gifts. *Allahu Akbar.*"

"*Allahu Akbar,*" Ali, Jamal, and Hakeem recited.

Sayeed's original plan called for placing a bomb at each of the three viewing points, but now that one of the bombs was smaller than he'd planned, he'd decided to target the cruise boat. *Allah's bombs will indeed make it a spectacular evening.*

Come and Take It

The Shootout at the Bartow Corral inflamed Second Amendment supporters, and it wasn't long before Tweets and Facebook posting began reminding them of an older travesty of justice related to guns—specifically, the unwarranted arrest of a decorated Iraq War veteran, U.S. Army Master Sergeant J. C. Grisham, by Temple, Texas police officers. A city of 70,000, Temple Texas is located near Fort Hood, a major U.S. Army base located in the heart of a state, where the right to bear arms has historically been upheld.

On March 16, 2013 Army Master Sergeant C. J. Grisham and his fifteen-year old son, Christopher, were walking along a rural Texas county road—a planned ten-mile hiking trip that would earn Christopher the last merit badge he needed to become an Eagle Scout. Having previously encountered cougars and feral hogs in the wild, Grisham was carrying a loaded AR15 rifle slung across his chest, and a .45 caliber semiautomatic pistol, openly displayed in a holster on his hip. Openly carrying a loaded rifle or shotgun is legal in Texas. In fact, a young adult can carry either one if accompanied by an adult. In addition, Sergeant Grisham had a concealed carry permit that allowed him to wear his holstered pistol.

According to an interview with FOX News reporter Todd Sarnes, Grisham stated he and Christopher were halfway into their hike, when two Temple police patrol cars approached them from the rear. Ordered to stop, by an overweight officer driving the lead car, Grisham complied and turned to face the officer, who got out of his car demanding to know what he and his son were doing.

Not satisfied with Grisham's explanation that they were hiking to help Chris achieve his merit badge, the officer asked, "What are you doing with the rifle," to which Grisham responded, "Does it matter, officer? Am I breaking the law?"

What happened next took Grisham completely by surprise, for with no explanation or forewarning, the officer stepped forward and grabbed Grisham's rifle. Instinctively reacting, when his combat training kicked in, Grisham held on to his rifle and stepped back. An action that quickly escalated the situation from bad to worse, when the officer drew his service pistol, slammed Grisham onto the hood of the patrol car, and forcibly held him there, until the two officers from the second car approached to assist.

Ordered to turn around and put his hands behind him, Grisham, who still had the rifle strapped to him and feared for his son's safety, complied under duress but gave the boy his video camera. "Keep the camera on me,"

Grisham reported telling the boy, hoping as he did that the video would document what he now felt was an illegal weapons seizure. Young Christopher followed his father's instructions to the letter and continued videoing his father, who was still bent over the front of the police car, repeatedly demanded to know why he was being cuffed and detained.

Finally one of the officers said, "We got a call from a concerned citizen." The officer then added, "In this day and age, people are alarmed when they see someone with what you have," referring to the rifle and declaring that anyone he encountered carrying a weapon was dangerous. Additionally the officer stated that people who called in to complain about someone openly carrying a weapon don't care what the law says; and that he was detaining Grisham until he determined there was "no issue."

Then, despite the fact Grisham had a concealed weapon permit and under Texas law open carry of a long gun was permitted; and a law enforcement officer cannot take a firearm from a citizen unless the citizen is pointing or waving the gun at others in a threatening manner—something the video recording clearly showed Grisham wasn't doing—the officer declared Grisham had resisted arrest and was guilty of "rudely displaying a weapon."

Audibly weeping while dutifully recording what was happening, Christopher watched his father being forced into the patrol car. When Grisham asked what was going to happen to his son, he was told the boy would be taken home in the other patrol car. Reassuring Christopher he would be all right, Grisham instructed the boy not to answer any questions until his mother was present. However, according Christopher's account, officers interrogated him throughout the ride home and refused to let him get out of the patrol car until he answered their questions.

Later in a FOX News radio interview with Todd Sarnes, Grisham stated the incident had traumatized and confused his son. "Every time he sees a police officer, he has a panic attack," he said. "That's unfortunate because we always taught our kids to respect police officers ... My son has his own copy of the Constitution ... He understands his rights (and) the concept of choosing the hard 'right' over the easy 'wrong.' It doesn't seem like our rights are being respected. For me it's a difficult turning point. I wonder what it is that I'm fighting for. If our basic rights are being violated this way—what is my purpose?"

When, subsequent to his father's arrest, Christopher bravely posted his recording on YouTube, the video of Grisham's arrest and illegal gun seizure went viral. Following that, on the morning of June 1, 2013, hundreds of citizens, supporting Sergeant Grisham's Constitutional right to own a gun, converged on Temple. After marching through the town carrying loaded rifles and shotguns, the protesters gathered for a rally, during which Master Sergeant Grisham spoke. Stating clearly that he held no malice toward the Temple police, the sergeant denied any truth to the rumor that he had anything to do with threats against the officer's lives.

The first "Come and Take It" event had occurred.

Tweets and Facebook postings, with links to the YouTube video, calling for a second "Come and Take It" on June 20th began in late May. Word spread like wildfire and Second Amendment supporters geared up to go. Most who planned to attend had watched Christopher's YouTube video that clearly showed the faces of the arresting officers. Thus many heading for Temple could recognize the police officers involved in Grisham's arrest—and some would be looking for them.

Temple, Texas
Saturday, June 20, 2015

The second **"Come and Take It" rally supporting Master Sergeant C. J. Grisham** began at dawn. This time the citizens had many more reasons to be angry: angry about what was done to the Bartow brothers; angry about unconstitutional gun laws; very angry at FEMA Corps; and by extension, furious with Temple's police force. Thousands of angry citizens from Texas and bordering states descended on Temple looking for a confrontation.

By eight o'clock large numbers of SUVs, pickup trucks and sedans began backing up along I-35 at exits leading into downtown Temple. Parked vehicles lined the shoulders of Adams Avenue, 31st Street, and North 3rd street. Every available parking place, public and private, was filled. Men and women carrying loaded rifles and shotguns headed toward rallying points at Wildcat Stadium and Halford Ball Field.

With no forewarning, the mayor and chief of police were taken by surprise when merchants began calling and asking what he was going to do. One storeowner reported that when he asked strangers to move their trucks from his parking lot, he was told to perform a physically impossible act. The police chief told the mayor untold numbers of demonstrators were ignoring his officers' commands. A major protest was occurring, but so far the chief and the mayor had no idea what demonstrators were protesting.

A group of armed protesters were walking north on 31st Street when they encountered a parked patrol car and a tall, overweight, scowling policeman stepped into the road and held up his hand and ordered, "PLACE YOUR WEAPONS ON THE GROUND AND STEP AWAY FROM THEM."

"GO FUCK YOURSELF," a man wearing camo pants and holding an AR15 at port arms, shouted back as he joined several other men who'd spread out on either side of the policeman.

One of the men recognized the policeman and yelled, "YOU'RE THE FAT FUCKER WHO ARRESTED SERGEANT GRISHAM."

Now the policeman compounded his first mistake by dropping his hand toward his service pistol, and instantly found twenty AR15s and three shotguns leveled at him.

"YOU TOUCH THAT PISTOL and we'll consider you're threatening us," a second man yelled.

"Yeah, rudely threatening us, and it'll take the medical examiner a couple of hours to count the bullet holes in your fat carcass," another man added with a menacing smile.

"Well, we got one of 'em," a woman said after the policeman raised his hands.

"Got any idea what to do with the asshole?" the second man asked.

"Yeah!" the woman replied, sneering and motioning for the three men to come close to her. While a brief whispered conference ensued, other men in the crowd held their rifles on the now cowed policeman.

Halford Ball Field's PA system had been turned on, and a rifle-toting protester, wearing a POW/MIA ball cap and an "Oath Keepers" T-shirt, was giving directions to the crowd. "When everyone gets here, we'll form up and march on city hall—DEMAND THE RETURN OF SERGEANT GRISHAM'S GUNS and then *punish* the people responsible for his arrest."

"WHAT'D YOU MEAN BY PUNISH?" someone shouted.

"HOW ABOUT A GOOD OLD FASHIONED TAR AND FEATHERIN'?" another shouted.

The what-to-do debate was just getting started, when the group with their captured obese policeman arrived. Elated by what they were seeing, the crowd erupted with thunderous hoots and shouts of approval.

"THERE'S THE ANSWER! That's what we'll do to the mayor, chief of police and the prosecuting attorney," the POW/MIA capped man hollered into the mike.

"YEAH," members of the burgeoning crowd shouted.

On the second floor of Temple's Municipal Building, the chief of police was attempting to explain the unexpected demonstrations to the mayor, when they heard a great commotion coming from somewhere outside the building. Rushing to the window, they looked for the source of the noise but saw nothing. Finally learning from an office worker they were hearing chanting from protesters marching down West Central Avenue toward them, they rushed down the stairs and out the Main Street entrance and stood waiting for the marchers to appear. As the protesters drew closer, the thundering words of their chant became understandable, "NO MORE NAZIS … NO MORE NAZIS."

"What the hell's going on?" the mayor asked, looking nervously toward the intersection of West Central and Main Street.

He was about to find out, because at that very moment, a cherry red pickup truck, with its license tag covered, turned left onto Main Street and proceeded slowly toward the front of the Municipal Building. Marching on both sides of the truck and heading up the first wave of chanting protesters, were the obvious leaders of the demonstration. For some reason though, there appeared to be a gap between the back of the truck and the full company of marchers. Standing on tiptoes and craning their necks to see what was behind the truck—because it certainly wasn't a float—the gawking city officials soon saw, to their utter shock and consternation, exactly what the truck was towing.

"OH MY GOD!" the mayor exclaimed. "CHIEF, DO SOMETHING!"

Stumbling along behind the truck, his hands cuffed behind his back, with one end of a rope noosed around his neck and the other tied to the truck's trailer hitch, was the fat policeman the protesters had captured earlier. Wearing only his birthday suit and his service belt slung around his neck atop the rope, the blubbering policeman hung his head in humiliation.

While some people lining the sidewalks on Adams Street began guffawing, others shouted for the man to be released. The reason for their reactions became clear to the mayor and police chief when the naked man passed by them. Painted on his back in large red letters were the words, "RUDELY EXPOSING A TINY WEAPON."

For several seconds onlookers on either side of Main Street in front of the Municipal Building were too stunned to do anything other than gape at the spectacle. However, once the shock wore off, their hoots, hollers, and laughter joined those of the parading protesters and drowned out the few shouts for the policeman's release.

Many residents of Temple either hunted game or enjoyed target practice and were well aware of what had happened to C. J. Grisham. Most had remained silent about their dissatisfaction with the police department for fear they too would be targeted and have their weapons confiscated. So, when they saw the humiliated police officer, most were glad he was finally getting his just deserts.

Shouts of "GIVE 'EM HELL ... DOWN WITH THE NAZI BROWN SHIRTS," arose from the crowd and several local citizens joined the ranks of protesters rapidly swelling up around the truck and onto the sidewalk in front of the Municipal Building.

In a matter of minutes, the stunned mayor and police chief found themselves surrounded by leaders of the angry, raucous protesters. Fearing for their safety the two men cowered as the protesters pinned them against the building's wall.

"We know who you are," the POW/MIA capped leader said to the police chief, getting in his face and grabbing hold of his uniform shirt. "But who is he?" he asked, releasing the chief and turning to jab the simpering man standing next to him in the belly with the barrel of his rifle.

"H–He's the mayor," the chief stuttered.

Grinning at the frightened pair, the leader sneered, "Good ... now— both of you *strip* and join your fat friend—and be quick about it.

"And, while you're stripping, tell us where we can find the prosecuting attorney?"

"H–He's not here ... H–He's in Dallas," the mayor said unbuckling his belt.

"*Damn* ... Well, I guess you two'll have to do.

"Now, where's Sergeant Grisham's rifle and pistol?

"T–They're in the evidence locker ... in the basement," the chief added as an afterthought.

"You heard him," the man said, and twenty men entered the building.

Fifteen minutes later, the mayor and police chief, both dressed in their birthday suites with their hands cuffed behind them and ropes around their necks attached to the pickup, were blushing crimson along with the police officer. For painted in red on all their backs appeared the same message—"RUDELY EXPOSING A TINY WEAPON."

While the crowd howled with laughter and the three mortified men stood sniveling in the street, the protesters who'd gone searching for Sergeant Grisham's guns rushed out of the building. Running up to their leader, they handed him the weapons.

"WE CAME AND WE TOOK 'EM BACK," the leader yelled, holding the weapons high for all to see before placing them inside the truck's cab with the driver. Then running to the rear of the truck and jumping up onto its bed, he grabbed a blow horn. "HEAD ON OUT—TELL 'EM WHY WE'RE HERE," he yelled to the throng of protesters, as the cherry red pickup slowly moved off on it's way up North Main Street toward Jackson Park.

"COME AND TAKE 'EM, JUST YOU TRY,
"TAKE OUR GUNS, WE'LL HANG YOU HIGH."

The crowd roared all the way to the park. Entering Jackson Park, the red pickup truck stopped near a large tree and several men untied the ropes from the truck's trailer hitch and tossed them over a limb. The crowd roared at the simulated hanging, while the three disgraced men stood with their heads hung in humiliation.

A pep rally followed the mock "hanging" and the crowd—later estimated to be over thirty thousand—having made their point quietly dispersed; leaving Temple and the nation with the memorable impression that no one messes with legal gun owner's right to bear arms under the Second Amendment.

Unfortunately, the gun control Nazis failed to get the message.

Protesters and a few townspeople had shot hundreds of videos of the three naked men stumbling along behind the red pickup truck. When the videos were posted on Facebook and YouTube, news of the event went viral. The second "Come and Take It" became a sensation on radio and TV news and talk shows across the nation and the world. Nonetheless, while Second Amendment supporters declared a victory and half the nation laughed, the other half scowled.

Chapter 28

Washington, DC
9 a.m. Sunday, June 21, 2015

Nellie Balogni and her husband Hughbie were eating breakfast, waiting for her favorite Sunday news show, *State of the Nation,* to begin. They'd returned home early in the morning, after a prolonged evening spent celebrating the huge commission Hughbie received for financing yet another sole-source-green-energy contract from the Department of Energy. The morning paper lay of the table unread.

Using her most solemn expression, *State of the Nation* hostess, Taffy Crow, opened the program by announcing the morning's top story—the second "Come and Take It" protest, and the outrageous spectacle that occurred in Temple, Texas.

After recapping Master Sergeant Grisham's 2013 arrest for "rudely displaying an AR15 rifle," which, according to Taffy, had "captivated the entire world's attention," she continued reporting what some called a "tongue-in-cheek" account of the second, "Come and Take It Protest" in Temple, Texas the previous day.

"In an event drawing an estimated thirty thousand people, the gun-totin', 'Come and Take It' folks protesting Sergeant Grisham's 'Rudely Displaying Arrest' have established a new Temple, Texas tradition for rude-crude behavior," Taffy said, batting her eyes and pursing her lips. "A tradition that might just result in the gun-toters changing the name of future events to 'Come and Take It *Off*,'" Taffy said, smirking and rolling her eyes.

"As you will see in the following video, provided by a private citizen, participants in the parade along with bystanders on the street were ecstatic with the protesters' crude behavior," she quipped, pausing to thrust her tongue in her cheek. Now before we play the video of the parade, which has been altered for propriety's sake, I caution anyone with young children that you might want to send them out of the room. What you are about see may be disturbing to some," Taffy concluded, wrinkling her nose.

After several seconds of showing front and side views of an approaching red pickup truck leading an enormous crowd of people, the camera zoomed in on front and rear images of a naked man. Stumbling along, with certain parts of his anatomy pixilated, the man had a rope around his neck that was attached to the red truck.

"**WHAT THE HELL IS GOING ON?**" Nellie screamed, jumping to her feet when the camera zoomed in on the words painted on the nude man's back, "What does that say ... 'Rudely displaying a–' ... **OH, MY GOD!** What have they done to that poor man?"

"Shush dear, let's watch and find out," Hughbie said, putting his index finger to his lips and pointing toward the screen, where Taffy, with a twinkle in her eye and trying not to laugh, was continuing with her report.

"Now I ask you viewers," Taffy said, frowning and staring intently into the camera lens, "Is that not *both rude and crude*? I don't know about you, but it looks to me like folks had one heck of a hot time in the streets of Temple, Texas yesterday.

"Let's ask our guest, Senator Dana Finkelstein in our Washington studio, what she thinks about this outrageous demonstration."

Scowling as the camera zoomed in on her, Dana Finkelstein radiated anger.

"Senator, what do you think of yesterday's events in Temple, Texas?"

"*Outrageous ... Contemptible*—An unbelievable exhibition by gun-nuts run amok. Those ruffians are guilty of kidnapping and should be prosecuted. This has to stop.

"American citizens are *not* going to be intimidated by gun—" Finkelstein paused, furiously scrunching her nose and turning red in the face, "By ... gun-toting ... anarchists!" she hissed through clenched teeth, while glaring at the camera.

"We *cannot* allow them to march through a town or city with *loaded assault weapons*."

"LOOK AT THAT HUGHBIE! Look at all those gun-nuts—thirty thousand of them? Those animals are anarchists. THE GOVERNMENT MUST DO SOMETHING!" Nellie squealed chopping the air with both of her hands.

"Yes, Dear," Hughbie sighed, rubbing his aching temples and realizing his wife was about to begin one of her hysterical rants.

"Look Hughbie ... I told you to *look* damn it—**HUGHBIE—you're not looking**," she screeched, flopping down in her chair and pointing to the TV, where a new video clip showing hundreds of protesters holding assault weapons filled the screen.

"Yes, dear," Hughbie muttered, and looking thinking, *"Bitch."*

Seconds later Taffy's face once again appeared, this time on split screen with Finkelstein. They listened as Taffy asked Finkelstein, "Senator, could it possibly be true, as I have been told that it's legal to open carry a rifle in Texas?"

"It may be, Taffy, but you can be sure of one thing—that's going to change. Tomorrow morning I plan to begin drafting legislation to stop this sort of thing. When I finish we'll have a federal law banning anyone other than law enforcement officers from carrying a weapon. This disgusting incident proves it's time to put an end to the *misinterpretation* of the Second Amendment."

"Senator, it seems the Second Amendment movement is growing. Remember what happened in Golden, Colorado, when police attempted to search a house for guns. Three SWAT operators were wounded and one was killed. FEMA sent a unit to take down the house and one of its vehicles was destroyed by an IED."

Finkelstein shook her head in the negative. "The governor ordered the National Guard to take over, and the commander placed the two men who owned the home under house arrest. This is a perfect example of why FEMA Corps is needed—a federal paramilitary corps loyal to the government. My new legislation will place all gun related issues under the Department of Homeland Security. No more meddling by locals."

Nellie Balogni had heard enough—more than enough. Fired up by Finkelstein's interview, she jumped up, and making chopping motions with both hands, stood before the television raving at the screen for several seconds; until finally gaining some self-control, she grabbed the unopened newspaper off the table and slung it across the room, screeching, "HUGHBIE! ... WHERE THE HELL IS MY DAMN PHONE?"

"Right here, dear," Hughbie replied, holding up her cell phone.

"Give it to me," she snarled, snatching the phone out of his hand and speed dialing her chief of staff.

"Carol, get the staff in right away ... *What?* Yes, *NOW, damn it!* I'm well aware it's Sunday ... *No!* It can't wait until morning. I want all of you ready to work with Senator Finkelstein's staff tomorrow morning, so you can get a gun control bill ready for me to introduce tomorrow afternoon ... *Yes, damn it!* You heard me right. I said tomorrow—*Monday!*"

Balogni's chief of staff hung up, shaking her head. She was use to the Speaker's hysterics.

The White House
11 a.m. Sunday, June 21, 2015

President Abomba and his inner circle of advisors, Attorney General Edison Helder, Vickie Barrett and Jane Incompentado were meeting in the president's study. Helder sat next to the president with Barrett and Incompentado on the opposite side of the table. They were talking via a speakerphone to Senator Realdick, who was saying, "Dana did a good job on *State of the Nation*. These gun protesters are getting out of hand.

"Nellie called with her panties in a wad during the show to tell me she planned to introduce a bill tomorrow. I told her to get a grip and wait for Dana's bill." Realdick paused for the chuckles around the table to die down. He was about to continue when the president interrupted.

"Yeah, Dana and I've got a lot of stuff to include in the drafts on 'no carry' legislation. Ed will review our stuff to make sure it'll stand up to challenges. I think that display of civil disobedience in Temple is working for us—takes the heat off Baghdad. Don'cha think?" Abomba asked, and before anyone could respond, abruptly sat forward in his chair.

Giving Incompentado a withering look, he said, "Jane ... I gotta say your Blue Shirts blew it in Golden." Holding up his hand to prevent a rebuttal, he stuck his chin out and continued, "I was playing golf with Gene Haggler the other day, and he mentioned something a guy named Sun Tuz wrote about military strategy—some stuff about knowing your enemy. Makes sense to me. Guess your Blue Shirt colonel failed to read Sun's book.

"I won't stand for anymore of this kind of stuff happening. For my plan to work, the Blue Shirts must be *feared*. We need a demonstration of real power." Glaring at Incompentado, he added with emphasis, "*No more screw-ups.*"

Nodding their agreement, but keenly aware of the president's surly mood, everyone shifted slightly in their seats.

Sighing and adjusting his chin, Abomba sat back in his chair, looked at Helder and changed the subject, "Ed, what's with Baghdad ... has your FBI team discovered who's responsible?"

"Several groups have claimed responsibility, but one name appears to be linked to the attack, someone called 'The Egyptian.' They did find the locations of the mortars and think they have the location of one of the rocket launchers—no trace of the shooters, and they still have twenty-one of our people."

"Yeah, we'll probably never know who did it. Is the Iraqi government cooperating?" Abomba asked.

"What you'd expect. Hell, it takes them a week to take a piss. They assigned a bunch of idiots to assist us. Even so, they did manage to find four of our people who'd been taken hostage."

"What about the request for medals for the killed and wounded?" Barrett inquired.

Abomba scowled, "Naw ... too many of 'em. It'd take me two weeks to pin on all the damn medals. Screw 'em, they knew the risk when they signed up.

"Does your gal pal have everything under control down at CENTCOM?"

"Yes, but I think I'll visit her for the Fourth of July weekend," Barrett replied and winked.

"Good idea. The First Lady's in Martha's Vineyard with the kids and that damn dog—wish I'd never agreed to get the thing ... he's great for photo ops, but he's always whining and wantin' me to pet him. Kids missed him so much I had order the Marines to fly him to the Vineyard in one of those tilt-propeller planes. Uh, where was I? Oh, yeah. I'm leaving to join 'em on Friday. Plan to return on July sixth. You got anything else?"

"One thing," the AG replied. "CIA has reported increased chatter concerning Iraq—probably has to do with the embassy attack. There's also been some chatter about a domestic attack."

Abomba stood, "Nothing new about that. They're always chattering about something."

The meeting ended.

Al-Sadr received a coded message from the grand ayatollah stating the morning of the July 5th would be an excellent time for a coup.

CENTCOM, MacDill AFB
Thursday, June 25, 2015

General Beck put the day's intelligence report on his desk and sat staring out the window. He couldn't shake the feeling trouble was brewing. Nothing concrete, but he had the old feeling: the sense of danger an experienced soldier who's survived repeated combat has; the sixth sense that keeps some alive while others die. Feeling an increased sense of foreboding since his visits to Little Creek and Fort Bragg, Beck reviewed what he'd learned.

The best of the best are also sensing something's wrong. Both officers and enlisted think the problem wears Blue Shirts. Then there's Baghdad, which can only be described as a clusterfuck. The FBI and administration are waiting for the Iraqis to figure out who did it. Names don't matter—they're all jihadis, and it has Iran's stench on it. I know in my gut something evil this way cometh. Master Chief Jefferson agrees. He also mentioned he's an Oath Keeper. Need to find out more about them.

Progressive-liberal state legislators, mayors, commissioners, school board members, school superintendents, and activists considered the second "Come and Take It" a challenge to their beliefs—beliefs they all held as articles of faith. Going into overdrive, they responded by writing new legislation, rules, policies, directives, and personnel policies. Pictures of any kind of gun were banned from many schools and violators would be expelled. Any student bringing a toy gun or water pistol to school was being charged with a felony. Discussion of hunting, shooting or anything related to guns became grounds for termination in liberal owned or managed corporations. Progressive-liberals were driving the nation toward a civil war, a war with no geographical boundaries. Abomba's administration saw the gathering storm as an opportunity to impose martial law and complete the transformation of America from a constitutional republic to socialist state.

A simple plan, but once again there would be unintended consequences.

Chapter 29

Chicago, Illinois
Saturday July 4, 2015

Sayeed skillfully maneuvered the dark colored 2012 Honda van through the heavy lakeshore traffic near Chicago's waterfront. Turning his head to look over his shoulder at Jamal, he said, "Turn on your cell phone." As soon as Jamal replied he'd done so, Sayeed pulled the van to the curb, and said, "May Allah be with you."

"*Allahu' Akbar,*" they all said in unison, and then, setting their plans in motion, Jamal opened the rear sliding door and got out. Slinging his backpack over his shoulders and following the crowd heading for Montrose Beach, he looked like just another young man wearing a backpack. After entering the beach, Jamal worked his way through the crowd, looking for the best location to settle down with the weighty burden he carried. He hadn't gone far when he saw a group of boisterous young adults sprawled out on blankets, drinking beer and smoking pot. Evidently they'd been partying a good while, because as he drew closer he noticed two empty drink coolers tipped on their sides with their lids open. *Allah be praised,* he silently exclaimed. *The space between coolers provides the perfect place for me to hide Your birthday present for the kafirs,* he decided, and working his way toward the coolers casually squatted near one to light a cigarette. A minute or so later, he sat down, and pretending to be drunk himself, eased the backpack off his shoulders, allowed it to slide the ground behind him, and used it as a backrest. Appearing to nod off every so often, he waited anxiously for darkness to fall, before reaching behind him to gently push the Allah's gift between two coolers. To make sure none of the revelers disturbed it, he decided to remain where he was until the fireworks began.

Forty minutes after leaving Jamal, Ali exited the van near the 63rd Street Beach. If things went according to plan, he and Jamal would use public transportation to leave the area. As soon as Ali joined the throng of revelers on the beach, he, like Jamal, appeared to be just one more young man among many wearing backpacks. Quickly noticing most of the infidels he was walking with were wearing identical patriotic T-shirts, Jamal figured they came together in a group, and staying with them provided him excellent cover. He became concerned however, once the group chose an area to settle down: first, because he discovered he'd taken up with a large Christian church group; and second, because the viewing area they'd chosen was filled to capacity. *Slipping away unnoticed from the midst of such a large group will be difficult if not impossible. I am trapped, unless I can work my way out and find a new location. If I leave my backpack with the bomb they'll notice it.*

"*Insha'Allah,* as Allah wills," he whispered. A statement that said it all for a Muslim, because Islam requires total submission, and Ali readily accepted his situation as being Allah's will. Easing his backpack off, he settled down and leaned into it for support. Warily looking around, he regrettably found himself sitting next to a detestable, half-naked *kafir* whore, who got in his face and asked—of all things, "Do you know Jesus?"

Disgusted by the woman's brazenness, but feigning a pleasant countenance, Ali shook his head and pretended to know only a few words of English. As time for the fireworks drew near, and the group began singing "God Bless America," Jamal became anxious about becoming a martyr. *I can't leave unnoticed before the bomb goes off.* "*Ihdena al siraat al moustaqueem,* Allah show me the way," Ali whispered in Arabic.

After dropping Ali off, Sayeed found a place to park his van near the Navy Pier. Like Ali and Jamal, he blended into the crowd and was able to find a spot to observe the fireworks. The morning newspaper had reported the extravaganza would begin at nine o'clock in all locations. Each display would last fifteen minutes and end with a spectacular grand finale.

Filled to capacity, the *Chicago Bell* cast off and slowly headed out into Lake Michigan. Before boarding Hakeem had turned on the cell phone taped to the pressure cooker, and sent the programmed text message—a message that told Sayeed his bomb was armed. The fact that receiving a text message would detonate the bomb was something Hakeem didn't need to know. Carrying a small duffle bag, he boarded with the crew at 5:30. If asked about the bag, he'd planned to say it was a change of clothes for a late night party, but to his relief no one asked.

A light breeze blew toward shore and the water was calm, a perfect night for a dinner cruise. Hakeem, however, had little time to enjoy the view as he bussed tables in the main dining room on the second deck. Once all the customers had been served, he took his break, and carrying his duffle bag climbed the stairs to the top observation deck. Once there, he looked around, and satisfied no one was watching, placed the bag inside a serving cabinet and covered it with a towel. After working on the boat for a month, he knew the cabinet was seldom opened.

Muttering praise for Allah, Hakeem spent the next few minutes leaning on the boat's railing, smoking a cigarette and gazing at the city. *Soon the kafirs will begin drinking and dancing,* he grinned, feeling proud of himself. *I've done it. The bomb is in place—Praise Allah. Soon the unbelievers will be blown to hell,* he gloated, listening to the sound of the revelers' laughter drifting up from below. *Yes, they will be dancing all right, but ... not for long.* "No—not for long," he murmured, but turning to walk toward the stairs, he stopped. Suddenly pricked by his conscience, he had a troubling thought. *For many on board it will be their last dance. Is it right to kill innocents?* "No, I will not question the deed. I am doing Allah's work," he muttered, suppressing the thought as he hurried down the stairs and returned to the galley.

"*HAKEEM, get to work.* You're not a paying customer," the steward yelled when he'd entered.

Waving in response, he headed for the main dining room.

Looking at his watch, Sayeed checked the time and turned on his cell phone, which he'd previously programmed to send a text message to each bombs' cell phone trigger. *All I have to do is press send ... Insha'Allah,* Sayeed sneered. *As soon as the cell phones I attached to each bomb receive the text message, they will activate the 'message received alert,' which will function the squibs inside the bombs and ignite the powder charges.* Sayeed snickered, visualizing the bloody carnage resulting from the explosions. Pleased with his work, he felt certain he would receive praise from his master, Grand Ayatollah Khomeini.

My master is very clever. After our meeting in Qom, he trusted me to carry out his plan. Nothing was written down. Nothing was sent by e-mail. No phone calls were made. Sayeed felt the warm glow of success. *Praise be to Allah, in a short time I will implement the plan and kill hundreds of kafirs.*

As the ninth hour approached, Sayeed gazed out across the lake and saw a brightly lit boat approaching. He hoped it was the *Chicago Bell.* When the first rockets fired from the barge Sayeed checked his watch. It was 9:01 p.m. *I have done all I can. Now it is in Allah's hands. Insha'Allah.* Selecting the stored message in his cell phone, Sayeed sat with his finger resting near the send button, watching the intensity of the fireworks display increase.

As soon as the first barrage of rockets lit up the sky and the spectators jumped to their feet, Jamal began easing his way toward the back of the raucous crowd. Ten minutes later found him near the beach entrance, where guards were so enthralled with the display he was able to silently slip away into the night.

Trapped in the middle of *kafirs*, Ali stood watching the display and grinding his teeth. *Infidels!* He seethed. *Infidels, who, like that stupid bitch next to me, worship Jesus as the Son of God, and something called the Holy Spirit. They're idol worshipers. At least the Jews know better—even if they are descendants of pigs and apes. Allah has no son. Christians can't be considered people of the book as long as they believe Mary is Jesus' virgin mother; Jesus is the son of Allah; and there is a Holy Spirit. May Allah send them all to hell,* Ali grimaced, *and thanks be to Allah, I am going to start them on their journey.* As the fireworks reached their glorious finale, Ali embraced the fact he was going to die for Allah, and unnoticed by the revelers who were looking skyward, strapped on his backpack, dropped to his knees facing Mecca, and assumed the position of prayer with his forehead touching the ground. *"Allahu' Akbar,"* he whispered, trembling with excitement and rejoicing in his last mortal thought, *Soon I will meet Allah as a martyr.*

Hakeem was busy serving drinks on the *Chicago Bell's* top observation deck, where he planned to martyr himself, but as the time for the bomb to detonate drew near, he was having second thoughts. The more he considered martyrdom, paradise and milk and honey weren't all that appealing. As for the *houris*, Allah's perpetual virgins, he'd already had all the women he wanted, and although the thought of having an eternal erection was enticing, he rationalized, *I can always purchase Viagra if needed.* With this thought in mind, he slipped down the stairs to the lower level and casually moved to the stern. Five minutes after the fireworks began, he removed his *Chicago Bell* T-shirt and dropped it over the side, intending to disembark with the surviving passengers.

Sayeed glanced at his watch. It was 9:13 p.m., and the fireworks display was reaching its finale. It was time. With his gaze fixated on the *Chicago Bell*, he pressed the send key on his cell phone. Several seconds passed with nothing happening, but then he saw a bright flash on the boat's top deck. While the crowd around him oohed and ahhed over the glorious pyrotechnic display above the lake, Sayeed's delight came from a puff of smoke he'd briefly seen illuminated by the boat's lights following the flash. *"Allahu' Akbar,"* he whispered, smiling with pleasure and cheering with the crowd. Continuing to watch the boat until the show ended, he mingled with the departing spectators.

Revelers on the lower decks of the *Chicago Bell* heard the explosion and felt the boat shudder. Lost in the screams and the noise caused by falling debris, Hakeem's whispered, "Praise Allah," went unnoticed. Yet it was what happened next brought his heart into his throat. Unable to prevent it, Hakeem felt himself being caught up in the surge of terrified passengers rushing toward the observation deck's staircase. Either out of curiosity or a desire to help, many passengers seemed desperate to reach and clamber up the staircase to the upper deck. Forced to go up the stairs or be trampled, Hakeem heard a passenger above him exclaim, "Oh my god," and then the passengers able to see the carnage on the top deck began screaming.

The screaming thrilled Hakeem, but when he finally stumbled onto the bloody deck, he relied on *taqiyya*, the Muslim's art of deception, to mask his delight and made a pretence of offering to help.

Captain Fazio heard the loud boom above the bridge, felt the boat shudder, and cringed at the sound of the screams that followed. Frantically placing the boat's propulsion system in neutral, he rushed to push his way up the observation deck's stairs toward the source of the screaming. Finally reaching the top he retched at the nauseating sight in front of him. Littered with broken bits of furniture, the deck was covered with blood, mutilated bodies and body parts. Too stunned to move, Fazio stood watching a man and two women checking bodies and using belts to fashion tourniquets. Later he would learn the man was a doctor and the women were RNs.

Gathering his wits, Fazio realized people must have been blown overboard by the explosion. Looking over the port side he saw four passengers treading water and several bodies floating facedown. "God in heaven," he uttered watching the ones still alive desperately thrashing about trying to keep their heads above water.

Cupping his hands to his mouth in an attempt to be heard over the wailing of the injured and hysterical passengers, Fazio screamed, **"PASSENGERS OVERBOARD."** A Steward on the lower deck heard him and looked up. Gesturing toward the water below Fazio screamed, "**HELP THE PEOPLE IN THE WATER. TOSS THEM LIFE RINGS.**"

Satisfied his order was being carried out, Fazio knew he had to return to the bridge and send an SOS, but that presented a problem because the stairs leading to the lower deck were clogged with passengers. Shouting, "MAKE WAY ... "CAPTAIN COMING THROUGH," and, "NO, I DON'T KNOW WHAT'S HAPPENED," he elbowed his way down the stairs to the bridge deck.

Once back on the bridge, he used the radio to call the Coast Guard on the emergency channel. "SOS! *Chicago Bell* declaring an emergency. Position one mile north of Navy Pier. Possible bomb detonation top deck. Many killed and wounded." Fazio repeated the announcement until it was acknowledged, and then concentrated on calming and organizing the passengers.

The Coast Guard chief monitoring the radio issued an alert requesting all vessels in the area to lend assistance.

Local TV stations covering the fireworks displays had most of their cameras zoomed in on the aerial bursts, however some cameras—in particular those covering the Montrose and 63rd Street Beach displays— picked up an odd flash amid the crowds at both beach locations. The few television viewers who'd noticed the flashes thought perhaps one of the fireworks rockets had fallen into the crowd. Security personnel monitoring the shows initially had the same thoughts, but quickly realized the explosions were too large, when people began screaming and scrambling for the exits. A cameraman at Montrose Beach was the first to notice the panicking crowd and zoomed in. His camera showed bodies and body parts strewn about with bloody clothes, coolers and other items. Word quickly spread and soon cameras for several networks were videoing the carnage.

While "Chicago Bombings" breaking news banners were appearing on national TV networks, Chicago's antiterrorism task force went into action following established protocols. Ambulances sped to the sites, along with every available police unit. Police and TV news helicopters quickly converged and hovered over the two detonation sites. Word of the attack on the *Chicago Bell* quickly spread and news helicopters headed for the boat.

A Coast Guard rescue helicopter was the first to arrive over the crippled vessel and report the damage. Guardsmen airlifted several severely wounded men and women off the ship's blood soaked upper deck, and then headed for the nearest trauma center. While the cameras on news helicopters were broadcasting live feed, Coast Guard boats began arriving and, using searchlights, located fifteen bodies and six survivors in the water—three with serious injuries and two complaining of ringing in their ears. Once assured all passengers in the water were out of harm's way, Captain Fazio eased his crippled boat out of the search area and headed at maximum speed for the Navy Pier, where ambulances and police units awaited the *Bell's* arrival.

FBI personnel arrived at the Navy Pier before the *Chicago Bell* docked, and detained all uninjured crew and passengers—including Hakeem. A large vacant nearby building had been commandeered and police directed all uninjured passengers and crew inside. The first order of business was to obtain the names of the passengers. According to the *Chicago Bell's* records there were 500 passengers and a crew of twenty-five on board.

Standing with the other crewmembers, Hakeem realized he had a problem. Someone in the crew would probably recall he had boarded carrying a small duffel bag—a bag he couldn't produce. *Perhaps I can pass myself off as a passenger. No ... my name is on the crew manifest. Allah, I have performed my task, please guide me.*

Sayeed slowly made his way to his van in a nearby parking lot, and patiently waited in line to exit and join the hundreds of vehicles leaving the area. An hour and a half later he pulled into the parking lot of an all night diner in Skokie, joined Jamal in a booth and ate a late dinner. After each paid their checks, Sayeed drove the van north to Dempster Street, turned west and then north onto I-94. Once they were safely away from Chicago, Sayeed drove toward Milwaukee and they exchanged stories of completing their missions.

It wasn't long before Sayeed saw a sign for a Motel 6 and exited onto U.S.-50. After paying cash for a room with two beds, he parked the van in front of their room. As soon as they entered, Sayeed turned on the TV, and he and Jamal watched news broadcasts on three local channels. Reports of the deaths and damage filled them with joy—their missions had been accomplished. Spreading prayer rugs on the floor they prayed to their vengeful god.

The next morning after showering and dressing in clean clothes, they placed their old clothes, including their shoes, into a plastic bag for disposal in a dumpster behind a nearby store. Sayeed gave Jamal a large envelope containing U.S. and Canadian bills, a passport with a different name, and plane tickets that would take him from Milwaukee to Detroit, and then onto

Toronto. Once there he would join the Muslim community and wait for new instructions.

"I wonder if Ali and Hakeem got away?" Jamal asked as they placed their suitcases in the van.

Sayeed shrugged, "Only Allah knows. They had different escape routes, and so far there have been no reports of anyone being arrested. Anyway, neither Ali nor Hakeem knows anything of value. Both were living here on expired student visas. Our brothers who purchased the gunpowder at different stores used false names and met Ali at clean locations. A brother using a false name and address rented both houses for cash. Ali never knew who any of these men were.

"A cleaning crew has already sanitized the Michigan house, and you disposed of the gunpowder containers before leaving. Arrangements with a local cleaning company have been made to clean your house in South Chicago. It will be done today.

"Even if Ali or Hakeem are caught, we have nothing to worry about."

"Where will you go after you drop me off at the airport"

"It is better if you do not know."

Chapter 30

Chicago, Illinois
Saturday night, July 4, 2015

Chicago gangs are part of the history and fabric of the city. A fact law enforcement and politicos accept, but something that presents a paradox for progressive-liberals. Gun control is supposed to reduce crime and murder; yet, ironically, even though Chicago has some of the strictest gun laws in America, it is also one of the top gun crime cities in the U.S. That being the case, there could be only one conclusion. Since the facts contradicted progressive-liberals' dogma, the facts had to be wrong.

The Fourth of July terrorist attacks attracted all the police units in the greater Chicago area to the attack sites like a super-magnet attracts paperclips; thus creating a perfect storm for gangs. Looting on a small scale had begun around ten p.m. in South Chicago, an area controlled by the Gangster Disciples. Looting in the Loop area by the Vice Lords followed.

It was pretty much business as usual, until 57 year-old Augustin "Big Tino" Zambrano, the leader of the Latin Kings gang, with the title of "corona" (crown), recognized the real opportunity. Newly released from a 51-year prison sentence because of overcrowding and good behavior, Big Tino had a brainstorm. While watching two members of the Kings struggling to jam a stolen 60-inch TV into a small sedan, a thought occurred to him—the real loot was in the rich suburbs. If all the police were at the bombings, the burbs were ripe for the picking.

Dreaming of gold coins, jewelry, watches, diamonds, silver, cash, and mink coats for the Kings' Queens, Big Tino, sneered, *Yeah, the Promised Land's waitin' for me 't come and take its treasure.* Elated by the thought of his new wealth, Big Tino knew the burbs were guarded by rent-a-cops. So he issued orders for the Kings to jack every SUV they could find, and follow him to the wealthy, gated communities surrounding Chicago. Within an hour, the Gangster Disciples—quickly followed by the Black P. Stones, Vice Lords, and Black Disciples—got wind of the King's treasure hunt and headed for the burbs too. After all, there was enough loot out there for all of them. Besides, why should the Kings have all the fun? Didn't they have a right to rape and pillage too?

It wasn't long before every phone line in the Chicago area's 911 emergency call centers lit up, and harried dispatchers were reluctantly telling frantic callers to be patient—no police units were available to answer their call. When one woman called hysterically pleading for help, because she was about to be raped, the dispatcher told her, "Don't resist. Let him have his way. If you don't fight, he may not hurt you."

"IT'S NOT A HE!" the woman screamed, "IT'S A THEM! I'm going to be gang raped. HELP ME!" Unfortunately, the poor woman was about to learn in times of emergency you have to help yourself.

A few citizens did understand and tried to defend themselves and their property by using golf clubs and baseball bats. One homeowner, who did defend himself and his property with a shotgun, would later be charged with attempted murder. It seems the homeowner managed to hit the intruder with a load of No. 9 birdshot, after the big man gained entry by breaking down the homeowner's front door. As a result the gang-banger sued the owner for assault, recovery of medical expenses, and lost wages.

Chicago's news media was in a dither. What to report? There were just too many stories to cover. Since every story was newsworthy, they solved the problem by jumping from one story to another. Rushing off in all directions from site to site, they first covered ambulance runs; then interviewed emergency technicians at the bomb sites; then vandalism, robberies, and stolen SUVs and automobiles in the city limits; then violent suburban home invasions and rape; and then live action video of gang members loading loot from multimillion dollar suburban homes into stolen SUVs and automobiles. It was altogether too much for Chicago's aggressive newshounds. Haggard reporters and television producers were working overtime, and much was made about the lack of police response.

While Chicago's mayor was attempting to deal with the looting, the governor was preparing to activate the National Guard. It wouldn't be long before the media would have another major story to cover.

At some point during the following months, a few progressive-liberals had an epiphany—without guns they were at the mercy of their attackers. Some individuals who'd been battered, abused and robbed, finally understood the old adage, "Sam Colt made all men equal," and decided guns did have a place in their lives. Most, however, chose to make excuses for the men who'd battered, abused and robbed them. After all, it always had to be someone else's fault. In the end they blamed the police for not doing the impossible—protecting everyone at the same time.

Martha's Vineyard
10:30 p.m. Saturday July 4, 2015

Tom Jenkins, head of President Abomba's security detail, listened to the voice in his earbud. *"Oh my god,"* he exclaimed and hurried to the president. "Mr. President, I must speak with you alone."

Abomba gave the large man a withering look. "I *told* you not to bother me tonight. Whatever it is … it can wait until morning," POTUS sneered and turned back to continue his discussion with director Stephen Spielberg about his latest movie.

Used to being snubbed by the president, Jenkins knew he had to tell someone. Frantically looking around, he saw the First Lady schmoozing with JLo. Deciding that telling the president's wife would the best course of action, he approached the singer from behind, looked over her shoulder, and waited for an opportunity to catch the First Lady's eye.

Finally noticing him nodding and winking at her, the First Lady frowned and snapped, *"What? ... What is it?"*

"Ma'am, excuse me, but I need to speak with you alone. It's *very* important."

"It better be. Excuse me darling, I'll be right back," FLOTUS told the singer, who gave Jenkins a withering look.

Standing off to the side with the First Lady and speaking softly, the agent told her about the attacks in Chicago.

"Why tell *me* … why not tell the President?"

"I tried ma'am, but he was too busy. I hope I'm doing the right thing by telling you."

Sniffing as though she smelled something offensive, the First Lady wheeled around, and without responding, headed for the president. Grabbing Abomba by his sleeve and jerking him away from Spielberg, who raised his eyebrows, she hissed, "There've been multiple workplace violence incidents in Chicago. You need to contact Rom. It sounds bad."

After several seconds, Abomba hissed back, *"Damn.* Why tonight? Yeah, I'll call Rom."

"You'd better call Jane Incompentado too."

Homeland Security was aware of the Chicago violence, however DHS's PR office was having difficulty deciding how to report it. Since the attacks occurred during public events it wasn't "workplace violence." Perhaps it could be labeled "recreational violence" or "eventplace violence"—however, there was some concern the new term would not apply to the cruise boat. Perhaps that attack could be described as "cruiseplace violence?" Desperately hoping no Muslims were involved, the senior PR official anxiously awaited guidance.

In Chicago, Mayor Rom Cristo was up to his ears in alligators when the president called. Abomba's first question was, "Is there anything linking the attacks to Islam?"

"So far the answer is no, Barry. We really have no clue who's responsible. Because all three bombs went off at the same time, we have to assume it was a coordinated attack, but no one has yet to claimed responsibility."

"Okay, good. Remember, I've declared the war on terror is over— ceased, done ... no more ... I *do not* want *anyone* trying to say otherwise. Do I make myself clear?"

"Yes, Mr. President."

"Good."

"Call Jane for support. Tell her I said to give you anything you ask for."

"Thank you, I will."

After speaking with Mayor Cristo, the secretary of homeland security immediately sent a Blue Shirt unit to Chicago to restore order.

Late the following day, a turf war of gigantic proportions erupted between FEMA Corps, the National Guard, and local police, which provided ample time for the gangs to complete their marauding through the burbs.

Chapter 31

Basra, Iraq
6:30 a.m. Sunday, July 5, 2015

Al-Sadr had been up for hours watching reporting the Chicago attacks on al-Jazeera. He was delighted, for the killings reaffirmed his faith in the Grand Ayatollah. *The Holy One's plan is working like a Swiss watch. The Great Satan's press and president are overwhelmed by multiple crises. First the minor shootout in a place called Golden in their Colorado state, and now the Chicago bombs. Gangs looting rich neighborhoods are an added bonus. Allah is indeed the best plotter, for only He could have caused all of these events to occur at once. Praise be to Allah. Everything is in place for my coup. The uprising will begin after morning prayers. Within a few months, Iraq will be The Islamic Republic of Iraq, and then I will be the Grand Ayatollah. After expelling the remaining kafirs, I will deal with the Sunnis.* "Allahu 'Akbar."

Baghdad, Iraq
7:30 a.m. Sunday, July 5, 2015

Mobs of Shiites exploded from mosques across the country demanding the expulsion of all *kafirs,* an end to the current elected government, and the formation of The Islamic Republic of Iraq. Two hours later, while the government struggled to deal with the mobs, al-Sadr's Mahdi Army appeared and all hell broke loose. After seizing government buildings and arresting Sunni and Kurdish ministers and representatives, they placed the president and prime minister under house arrest. Violence exploded across Iraq. Sunnis were massacred and a civil war loomed on the near horizon. Al-Sadr had become Iraq's new strong man, and one of his first orders was for Western embassies to reduce staff. U.S. Embassy survivors and the remaining MPs had relocated to an indefensible building in the Green Zone. Al-Sadr ordered the MP detachment to leave the country within forty-eight hours, leaving the survivors defenseless.

Iran offered to provide "stabilizing" troops and the offer was accepted. Within a month Iran would effectively control Syria and Iraq.

Israel and Jordan braced for the storm they knew was coming.

China discreetly notified al-Sadr that as long as Iraq's oil continued to flow and no harm came to Chinese personnel or property, they would remain neutral and veto any UN actions.

Iran's terrorist organization, Hezbollah, based in Lebanon and Syria, was turned loose on their Sunni rivals, al-Qaeda, al-Nusra Front, Hamas, and the PLO.

If America did not act quickly, Iranian dominance of the Middle East would be secured; thereby setting the stage for a regional war between Sunni and Shi'a nations, and making Iran an unacknowledged nuclear power possessing a stockpile of untested warheads—well, untested if you didn't count the North Korean tests.

Martha's Vineyard
Early Sunday morning, July 5, 2015

Tom Jenkins dreaded having to awaken President Abomba, but he had no choice. Iraq was on fire and the president had to make immediate decisions—something he avoided whenever possible. Taking a deep breath, Jenkins wondered how his boss would react to the bad news he was about to deliver. Tapping gently on Abomba's bedroom door, he softly called through the door, "Mr. President ... Uh–Mr. President."

"Huh, what is it?"

"Mr. President, there are major developments in Iraq."

"*Oh, hell* ... What time is it?"

"It is one-fifty-two, Mr. President, and the Secretaries of Defense and State are on the phone."

"Damn it Jenkins, I just got to sleep. Tell them to handle it," Abomba said yawning loudly and rolling over.

Shaking his head, Jenkins stood staring at the president's door. "Yes, Mr. President."

Returning to the temporary communication room in the library of Abomba's vacation residence, Jenkins used the speakerphone to inform Heinz and Haggler of the president's instructions. Neither was surprised, and neither had any good ideas about what to do. Finally Heinz said, "Gene, I'm closing the embassies and consulates. Arrange for C-17s to pick up our people ... and any other westerners who need a ride."

CENTCOM, MacDill AFB
Sunday, 5 July 2015

The imminent danger alert from the temporary U.S. embassy in Baghdad sounded at 0129 hours. Most of the staff was already at their posts when it arrived. General Beck had summoned them when news of the Chicago bombing appeared on the major news networks. Once the three coordinated bombings were confirmed, Beck was sure it was another jihadi attack, and no one disagreed with him. Now a second front had opened in Iraq.

General Doughberry reported CENTCOM's readiness to the chairman of the Joint Chiefs, but instead of receiving orders he was told to stand by.

Beck noted Colonel Collins' late arrival at 0812 hours. Later, hearing her explain she'd been in St. Petersburg when he issued the summons, Beck smiled, correctly guessing she was with her gal pal.

As the clock on the wall approached 1100 hours, it became apparent to everyone no alert or action orders were going to be issued Even Doughberry was shocked by the apparent surrender to al-Sadr. The meeting ended at 1105.

Beck had just entered his office when the phone rang. Glancing at the Caller ID he saw it was Rockford, and was pretty sure he knew why the colonel was calling. Picking up the handset and attempting not to show his disgust with the lack of orders, he answered, "Good morning, Rocky."

Wanting to ask what the hell was going on, but sensing this time wasn't the right time to do so, Rockford restrained himself and said, "Good morning, sir."

"An interesting morning it is … but I'm not so sure how good it is. To answer your unasked question, we have received no orders of any kind." He paused when he heard Rocky heave a sigh. "Yeah, I know how you feel, but our only instructions are to stand by. The Air Force has been tasked to send C-17s to evacuate embassy personnel and the MP detachment. Al-Sadr ordered the MPs to leave."

After several seconds of silence, Rockford, his voice was husky with emotion, mumbled, "Damn … sir, this means we've lost Iraq. Afghanistan is under Taliban control, and Syria is now a client state of Iran and Russia …" he hesitated, struggling to control himself.

"Sorry sir," he finally managed to say, "But I personally can't help feeling all the blood we spilled was for nothing, and our men and women are beginning to realize it."

"Are you referring to loss of morale?"

"No, sir ... worse. The troops are beginning to question the President's decisions. They're losing confidence in him as Commander in Chief, and that's a serious problem."

Beck had anticipated this, but he needed to gauge the extent of the problem. "Are you referring to Delta?"

"Yes ... and the entire post. There's open grumbling at the officers and NCO clubs—even during formations and training. The men don't seem to care if anyone hears them."

"How about other commands?"

"I have secondhand reports it's the same at many other bases. The Blue Shirts put a bad taste is a lot of mouths; and the near shooting of protesters in Golden confirmed the men's opinion of them. The Blue Shirts use of heavy machine guns near Chicago cinched it. There's no way our men and women will work with the Blue Shirts. In fact, there may be violent clashes if they're ordered to."

Beck stared at the top of his desk for a couple of seconds. "Anything else?"

"No, sir. We're ready to go to Iraq and kick al-Sadr's butt, but I don't think that's going to happen."

"Neither do I, Rocky," Beck agreed. "I'll let you know as soon as we get any action orders. Give my best to Jill."

Rebecca Collins was also using her office phone to call her gal pal Vickie Barrett at the White House. The pair had been enjoying a romantic weekend at the Grand Plaza Hotel on St. Pete Beach when Beck's summons arrived. Rebecca had dropped Vickie off at flight operations at 0700 on her way to CENTCOM.

Vickie answered on the third ring, "Hi, lover, just got here. Miss me already?"

Rebecca smiled, "Yes I do. We had a great time. Looking forward to next time.

"Vickie, what's going on regarding Bagdad? We were told to stand by early this morning ... since then nothing, and I gotta tell you the natives are getting restless."

Barrett liked Rebecca, especially their sex. She was a wonder in bed, but that didn't give her access to the president's inner circle. On the other hand, Rebecca did provide her access to the senior military generals' thinking; and Barrett wasn't surprised the troops were unhappy. *Hell, I'm unhappy too. No one told me a coup in Iraq was planned. Hmmm, I wonder if the Ayatollah is running his own game. Wouldn't surprise me, the Iranians are a duplicitous lot. Abomba's floundering, letting events control him. Damn the CIA. First they failed to warn us about the terrorists' attacks in Chicago, and then they missed al-Sadr and his Mahdi Army's coup. And, to top it off, I've just learned Abomba is leaving for Brazil on Friday. Damn him too—he always leaves town when there's a crisis. What do I tell Rebecca? I need her input to stay on top of things.*

"Rebecca, the President is on his way back from Martha's Vineyard. From what I've learned, we suffered a double intelligence failure—both Chicago and Iraq. Once the President gets past the reporters, he'll be able to meet with his security team and formulate his response. Tell everyone to hang in there and wait for orders."

"Thanks. Hope we can get together again. You're the best lover I've ever had. Bye."

Vickie remained seated, remembering their last two weekends and Rebecca's last comment. *And you, my darling girl, are the best lover I've ever had. Now how can I arrange for us to meet on a regular basis? Hmmm.*

President Abomba and his large contingent of hangers-on and security personnel were helicptering from Martha's Vineyard to the airport where Air Force One waited for them. So far the president hadn't declared a position on either the Fourth of July attacks or the coup in Iraq. The rabid press wanted answers, and Abomba knew they'd be waiting to greet him when at Joint Base Andrews the White House. In fact, the First Lady was furious at the press for intruding into her space.

Washington, DC
Sunday morning, July 5, 2015

The White House switchboard was jammed with calls from television producers seeking guests—someone, anyone to appear on the morning news shows. Reporters were demanding statements and interviews with anyone the White House could provide. With no guidance from the president, Jay Schpinmeister, Abomba's press secretary, was frantic. When he finally reached the president on Air Force One, Abomba directed him to say everything was under control, and he was coordinating with world leaders.

"Very good, Mr. President, but I strongly advise you to return to Washington as quickly as possible," Schpinmeister urged, even though he knew it wasn't going to happen. He was all too familiar with Abomba's penchant for avoiding responsibility and knew Washington was the last place the president wanted to be.

Schpinmeister had no idea how right he was, for unknown to him his boss was already planning his next vacation boondoggle.

After hanging up with Schpinmeister, Abomba sat staring at his golf clubs. *I'm overdue for a trip to Brazil,* he reasoned. *I've heard there's a beach near Rio that's a nice place to vacation. Wonder if they have any decent golf courses ... Hmmm?* Frowning, when an aide interrupted his scheming to tell him the king of Jordan was holding, he muttered something unintelligible and took the call.

"Mr. President, I am very concerned about events in Iraq. Al-Sadr is Grand Ayatollah Khomeini's puppet. If you don't deal with the Mahdi Army, Iran will own Iraq," the king said, but chose not to add, *And Jordan will be next.*

"Hezbollah has taken credit for the three bombings in Chicago," the king continued. "Which means the attacks must have been part of Khomeini's plan."

"I suppose they could have been," Abomba, muttered. He hadn't considered that possibility.

After ending the call, Abomba sat brooding. *Yes, a trip to Brazil is just what I need. Can't ignore our South American neighbors can I? Besides, it will make me look presidential.* Picking up his cell phone he called his chief of staff and directed him to schedule a trip to Brazil, departing Friday morning.

The president of Brazil would not be thrilled when informed of President Abomba's sudden desire to visit her.

The major networks' morning news talk shows were pure comedy. There were so many hot topics hosts didn't know where to begin.

Senators Dana Finkelstein and Betty Boxnutter were guests on *Meet the Press*. After five minutes of inane prattle over Chicago's gangs, the host had finally given up trying to get them to discuss Iraq when Boxnutter dismissed the topic by saying, "The Chicago bombings were caused by America's deplorable treatment of Muslims."

Gun control was their only interest. "Anyone with a grain of intelligence can see the presence of guns was responsible for the dead and injured Chicago citizens living in the suburbs. If there were no guns, gangs wouldn't have gone on their rampage," Boxnutter stated, slapping the interview table top for emphasis.

After several more similar pronouncements, the host—almost choking on his words—finally pointed out, "Senator, with one exception, Chicago's citizens didn't have guns. They attempted to fend off the gangs with golf clubs and baseball bats. Many are now demanding the right to have guns for protection."

"That's totally *preposterous,*" Boxnutter snapped, and was about to launch into a tirade when Finkelstein interrupted.

"What Betty means is gangs wouldn't have had guns, if all the guns had been confiscated."

"*What* ... are you saying you don't believe illegal guns will be smuggled into the country?" the host blurted out.

Things went down hill from there.

FOX News Sunday featured Senator Crux, who clearly stated the danger lurking in Iraq. "If Iran gains control of Iraq, Jordan is next. Then Israel will be surrounded and there will be a nuclear war. Israel will have no choice."

"What do you think we should do?" the host asked.

Crux sighed and slowly shook his head. "There are no good options left. In order to stop al-Sadr and Iran, we'll have to launch a third Gulf War, and that's not feasible. I think we have two choices—let Iran win, or bomb Iran."

The host sat staring at his guest for five long seconds, and then changed the topic to the FEMA debacle in Golden, Colorado. During the second segment, FOX—along with the other networks—received an e-mail from Hezbollah claiming credit for the Chicago bombing and providing more details than the FBI had managed to accumulate.

Senator Crux concluded his interview by saying, "Now there can be no doubt about Iran's involvement in the Chicago attacks.

Secretary of State Jerome Heinz appeared on ABC's "This Week." He'd learned from his predecessor's mistakes and wasn't going to allow a Susan Rice spectacle to occur on his watch. Expecting a friendly reception, Heinz was surprised by the host's hard questions. "Mr. Secretary, the administration's policy of supporting the rebels in Syria has resulted in Iranian dominance with Russian support. How will the United States respond to the coup in Iraq?

"George, our first action will be to present the matter to the United Nations. The President is working with his advisors, evaluating options. It's too early for me to provide an answer."

"Mr. Secretary, over three months have passed since our embassy was destroyed. So far the President has taken no action. Was al-Sadr's Mahdi Army responsible for the attack?"

"We've been working with the Iraqis and have yet to determine who was responsible. The President has stated those responsible will be brought to justice."

"Mr. Secretary, it appears that al-Sadr is now in charge in Iraq. If his Mahdi Army conducted the attack on our embassy, what kind of cooperation can we expect from him?"

"I think we should wait to cross that bridge until we come to it. However, I'm sure we can count of his cooperation.

"Getting UN support is going to be difficult. The Organization of Islamic Cooperation, commonly referred to as the OIC, has 57 members and is a powerful voting block in the UN. At present they aren't pleased by our failure to ratify the UN Arms Trade Treaty I signed last year. It will be difficult to obtain their cooperation until the treaty is ratified. Senator Realdick is two votes short of the two-thirds vote required."

"Do you mean we're being held hostage by the UN until we ratify the treaty?"

"Well, I wouldn't put it that way. Let's say we'll receive more cooperation if we do."

After the break, the interview continued.

"Mr. Secretary, the issue of gun control is dividing the nation. It's no longer a Democrat versus Republican issue. Gun owners belong to both parties, and they're becoming more vocal regarding the Second Amendment. In fact, gun control has sparked violence from gun ownership supporters. Several men have been killed. What is your position regarding the Second Amendment?"

Now clearly uncomfortable, Heinz's brow was sweating and he was showing other subtle signs of anxiety. "George, I'm not a Constitutional scholar. The attorney general has ruled the Second Amendment's purpose was to protect the rights of hunters, and hunters don't need semiautomatic weapons."

"Mr. Secretary, a large percentage of our citizens are rejecting his opinion. It now appears that the six northern counties in Colorado intend to secede and form a new state, North Colorado. In fact, they've already set up a new state government.

"A similar movement is underway in northern California."

Heinz was squirming in his seat. "George, I doubt the U. S. government will recognize the new state. It's an issue to be decided by the U. S. Supreme Court ... as will the interpretation of the Second Amendment."

Marine One landed on the White House lawn at 4 p.m. and President Abomba's security detail opened a corridor through the shouting reporters for the president and the angry First Lady, allowing them to enter the White House without answering any more stupid questions. "Damn them all," the president grumbled. *I answered their annoying questions at Andrews. Why should I have to repeat stuff I've already told them? What the hell do they think I can do ... invade Iraq for a third time? I told Haggler and Heinz to take care of it. Hmmm ... wonder if I can get in a round of golf before leaving for Brazil?*

"Mr. President, you security team is waiting for you in the Situation Room," his aide told he when he entered the building.

Abomba glared at the aide. "Not now, we're tired. Tell Sandra Wheat to come to our quarters and brief me in an hour."

"Yes, sir," the aide replied and notified National Security Advisor Sandra Wheat POTUS was tired and required a briefing in his private quarters in one hour. Wheat replied she'd be back to brief him at five-thirty.

Wheat was halfway through her briefing when FLOTUS, the First Lady, breezed in declaring she was starved. Instantly standing, because he was bored and wanted to get rid of Wheat, Abomba laughed. Then, grinning at his pouting wife he said, "Well so am I.

"Sandra, you'll have to excuse FLOTUS and me—She loves it when I call her that ... Don'cha Hon?" he joked, continuing to grin at the frowning First Lady.

"She *can* be a bit of a sourpuss though," he shrugged, snickering.

"Uh—yeah ... well, Sandra, how 'bout you come back later this evening, after we've popped over to Arlington for some Hell Burgers? She loves 'em ... don't you Hon?" he asked, knowing full well FLOTUS was worried about the ten pounds she said she'd put on her butt during this month's vacation.

Receiving a glare from FLOTUS that could flash freeze Lake Michigan, POTUS looked down and muttered, "Uh ... yeah—I uh, sorry Hon, I forgot."

"Uh, Sandra, when you come back, be sure to bring me some stuff I can read to the press. Make sure it says Secretary Heinz is establishing a working relationship with—what's his name again? Al—uh ... something-or-other. Yeah ... Secretary Heinz is going to travel to Iraq and meet with him. Sorry to rush off like this but can't keep the *little* woman waiting."

Damn it! Another afternoon shot to hell preparing a report he won't read. Well I'll be damned if I'm going to hang around waiting for them to get their burger fix. "Very well, Mr. President, I'll just drop off your stu—" Wheat caught herself before saying stuff. "I'll drop off your *statement* for the press with your aide before I leave this evening."

"Enjoy your burgers," Wheat sneered at FLOTUS and POTUS backs as they hurried out the door.

"God help me, I don't know which one of them is more insufferable," Wheat muttered, after the door closed. Then, continuing to silently bellyache, she collected her stack of briefing papers. *That woman never speaks to me—and the President always has some lame excuse like his monthly vacation or a golf date to keep me from finishing my report ... never sits still long enough to listen to anything. Oh, well, I guess that's what they mean by "plausible deniability,"* she decided, departing for her office.

Chapter 32

Capitol Building, Washington, DC
Monday morning, July 6, 2015

Republican minority leaders in both houses began the day with demands for investigations: Investigations of the bombings in Chicago; investigations of the looting in Chicago suburbs; investigations of FEMA Corps using heavy machine guns on gangs inside gated communities; investigations of the clash between FEMA Corps and the Illinois National Guard; and investigations of the coup in Iraq. One congressman tweeted there were not enough hearing rooms to accommodate all the hearings.

By noon almost every legislator's phone lines were jammed with callers demanding action. Their e-mail and message boxes were filled to capacity, and fax machines were running out of paper. The American people on the left and right were expressing their anger—a large percentage of them about pending gun control. Conservatives demanded an end to gun control legislation, while progressive-liberals demanded banning all guns. Conservative and progressive-liberal values were grinding against each other like two gigantic tectonic plates. Fault lines in the fabric of America were becoming active—fault lines that ran through every community in every state. Was a catastrophic sociopolitical earthquake imminent? Time would tell.

CENTCOM, MacDill AFB
Monday evening, 6 July 2015

General Beck had just poured three fingers of Famous Grouse scotch over ice cubes in his glass, and was settling down in his favorite easy chair to watch the evening news when his home phone rang. Setting his glass aside, he reached for the portable receiver, read the word 'encrypted' on the display screen, and activated his encryption device. A few seconds later, after waiting for the units to shake hands and identify the caller, he read 'Hazzard,' and pressed the talk button.

"Evening, Tom ... How goes it?" he asked, attempting to sound upbeat, even though he knew the reason for the call.

"Sir, I just talked to Rocky," Hazzard responded, dispensing with pleasantries. "We have a similar situation here. The men are asking why there've been no alert orders."

"Nothing's changed since I spoke with Rocky this afternoon."

Beck heard Hazzard mutter, "Damn it."

"I'll let you know if we get orders."

"Thank you, sir. Are you up for some fishing?"

Realizing what Hazzard was suggesting, Beck responded, "You know, that sounds like a great idea. Let's do it as soon as the Iraq and Chicago situations calm down."

"Yes, sir. Sounds like a plan."

The O'Rippley Quotient
8 p.m. Tuesday, July 7, 2015

O'Rippley opened his show with his talking points, chief among them being the president's apparent inability to make hard decisions and level with the American people. Staring into the camera's lens, O'Rippley declared, "America is a ship adrift without a rudder, a ship in danger of being driven onto a rocky shore. This will be the subject of tonight's show. Now it's time to enter our 'No Centrifugal Force Zone.' My first guest is Texas Senator Carlos Crux, who's here to enlighten us on his position on recent events, and their impact on our safety and security."

"Good evening Senator," O'Rippley said as the camera pulled back to focus on the earnest expression of Carlos Crux who sat across from him.

"*Is it* Bill? I wish I could agree that it is a good evening." Crux paused to stare into the camera's lens, "But unfortunately it's *not*. America is in trouble. In fact this may well be the worst period in America's history. Where once we were strong and united, now we're a divided nation. The last time America found itself in this situation the issue was clear. The issue was slavery. Southern states used slaves to work plantations, thus there was a geographical dividing line, the Mason-Dixon line.

"Northern states fought to maintain the union for two main reasons: first, if the United States of America had split into two nations, both would fail—or one or both could be conquered; and second, to end the practice of slavery, a practice that violated America's most basic founding principal— namely that all men are created equal.

"Southern agrarian states required slave labor, and plantation owners, the elite class, fought to maintain their privileged life style."

"Yes, 155 years ago the slavery issue violated both the Declaration of Independence and the Constitution," O'Rippley interjected. "And that's what's different today. Today the issue is civil rights as they apply to the Constitution."

Crux nodded his agreement. "Yes, the Constitution *is* the dividing issue today. Progressive-liberals' ideology is incompatible with our Constitution. Why? ... because their ideology is based on a socialist philosophy, which is similar to Communism or National Socialism. In short it advocates a system in which the government controls everything—runs businesses, provides services and even products, something the Founding Fathers never intended. I believe we're seeing a civil war brewing—progressivism verses conservatism ... or perhaps progressive-liberals versus Constitutionalists.

"It boils down to how the Constitution is interpreted. Is it as progressive-liberals assert, a so-called 'living document?' "

O'Rippley leaned forward, frowning. "If this is true, then—with very few exceptions—there will be no geographical separation. A new insurrection could pit neighbor against neighbor."

"Yes, a conflict that becomes both a civil war and a revolution. The revolution will be against our increasingly tyrannical government. The crown's stamp tax triggered out first revolution, which began with 'the first shot fired at Lexington Common.' I fear the coming revolution will be triggered by attempts to enforce gun control laws, and like the first revolution, this war will be against tyranny.

"Our first revolution also had a civil war component, rebels against royalists. This time it will be Constitutionalists against progressive-liberals.

After the station break, the discussion continued with O'Rippley recapping the first segment, and then saying, "So Senator Crux, you see parallels between King George III and President Abomba."

"Not just the President, progressive-liberals as well—the royalists of today, who are forcing their socialist agenda on all Americans. An agenda half of our citizens—the half that pay taxes—do not want. Even though history and current experience clearly demonstrate progressive-liberal dogma is false, the 'royalists' refuse to admit they're wrong. The idea that private gun ownership is bad, and ending it will prevent crime, is an article of faith for them—an indisputable fact that cannot be challenged.

It was time to change the subject and O'Rippley asked, "Let's move on to Iraq. What is your take on recent events?"

"Bill, we have effectively been kicked out. Not just out of Iraq, but out of the Middle East. Our credibility and influence is gone. The President's failure to publically condemn the attack on our embassy is a disgrace. Abomba's indecisiveness emboldened al-Sadr to take over the country, and our President has done nothing to stop him. In the eyes of the world we are the Keystone Cops.

"American blood spilt to free a country from a tyrant has been wasted. Over 33,000 have been killed and more than 100,000 wounded. The President's rules of engagement are the main cause for the deaths and injured. I also suspect they are the cause of the unacceptably high suicide rate in our military. It is estimated that eighteen veterans and active duty military commit suicide each day. While our men and women in the military put their lives on the line, the President plays golf.

"President Abomba is perceived as a weakling; and his lack of a military response to the attack on our ... No—the destruction of our Baghdad embassy told the Muslim world it's open season on Americans. The Chicago bombing is just the beginning. I fear there will be more."

"I'm afraid we'll have to leave it with that. Senator, thank you for taking time to be on my show."

Colonel Albert East was the main guest on the Sean Haddley Show. Haddley began by asking, "Colonel, give us your opinion on what's happening in Iraq?"

East grimaced and took a couple of seconds to collect his thoughts before answering. "Sean, Iraq clearly establishes the President's Middle Eastern policy is a complete failure. President Abomba inherited a relatively stable Middle East. While most of the leaders could be considered dictators, the people enjoyed varying degrees of freedom. By supporting the Arab Spring, Abomba has allowed religious fundamentalists—Islamists—and the Muslim Brotherhood to impose a far more restrictive form of government, on their people—one based on Islamic Shariah law. The Egyptian people rebelled after the Muslim Brotherhood took over, and we did nothing to support the rebellion—just as we failed to support the Green uprising in Iran. Remaining Christian and Coptic churches are being destroyed and members of both faiths murdered. The same is true for Jews.

"Allah's words, as recorded in the Qur'an, say He selected Muhammad to bring the true words of the one true god to the world. The

Qur'an is composed of Muhammad's recitations—only Muhammad's, no one else's. Muhammad created the Islamic religion in twenty-two years. Allah's words recorded in the Qur'an instruct all Muslims to fight until all say there is no god but Allah. Muslims believe Islam is the only true religion and it's their duty to impose Islam on the entire world.

"We see this command being fulfilled in the Middle East today."

"Is that why our embassy was attacked in Baghdad?" Haddley asked.

"Yes, Sean, because fanatical followers of Islam believe there is no authority but Allah's, there should therefore be no foreign influence in Islamic lands. Other faiths, for example 'People of the Book'—a Muslim term meaning Christians and Jews who worship the God of the Bible and Torah—are allowed to exist under draconian rules, as long as they do not proclaim Jesus is the Son of God or worship the Holy Spirit. Such people are known as *dhimmis,* non-Muslim citizens of an Islamic state, who pay a special tax called a *jizya* for the right to live there. In reality *dhimmis* are subjects of the Muslims, one small step above slaves.

"The United States Embassy was an intolerable symbol of Western decadence and had to be removed. Al-Sadr is Ayatollah Khomeini's puppet. As soon as he consolidates his power, he'll turn Iraq into another Iran and impose Shariah law on the people."

"What about Afghanistan?

"Sean, once again we've turned victory into defeat. It seems to me progressive-liberals crave our defeat and will do whatever necessary to ensure we always lose.

"The Taliban has regained control of Afghanistan and is methodically killing everyone who worked for or with us—the same thing happened in Vietnam."

Returning to the discussion after a station break, Haddley asked Colonel East, "What is the mood in our military? I'm getting reports of low morale."

"Unfortunately, Sean, what you're hearing is true. Morale is low, and this is a very serious problem, but more to the point, our military is losing faith … not in our God or Country—but rather in our President. They are questioning his judgment and his willingness to defend our nation."

Haddley stared at East for several seconds, his expression mirroring his concern as he evaluated his guest's statement. Finally he asked, "Is it that bad?"

"Yes, Sean, it is. Over the last six years President Abomba has promoted men and women loyal to him into senior leadership positions. Men and women with, in many cases, less experience and qualifications than those they now command.

"Our best and brightest are beginning to remind each other the oath they swore was to support the Constitution, not the President, not the Congress, and not the Supreme Court.

"They are beginning to ask themselves, 'Has our government become the domestic enemy of the Constitution?'"

Frowning and shaking his head, Haddley whispered, "God in heaven."

East and Haddley looked at each other in silence. Finally East asked, "Sean, what do you know about Oath Keepers?"

"Not much. Tell me about them."

East nodded, and said, "Oath Keepers are a non-partisan association of currently serving military, veterans, peace officers, and firefighters who pledge to fulfill the oath they swore. An oath ending with these words, 'To support and defend the Constitution against all enemies, foreign and domestic, so help me God.'

"The founding principal of Oath Keepers is that members *will not* obey unconstitutional, illegal and immoral orders—such as orders to disarm the American people or to place them under martial law and deprive them of their ancient right to a jury trial. Oath Keepers have drawn a line in the sand. They will not 'just follow orders.'

"Their motto is 'Not on our watch!'

"Men and women in our military and law enforcement are starting to ask each other, 'Are you an Oath Keeper?' "

Once again the host and guest sat in silence for several seconds.

Finally Haddley said, "So, if a revolution does occur the military may split into opposing armies, just like the civil war."

East nodded, "Yes the Blue and the Red instead of the Blue and the Gray."

"Colonel, thank you for sharing your opinion and wisdom with us. I pray it doesn't come to this."

"Sean, thank you for having me on your show. And I too am praying reason will prevail."

Instead of seriously considering the messages delivered on the O'Rippley and Haddley shows, progressive-liberals in Congress and the

White House went ballistic. New and resubmitted failed bills were introduced. Gun laws would be strengthened and enforced. Consequences be damned.

Chapter 33

Kookie Robats opened the show with a monolog about guns destroying American culture. If America was to survive as a diverse, politically correct, multi-cultural, racially inclusive nation it had to forswear its militaristic history, and reduce the size of its military and nuclear weapons stockpile. The fact that the Abomba administration had and was doing just that wasn't enough. Smirking at the camera, Kookie concluded, "We still have *one thousand* nuclear warheads. If we really must have these disgusting things, then a couple of hundred is more than enough." Kookie was an astute student of war and military tactics—after all she had watched ten one-hour shows on the Military Channel.

"I am very happy to report that our congress is responding to the gun crises. The following is a summary of all the bills that have been submitted in the last two weeks. Some had been defeated in the last sessions," she said, as the screen filled with the list.

- Fix Gun Checks Act (S. 325)
- Ammunition Background Check Act (S. 334)
- The Gun Owner Licensing Act (H.R. 255)
- Buyback Our Safety Act (H.R. 259)
- Handgun Licensing and Registration Act (H.R. 257)
- Tiahrt Restrictions Repeal Act (H.R. 258)
- Support Assault Firearms Elimination and Reduction from our Streets Act (H.R. 260)
- Firearm Safety and Public Health Research Act (H.R. 263)
- Large Capacity Ammunition Feeding Device Act (H.R. 273)
- Stop Online Ammunition Sales Act (H.R. 301)
- Assault Weapons Ban (S. 350/H.R. 591)
- Firearm Safety and Buyback Grant Act (H.R. 307)
- Firearm Risk Protection Act (H.R. 311)
- The Gun Owner Licensing Act (H.R. 314)

- Equal Access to Justice for Victims of Gun Violence Act (H.R. 322)
- Prohibit the Possession or Transfer of Junk Guns, a.k.a. "Saturday Night Specials" Act (H.R. 340)
- The Explosive Materials Background Check Act (S. 411)

"Once these bills are passed and combined with the new gun control laws scheduled to go into effect on January 2nd, America will be gun free by this time next year. Once again we'll be able to leave our doors unlocked."

Progressive-liberals hate being bothered with details, especially any details indicating their ideas could be unworkable—a brain numbing compulsion that might be better explained by the old saying, "My mind's made up, don't confuse me with the facts."

U. S. Congresswoman Diana DeGette, a Democrat who'd represented Denver since the 1990s, provided an example of this mindset. According to *The Denver Post*, DeGette attended a 2013 Public Forum on Guns in America, part of the National Debate on Guns, and made the following statement regarding how banning magazines holding more than 15 rounds would reduce gun violence, "What's the efficacy of banning these magazine clips? I will tell you these are ammunition, they're bullets, so the people who have those now, they're going to shoot them, so if you ban them in the future, the number of these high capacity magazines is going to decrease dramatically over time because the bullets will have been shot and there won't be any more available."

The *Post* went on to say, "One of the most bizarre moments of the forum came when DeGette was speaking about why a ban on large-capacity magazines would be effective in decreasing killing and seemed not to understand that the magazines are reloadable rather than one-time use."

Progressive-liberals celebrated the newly introduced bills, while those with common sense knew a line had been drawn. High on the narcotic of success, anti-gun fanatics weren't content to wait for January. New rules, ordinances, policies and regulations were quickly written, voted on and implemented by state and local governments, and school boards. The first to feel the sting of the new wave of laws and rules would be the schools, when the fall session began in August.

Joint Base Andrews
23 July 2015

Air Force One touched down, marking the president's return to the capital. Ecstatic over his visit to Brazil where he discovered South American countries had excellent golf courses, Abomba had decided to continue his boondoggle by visiting Argentina and Peru before returning to Washington and another much needed vacation.

Grumbling when he saw the throng of reporters waiting for him, POTUS— followed by FLOTUS, his mother-in-law, the children and innumerable members of his entourage—descended the big plane's portable stairs. Stopping to address the reporters, the president recited his press secretary's prepared report on the importance of his trip.

"It is with great optimism I report my trip has unquestionably cemented relations with three of our most important friends in South America. Soon we will sign new trade agreements, resulting in thousands of new jobs. My visit to these three countries demonstrates my administration cares about our southern neighbors. I—"

"WHAT ABOUT IRAQ? ARE YOU GOING TO VISIT IRAQ AND MAKE AL-SADR OUR FRIEND?*"* a SUN news reporter shouted.

"Yeah, I'd really like to see him do that," another reporter whispered.

"Me too. I wonder where he'll go to hide from us next time?" another reporter chimed in, and his comment drew chuckles from all who heard it.

"To answer your question, Secretary Heinz has met with Mr. al-Sadr and reports progress. I'm confident we will soon have excellent relations with Iraq's new government," President Abomba posited, thrusting his chin forward. He was about to continue when the First Lady locked her right arm around his left and unceremoniously began pulling him toward Marine One.

"Thank you for coming to meet us," Abomba called over his shoulder, "I'll schedule a press conference in the near future," he managed to say, before FLOTUS propelled him up the steps and into the waiting helicopter.

J. Edgar Hover Building
Friday, July 24, 2015

Preliminary copies of the FBI's Chicago field office report on the Fourth of July bombings arrived at nine o'clock. The director received his copy and began reading it after lunch. The bombs were similar to the bombs used in the 2013 Boston Marathon bombings, however the energetic material was a mix of several commercially available pistol, rifle and shotgun propellants used for handloading cartridges. Agents were interviewing sellers of the various propellants to see if there was any connection. Analysis had determined two eight-quart and one six-quart Presto pressure cookers had been used as containers. *So, it was a six-quart cooker that detonated on the top deck of the boat. Presto pressure cookers are available in stores throughout the U. S.* The director rubbed his chin. *Nothing unexpected here,* he decided as he read on.

Uninjured passengers and those with minor injuries had been interviewed at the Navy Pier. No one remembered seeing anything suspicious. The *Chicago Bell's* crew was efficient and pleasant. Passengers were watching the fireworks display on the top deck, through windows on the middle and lower decks, and on the fantail when the bomb exploded on the top deck. All witnesses later agreed the boat shook or shuddered after the blast. Based upon their personal experiences in Iraq and Afghanistan, several men and two women positively stated it was an IED.

Injured survivors were interviewed in their hospital rooms, as soon as they were able to speak. *Hmmm ... The fact that two remembered the explosion is surprising. I know that the mind normally doesn't record a severe trauma caused by a nearby explosion—apparently the brain blocks the memory.* Reading on, he discovered two had been blown off the top deck into the water by the pressure wave. Satisfied, the director moved on to the crew section.

Three crewmen working on the top deck had been killed. All remaining crewmembers were accounted for and had been interviewed before being released. *So far, nothing of importance,* the director decided, however he was becoming concerned. *There's no indication of who the suspect or suspects are, or how they got the bomb on the boat.*

Reading on, he found the first useable information. The boat's chef had stated that a new crewmember, Hakeem, was assigned to the top deck, yet he'd told the interviewing agent he was on the fantail when the bomb exploded. *That's odd. I wonder why he wasn't at his station,* the director thought. Reading on, he learned another interesting fact. The interviewing agent had noted Hakeem wasn't wearing a T-shirt identifying him as a crewmember. When asked why, Hakeem had said he'd gotten sick to his stomach and vomited on his shirt. Thinking it better to remove it because of the smell, he'd gone to the fantail to recover and thrown the shirt overboard. *A possible explanation, but I still find it odd. Let's see what else the report has to say about this Hakeem fellow.*

Two pages later, under follow-up interviews, the report noted the address listed for Hakeem was an unoccupied house in South Chicago. The forensic team reported a cleaning company had cleaned the house and no evidence had been recovered. "Ah ha!" the director exclaimed. The following paragraph stated Hakeem had disappeared, and his name appeared to have been false. Worse, the director noted, there were no photographs of Hakeem, and the artist's sketch was lacking sufficient details for a positive ID. Leaning back in his chair, the director knew he was in for some stormy weather, and worse still, Hakeem was in the wind. "Damn it," he muttered.

Moving on, the director began reading the description of the 63rd Street Beach explosion. Parts of coolers, duffel bags and backpacks were spread in a pie shaped path toward the southwest. Roofing nails were discovered embedded in three backpacks. The pressure cooker pot had split open forming a strip of stainless steel, which was typical of this type of propellant bomb. High explosives would have turned the pot into shards of metal. The combination of roofing nails and blast had ripped nearby human bodies into pieces. Nails from the blast shredded viewers standing farther away from the explosion. Twenty-six viewers had been killed and over sixty injured.

The director sat visualizing the carnage. *It appears the bag or backpack containing the bomb was placed next to coolers and bags. Smart, in the excitement no one would notice an extra bag, and the bomber could walk away unnoticed.*

Turning to the next site, Montrose Beach, the director found another significant piece of information. One body was lying face down at the point of detonation. It appeared the bomb had exploded on top of him. The body was mangled, but the investigators thought it belonged to a suicide bomber. Identification efforts were underway. *If this was a suicide bomber, were the other two also?* The director wondered. *If true, there should be two more bodies showing similar damage.*

The director mentally reviewed the report and decided the attacks had been very well planned—no warnings, no chatter, and no intelligence agency had picked up anything specific indicating an attack. *I don't have very much to report, and that's bad.* His conclusion proved correct. Once again the Washington blame game was on, and the FBI report bounced like a ball in an old pinball machine between Congress, CIA, NSA, DIA, DHS, and the White House. Another distraction from the coup in Iraq—just as Ayatollah Khomeini had planned.

As the month drew to a close, the average citizen worried about the economy, inflation, and another terrorist attack. Parents of school age children began purchasing clothes, spiral notebooks, cell phones, software, and computers. Parents with high school juniors and seniors worried about the pending cost of college.

Progressive-liberals were also worried about the coming school year. However their concerns centered less on mundane things like supplies and more on how to ban any and all things related to guns. The list included: pictures of guns; the textual use of the dreaded "gun" words, such as assault weapon, rifle, shotgun, pistol, revolver, hand gun, AR15, M16, M4, semiautomatic, musket, and muzzle loader; and finally any drawing, carving or hand motion that could be considered representative of a gun. Students committing such egregious transgressions would be severely punished, regardless of their age. Zero tolerance had become the progressive-liberals' credo.

Like all decisions made in haste, progressive-liberals soon found their thoughtless plan for sanitizing all library and textbooks had unintended consequences. Since cutting pictures out of books usually deleted sections of text on the other side of the page, the architects of censoring library and textbooks were left with the problem of how to retain readable material.

A number of congressional committees had been formed to address the problems, and several outlandish suggestions were under consideration. The idea with the most traction entailed removing library books and textbooks containing pictures of, or references to, guns from school property.

After hours of debate the idea was deemed unworkable because it would eliminate many of the required textbooks, as well as required books, magazines and newspapers.

As if the previous ideas weren't outlandish enough, one committee leader, a woman with six PhDs, proposed removing the horrible "gun" word and "pictures of guns" from electronic books. While most on the committee thought the idea would be far too difficult to implement, one wag came up with the brilliant idea of making NSA responsible for removing gun photos and language from e-books. Instantly resonating with other members, a quick vote of approval directed the committee's leader to request that Senator Boxnutter draft and submit a bill requiring NSA to sanitize all e-books used by school children.

Boxnutter, who was thrilled with the idea, enthusiastically agreed, and immediately set her staff to work drafting "The Delete Words and Pictures of Guns in Electronic Books Act." As suggested, the bill assigned NSA the responsibility for implementing the law, with a completion deadline of January first.

All societies, no matter their religion or race, harbor wannabe Nazis. Men and women who will, once given a small amount of power over others, become mini-dictators, drunk on their newfound power. Police departments are no exception. The "Shootout at the Bartow Corral," and the first "Come and Take It"—as they came to be known—are but two examples. When a few over-zealous or power crazed police officers exceed their authority, the rights of the individuals they're sworn to protect are violated.

Incorporating politically correct values into laws and regulations increasingly ground against liberties guaranteed by the Constitution. As one egregious over-step piled on top of another, anger and resentment grew and the divide between opposing political views widened.

There are two legal approaches to guilt and innocence—guilty until proven innocent, or innocent until proven guilty. For 19th Century immigrants coming to the new United States of America, the appeal was the latter. Innocent until proven guilty is a fundamental principal of American law. Freedom of religion, the right to worship as one chooses is another. Sometimes these founding principals get in the way of forming the politically correct, inclusive, multicultural society progressive-liberals seek. After all, individual rights have no importance in a country where the government controls everything for the good of all—whether the people like it or not.

Chapter 34

Ontario, California
August 1, 2015

Hector Gomez and his pal, Jesus Hernandez were blowing the last of their paychecks at the El Farol Rojo bar. At closing time the pair staggered out in search of Hector's car, but it wasn't where Hector remembered leaving it.

"Ish that it over there?" Jesus drunkenly asked, pointing to a car he thought looked like Hector's.

"Zat look'sh like it," Hector slurred, hanging on to Jesus as they stumbled toward the car, "but I'm sh're I didn' park it here."

"Try y'r key, shee if it fits."

Surprisingly—at least to Hector—the engine started and the pair began slowly riding through the city, attempting to find their apartment building. This time Jesus wasn't much help. A month earlier Hector had found an empty ground-floor apartment with an unlocked rear window and moved in—squatted actually. Jesus joined him there two weeks later.

After several false stops, the pair finally located the building they were looking for and stumbled inside the entry hall. "Hector, thi'sh look'sh like our door," Jesus said, inserting the key they'd found in a kitchen drawer in their commandeered apartment's kitchen. Frustrated when the key wouldn't turn, Hector began pounding on the door. Why he thought there would be someone inside to open it remains a mystery.

Derrick Johnson was sound asleep when a loud pounding on his apartment door awakened him. Groggy, he looked at his alarm clock. It was 3:12 a.m. "What the hell is going on?" he muttered getting out of bed and stumbling toward the door. Looking through a wide-angle peephole in the door, he saw a stranger—no there were actually two strangers—in the hall. Opening the door with its chain lock attached, Johnson peered through the crack and asked, "What do you want?

"Want inshide," Hector slurred, attempting to push the door open. But deterred by the chain lock and too drunk to react, he cursed in frustration as Johnson quickly slammed the door shut and locked it.

"GO AWAY, DAMN YOU ... YOU'RE AT THE WRONG APARTMENT," Hector heard Johnson shout through the door.

"ASH'HOLE," Hector yelled back.

"What's going on Dad?" asked Johnson's sixteen-year-old son, Tom, who'd also been awakened in his rear bedroom by the pounding.

"Nothing to worry about, son, just a couple of drunks at the wrong door. Go back to bed."

Jesus Hernandez, who was slightly more coherent than his friend, said, "Hesh'tor, they must've changed the lock. Le'sh climb in the back window like you did the firsh time."

"Good idea."

Staggering down the hall, the pair found the back exit and entered the alleyway. Once behind the building, it took them some time to determine exactly which apartment they'd squatted in—a difficult task for two drunks on a dark night.

"Dish is it," Hector said pointing up to an open window. "Boosh me up," he said reaching up to grasp the window ledge.

"*Ughhh* ... Get your fat assh up in t'ere," Jesus, grunted. "I can't holt choo forever," he groaned hefting Hector up with such force that his drunken buddy tumbled through the screened window.

"WHAT THE HELL!" Tom exclaimed, as Hector landed on top of him.

"WHATCHA DOIN' IN MY BED?" Hector shouted, viciously battering Tom in the face.

"GET OFF ME," Tom screamed, shoving Hector off the bed and fighting back with all his strength. "GET OFF ... GET OFF ME," Tom continued screaming as the violent struggle spilled out into the hall, and the pair fell to the floor with Hector on top.

Awakened by Tom's screaming and the sounds of the fight, Derrick Johnson sprang from his bed, threw open his bedroom door and turned on the hall light. What he saw horrified him, not only was the man from the hall straddling his son and beating him bloody, but he was pretty sure he saw the other man standing in Tom's bedroom doorway. Determining he had to do something because a stranger—maybe two strangers—had broken into his apartment and one was beating his son, Derrick shouted, "HOLD ON TOM," and rushed back in his room to retrieve his pistol.

"I'M HERE, TOM," Derrick shouted, running toward the man on top of his son.

"GET THE HELL OFF HIM! Stand up. I have a gun. DO IT NOW, OR I'LL SHOOT."

Hector was too drunk and too angry to listen to the man he thought was in *his* apartment. How the man moved in and changed the locks in one evening was beyond Hector's capability to comprehend. All Hector knew was that he had to beat the man he found in his bed—teach him a lesson.

"Dad! Help!" Tom pleaded, looking at his father with blood streaming down his face.

"**STOP! STAND UP, OR I'LL SHOOT,** Derrick screamed, but the man continued his violent attack. Frantic to save his son, Derrick realized he had no choice and triple tapped the man, just as he'd been taught to do.

Hearing the sound of gunfire, Jesus, who'd ducked back into the bedroom when the man appeared with the gun, dived out the window and ran.

After seeing to his son's injuries, Johnson called 911 for an ambulance and reported he'd just shot someone—a man who'd broken into his apartment and violently attacked his son. The recording set the time at 3:59 a.m.

Officer Pat Snyder arrived before the ambulance. As soon as he entered the apartment, Derrick pointed to the table where he'd placed his pistol. EMTs arrived a minute later, and once they'd checked the intruder and pronounced him dead, Officer Snyder began questioning Derrick.

"Was the intruder armed?"

"I didn't know if he was armed. He was on top of my son, so how could I know?" Derrick answered.

"Did you see a weapon?"

"No."

"You said you told the intruder to stand, and that he didn't."

"Yes. He kept bludgeoning my son."

"So you shot him?"

"Yes."

"At any time did you consider any other course of action, before shooting an unarmed man three times?"

Derrick didn't like where the officer was going. "What other course of action are you referring to, Officer?"

"Pulling him off your son would have been one alternate action."

"What about the other man. I didn't know where he was."

"Did you see him?"

"I thought I did."

"So, you killed an unarmed man, because you thought you saw another man."

At this point, Derrick Johnson realized he was being accused of murder and refused to answer any more questions until his attorney was present.

Officer Snyder recommended Derrick Johnson be charged with manslaughter. Progressive-liberals applauded Snyder and denigrated Johnson for murdering an unarmed Hispanic man. Defenders of the Constitution—the right of a citizen to protect his home and family—screamed foul. Officer Snyder had interjected personal values into his investigation and recommendation—specifically, that he felt citizens should not possess firearms.

Within hours of Derrick's arrest, twenty-five Second Amendment supporters rallied in his defense at the police station on South Archibald Avenue. The next day, demonstrators numbering in the hundreds stood outside demanding dismissal of all charges. The mayor ignored the protesters, setting off nationwide Facebook postings and tweets. The following day thousands of Second Amendment supporters descended on the city of Ontario, causing major traffic disruptions and attracting national news media. After a review of the evidence against Derrick Johnson, charges were dropped.

Good judgment and common sense prevailed, but not all similar clashes would be peacefully resolved.

Denver, Colorado
August 3, 2015

Colorado's new attorney general, Robert Langford, a retired Marine Corps legal officer, announced the grand jury had refused to indict Orville and Arthur Bartow for second-degree murder, manslaughter, and resisting arrest—a decision that outraged progressive-liberals. The Grand Jury found the facts in evidence did not support the charges and sighted the following reasons: the brothers had allowed National Guardsmen to search their house for a sniper rifle and none was found; a CBS camera was recording the front of their house when the shots were fired and the video showed no muzzle flashes; all the rifles in the Bartow's house were either .30-06 or .308 calibers; and the sniper's bullets were .338 caliber; thereby establishing the shots which killed the machine gunner and Zapata had been fired from a different, yet to be identified location.

Since the Grand Jury had decided that because the Bartows had agreed to allow a search once a proper warrant was presented, both the SWAT and FEMA attacks were illegal; and the brothers' right to self-defense prevailed. The brothers pleaded guilty to detonating an explosive device without a permit, received suspended sentences, and were each placed on five years probation. Photographs of Orville and Arthur standing with Rex in front of their bullet-riddled house appeared on the Internet and in local newspapers and TV.

Left wing bloggers, MSNBC and CBS news quickly vilified Colorado Attorney General Langford. On the floor of the House, Speaker Nellie Balogni denounced Langford's decision as incomprehensible, shameful and an act of cowardice. The following day, Senators Betty Boxnutter and Charles Simmerman repeated the denouncement on the floor of the Senate. Governor Hickengooper's office issued a bland statement to the effect that he respected the Grand Jury's decision.

Norfolk International Airport
9:45 a.m. Friday, August 7, 2015

Tom Hazzard and Harold Rockford watched General Beck enter the main terminal. Hazard waved a greeting, "Good morning, Tony"

"Good morning gentlemen," Tony Beck replied. "I'm ready for some serious fishing. What's biting?"

Hazard grinned and replied, "Blues, some big ones in the mouth of the bay. Been catching them with cast spoons. Average around ten pounds."

Beck's face split into a broad smile, "Now that really does sound like fun. I can't wait to tie into one."

"Me, too," Rockford added. "Tom's been feeding me fish tales ever since I arrived."

The men headed for Rockford's SUV. On the way to the *Fish Finder* they stopped at McDonalds to purchase lunch. Two hours later found them cruising at ten knots on the east side of the Chesapeake Bay Bridge. All three were looking for sea gulls hitting the water—a sure sign a school of fish was busting bait on the surface. Rockford was the first to mention the real purpose of their fishing trip. "Tony, it appears the President isn't going to take any action against those responsible for destroying our Baghdad embassy and the deaths of our people. A clear signal to other nations we're weak."

"Obviously Iran thinks so—hell, the jihadis proved it. Al-Sadr pulled a coup and now our Secretary of State is in Baghdad kissing Sadr's ass," Hazzard added.

Beck remained silent for several seconds before answering, "Intelligence has some information linking the Chicago bombings to Khomeini. Nothing firm, but it tracks."

Hazzard shook his head, "President Abomba's vacations and boondoggles are riling the troops. Every time a crisis occurs he takes a trip. He and his family went to Africa while the first Muslim Brotherhood's Egyptian government was being overthrown."

"And he only made a token attempt to support the Egyptian military when they called for new elections. A new president was elected and then assassinated by the Muslim Brotherhood—just like Nasser," Rockford added.

"Yes," Hazzard agreed, "and this time the MB played the *fatwa* card. Clerics issued *fatwas*, legal pronouncements based on Shariah, Islamic religious law. After a brief but brutal civil war, the Brotherhood managed to regain power. Now Egypt's becoming an Islamic dictatorship. After the MB regained power they purged the senior military and Western leaning intellectuals.

"Tony, our reenlistment is dropping and officers are requesting release from active duty or resigning their commissions. There's still a lot of discontent over the thirty special ops men killed in Afghanistan in that old CH-47 helicopter. Lots of unanswered questions." Hazzard let his comments hang in the air a couple of seconds before asking, "Are you two getting similar reports?"

"Yes, I have received—"

"Fish breaking at two o'clock!" Hazzard exclaimed, cutting Beck's reply short.

"About a mile away ... *HANG ON!*" he yelled, pushing the twin throttles forward. *Fish Finder* exploded out of the water onto a plane and streaked toward the flock of diving gulls. "I'll cut the engines and let the boat drift into the action. Cast as far as you can, let the spoon sink for five seconds, and then start reeling in with a jerking motion."

A few minutes later Hazzard pulled back on the throttles, allowing the *Fish Finder* to settle into the water. Then advancing the throttles far enough to gain forward motion, he turned toward the patch of boiling water. As the boat neared the action, he cut both motors and the *Fish Finder* drifted toward the feeding fish. "Cast," he told the others.

Each man cast his two and a half ounce Hopkins spoon in a different direction. Beck counted to five and jerked his rod. His second jerk resulted in a solid hit. His rod bent and the drag started screaming. "I'M INTO A GOOD ONE," he yelled.

Within seconds, all three men were fighting large blue fish. Beck was the first to bring his fish next to the boat. Grabbing the stainless steel leader with a gloved hand, he swung the twelve-pound blue fish onto the deck. Flopping around on the deck with its jaws snapping, the fish promptly freed itself from the hook. Blue fish have evenly spaced, razor-sharp, intimidating teeth, shorter in length than a barracuda's, but no less dangerous. Blues have been known to dine on the toes of any fisherman foolish enough to go barefoot or wear flip-flops.

Hazzard's fish wasn't bleeding, so he released it and put the other two into the ice chest. By the time he'd completed his task the school of fish had moved on and the water was calm. "Now we start looking again," he said, starting the motors and cruising to the northwest at six knots.

"Rocky, break out our lunch … I'm starving," he added.

Rockford retrieved the McDonald's bag and three bottles of water. Once everyone had their burgers, he brought up Beck's earlier conversation. "Just before Tom saw the fish you started to tell us something, Tony. I remember you saying, 'you'd received.' "

"Yes. I've received several phone calls from other senior commanders. Each, to varying degrees, expressed carefully worded concern about our reaction to the embassy attack and the bombing in Chicago. A couple of callers brought up the Blue Shirts … " Beck paused to stare at a distant pelican diving into the water for lunch. After collecting his thoughts, he continued. "The most disturbing elements of the calls—all the calls actually—was the possibility of the military being ordered to suppress civilian protests. How far would we be ordered to go?"

Hazzard and Rockford looked at each other, and then Rockford asked, "Do you mean fire on civilians?"

Again Beck paused to look at the pelican hunting lunch before answering. "Uh … Yes, but no one actually phrased it that way—mostly hints and innuendos." Beck pursed his lips before continuing, "That was the real reason for the calls … How to meet and discuss the issues without violating regulations pertaining to questioning civilian leadership."

"So the unasked but implied question was … would such an order be legal?" Rockford commented.

"Yes that *is* the real question," Hazzard added. "My people aren't afraid to ask. In fact they are asking."

"As are mine," Rockford agreed.

By then all three men had turned to watch the pelican, which had now been joined by a second one. After a long minute, Hazzard said, "My men are joining an organization called 'Oath Keepers.' A non-partisan association of currently and formerly serving military, police, and first responders, who pledge to fulfill the oath they all took to defend the Constitution against all enemies, foreign, and domestic. They believe the oath only applies to the Constitution—not to politicians—and refuse to obey unconstitutional orders such as warrantless searches or detaining Americans as enemy combatants; both of which they believe violate the Fourth and Fifth Amendments. In short, they won't do anything to violate their oath to protect the Constitution."

"The same in my shop," Rockford added. "In fact, I suspect many will support the protesters." Hazzard nodded, indicating the experience in his shop was the same.

Beck was rubbing his chin, contemplating his response, when Rockford pointed and exclaimed, *"Diving gull!"*

"Hang on," Hazard said, as he grabbed the steering wheel and pushed the throttles forward. Slowly turning to the west, they repeated the tactics used on the first approach and found themselves in another school of blue fish churning the surface in a feeding frenzy. In a matter of seconds all rods bent as unhappy blue fish attempted to depart the area.

Fifteen minutes later, there were three more big blues in the cooler. Before calling it a day, the trio had found two more feeding schools. That night Beck and Rockford feasted on fresh baked blue fish at Hazard's quarters.

The next morning, Beck and Rockford visited SEAL Team Six before heading to the airport to catch the afternoon flight to Charlotte. Rockford had a tight connection and departed half an hour before Beck's flight to Tampa. Once his plane was airborne, Beck settled back in his seat and chuckled, remembering discussions about Blue Shirts he and Rocky had with the SEALS. *Seals and Deltas sure aren't bashful about voicing their opinions.* Still chuckling, he opened the novel he had been trying to read for two months.

Chapter 35

Truman, Arkansas
Wednesday, August 19, 2015

$\mathbf{T}$**ommy Randall's first day of school ended at 2:45 p.m.** Tommy was in the fifth-grade and liked his teacher, Ms. Butterworth. After school, Tommy rode the school bus home to the farm five miles out of town, where he lived with his parents. Hopping off the bus at the entrance to his family's farmhouse, he ran up the long driveway and waved to his father driving their John Deer tractor in a nearby field.

Inside the house, Tommy found his mother in the kitchen snapping green beans. "How was your first day at school?" she asked.

"Great. I like Ms. Butterworth. She's new. She's from New York City—so's the new principal."

"That's nice," his mother absentmindedly replied.

"Yeah. She wants each of us to stand up and tell the class about our family on Friday. She said we can bring in something of interest to show the class."

"That's nice," his mother replied, again half listening.

"Oh, I almost forgot. Ms. Butterworth told me to give you this," Tommy said, removing a large envelope from his backpack and laying it on the kitchen table."

"What is it?"

"I don't know. She gave each of us an envelope to bring home. I didn't look inside.

"I'm going outside and ride on the tractor with dad."

His mother nodded and placed the envelope on a pile of magazines on a nearby table.

That night, Tommy lay in bed thinking about what he'd take to school on Friday.

Oak Grove Elementary School
Friday, August 21, 2015

Tommy and his friend Paul were the last students to enter the classroom and find a seat before the bell rang. Snickering softly, Paul, who'd taken a seat behind Tommy, poked his friend in the back as Ms. Butterworth walked to the front of the class. "Think her skirt's short enough?" Paul whispered.

A thin woman with mousy brown hair that fell limply to her shoulders, their teacher wore high heels, a white blouse and a tight, blue mini skirt that accentuated her bony legs. At five-feet-five some might have considered her attractive, especially Ms. Hamm the school principal—if you could believe what Paul whispered to Tommy on the bus that morning. According to Paul's dad, a detective in Jonesboro, Ms. Butterworth and the new principal, Ms. Hamm, shared a house. "So what?" Tommy had replied.

"Don't cha get it? They're from New York City. Bet they're gay … you know—*Lezies,*" Paul replied, bursting out laughing.

Tommy hadn't replied, for he wasn't sure what Paul meant by gay. *Gay? Lezies? What are they?* he'd wondered.

"Good morning class," Ms. Butterworth said closing the classroom door.

"Good morning, Ms. Butterworth," the children responded.

"This morning we'll be working on fractions. After lunch you'll tell your classmates and me about you and your family. I'm looking forward to learning more about each of you.

"Ms. Butterworth, can I ask you about something?"

Butterworth suppressed her annoyance and replied, "Of course you can, Mary."

Mary was the smartest kid in the class—probably in the school. Her father was a retired colonel, and she was very patriotic. "Ms. Butterworth, why aren't we saying the pledge of allegiance to the flag? We always did until this year."

Staring down at the pretty little girl with big brown eyes, Butterworth offered a condescending smile. "Mary, reciting a pledge to a flag can offend someone. And we wouldn't want to offend any of our other students … now would we?"

"Ms. Butterworth, how can pledging allegiance to our flag offend anyone? My father says the flag represents our Constitution."

"Some people are offended by our flag. After all, our country has done a lot of bad things.

"Now, let's get on with the lesson. Today we're going to learn how to add fractions."

Ms. Butterworth's answer troubled Tommy. *How can saying the pledge of allegiance offend? I was taught to stand up and place my hand over my heart when saying the pledge and when the National Anthem is played. My dad, granddad, and great granddad were in the Army. Great granddad was awarded lots of medals. I brought his Silver Star and his photograph to show the class. I'll ask Mary. She'll know. She's real smart.*

After lunch Tommy and his eleven classmates were ready for show and tell. Paul was the second student to stand up in front of the class. "We've lived in the Jonesboro area for the last fifteen years. My mother works at the library, and my dad's a police detective. He catches bad guys. When I grow up I'm going to be a policeman, too."

Ms. Butterworth smiled and said, "I'm sure you're proud of your father. We need policemen to keep order and protect us. Thank you, Paul."

Mary Steinberg was next. "My father retired from the Army and is now a banker. He's the president of the First National Bank in Jonesboro. His father was also a banker, and our family has lived in the area since 1985. My mother's a lawyer and my big sister, Sarah, is a junior in high school. She's going to be doctor, and I'm going to be a banker like my father."

Ms. Butterworth smiled at the serious young lady, realizing she was from an influential family. "Thank you, Mary."

Tommy Randall, your next."

Tommy stood, and carrying a photograph and a box to the front of the classroom, placed them on a table. "My dad's a farmer, like his dad and granddad. Mom helps him run the farm. I plan to be a soldier and then a farmer, just like my dad.

"My dad, granddad and great granddad were all soldiers. My great granddad fought in the Second World War and received several medals." Tommy picked up the box from the table, opened it, and held it up for the class to see. "This is a Silver Star. Great granddad Thomas—I'm named for him—was awarded this medal for bravery in France."

"That's a very important medal," Paul said.

"Tommy, what did your great grandfather do to earn it?" asked Ms. Butterworth, who was unfamiliar with military medals.

"Ms. Butterworth, you don't earn a Silver Star. It's awarded to a soldier when other soldiers report they've performed extreme acts of bravery. Great granddad Thomas attacked a German machine gun nest and killed all the Germans. He did it with no help, all by himself."

"Did you say he killed all the Germans?" Ms. Butterworth asked with a shocked expression.

"Yes, ma'am, he sure did," Tommy replied with a big grin.

Returning his grin with a frown, Ms. Butterworth stared at Tommy in disgust.

Reacting to her expression, Tommy asked, "What's wrong with that?"

"Well, I don't think killing all of those men was necessary. He could have taken them prisoner. There's simply no excuse for killing."

Tommy and his classmates stared at their teacher. What did she mean, they all wondered?

Finally, Tommy set the box containing the medal on a table and picked up a picture frame laying face down beside it. Holding up the photograph to the class he said, "This picture of my great granddad was taken in France during the war," he said, and then, walking from one side of the room to the other, he showed the students a photo of a fierce looking young sergeant thrusting an M1 rifle with fixed bayonet toward the camera. Turning to proudly show the photo to Ms. Butterworth, Tommy smiled.

"That's a gun!" Ms. Butterworth gasped. "You brought a picture of a *gun* into the school."

"What's wrong with a picture of a gun? My great granddad was holding his rifle. The same rifle he used to kill the Germans."

"That's enough," Butterworth hissed, grabbing Tommy by the arm with her right hand and jerking him hard. "Come with me young man ... we're going to the principal's office," she said snatching the photo from him with her left hand. Then, roughly pulling him toward the door, she stormed, *"OPEN IT!"*

Astonished by their teacher practically dragging Tommy out of the room, almost every student in the room was too stunned to react—every student that is except smart, little, patriotic Mary Steinberg, who wasn't going to simply sit there and do nothing. *We can't say the Pledge and can't show a picture of a gun? This isn't right and what Ms. Butterworth did was wrong. She had no right to treat Tommy that way,* Mary decided, jumping up from her desk.

"What're you gonna do Mary?" Paul asked.

"I'm going to call my mother and tell her what happened," she exclaimed, running to the coatroom to get her cell phone from her backpack.

Bolstered by Mary's courage, Paul followed her example and quickly used his phone to call his father.

At the Randall's house Tommy's mom Betty answered the telephone,

"Hello."

"Mrs. Randall, I'm Ms. Hamm, principal at your son's school. Please come and pick him up."

"Has Tommy been hurt?" Betty gasped.

"No! He violated school policy, and he's being expelled. I want him *off* school property. Can you come and get him?"

Betty was too shocked to ask any more questions. "Of course, I'll be there in twenty minutes."

"Good, he'll be in my office." The line went dead.

Tommy's father was in Jonesboro and had forgotten his cell phone. Something Betty discovered when she called him and heard his cell phone ringing in their bedroom. Not knowing what to do, she drove to the school and headed for the principal's office. Entering, she saw her son's anxious expression, gave him a small smile and nodded reassuringly. She knew her boy and while he could be rambunctious at times, he was a good boy, respected adults and followed the rules. He'd never been in trouble at school before.

"I'm Tommy's mother. What's he supposed to have done?"

"He brought a gun to school," Ms. Hamm declared, her tone and body language radiating her feeling of superiority.

Turning to her son, Betty calmly asked, "Tommy, did you bring our shotgun to school?"

"No, ma'am. I didn't bring a gun to school. I know better than that."

Turning to the tall, butch-looking, shorthaired woman wearing a pants suit, Betty demanded, "Show me the gun."

Ms. Hamm looked down at the shorter woman, held up the offending photograph and sneered, "This gun."

Betty looked at the framed photograph that normally sat on their fireplace mantel, and then at the overbearing woman. "That's *not* a gun … that's a photograph," she said. "Don't you know the difference?"

Expecting this kind of answer from a local hick, Hamm picked up several sheets of paper stapled together. "Our new gun policy is clearly defined in these rules," she said, shaking the papers in Betty's face. "Every student was given a copy of the rules to take home. Guns are defined on page three," she said reading the policy out loud. "'A gun is any firearm, BB gun, pellet gun, replica or model of a gun, picture of photo of a gun, or any hand gesture representative of a gun. Having a gun, or any discussion of a gun on school property is grounds for expulsion.'

"Didn't you read our rules—or can't you read?"

Betty glared at Hamm. "I won't even dignify that with a response. You can't be serious. You're telling me that showing a photograph of a decorated war hero is grounds for expulsion. Lady, it's you who're going to be expelled," Betty said, and taking her son's hand was about to leave when Tommy stopped her.

"Mom, the medal's still in my classroom."

"We'll get it on the way out."

"No, you won't. You are not permitted to go back into the classroom—neither of you can."

The next thing Betty Randall said shocked her son. "Try and stop me, *bitch*."

Grabbing Betty by the arm and twisting it up behind her, Hamm marched her out her office toward the school's front entrance. "Didn't take much effort to stop you—Did it *bitch*?" she said, viciously shoving Betty out the door.

"MOM!" Tommy yelled, pushing past the principal and out the door to help his mother up from where she'd fallen.

"Don't ever set foot on school property again, or I'll have you arrested." Hamm stormed, pulling the door shut.

What Hamm didn't know was that one of Tommy's playmates, Howie, was returning from the bathroom when he saw Mrs. Randall enter the building. Following her to the principal's office, he'd hung around the hall outside Hamm's open door trying to hear what was being said. When Hamm burst into the hall shoving Mrs. Randall toward the school's entrance, he'd scurried away to hide and watch.

Already intimidated by Hamm's masculine appearance and perpetual scowling, Howie was terrified; for now he was seeing Tommy's poor sweet mom—a grownup woman no less—being violently shoved around by the new principal. *What would she do to me—a little kid—if she caught me snooping?* Howie shuddered to think as he stood watching Mrs. Randall go flying out the door. Suddenly having to pee again, he ran back to the restroom to relieve himself and call his father.

By the time Betty and Tommy reached home, word of the incident was rippling through the community. John Randall found out when he entered Jonesboro's bank and Mary's father motioned for him to come to his office.

Five minutes later John Randall was speeding through Jonesboro heading home. When he arrived, he found several of his neighbors talking to Betty. After listening to his son and wife's description of what happened, he headed for his truck.

Chapter 36

Oak Grove Elementary School
Friday, August 22, 2015

A **caravan of pickup trucks and SUVs arrived** at the school just as the school buses were departing. John Randall, a powerfully built man who stood well over six-feet, got out of his truck. Followed by ten other men, he entered the school and headed for the principal's office. Turning to his followers, he said, "See if you can find me a text book with a picture of a gun or a cannon—a nice big text book."

When Ms. Hamm heard men's voices in the hall, she'd opened her office door and looked out. Surprised to see men opening classroom doors, she was about to ask them what they were doing, when she noticed a large man followed by four other men striding toward her. Disturbed by their angry expressions, she quickly closed and locked the door.

John Randall saw a large, shorthaired woman standing in an open doorway looking at him, and recognized her from Betty's description. When the woman ducked back into the room and closed the door, he knew he had her trapped. Tuning the doorknob and finding the office locked he began pounding on the door and shouting, "OPEN THIS DOOR, I know you're in there and I want to talk to you."

"What do you want?"

"I'm Tommy Randall's father and you're going to explain your actions toward my son and my wife."

"Mr. Randall, you'll have to take that up with the superintendent. Now leave or I'll call the police."

"Like hell I will," Randall muttered, and taking two steps backward, he surged forward and used his right foot to shatter the door's lock. Bursting through the door, he saw the woman standing in front of a desk pushing buttons on her cell phone. Fueled by anger and without conscious thought, Randall's muscle memory took over, and dropping his shoulder, he charged. Randall, who'd been an all-state star tackle on his high school football team, hadn't forgotten how to throw a block. Surprised by the swiftness of Randal's attack, Hamm grunted when the big man's shoulder impacted her sternum, knocking her to the floor and leaving her gasping for breath.

"Calling the police were you? I don't think so," Randall snarled, grabbing her cell phone and ripping the desk phone's cord out of the wall. Leaning over Hamm he snarled, "NOW, GET UP. Get up and explain your actions … or I'll beat the answer out of you."

"NO, please don't hit her again!" a woman behind Randall yelled.

Surprised to hear another woman's voice in the room, Randall whirled around toward the sound, "Who the hell are you?" he asked the skinny, stringy-hired woman standing off to the side of the battered office door.

"I–I'm Tommy's teacher, Ms. Butterworth."

Randall grinned and said, "Good, you've also got a lot of explaining to do. Get over here next to your boss."

Constance Butterworth cowered. She didn't like the man's grin, and he frightened her.

Turning back to the temporarily cowed principal, Randall said, "Now, *get up* … get in your chair and tell me where this stupid gun policy came from? In case you've forgotten, you're not in New York City anymore."

Scrambling to her feet Hamm plopped down in her chair and defiantly squared her shoulders. Attempting to assert her authority, she hissed, "You'll pay for what you've just done to me—the school board will not stand for this."

Randall's angry expression caused her to add, "But in answer to your question, the board hired Mr. Grover Smythington as superintendent of schools, because your county schools had fallen below the national average. His job is to upgrade FCAT scores. He hired Ms. Butterworth and me to help him—in fact, he hired twenty teachers from the New York City area for the same purpose."

"That's not what I asked you … answer my question, damn it. Explain the so-called 'gun policy.' How in God's name can you say a photograph of a gun is a gun?"

Hamm puffed up and proclaimed, "That's our policy. Your son was given a copy of the new policy to take home and today he violated it. We have *zero tolerance* for mistakes that involve guns. I explained it to your wife. Tommy is expelled. That's all there is to it."

"I've found one," a man declared, entering the room and showing Randall the cover of a large book entitled *American History*. "Look at this," he continued opening the book to a picture of George Washington leading a column of men carrying muskets.

"Well I'll be damned," Randall said, smirking as he looked at the picture. "Isn't this amazing? Take a close look a this," he said turning the big book around so Hamm could see it. "Aren't those guns?"

Hamm averted her eyes, refusing to look at the picture.

Stepping around her desk to get closer to her, Randall held the book so the picture was half a foot from her face. In response Hamm glared up at him and turned her head away. Disgusted with the woman, Randall shook his head, stepped back, and began flipping pages until he found a picture of another gun. This time it was a WWI soldier holding an Enfield rifle.

"What about this photo?" he asked, again showing Hamm the picture.

Glancing at the photo, Hamm sneered and refused to answer.

Randall continued flipping pages until he found a WWII photo of men holding M1 rifles. "And this photo?" he asked.

Still glaring at Randal, Hamm continued refusing to look at the photo or to speak.

"You're either as stubborn as a mule or just plain stupid ... or maybe you just need a closer look," Randall snarled, leaning over Hamm and shoving the open book against her face—literally rubbing her face in it.

"Is that or isn't that a picture of a gun?" Randall stormed.

Hamm still made no reply.

"By God you really are an officious bitch," Randall snarled jerking the book away.

Hamm curled her lips, baring her teeth.

"Cat still got your tongue? Maybe we need to do something about that," Randall sneered, snapping the book shut and hefting it with his right hand.

"If I'm not mistaken you said the new gun policy is 'zero tolerance.' Well, I have zero tolerance for idiotic bureaucrats who refuse to answer their employer's questions. In case you've forgotten ... you work for me."

Glaring at Hamm, Randall closed the heavy book and looked at its cover. "And just as your zero tolerance policy has consequences—SO DOES MINE," he stormed, lunging forward and striking the domineering woman on the side of her head with the flat side of the book.

Knocked out of her chair and stunned by the blow, Hamm lay face down on the floor, her thoughts whirling in an attempt to grasp what just happened. Groaning and rolling over, she squinted up into Randall's hard face.

"As I said, I have *zero tolerance* for fools like you. Now, get up and sit in your chair ... I have more questions, and I expect straight answers—not some pinko, commie, socialist, progressive-liberal bullshit."

Groaning softly, Hamm continued lying on the floor, but no one—not even Butterwort, who was cowering in a corner behind Hamm's desk—attempted to help her.

Finally able to stand, Hamm managed to get back in her chair. Once self-assured, overbearing and authoritative, Hamm was, for the first time in her life, frightened. Feeling as though she was living a nightmare, she was conflicted. *This can't possibly be happening to me,* she told herself, but it was. *Here I am in this podunk, hick town, attempting to enlighten the rednecks, and this my reward.*

Carl, the man who'd found the history book, spoke to her for the first time. "My son tells me you no longer say the pledge of allegiance at the start of the school day—*Explain that.*"

Hamm hated having to deal with these uneducated bumpkins, but, warily looking at Randal, who still held the heavy history book; she also didn't want to be hit on the head again, so she reluctantly muttered, "Some students may find the pledge offensive."

"Well, I not only find your policy offensive, I find you offensive as well," Carl responded, shaking his fist at her.

"So do I," another man added.

"Me too."

Carl leaned forward and looked into the woman's eyes. "You and your little sniveling squeeze are more than offensive—you're disgusting. So, I suggest you both go back to New York ... Go back today ... because if you're still here tomorrow, I'll personally tar and feather both of you—with *real* hot tar and real feathers," he said, emphasizing the word real and prompting the other men to roar with laughter.

Looking aghast at the laughing men, Hamm's eyes were suddenly drawn to where Butterworth sat on the floor sobbing.

"That's very good advice," Randall said, grabbing Hamm's shirtfront and yanking her out of her chair. "But enough of this! I have some zero tolerance issues myself: first, there's your unwarranted expulsion of my son, and your abuse of my wife; and second, your illegal seizure of my family's cherished personal property.

"Understand this bitch ... my son *will be* in school tomorrow. If he has any problems with you, this little episode will look like child's play compared to what will happen next. Now, where's our photo and my grandfather's medal?"

Despite her pompous demeanor, Hamm had never been manhandled. Now, with her brow dripping sweat and insides shaking like jelly, she was terrified. *This man is crazy ... Hell! ... They're all crazy ... crazy enough to do whatever they want to us.*

"The photo is over there—*Take it,*" she said, pointing to a worktable.

"Where's the medal?"

"I–I don't know. I–I haven't seen it."

"You're the teacher—" Randall said, whirling around and glaring down at Butterworth. "WHERE'S THE MEDAL?"

Cringing and raising her forearm over her head in fear, Butterworth whimpered, "I–In the trashcan. I–I threw the disgusting thing away."

"Disgusting thing?" Randall hissed through clenched teeth, reaching down to grab hold of her hair and yank her to her feet. "Take me to the trash can. And you'd damn well better pray it's there." Still holding Butterworth by her hair, he marched her out of Hamm's office into the hall. "Now, where's the damn trashcan?"

Sobbing and stumbling, Butterworth led the men down the hall to her classroom, "It's in there."

Randall opened the door and shoved her into the classroom, causing her to slam into a student desk and fall.

"Now," he said following her into the room, "CRAWL!"

"What?" Butterworth mumbled.

"I said crawl, " he repeated in response to the look of disbelief on Butterworth's face. "Crawl to that trashcan and get me that medal."

Randall and his friends watched Butterworth sniveling and whimpering her way to the trashcan and begin fumbling through its contents. "Here it is—take it," she mumbled pulling the black leatherette presentation box out of the can and handing it up Randall.

Reverently taking the box and holding it near his mouth to blow pencil shavings and graphite off the box, Randall flipped the hinged lid open and sighed in relief. His grandfather's venerated WWII medal attached to a red, white, and blue ribbon was inside.

"Disgusting thing, eh?" Randall said, holding the box so Butterworth could see it. "You call the third highest military decoration for valor awarded by the United States Armed Forces 'disgusting?' It looks to me like you're the one who's disgusting. I strongly suggest you leave the state before tomorrow morning."

Tucking the box in his pocket, Randall turned and led the others out of the school building.

Eleanor Hamm and Constance Butterworth called their boss, Superintendent Grover Smythington using Butterworth's cell phone. After reporting their altercation, they listened to the superintendent's reply. "This is an outrage. I will not stand for you being treated this way. Meet me at the sheriff's office and file a complaint. *These men are going to prison.*"

Shaking her head and looking at Butterworth, Hamm replied, "You don't understand. The men in this town are savage bullies. There's no way we're staying here. We're leaving. I suggest you do the same."

The next school board meeting resulted the in entire school board being forced to resign. Superintendent Smithington had already done so. Like citizens all over America, the good people of Jonesboro were finished with political correctness and inclusiveness. More significantly they were fed up with state and federal governments seeking to control every aspect of their lives. They were beginning to understand the root of America's problem was no longer about Democrats and Republicans. Both parties had failed them. No, it was now about American values versus progressive-liberal values, and most citizens considered themselves Americans.

The national media procrastinated for two days before reporting the story. A story quickly followed by similar instances occurring across the nation. A few states were turning red or blue, but most remained white, with the red and blue divisions occurring at the local level. Texas was the poster child for this phenomenon. Progressive-liberals fleeing stagnating eastern states had moved to Texas to take advantage of the state's low taxes. And, like newcomers to Temple, they sought elected office and began imposing the same type of dictatorial rules that had ruined their former states. Modern-day carpetbaggers from the north had overrun Texas, and the citizens had finally noticed.

Chapter 37

New gun rules created zero tolerance incidents all across the nation. Banning toy guns, action figures, photographs, and clothing with pictures of guns resulted in children being arrested for breaking these ridiculous rules. For example, police were called when one young boy used his hand to simulate a pistol. Out of all the similar incidents, only one involved a real gun, and it was unloaded. A growing number of parents throughout America were developing zero tolerance for inane zero tolerance policies.

A young man, an Eagle Scout and a high school senior, made a life-altering mistake one Monday morning after parking his truck in his school parking lot. Running late for homeroom sign-in, the young man reached behind his seat to retrieve his book bag and cringed. Lying on the floor next to his bag was the shotgun he'd used Sunday afternoon, while shooting skeet at a gun club with his friends. Suddenly remembering he was supposed to be at a family cookout, he rushed home. Afterward, he helped clean up and forgot to take his shotgun in the house.

Now standing beside his truck and knowing the schools' zero tolerance gun policy, the young man panicked. Fearful of the consequences for not doing the right thing, he considered his options. Having a gun on school property was an offense, leaving school property was an offense, and leaving the shotgun in his truck was an offense. Perhaps he could call someone to come and get the shotgun, but this also presented another problem, because use of cell phones on school property was not allowed.

After several agonizing minutes, he decided to leave his shotgun in the truck and use the phone in the school office to call his mother to come and get his shotgun. Unfortunately, a member of the PC police in the office overheard his phone call and reported it to the principal, who made a mindless, bureaucratic decision and gave the young man a one-year suspension. By choosing to follow zero tolerance dictates instead of giving the young man a good ass chewing, the principal's punishment negated the boy's applications to colleges and ended any chance he might have had for a scholarship.

What, if anything, did this zero tolerance incident accomplish toward helping a young man become a productive citizen and making society safer from gun owners? What lesson did the young boy learn from his unwarranted punishment? More importantly, what lesson did it impart to other young people? If he'd simply left his shotgun behind the seat and gone on with his school day, no one would have been the wiser. However, because he tried to do what was right, the boy and his parents learned the irony of the lesson zero tolerance conveyed. Doing the right thing was wrong, and doing the wrong thing was right. A lesson that could have had positive results, if common sense had prevailed—something that would never be allowed to happen when zero tolerance dictates were strictly imposed.

In another zero tolerance anti-gun incident, the father of a third-grader was arrested, after becoming enraged with a school administrator for calling police and having his son handcuffed and arrested for using his hand to simulate a gun. According to court records, the father willingly admitted bashing the school's superintendent in the head during a heated discussion over the stupidity of the arrest.

"I tried repeatedly to get Dr. Cranston to understand a nine-year old couldn't be expected to understand the complexities of these new rules," the father told the investigating officer. "I tried to tell Dr. Cranston having my son arrested was excessive. I really did … but no, instead of listening to me, he kept quoting the school's zero tolerance policy and waving the rules in my face. After several attempts to make him see reason, I picked up an autographed baseball bat he kept by his desk and I used it to get his attention."

The arresting officer reportedly told the father he understood his frustration, but giving the superintendent a concussion was excessive. In the end, the officer said he had no choice but to arrest the father and charge him with assault.

While Anti-gun progressive-liberals celebrated the high school student's expulsion and the irate father's arrest, citizens with common sense began recognizing the absurdity and unintended consequences of zero tolerance rules. As the months passed, more zero tolerance incidents occurred, triggering increased numbers of citizen protests and demonstrations, and ultimately resulting in violent clashes with law enforcement. Soon police found themselves pitted against the very people they were paid to protect, prompting many officers not only to question the law, but also to object to enforcing it. Progressive-liberals, however, continued employing their illogical logic, declaring that protests validated the need for more laws and the elimination of all guns.

As time wore on and more anti-gun related violence occurred, the nation grew increasingly divided on the issue of government control over private gun ownership. Planned protests pushing racial inequality became a focal point for anti-gun protesters to push their agenda. For an administration bent on gun control and a media looking for sensational headlines, racial friction was added ink for the press and fodder for anti-gun fanatical ravings. No effort—no matter how outrageous the scheme—was overlooked in the administration's plot to disarm America's gun owners. Pitting white against black soon became the norm.

The much-publicized George Zimmerman trial was a prime example of how far an administration's progressive-liberal agenda is willing to go to use racial tension to achieve their agenda.

In what turned out to be one of America's most poorly prosecuted white against black murder trials in recent times, twenty-eight year old Neighborhood Watch captain, George Zimmerman was charged with maliciously stalking and shooting a hoodie-wearing, seventeen-year old "black child," Trayvon Martin, at point-blank range.

Dubbed a "White Hispanic" by the New York Times," Zimmerman was portrayed as a "wannabe cop" by prosecutors, who—in a case based more on fiction than facts—alleged Zimmerman had it in for blacks. The prosecution, ignoring the numerous break-ins in the townhouse community where the shooting occurred, alleged Zimmerman was angry because nothing ever came of him reporting young black men hanging around and being up to no good in his neighborhood: he thought they were always getting away with some illegal activity. According to prosecutors, Zimmerman was determined to see that this black "teenaged-child"—so named by the prosecution—wasn't getting away. In attempting to prove it's fiction, the prosecution turned a simple self-defense case into a racially motivated murder trial.

Such were the prosecution's allegations.

What follows are the facts.

According to investigative police reports presented during the trial, George Zimmerman had reported other incidents of seeing suspicious looking young men in his neighborhood. There had been several robberies in the months prior to the night he shot Martin. However, the implication that Zimmerman maliciously set out to stalk Martin, a black "teenaged-child," was categorically untrue.

The truth of the story lies in the jury's not guilty verdict, which was based on the following facts in evidence presented in sworn testimony during the trial. George Zimmerman was driving to the store that dark rainy night, when he spotted a hoodie-wearing figure apparently prowling and loitering near the townhomes. After contacting the non-emergency police dispatch number to report he'd seen a suspicious acting person who'd run off and disappeared, Zimmerman left his truck to locate a street sign that would designate a clearer location for the police. Told by the dispatcher not to follow the individual he'd seen, Zimmerman was returning to his truck when, without warning, the five-eleven, 158 pound, black, "teenaged-child" jumped out from behind some bushes and accosted him by yelling, "What the fuck's your problem homie?"

Telling Martin he didn't have a problem, Zimmerman was getting his cell phone out to call 911, when Martin suddenly knocked him to the ground with a bone-breaking punch to his nose. Then, straddling a screaming Zimmerman and telling him, "You're going to die tonight," Martin began pounding his face and painful broken nose and bashing his head bloody on a concrete sidewalk—a style of assault one witness described as "ground-and-pound."

Stunned and unable to free himself from the unexpected assault, Zimmerman—whose personal trainer described him as "physically soft"— lay pinned to the ground, fearing for his life and screaming for help, while Martin viciously beat him. Ultimately wriggling free enough to reach for his permitted, concealed handgun, George shot and killed his attacker.

Sanford police arrived shortly after the shooting and interviewed witnesses and Zimmerman. After receiving limited medical treatment from an EMT, Zimmerman was taken to the police station and interviewed a second time. Carefully reviewing both statements, investigators initially determined Martin's shooting was a clear-cut case of self-defense and Zimmerman was released. In a rational world, that should have been the end of the story, but for the rabid media and certain high-profile civil rights agitators this was only the beginning.

Progressive-liberals, black activists and the Pulitzer hungry media immediately blamed Zimmerman, a white man, calling him a murderer. Later when the media realized Zimmerman was Hispanic, they invented a new term, "White Hispanic," thereby making George Zimmerman the first

"White Hispanic" person in the U.S. Once again, facts contradicted ideology, so facts had to be ignored.

The liberal media went into a feeding frenzy, and complete with a much-publicized innocent looking photo of a twelve-year-old Trayvon, immediately convicted Zimmerman by reporting that he was a stalker who murdered a "child." Facts didn't matter, only sensational coverage did. A few conscientious reporters attempted to investigate before reporting, but they were ignored.

Spurred on by the likes of two leading, race-baiting reverends, Jesse Jackson and Al Sharpton, Trayvon's mother wasted no time joining the race-baiters in stirring up racial tension and starting protests. Jackson and Sharpton—assisted by the U.S. Justice Department's Community Relations Service unit—organized marches in Stanford, Florida and demanded justice for Trayvon.

As it happens, Florida is divided into twenty Judicial Circuit Court Districts. The city of Stanford is in the 18th Judicial Circuit, and Jackson, Sharpton and the media were enraged over Zimmerman's release, and the slow, methodical approach to prosecutorial justice the 18th Circuit was taking. The race-baiters and their supporters wanted blood, and determined to get it, began putting pressure on Florida's governor to appoint a special prosecutor—a scalp hunter from out of the area who would better serve their goal of getting Zimmerman indicted. A little over a month after Trayvon Martin was shot, Florida's Governor Rick Scott and Attorney General Pam Bondi worked together to appoint Angela B. Corey, State Attorney for the 4th Judicial Circuit, as the special prosecutor.

Thus began a prosecution driven by emotion and politics, rather than facts and evidence. Why emotion you may ask? The answer quite simply is that's all the prosecution had—lots of emotion and very few facts to support a conviction. Later, the Zimmerman case would be labeled one of the most mishandled and politically motivated prosecutions in recent U.S. history. Prompting one local wag to suggest the three prosecutors, might be better described as bounty hunters, and should star in a movie entitled, *The Three Stooges Prosecute.*

In a related incident, Zimmerman's defense team subpoenaed whistle-blower Ben Kruidbos, former director of information technology for the 4th Judicial Circuit State Attorney. Testifying at a pre-trial hearing, Kruidbos stated he believed his boss, State Attorney Angela Corey, purposely excluded evidence he'd extracted (recovered) from Trayvon Martin's cell phone.

Saying he was concerned he would be held liable if all the information he'd recovered wasn't presented to the defense, Kruidbos testified his report was more than three times the size of the one prosecutors gave the defense. For example, he said the prosecution only gave 2,958 photos to the defense when his report contained 4,275. According to Kruidbos testimony, prosecutors excluded (deleted) photographs and text messages he'd recovered. Evidence that included: a picture of a hand holding a semi-automatic pistol; pictures of what appeared to be marijuana plants; and text messages pertaining to buying and selling pistols. Also excluded were messages pertaining to Martin's fights and him bragging about winning a fight by punching his opponent on his nose, mounting him and giving him a pound down. Kruidbos was later fired for his testimony and is suing the state, citing a statute that makes it illegal to fire someone for testimony given under subpoena.

In one of several rulings seeming to favor the prosecution, the judge in the case excluded Trayvon's school records from the record—even though they included his two suspensions. The last suspension came after Trayvon was caught on a school surveillance camera using a marker to write graffiti on a door. When police searched his book bag looking for the marker, they found suspicious items in his book bag: items, which included what appeared to be burglary tools and numerous pieces of women's jewelry tied to a list of stolen property from a residence near the school.

After his second suspension, his mother, who was divorced from his father, ordered Trayvon out of her house and arranged to have him sent to Stanford to live with his father's girlfriend. When commenting on the Trayvon's poor record in a March 26, 2012 article, *The Miami Herald* stated, "Multiple suspensions paint a complicated portrait of Trayvon Martin."

Despite the fact a jury acquitted George Zimmerman based on the facts in evidence, progressive-liberals ignored the prosecutorial mistakes and the growing hostility of conservatives. Charging ahead with their agenda, civil rights activists insisted on inciting racial conflict.

Now a similar incident had occurred.

Chapter 38

Mudford, Alabama
September 17, 2015

Larry Puckett, a middle-aged man of medium height, stopped at a Quick Shop for gasoline on his way home from his night shift at Mudford's cattle feed plant. After paying for his gas, Puckett left the store with a cup of coffee and a doughnut. No sooner had he reached his vehicle than a pair of hoodie-wearing "teenaged children" appeared out of the dark. Slamming five-foot eight Puckett against his truck the six-foot plus "teenage children" demanded his money and keys. When Puckett refused their demands, one of the "teenage children" punched him in his face and knocked him to the ground, where the other "teenage child" set about viciously kicking him in his ribs and kidneys.

Like George Zimmerman, Puckett also had a concealed weapons permit and was packing a small .45 semiautomatic pistol; however, unlike Zimmerman, Puckett was physically fit from heavy labor in the feed plant. Wiry and determined to defend himself, Puckett managed to roll away from his attacker's heavy boots, draw his pistol from behind his right hip and fire two rounds into the "teenage child's" chest; just as the youth raised his heavy boot to stomp him in the face. Hearing the gunshots and seeing his fellow gangbanger double over and slump to the ground, the other "teenage child" lunged forward screaming in rage and jumped on Plunkett. Still pointing his gun upward, Puckett quickly jammed it into his attacker's chest and shot him point blank.

Regrettably, both "teenage children" perished before the ambulance summoned by the Quick Shop's clerk arrived. Later, the two "children," both seventeen-year-olds with long rap sheets, were identified by their first names as Artavius and Scandale.

Shortly after the "children's" shootings, Reverend Tobias Dullston, a black activist preacher renowned for stirring up racial trouble, arrived and quickly demonstrated his skill. Egged on by the reverend and the media, protesters from several states—their transportation paid for by anonymous donors—began pouring into town demanding Puckett's arrest. Their calls for a second-degree murder indictment echoed through Mudford's normally peaceful streets. Nonetheless, given the evidence against the "teenage children," the local police and prosecutor's office decided Puckett acted in self-defense.

Within days violence erupted. Community organizers from Chicago and California led "bash mobs" through the quiet town, reeking havoc, robbing, and destroying local businesses. After two days and nights of anarchy, Mudford's police force was exhausted. As the influx of protesters and rioters continued, the police were unable to maintain the peace, and local citizens took up arms in the defense of their town.

On the third morning after his arrival, Reverend Dullston was ranting at a rally in the town's park: a rally demanding racial justice for Artavius and Scandale. It was readily apparent to authorities that Dullston was inciting another riot. However, even though local law enforcement was standing by, nothing could have prepared the town for what happened next.

The good reverend was waving his hand in the air to make a point, when to everyone's horror a sniper's bullet punched a hole between the reverend's eyes. Chaos ensued. Enraged by seeing their leader killed, Dullston's followers exploded from the park, intent on burning the town to the ground. Rioters blew through the police lines, set several stores on fire; and then, with lit Molotov cocktails in hand, headed for residential houses on adjoining streets.

Determined to save their town from destruction and prepared to introduce the angry mob to southern justice, homeowners, armed with shotguns, rifles and pistols awaited the madding crowd's arrival. Before the police and newly arrived sheriff's deputies could restore order, a bloodbath had occurred.

The following day, with the town reeling from death and destruction, Department of Justice investigators arrived and began building a case to prosecute those who'd shot demonstrators, completely ignoring the fact that the demonstrators were clearly attempting to burn houses.

Mudford's mayor, who'd had enough of outsiders, quickly put a stop to federal intervention in a local issue. Calling a public hearing to declare his refusal to allow DOJ to prosecute innocent citizens, the mayor instructed the sheriff to take the investigators into custody, escort them to the airport, and send them back to Washington, DC. At the entrance to the boarding ramp, the sheriff handed the senior FBI agent a message for U.S. Attorney General Helder—"DON'T COME BACK."

"Who does this asshole think he his?" President Abomba raged after reading the Alabama sheriff's message. Determined not to tolerate such insubordination by mere peons, President Abomba decided to employ JFK's solution to what he considered a similar problem and federalized the Alabama National Guard. It seemed like a good idea at the time, but there was a slight problem.

Whereas JFK federalized Alabama's National Guard to force the Governor George C. Wallace to comply with federal court orders to allow Negroes admission to a state university, Abomba intended to use federal troops to force the conviction of an innocent man. He'd failed to recognize the difference between two young black people seeking an education, and two young black thugs attempting a robbery.

Learning of President Abomba's order, Governor Todd promptly de-federalized his National Guard, consequentially setting up a Constitutional challenge. Other southern states expressed support for Alabama, and hinted at seceding if the president didn't back down.

The president called a council of war.

The White House
October 1, 2015

Secretary of Homeland Security Incompentado, Attorney General Helder, Secretary of Defense Haggler, and Vickie Barrett entered a secure White House conference room and waited for the president to arrive. When the door opened a few minutes later, Abomba strolled in and sat facing the others in a chair next to Barrett. Frowning and glaring around the table, Abomba wasted no time on pleasantries, "The 'Mudford Incident,' as it's been dubbed by MSNBC, is unacceptable.

"Totally unacceptable!

"We're here to decide how to respond. *I want ideas*, people," he barked.

While everyone sat in silence, the president impaled his secretary of defense with angry eyes.

Seeming to shrink in size, Haggler bit the corner of his lower lip and attempted to phrase his response. Finally he said what he'd been thinking, "Mr. President, you have the authority to declare martial law—order the Army to occupy the town. Then federal agents can take the troublemakers into custody."

Liking the idea, Abomba pursed his lips, squinted and nodded his head.

"However, Mr. President, I am not sure how the Army commanders will respond. Governor Todd will activate the Alabama National Guard, and he may order the Guard to prevent federal troops from entering Alabama or the town.

"Sir, I hate to think what will occur if National Guard and U.S. Army units engage each other."

Squinting and obviously annoyed, Abomba stared at Haggler in disbelief. "You can't be serious. Do you really think a state National Guard would fight a U.S. Army unit? They wouldn't stand a chance."

Staring back in amazement, Haggler suddenly realized how little his boss—the military's Commander in Chief—actually knew about the military he commanded. *What the hell do I say now? He doesn't take criticism well. On the other hand, it might be better to get fired, before he starts a second civil war. Oh well, here goes.*

"Mr. President," Haggler paused to bite his upper lip and look at the tabletop. "Mr. President, our Army is partially composed of National Guard units. They have the same training, experience, and equipment as the regular Army. If an engagement ... er, a battle were to occur, it would be brutal." *Brutal, that is, if an Army unit would actually engage the Alabama National Guard, and I'm not sure that they would,* a thought Haggler did not dare to vocalize. However the president picked up on the "if."

"What'd you mean by *if?* Are you implying that *my* Army would disobey orders from *me,* their Commander in Chief?" Abomba stormed, standing and slapping the table.

Barrett, who'd been quietly wondering the same the same thing, decided, *If Gene brought the topic up, that means he's worried about it. I'll call Rebecca and ask her to give me an opinion. One thing's for certain, it's way to early for such a confrontation to occur.*

Always looking for an opportunity to increase her power, Jane Incompentado spoke up, "Barry, we don't want the Army and the National Guard tangling. It would become a political nightmare and conservatives would have a field day." Abomba nodded and sat down, "I can send my Blue Shirts to maintain the peace and ensure the town's security. That's part of Homeland Security's job," Incompentado continued. "The governor will be reluctant to challenge DHS. Ed can send his FBI agents with my Blue Shirts to investigate the shootings and make arrests. The local police will not be a problem."

Glad to be off the hook, Haggler heaved a silent sigh of relief, and together with Helder, who wanted in on the action, voiced agreement.

Abomba stuck out his chin and declared, "Make it so," a phrase he'd learned watching *Star Trek*.

"Now, let's discuss this seceding business. Don't these fools know I'll *never* give them permission to secede?" Abomba asked, glaring at Helder.

Inwardly cringing, for now it was his turn to worry about how to inform the president he was wrong without causing him to melt down, Helder cautiously said, "Uh ... Barry, the Constitution is silent on the issue of a state withdrawing from the Union. Article Five, Section Three establishes how new states can join or be formed, but there's no mention of withdrawing.

"The Articles of Confederation, which preceded the Constitution, contained the words, 'By these, the Union was solemnly declared to 'be perpetual,' however, these words were not incorporated in the Constitution; and thus, secession arguments have raged since the Union was formed. Many have asked whether secession is a constitutional right, or is secession a natural right of revolution?

"*Let me get this right*," Abomba said, a sharp edge in his voice and holding up his hand to interrupt Helder's comments.

"You're telling me I don't have the *right* to approve or disapprove secession? You mean they can just secede?"

"Uh, Barry," Helder said knowing a tantrum was in the making. "There's uh ... no definitive answer. So the question is, what will we do if they do secede?"

Abomba's temper, kept hidden from the public, instantly flared. "Then *damn it* ... I'll do what Lincoln did. *Preserve the Union,*" he caustically said, rising and stomping out of the meeting.

With the war council effectively ended, most of the attendees dismissed the president's declaration as boastful rhetoric, but not Haggler and Barrett. With thoughts of another civil war sending chills down their spines, they hurried off to do damage control—Haggler to talk to Pentagon powers-that-be, and Barrett to call Colonel Collins. She wasn't sure where the military stood, and she desperately needed to find out.

Colonel Collins checked the caller ID on her phone. The White House was calling. *Hmmm, hope it's Vickie.* Picking up the receiver she answered, "Colonel Collins."

"Hi, lover … need to talk to you. Are you free tomorrow?"

"No, but I've nothing planned for the weekend."

"Sounds yummy. Can you come to Washington?" Barrett ask and was sure she heard Rebecca gasp.

"Of course. I'll catch a late afternoon flight from Tampa to Reagan National … e-mail you my arrival time. Any suggestions for a hotel?"

"No," a smiling Barrett coyly said, "You won't need one."

"Now that's what I call a plan," Collins replied, squeezing her legs together.

Barrett chuckled, "Yes, a good plan, however, this is about business. I, uh … we're concerned about the military's view on controlling civilian unrest … need to take their temperature so to speak."

Realizing the conversation had become serious, Collins chose her words carefully, "I understand. There's concern here about the Golden incident … and now the events in Alabama."

"Good. You understand. I'll meet you at the airport."

Chapter 39

Reverend Joseph Scoundrell, president of the SPECTRUM SHOVE COALITION, was holding an organizational meeting with his senior staff to plan a response to the assassination of Reverend Dullston, and the murder of Dullston's demonstrators in Mudford, Alabama. "It's been decades since white men, like those in the KKK, have shot black men on city streets, and this racist act must be dealt with—dealt with quickly," Scoundrell declared. The fact that some of the men doing the shooting were black somehow escaped the reverend's attention.

"After much prayer and deliberation, I have decided we cannot wait for the President and Attorney General to act. Instead, I plan to lead a convoy to Mudford and march through the town. I want to lead a million-man march from Atlanta to Mudford, Alabama. Put out a call for supporters and demonstrators." he told attendees.

Immediately after the meeting, Scoundrell's secretary posted the following announcement on SPECTRUM SHOVE'S Facebook page: "After much prayer and deliberation, Reverend Scoundrell announces plans to lead a Million-Man March to Mudford, Alabama to honor the lives of Reverend Tobias Dullston, and the two children, Artavius and Scandale. Marchers will protest these racist murders and demand justice be served on their killer or killers. All interested parties are directed to assemble near Atlanta at a location to be tweeted on Thursday. The convoy will depart Friday morning, driving slowly west on I-20 into Alabama, and then north on U.S. 27 to Mudford. In addition, the reverend plans to lead a foot march through the town on Saturday, October 10th." Tweets followed the Facebook posting and SPECTRUM SHOVE began chartering buses.

Later that evening, Reverend Scoundrell could be found relaxing in his expensive executive desk in his home office, reading postings coming on SPECTRUM SHOVE'S Facebook page. Sipping 91 proof Wild Turkey Bourbon the reverend was ecstatic over the overwhelming number of responses he was getting to the announcement of his Million-Man March.

Humming, "Happy days are Here Again," he leaned back with his eyes closed, envisioning miles of automobiles and buses rolling along two abreast, flowing west on the interstate into Alabama. Always looking for an opportunity, Scoundrell gloated over his secret plan to use Dullston's passing to turn the good reverend into a martyr for the liberal cause. *Ah, yes, this truly is, like that last Facebook posting says, a "noble cause."* Scoundrell sighed, but then, amused by his real motive for the march, he chuckled. For years he'd secretly hated Dullston for constantly stealing the limelight from him. Chuckling again, he sat forward to take another sip of bourbon before leaning back to scheme. *With Dullston gone, I can absorb his organization. Hmmm, I can name the new organization the SPECTRUM KINETIC SHOVE COLLATION.* Smiling at the thought, and with dollar signs floating in front of his eyes, the reverend drifted off to sleep.

Washington, DC
Friday morning, October 2, 2015

Secretary of Homeland Security Jane Incompentado was discussing recent events in Mudford with her FEMA Corps commander, General Sherman, a retired Army brigadier general. A map showing Alabama and Georgia was projected on a large screen in her office. "General, we need to establish a presence in Mudford as quickly as possible.

"Yes, ma'am, I understand. I plan to assemble a company size force here," Sherman said, gesturing to the map and placing the red dot from a laser pointer on Cartersville, Georgia. "Our convoy will proceed southwest on State Road 113, and then turn west on U.S. 278," he said, continuing to use the laser pointer to trace the route. "We turn south on U.S. 27, which takes us to Mudford."

Incompentado nodded, "What is your time table?"

"Orders have been issued. We'll depart Cartersville Friday morning, October 9th, and arrive in Mudford Friday afternoon. My commander will meet with the mayor and city council and establish the rules. FBI agents will arrive the next day."

"Who is your commander?"

"Madam Secretary, you said you wanted to make an example, so I've placed Colonel Savage in command."

Incompentado started to object, but then thought better of it. Colonel Savage was brutal, and Abomba wanted to make an example. After weighing the alternatives, she said, "Good."

Ronald Reagan Washington National Airport
8:09 p.m. Friday, October 2, 2015

Colonel Rebecca Collins, wearing a low-cut, bright green dress with a very short skirt and four-inch platform heels, headed for the terminal exit carrying a small travel bag. With her shapely figure and her long brunette hair falling softly around her shoulders, Collins presented a striking figure: one that attracted several men's eyes as she walked toward the nearby VIP parking area. Vickie Barrett saw her, waved from her silver Mercedes SL560 and popped the trunk.

"Nice ride," Collins said, placing her bag in the trunk and closing it.

"Thanks, how was your flight?"

"Cramped. Had to fly coach."

"Hungry?"

"You bet. Haven't eaten since noon."

"Good, we'll stop for dinner at one of my favorite restaurants in Old Town Alexandria. My condo is close by."

"Good," Rebecca said, favoring Vickie with an alluring smile.

Twenty minutes later, the women left the Mercedes with the parking attendant at Bristol Lafayette. "*Bonsoir, mademoiselle*, it is a pleasure to serve you again," the maitre d' greeted Vickie as they entered, and then, turning to acknowledge Collins, continued, "and you as well, *mademoiselle*."

"Thank you, Andre, this is my friend, Miss Rebecca Collins."

Andre nodded to Barrett's companion. "This way, *s'il vous plaît*, I have a table for two in a secluded area." Andre said, casting an admiring glance at the striking brunette, and thinking she was by far the best looking woman Barrett had ever brought with her.

"*Merci, vous êtes à la nature*, Thank you, you're very kind," Barrett replied.

Vickie and Rebecca sat studying the menu. "Hmmm, everything looks delicious. I think I'll start with *Le Thon Tartare*," Vickie said.

"Hmmm … Good choice—think I'll join you," Rebecca smiled.

"You'd better," Vickie said, giving Collins a smoldering look that promised a steamy evening ahead. *Can't wait to get her in bed."*

"*Bonsoir Mademoiselle* Barrett," their waiter Pierre said, temporarily breaking the spell. "Are you and your companion ready to order?"

"*Oui*, Pierre ... we're starved." Barrett said, continuing to gaze at Collins. We'll both start with the *Le Thon*, and I'll have the Sea Scallops."

"And you, *Mademoiselle?*"

"I'll have the fresh grilled salmon, Pierre."

"Both are excellent choices. *Merci*."

"Pierre, please ask Andre to select a wine for us. We both like dry wines."

After the appetizers arrived and the wine was poured, Barrett's expression changed. Lowering her voice and giving Collins serious look, she asked, "What have you heard about the Blue Shirts and FEMA Corps?"

"The subject recently came up in a meeting. General Doughberry cut the questions off, but I don't think it ended there. I've walked in on a few conversations and heard the words Blue Shirts or FEMA mentioned, but as soon as they saw me they changed the subject." Collins knotted her brow. "My guess is there are a lot of unofficial questions being asked.

"Is there something I should know?"

"Perhaps. We expect civil disobedience to increase as new gun control regulations go into effect. Demonstrations that may prove to be more than police can handle."

"Yes, General Doughberry made that clear when he arrived. He said we're to be prepared to back up DHS. He mentioned several right wing organizations were being designated as domestic terrorists."

Barrett nodded. "Yes, that's true. Our concern is whether the military will follow orders and—"

"And suppress civilians if ordered to do so," Collins finished for her.

Barrett locked eyes with Collins and said, "Yes."

Collins contemplated the question for several seconds before answering, "I don't know. And, I don't think anyone at CENTCOM knows, and that's what most of the hushed discussions are about—that and FEMA Corps almost shooting civilians in Golden." Collins looked into Barrett's eyes and asked, "Is it true that the President federalized the Alabama National Guard, and then the governor de-federalized it?"

"Yes, and if there's more trouble, Homeland Security will take control of the town.

"What's your take on General Beck?"

Again, Collins took her time before answering, "He's very hard to read—quiet and seems to know everything that's going on ... He's visited all the commands in the last month, and I think he was at Little Creek a couple of weekends ago. Something about going fishing. He took leave."

Their dinners arrived and the conversation reverted to lighter issues. Both were anticipating a night of lovemaking.

After a leisurely breakfast, the two drove to Annapolis for a day of sailing on the bay. They dined there with another couple from Annapolis, and then headed back to Vickie's condo for another night of lovemaking. The next morning while they sat in the kitchen talking, Barrett brought the conversation back to business. "This has been a fun weekend, but it's time to talk shop. We're getting reports about an organization called the Oath Keepers. Seems as though a number of military men and a few women are joining. Know anything about it?"

"No, but I've heard the name mentioned. What oath are they keeping?"

"As I understand it, their oath is a pledge to uphold the oath we swore to protect the Constitution—" Barrett paused to see how Rebecca would answer and to gauge her reaction.

"Do you mean the part that says we swear to protect the Constitution from all enemies, foreign and domestic?"

Barrett was watching Rebecca's face but only saw confusion. "Yes, that's what their website says ... but the question is, who do they consider the enemy?"

Collins thought about the question. She knew it was significant, but was having trouble understanding why it was important. Finally the answer dawned on her, and she replied, "Are you referring to the right wing groups and those people the AG has labeled domestic terrorists?"

Barrett's intense expression softened, and she replied, "Yes. So the question is, will the men and women who've joined the Oath Keepers follow orders, if those orders call for suppressing or arresting domestic terrorists?"

Collins sat contemplating the implications for several seconds, having trouble classifying some of the groups as domestic terrorists— especially veterans. Nevertheless, aware her star rested with her answer, she carefully worded her answer, "I'll keep my eyes and ears open and quietly investigate."

"Good," Vickie said, standing with a wanton expression and stretching: her blue negligee clinging to her like a second skin and her erect, dark nipples clearly visible through the sheer, silky garment. "It's too early to go to the airport," she said, giving Collins a smoldering look and walking toward the bedroom.

On the way to the airport Collins agreed to watch General Beck and keep her ears open for talk about the Blue Shirts, FEMA Corps and Oath Keepers. Pulling into a VIP parking slot, Barrett leaned over to kiss Rebecca and whispered, "I think you should plan on coming up to brief me every other weekend. I'll take care of issuing orders to your boss."

On the return flight to Tampa, Collins began to worry about where her loyalties lay. *This Oath Keeper business requires a lot of research. Using the military to control and even suppress civilians ... I just don't know. I want my star, but will I have to violate my oath to get it?* For the first time she felt conflicted. *I find myself in a game I don't fully understand.*

Chapter 40

I-20 West of Atlanta
Friday morning, October 9, 2015

A red 1960 Cadillac convertible cruised along I-20 toward the Alabama state line. It was a beautiful, crisp fall day. The top was down and Reverend Scoundrell, riding in the front passenger seat whistling *Oh, Happy Day*, was enjoying the open air and blue sky. Turning to look back over his shoulder, he gloated at the sight of all the automobiles, SUVs and buses driving along side by side behind him, filling both lanes for as far as his eyes could see. "PRAAAISE THE LAWD," he shouted, pumping his fists and rocking from side to side in his seat.

Overhead a local CBS affiliate's helicopter caught up with the procession as it crossed into Alabama and begun videoing. The reverend's antics usually made news and the national network picked up the broadcast when the helicopter reached the head of the mile long column.

Looking up Reverend Scoundrell heard the helicopter, waved, and shouted, "HAAALLELUIAH!"

Inside the State Capitol building in Montgomery, Governor James Todd and Alabama's Senate president were deep in conference over the situation at Mudford, when an aide suddenly opened door. "Excuse me, Governor, Senator ... you need to turn on the TV, Channel 8," she said.

"What's happened now, Mary?" the governor asked, anxiety evident in his voice.

"Governor, you need to see it with your own eyes," the aide said, entering the room and turning on the TV.

As Mary stood off to the side, the governor and the senator watched a video showing a long parade of vehicles moving along a four-lane highway. Obviously filmed from a hovering helicopter, the camera zoomed in on the lead car in the parade, a red convertible driven by a man wearing a chauffeurs' uniform. Seated next to the driver and looking up to wave at the cameraman was none other than the famous Reverend Joseph Scoundrell.

"What in the world is that all about, Mary?" the governor asked.

"Wait a minute … the announcer will explain. They've been running this clip for the last half hour," she said as the video ended and the station picked up the story.

"Well folks," the news anchor said, "From the looks of it, that's quite some parade Reverend Scoundrell is leading to Mudford. According to SPECTRUM SHOVE'S Facebook page, he fully intends to proceed with what he's billed as a Million-Man March to Mudford, where he and his marchers intend to demand justice for Reverend Dullston, Artavius and Scandale. Once there he plans to hold street parades and demonstrations for as long as it takes to get Reverend Dullston's killer and Larry Puckett arrested and put on trial for murder."

"*Oh my god,*" the governor exclaimed, and the senator gulped in distress.

"Mary, get the mayor of Mudford on the phone right a way. Tell him to watch CBS, and then have him call me back—I doubt he knows what's coming his way.

"Then get me Colonel Callahan at the Department of Public Safety."

Five minutes later Mary returned and said, "Colonel Callahan is on line three. I gave the mayor's assistant your message."

"Thanks, Mary."

Pushing the blinking button, and then the speaker button on his phone, the governor said, "Harry, do you know what's coming our way on I-20?"

"Yes, Governor. I was about to call you. Looks like trouble."

"Yeah, trouble with a capital T. We need to get troopers to Mudford."

"Yes, sir. I'm working on it.

"However, there is more bad news—"

"What the hell could be *worse?*" the governor interrupted.

"Ten minutes ago a column of FEMA buses, Humvees and three Bradley Fighting Vehicles on flatbed trailers entered Alabama on U.S. 278. I think they're headed for Mudford. Looks like we're being set up by the feds.

"Oh my god! Are we going to be the next Golden?" the senator muttered, stating the other's unspoken fears.

"Mary, get me General Jones."

Major General Jones was Alabama's adjutant general and the commander of Alabama's National Guard.

Mary was about to place the call when the mayor called back.

"Governor, thank you for calling. It's an honor to speak with you."

"Robert, you may not think so after I bring you up to date.

"The *famous* Reverend Scoundrell is leading a mile long parade of demonstrators along I-20 heading for Mudford."

"Shit!" Oh, pardon me, Governor."

"Robert, it gets worse. FEMA Corps is also heading your way. They'll probably arrive this afternoon, coming down U.S. 27. Looks like they're loaded for bear.

"I think we're being set up as an example of what happens when you defy the feds. Try to keep your citizens calm. If they react to Scoundrell's protesters they'll give FEMA an excuse to intervene. Get the word out fast. No matter what happens—*Do not react!*"

"Can you send me some help?"

"Working on it. Let me know when your company arrives."

"Governor, General Jones is holding," Mary called from the door.

"Robert, have to go. Good luck."

Mayor Robert Bowden heard Mary's words and felt somewhat relieved. If the governor was calling the commander of the National Guard, he was taking the situation seriously.

As soon as General Jones finished his conversation with the governor, he decided to call his counterpart in Colorado. The conversation left him shaken. FEMA Corps was bad news, and now they were his bad news.

After ending his call with Jones, General Morrison decided to call General Beck.

General Beck bid General Morrison good-bye and hung up the phone. *The shit is about to hit the fan. I wonder how the Governor's going to react. Guess I'll find out tomorrow. Better go home and use my encrypted phone to call Hazzard and Rockford.* Standing in preparation to depart for his quarters, he placed the classified documents he'd been reading in his safe.

Beck opened his door and was surprised to find General Ulrich, with his hand raised ready to knock on the door. "Well ... good morning John, come in."

"Yes, sir. Do you have a couple of minutes?"

"Of course. What can I do for you?"

"Tony, I'm really worried about this mess in Mudford, Alabama. Sounds like a combination of the Zimmerman-Martin shooting in Sanford, Florida and the Golden mess. Just saw a report on CBS about Reverend Scoundrell leading a convoy to Mudford. He's going to start a riot. If he does, the citizens may react with more violence, and then the Blue Shirts may appear."

Beck sighed, "John, your dead on. In fact, FEMA Corps's on their way to Mudford as we speak. The news media hasn't learned what's happening, but I'm sure they're going to any time now."

Ulrich stared at Beck, shook his head and whispered, *"Damn!"* Continuing in a normal voice he asked, "Are we going to become involved?"

"Let's hope not. I doubt we will." *At least not this time,* Beck thought.

Chapter 41

As soon as Reverend Scoundrell led his caravan into Mudford, his followers promptly rented every available room. Scoundrell's personal assistant had already called ahead to book him the best hotel suite in the town under a different name.

After the hell they'd just experienced at the hands of Reverend Dullston's followers, jittery citizens watched the invading demonstrators with disgust and trepidation. The mayor's instructions had been spread through downtown and were now reaching residential areas. Mudford's citizens remained quiet as the invaders settled in. Occupiers and anarchists had also arrived and were displaying signs reading "Occupy Mudford," but so far there'd been no demonstrations. Grumbling began when a large number of typically filthy Occupiers began pitching tents and placing sleeping bags in the park.

The first signs of trouble began around mid-afternoon, when the Occupiers started looking for firewood, and a homeowner heard pounding behind his house. Looking out his rear window, he saw several men ripping boards off the side of his old garage. Shouting for them to stop only resulted in one of them hurling rocks and breaking his downstairs windows. A 911 call brought a quick response by Mudford's police, followed by a scuffle in which one of the Occupiers was cuffed and arrested.

While police were dealing with similar incidents in neighborhoods surrounding the park, FEMA Corps arrived and found a patrol car waiting to greet them at the city limits. After showing Colonel Savage where to park his column, the officer told Savage he'd lead him to the mayor's office. No tents and sleeping bags had been issued to Savage's men, and they'd soon discover no motel rooms were available.

Inside City Hall, Mayor Robert Bowden was watching through a glass partition, as a man wearing blue camouflage BDUs entered his outer office, spoke with the his assistant, and headed for his office door. Standing to greet the man when he entered, Bowden introduced himself, "Good afternoon, I'm Mayor Bowden."

"Pleased to meet you, Mr. Mayor. I'm Colonel Savage, the commander of the FEMA Corps unit. We're here to restore order."

Bowden quickly evaluated the burly man and decided he was overbearing and arrogant. "Colonel, there is no disorder for you to restore."

"Even if there were *disorder,* my police force is perfectly capable of dealing with it. If assistance is required, the Highway Patrol will provide it. Therefore, I see no need for—what did you say you were ... FEMA something or other—for you to stay?"

Savage puffed himself up, "Mr. Mayor, a world renowned black leader and many of his followers were just killed in your town. The guilty parties haven't been arrested and the assassin hasn't been found.

"The government *will not* stand for another such occurrence."

Bowden took his seat without inviting Savage to do the same. Looking up, he pursed his lips and said, "If you and the *government* are so concerned about the safety of Reverend Scoundrell and his activists ... you should have prevented them from coming to Mudford in the first place.

"Now that they *are* here, I'm responsible for their safety and *they*'re responsible for obeying our laws. Reverend Dullston was inciting a riot *when he was shot.* His troublemakers burned down several businesses and were attempting to loot and burn houses *when they were shot.* Our homeowners rightly defended themselves and their property.

"If Reverend Scoundrell and his followers repeat the actions of Reverend Dullston's gang, the results will be similar."

"Mr. Mayor, my orders are to keep the peace. That means protecting the rights of protesters. If any of your citizens resort to violence, I will take harsh action."

Turning red in the face, Mayor Bowden stood and glared at Savage, "If any of your men even think about interfering with my police, they *will be* arrested. Now, I want you and your FREEBEE Corps to get out of Mudford."

Savage laughed in the mayor's face and stomped out of his office.

Lines had been drawn, and the only thing necessary was for someone to fire the first shot.

An hour later, Captain Vandergriff and a sergeant from the Alabama Highway Patrol arrived, followed a few minutes later by the county sheriff.

After meeting with the mayor, Captain Vandergriff and Sheriff Barringer sought out Colonel Savage and relayed the governor's concerns about FEMA Corps' presence. Savage repeated what he'd told the mayor, and the captain relayed the conversation to his boss, Colonel Callahan, at the Department of Public Safety. After the call, Callahan met with the governor and General Jones in the governor's office, where Jones reported he'd sent Lieutenant Colonel Able to Mudford to evaluate the situation. All three men expected events to get out of hand the next day. "General," the governor asked, "is FEMA Corps a military unit? If not, how can DHS have units armed with military weapons and wearing military type uniforms?"

General Jones had been wondering the same thing. "I don't know, but I'll call the Pentagon and try to find out."

"Try?" the governor asked.

Jones shrugged, "Governor, getting a definitive answer from the Pentagon has been difficult since the current administration took over. Lately it's been almost impossible."

The governor frowned and shook his head in anger, "General, assemble a force sufficient to expel FEMA Corps, and locate it within striking distance of Mudford. I've had enough of Washington's meddling. Assemble whatever force you think necessary to kick them out of Alabama."

"Yes, sir."

After leaving the governor's office, General Jones returned to his headquarters to expedite his orders. Shortly thereafter, he received a call from Colonel Able, who reported the results of his meeting with Colonel Savage, which turned out to be a replay of Savage's meeting with the mayor. Jones sat evaluating Abel's report, including the number of FEMA Corps men and their weapons. *Damn, I'm going to need a large unit. Hopefully, when Savage sees a battalion-sized force, he'll pack up and leave. If not, I'll have to quickly finish him off. Can't have a prolonged engagement.* Jones sighed. *I can't believe I'm even thinking about engaging a U.S. government force in Alabama. What the hell is going on? Maybe Morrison in Colorado knows. Oh well, time to do my job.* General Jones decided, calling for his staff and issuing orders to form a battalion that included a platoon of M1A2 tanks. The battalion would take up a position three miles from Mudford. Surprised by Jones' unprecedented orders, his staff initially thought he was putting them on. Not since the civil war had a state taken up arms against the federal government.

After the staff meeting, Jones called General Morrison to discuss the latest turn of events. When the conversation ended, Morrison called Beck.

Chapter 42

Mudford, Alabama
Saturday morning, October 10, 2015

The morning got off to a slow start. Townspeople were appalled at the condition of their once pristine park. Trash littered the grounds, bushes had been crushed, trees damaged, and a black anarchists' flag draped over the statue of the town's civil war hero. A park attendant reported finding: both bathrooms trashed, all toilets stopped up and overflowing; mirrors broken; and water left running in all the sinks. When the attendant placed "Out of Order" signs on the doors, the Occupiers promptly ripped them off.

Word of the Occupier's presence and conditions in the park quickly spread and more curious locals began arriving. Standing on the sidewalks around the outside of the park, Mudford's citizens were treated to sights of naked and scantily clad men and women—some using the bushes for toilets. A few boomboxes were playing rap songs at ear damaging decibel levels, and it wasn't long before the Occupy crowd began taunting local citizens.

Mayor Bowden, the police chief, and three city councilmen mingled with the townspeople, encouraging them to keep quiet or go home. Every police officer and reservist was on duty. Bowden looked at the mess in the park and sighed, *Damn, and it's only nine o'clock.*

TV vans from ABC, CBS, CNN, NBC, and FOX were positioned around the park, but so far there was nothing to video. Reverend Scoundrell was still enjoying breakfast in his suite. He planned to enter the park and speak to his followers at eleven o'clock.

As the men and women from Scoundrell's convoy began arriving at the park to hear his speech, they walked by a rental box truck where several community organizers were passing out a variety of handheld and stick-mounted signs. Several different messages appeared on the signs. Some called for justice for the murdered party and bore a picture of either Reverend Dullston, or an elementary school picture of an eight or nine year old Artavius or Scandale. Others simply read, "No Guns," "Guns are for Racists," and "Kluckers have illegal guns"—a reference to members of the white supremacist organization the Ku Klux Klan (KKK), people who hate Jews, Catholics, gays, blacks, Latinos and other non-whites.

The last item to come off the truck was a twenty feet long banner with the names Dullston, Artavius and Scandale on the top line and the slogan "Justice for All" below the names. Community organizers quickly displayed the banner in front of Reverend Scoundrell's speaker's stand in the park.

It wasn't long before the park was overflowing; and the increased number of boomboxes had raised the noise level from very loud to deafening. Adding to the cacophony, and causing locals' tempers to flare and harsh words to fly, was the arrival of a demonstrator's van, with bass blaring so loud from vehicle-mounted speakers, store windows began to vibrate. As time for Scoundrell's speech drew near, tension between the reverend's marchers, who for the most part were clean and orderly, and the filthy, disrespectful Occupiers escalated—several times to the point of violence.

By ten-thirty Mayor Bowden was ready to scream. Walking along a street bordering the park, trying to calm his citizens, Bowden was sure things couldn't get worse. Then he received word that ten FBI agents had arrived at City Hall. According to his aide, the senior FBI agent, who'd met with the police chief, had demanded to interview homeowners involved in the shootings of Reverend Dullston's followers. They'd also said they planned to arrest Larry Puckett, the man who shot Artavius and Scandale, for Civil Rights violations. Rebuffing the senior FBI agent's demands, the chief told the agent his department was handling the investigation, and he and his nine other agents should go back where they came from. Incensed by the chief's attitude, the FBI leader got his back up and words started flying.

What the aide didn't report, because both he and the angry parties inside City Hall missed seeing them, was the presence of an NBC reporter and his cameraman who'd slipped in unnoticed. Tipped off about the FBI's arrival, the pair had arrived just in time to video what quickly turned into a heated exchange. After watching the cameraman's feed for a few minutes, the network picked up the video and the report went live on the national network.

Worried a turf war was in the making, Mayor Bowden hurried back to City Hall and cringed when he spotted the NBC van in front of the building. *Damn it! The aide didn't tell me about the TV van being here. Just what we don't need—more national news,* he thought. Rushing inside to investigate, he entered the building's foyer, found the two parties squared off, and heard the senior FBI agent issuing his final statement. The Justice Department was taking charge of the investigation. Not only did they plan to question the homeowners, they intended to arrest everyone involved in shooting the demonstrators. Carrying out previous instructions, one of the FBI agents had called Colonel Savage as soon as the argument began.

Sheriff Barringer had also noticed the NBC van as he approached City Hall. Seeing Savage and two armed men with stripes on their sleeves exit the colonel's FEMA Humvee, he followed them into the building and walked right into the middle of the heated argument.

Confused by all the shouting, he stood back listening for a minute, trying to sort out the reason for the dispute. Finally realizing what was going on when he heard the senior FBI agent claiming authority, he was appalled. "*No way!*" he interjected, getting in the agent's face. "You have no authority in this matter whatsoever. If you and your people aren't out of this town in the next hour, I'll have my men arrest you."

Barringer's statement was exactly what Savage wanted to hear. Storming up to the sheriff and getting in his beet-red face, Savage shouted, "YOU'LL DO NO SUCH THING! I'm here representing FEMA corps under the direct authority of Secretary of Homeland Security, Jane Incompentado. My orders direct me to support the FBI in arresting and transporting those individuals involved in shooting demonstrators and murdering Reverend Dullston and the two young boys. I will *not* permit your deputies, nor anyone else for that matter, to arrest any FBI agent."

Outside City Hall, ten highway patrol cars, each containing four officers, pulled to a stop in front of the building. Lieutenant Bale got out of the first cruiser and reported to Captain Vandergriff, who stood waiting for them near the front entrance. After a brief greeting, Vandergriff said, "Tell the troopers to remain near their cars, then we'll go in together."

Vandergriff and Bale headed inside and were alarmed by what they saw. The police chief and the sheriff were standing, with their hands resting on their pistols, glaring at ten men in dark suits with their hands inside their jackets. The FEMA colonel had his hand resting on his pistol, and the two men with him were un-slinging their M4 carbines. Mayor Bowden, the only unarmed man there, stood behind the police chief with his mouth hanging open.

Feebees, Captain Vandergriff correctly assumed, and stepping forward with his hands on his hips demanded, "What the hell's going on?"

When no one responded, he shouted, "STAND DOWN!"

Lieutenant Bale, who'd finally realized the trouble they'd been sent to control was occurring, used the confusion to quietly slip outside. After quickly ordering the newly arrived highway patrolmen to arm themselves and form a line in front of the building, he returned to the confrontation still raging inside. Joining his captain he shouted, "I HAVE FORTY ARMED MEN OUTSIDE. NOW, FOLLOW CAPTAIN VANDERGRIFF'S ORDERS."

NBC was now broadcasting live feed of the clearly volatile situation nationwide, along with their on-the-scene reporter's running commentary. Needless to say, the broadcast had many interested viewers. Among those watching were: President Abomba, Jane Incompentado, and Vicki Barrett in their Washington offices; Governor Todd and General Jones in the governor's Montgomery office; millions of Americans in homes, offices, restaurants and bars; and a surprising number of folks in other parts of the world. All were engrossed by a drama that could only occur in America.

Unaware of the drama going on in City Hall, Reverend Scoundrell stood next to the anarchist's flag draped statue in the park addressing his followers. "We're aaaaall here today to celebrate the remarkable life of that great American, Revereeend Tobiiiiias Duuullston," he solemnly began, drawing out each word in his famous quaking voice, "who was *murdered* here—right here where I'm standing ... *murdered* by a cowardly white man ... *a raaacist.*" Scoundrell paused, letting his eyes sweep the crowd, allowing his words to sink in. "Yes, he was *murdered ... muuurdered ...* by a *whiiite* man, a *maaan* who hated black men and women."

Scoundrell paused again, and then thundered, "WAS HE MURDERED BY THE KU KLUX KLAN?" After another long, dramatic pause—complete with raised eyebrows and rolled eyes—he continued, "*MAAAYBE ...* maaaybe not, but it *doooesn't* matter. He was murdered ... *muuurdered* right here in Mudford.

"WE DEMAND JUSTICE. We demand his murderer be arrested and *triiied* for murder.

"WE DEMAND JUSTICE NOW!

"It's *tiiime* to march for justice. FOLLOW ME! We'll march through downtown and then into the residential streets ... where our brothers and sisters were *muuurdered* by these *whiiite* crackers. FOLLOW ME!"

ABC, CBS, CNN and FOX went live nationwide.

Just as tempers were about to explode inside City Hall, the standoff was interrupted by a thunderous cadence of many people chanting,
"JUSTICE FOR DULLSTON, NO MORE GUNS!
"JUSTICE FOR ARTAVIUS, NO MORE GUNS!
"JUSTICE FOR SCANDALE, NO MORE GUNS!"
Hearing the ruckus outside and seeing a possible way to break the stalemate, Mayor Bowden seized the moment. "OH MY GOD ... Listen—they're coming. They're going to tear this town apart. HELP ME STOP THEM!" he yelled, bolting right through the middle of the angry men and running out of the building.

Running after him the police chief, sheriff and other assorted turf-battlers dashed out of the entrance, but stopped short, stunned at what they were seeing—Lieutenant Bale wasn't bluffing when he said he had forty men outside. Standing on the lawn with his hands in the air was a white-faced Mayor Bowden shouting, "DON'T SHOOT! I'M THE MAYOR," to the line of forty state troopers pointing their AR-15s at him.

"STAND DOWN!" Captain Vandergriff ordered, stepping in front of the mayor. "Step aside. We need to observe the demonstrators."

So, the mayor's ploy to stop the turf war worked, the police chief snorted. *However, I'll bet after the scare he just had, he sure could use a change of briefs right about now.* Still chuckling, he watched the troopers move away from the mayor.

"That was quite some stunt you pulled Mr. Mayor. Now let's go see what's really happening with those demonstrators," Vandergriff told a wild-eyed Bowden, grabbing his elbow and leading him to join other onlookers waiting for the parade.

Though still some distance away the leader of SPECTRUM SHOVE Coalition's Million-Man March, Reverend Joseph Scoundrell could clearly be seen marching toward City Hall, using a bullhorn to direct the chanting. Following Scoundrell, and carrying the long "JUSTICE FOR ALL" banner that stretched across the street, were the six community organizers responsible for coordinating the event; and behind them marched innumerable—certainly less than the reverend's hoped-for million—sign-bearing, flag-waving protesters chanting demands for justice and the elimination of guns.

Carefully observing the reaction of the townspeople, Mayor Bowden could see some were visibly unnerved by the cadence of the marchers' chanting, while others calmly watched in amazement. All in all, Bowden concluded, the demonstration, though loud, was actually peaceful. So leaving the turf-battlers to watch the spectacle, he motioned for the police chief and sheriff to join him inside City Hall. They'd just started walking back toward the building, when they heard the senior FBI agent causing a disturbance behind them. Turning around they saw him standing beside Colonel Savage and pointing toward the marchers.

"YOU SEE THAT! THESE PEOPLE WANT JUSTICE," the agent shouted, and then, moving closer so Savage could hear, added. "And we're here to make sure they get it. Go get your men ready to back us up. We're not leaving till we've arrested those individuals responsible for committing the murders in this town.

Savage, who was certain violence was in the making and itching for it to start, motioned for his men to follow and departed to join his unit. He planned to be ready when trouble occurred.

Still in a huff over his earlier confrontation with the FBI and Savage, Sheriff Barringer was standing close enough to hear the senior agent's comments and watched Savage leave with his men. Stomping up to the agent, he yelled. "STAY HERE, AND I'LL ARREST YOU. I TOLD YOU TO GET OUT OF MY COUNTY."

Hearing the sheriff's comment Captain Vandergriff stomped up said, "No! Get the hell out of Alabama. Do it now—or *I'll* arrest all you."

Sneering, the senior agent replied, "Try to. We're backed up by Colonel Savage!"

"GENTLEMEN, CAN WE TAKE THIS BACK INSIDE," yelled the mayor, trying once more to defuse the situation, but no one listened.

Instead the angry agent stepped closer to the sheriff and captain and said through clenched teeth, "Savage is here with orders to stop any interference with our arrests. He will use the full force of his heavily armed Homeland Security unit if you interfere. I hope you're not foolish enough to take on our armored vehicles."

"Are you telling me Colonel Savage has orders to fire on Alabama law enforcement officers?" the sheriff snarled.

"Ask him yourself. Why don't you?"

Sheriff Barringer and Captain Vandergriff looked daggers through the agent who was looking at them with a satisfied expression.

Finally Vandergriff said, "You can't be serious."

Enjoying himself immensely, the agent replied, "Interfere and you'll find out."

Colonel Able, standing within earshot, decided the agent wasn't bluffing and called General Jones to report the conversation.

Twenty minutes later, tanks were moving forward to a position that would allow them to engage the FEMA vehicles from cover.

Chapter 43

CENTCOM, MacDill AFB
1100 Saturday, October 10, 2015

Colonel Collins had been flipping channels watching the morning news on CNN and ABC since 0630. She'd seen snippets of news about Scoundrell's Million-Man march and was curious as to what else was happening. Flipping to NBC, she caught the coverage of the near shootout in Mudford's City Hall. Returning to CNN she watched portions of Reverend Scoundrell's speech and saw the large boisterous crowd preparing to march through downtown Mudford.

Realizing the seriousness of the situation and that something bad could happen, she decided to go to headquarters and see who was there. When she arrived, she found Generals Beck, Roberts, and Ulrich in one of the small conference rooms watching the news on three different TV screens.

"Beck saw her and waved a greeting, "Come on in, there's coffee and doughnuts on the table."

"Thanks ... I'd been watching the news in my quarters and decided I better come in."

"Good morning, Rebecca," Roberts and Ulrich said, waving too.

Once Collins had her coffee and doughnut, Beck asked, "Were you watching NBC?"

"The confrontation in City Hall? I watched a bit of it."

"Did you catch the senior FBI agent threaten FEMA's armored vehicles would fire on Alabama law enforcement if they interfered."

"No, I missed that," Barrett said and almost laughed at the ridiculousness of the statement, until she saw the serious expressions on the men's faces. "You think they actually *would?*"

Ulrich answered, "With Colonel Savage in command, yes. I think he would."

"Colonel Savage? Who's Colonel Savage?"

"He was the commander of the FEMA Corps unit that almost fired on civilians in Golden, Colorado. He ordered his men to fire on a house with

M2 machine guns. Now he's in command of the FEMA unit at Mudford. This time they have a three Bradleys, plus the armored Humvees."

"Oh! Does General Doughberry know?"

No one answered.

"Tony, I think I'd better bring him up to speed," Collins said, and Beck nodded his agreement.

After updating her boss-lover and promising to call him if anything important occurred, Collins sat at her desk gaming events. *If FEMA Corps fires on law enforcement or civilians, what will happen? Unknown. Oh my god! That's what Mudford's all about. In order to plan how to enforce gun regulations in January, Abomba's running a test to see how far the federal government can push the states. That's why Savage is in command. They know he's a hothead. This may be my chance to find out what Beck's thinking.*

Collins returned to the conference room in time to see Reverend Scoundrell leading the marchers. Settling into a chair she asked Beck, "Has anything happened?"

"No, but it looks like it's about to."

Two of the TV screens showed the last of the marchers passing City Hall, and then switched to a scene in which a group of bedraggled young men and women Occupiers were milling around in front of a storefront.

"Anarchists," Roberts commented. "See those men off to the side holding liquid filled bottles with fabric wicks sticking out of them—Molotov Cocktails."

Mudford, Alabama
Saturday, October 10, 2015

Mayhem was building in Mudford. Almost every riot, uprising and revolution has its provocateurs. Destroying personal property and buildings is their forte, and usually the main item on their agenda—Mudford would be no exception. When one man in the group of Occupiers milling around in front of a store suddenly threw a brick through the window, others joined in. Completely shattering the glass, the group stormed through the opening to smash and loot inside. When a policeman saw them breaking in and attempted to arrest them, the miscreants brutally attacked and beat him and the owner.

Leaving the scene before police backup arrived, the troublemakers continued attacking other business owners and vandalizing property. A short while later city police and highway patrolmen caught up with them, and after enthusiastically introducing the Occupiers to nightsticks, corralled them. Everything appeared to be under control, until a FEMA Humvee arrived, and a burly man wearing a blue camouflage uniform got out.

Using a bullhorn, Colonel Savage glared at the police, and barked an order for them to release the Occupiers and leave. When the order was refused, Savage ordered the Humvee's machine-gunner to aim his M2 at the local law enforcement officers, and a highway patrol sniper zeroed in on the gunner.

Was this going to be a replay of the Golden shootout?

Fortunately, the standoff ended when police heard the sound of gunfire coming from a residential area and received a frantic call on the radio net for assistance, "Citizens blocking the marchers—Warning shots fired into the air. Request backup."

After most of the police and highway patrolmen sped off in response, Colonel Savage ordered his men to followed.

The mood in CENTCOM's conference room had become tense as everyone silently watched the M2 machine gun swing around and point at the police.

Looking at Beck's expressionless face, Collins asked, "What will happen if FEMA Corps fires?"

"Unknown, Rebecca. If the police or Highway Patrol returns fire they'll be massacred."

Collins didn't reply, but continued watching Beck, trying to figure him out and waiting for him to continue.

Finally Beck said, "What will happen if they do … is that your question, Rebecca?"

"Yes, sir."

Everyone in the room waited for Beck's answer.

Beck sighed, "Several possibilities, a law suit, Congressional action, or direct intervention by the Alabama National Guard."

"That's what happened in Colorado," Ulrich interjected. "But the difference there was Savage only fired on the house. He didn't kill anyone. He was getting ready to order his gunner to fire on civilians, when an unknown sniper took the gunner out."

Collins studied Beck carefully, hoping to catch a sense of what he was really thinking.

Beck pursed his lips and said, "Worse case, the Guard takes out FEMA Corps."

Collins hadn't thought of this option, and now wondered what Beck knew. After waiting for him to continue, she realized he'd said all he intended to. "Tony, in that event, will we become involved?"

"What do you mean by involved?" Roberts asked.

"Do you mean we'll be ordered to attack the Alabama National Guard?" Ulrich asked standing. Collins nodded yes.

All eyes turned to Beck, who'd suddenly found some interesting doughnut crumbs on the tabletop to study. Finally, he looked up and replied, "I guess we'll have to wait and see what our orders are."

Collins purposefully frowned, baiting Beck, "Orders are orders. We have to follow them. Don't we?"

Before Beck could answer, Ulrich said, "Yes, if they're *legal*."

Collins held her breath, waiting for the next comment. When, after a long silence, Beck changed the subject, Collins had her answer. *My problem is ... I agree with him—them. What do I tell Vickie?*

Mudford, Alabama
11:45 a.m., Saturday, October 10, 2015

Colonel Savage, riding in the first of four Humvees, arrived at the line of armed, angry homeowners, who'd congregated behind a hastily assembled makeshift barricade—trashcans and lawn furniture they'd piled up to block Reverend Scoundrell's march route.

Flinging open the passenger door of his Humvee and jumping out, Savage stood, legs splayed apart, bellowing into the bullhorn at the armed men and women.

"**DISPERSE!**"

"** Do it now or I'll fire on you.**"

Colonel Able, who'd been standing off to one side awaiting Savage's arrival, quickly approached the burly colonel from behind, grabbed hold of the bullhorn and jerked it out of his hand. Enraged, Savage spun around ready to give somebody hell, but stopped when he saw Able's hand raised to silence him.

"Colonel, you *don't* want to do that," Able calmly said.

"**FUCK OFF!**" Savage yelled. "What are you gonna do to stop me?"

Able grinned and replied in a low, menacing voice, "If even one of your vehicles fires, every last one *will be destroyed.*" Handing Savage his binoculars and pointing to a hill about a mile and a half away, Able added, "Now look carefully at the tree line on the military crest."

Savage grabbed the glasses and quickly scanned the hill.

"I don't see a damn thing up there but trees."

"Look harder."

"Still don't see anything."

"Keep looking," Able said, pulling a small handheld radio from its holder on his belt. "Firedog Actual, this is Able," he said speaking into the radio's mike. "Move forward until you're visible."

Both men heard a microphone click.

So angry he was shaking, Savage studied the military crest and caught his breath at the sight of an M1A2 tank partially emerging from the undergrowth. Even more shocking was the fact that he was looking directly into the business end of the 120mm main gun barrel.

"There are three tanks up there with orders to destroy all your vehicles. In addition, there are two companies of armored cavalry three miles distant.

"Now pay attention to what I'm saying. I'm relaying our Adjutant General's orders—Be out of Alabama by sunset, or you'll be taken by force."

Able grabbed his glasses from Savage's hand and stood there waiting for him to move.

Savage was furious. Red-faced and huffing, he inwardly raged that once again he'd been outgunned and had no choice but to leave. Then, swearing to himself, *This will never happen to me again*, he gave Able a withering look, stomped away and got in his Humvee. Two hours later, FEMA Corps found itself once more in retreat with its tail between its legs.

Reverend Scoundrell had watched the exchange between Colonel Savage and another officer and wondered what was going on. When Savage suddenly got into his vehicle and left, Scoundrell didn't know what to think. He'd been promised armed support, but now that support was leaving. If he backed down, he'd lose face. His power would be weakened. *What should I do? Maybe I can schmarm my way through*, he thought, deciding to press on.

Smiling cordially, he walked toward the line of locals blocking the street. Noting that almost all the men were armed, and feeling apprehensive because none of them were smiling back, Scoundrell cheerfully said, "Good afternoon friends, I am Reverend Scoundrell, and my fellow protesters and I are here to peacefully march through your lovely town in support of our murdered brothers and to seek justice for them," he said extending his hand to a giant black man, cradling a double barrel shotgun who had stepped forward to meet him.

Built like a tank and standing well over six feet, the man scowled down at Scoundrell for several seconds before responding. "Them two young gangbangers already done received every bit of justice they deserved. Fact is ... I 'spect them dyin' the way they did, saved us taxpayers the expense of a *trial,*" he added, opening his eyes wide and pursing his lips.

"Reverend Dullston's so called *peaceful* demonstrators was burning stores and houses and we protected our property. We's prepared t' do the same thing now—if'n your folks there makes more trouble," he said nodding toward Scoundrell's marchers.

"Brother, I—"

"*I ain't yo Brotha,*" the big man growled.

Scoundrell blinked. He wasn't expecting such an abrupt response. To save face he had to find a way to finish the march. "Mister, we're *not* here to make trouble by burning or damaging your homes. We're here to march in protest. These people—" Scoundrell paused to use his head to indicate the demonstrators filling the street behind him, "should be allowed to complete their march. Some have come hundreds of miles. If you allow us to march through your neighborhood, we'll leave and there'll be no trouble."

"What about them animals in de park—them Occupias. Mudford don't need, and don't want no Occupias. From what we's hearin', they's already done tore up our park, beat a store owner and police officer haf't def, set more sto'es afire and are still bustin' up the shoppin' area. We ain't gonna stand for that kind o' doin's in our town."

"Those Occupiers are not with me. I have no control over them."

"Okay," the big man said, again squinting down at Scoundrell. "I hear ya." Then, pausing to scratch his head and think, he looked at Scoundrell's marchers and at his armed neighbors standing behind him. Finally he spoke, "All right gimme a few minutes t' talk t' my neighbas."

Scoundrell heaved a sigh and nodded as he watched the man lumber away. *Looks like I may've done it ... we'll have to wait and see.*

A few minutes later the giant returned, "We's agreed to allow ya'll t' march a few blocks—providin' there be no chantin' or yellin'. When y'all's done marchin', y'all 'll have 't leave," he said, leaning over and looking the reverend in the eye.

Scoundrell contemplated his response. This arrangement wasn't what he wanted, and it certainly wasn't why his marchers had come all this way. But it sure beat getting shot. "Thank you kindly, sir. We accept."

"Good, I'll lead the way. Tell yo' people t' follow me, but know this ... if them Occupias makes trouble—we's gonna shoot 'em."

Shaking his head slowly and swallowing hard, Scoundrell nodded he understood. Five minutes later, the marchers, their enthusiasm dampened by the sight of armed townspeople lining the streets, quietly followed the big man with the double barrel shotgun. They would complete their march with no further incidents and depart.

The senior FBI agent watched FEMA Corps' Bradleys being loaded on flatbed trucks and the blue camouflage BDU clad men boarding busses. *What the hell is going on?* Using his cell phone, he called Savage, but got no answer.

Observing the agent's look of consternation and wearing a wicked grin, Sheriff Barringer strolled up to him. "Seems as though your FEMA buddies just got kicked out of Alabama. Now, I'll give you and your agents thirty minutes to get the hell out of *my* county. If not, you're all going to be my guests for a while."

Realizing he had no real options, the agent sneered at the sheriff, who simply continued wickedly grinning with delight. Finally, signaling his men to board their vehicles, the agent joined them and they departed. An escort of Highway Patrol vehicles led the way, with Mudford police and county sheriff vehicles following close behind—their multicolored lights flashing and sirens wailing all the way to the state line.

While most of the police had moved on to deal with Reverend Scoundrell and his marchers, the captured Occupiers, who were being held by only two city policemen, saw an opportunity to escape and ran in search of the marchers. However, instead of finding them, they ran headlong into the angry, armed homeowners' barricade. Quickly corralled by the authorities—with a lot of eager help from the homeowners—the stinking Occupiers were appropriately placed—for lack of a better place to keep them—in a swine holding pen at a nearby pork processing plant. Kept there over night, they were none too happy when the mayor ordered them to clean up the city park: a task they found extremely onerous, having never done an honest day's work in their lives. Later the troublemakers would learn a large percentage of TV viewers across the country had laughed and cheered while watching their humiliation—particularly those news clips showing them incarcerated with hogs.

All in all, it should have been a good learning experience.

Well ... maybe not so good for everyone.

Chapter 44

President Abomba could never remember being so angry. He and the First Lady were in his private office watching Alabama Highway Patrol cars, their lights flashing, escorting the FEMA vehicles east on I-20. A Mudford patrol car and a Sheriff's cruiser followed.

"THEY'RE BEING RUN OUT OF THE STATE.

"WHAT THE HELL HAPPENED?" the president screamed.

The First Lady didn't know what to say, so she said nothing.

"Somebody's going to pay for this," he snarled, grabbing his phone and speed dialing his Secretary of Homeland Security.

Jane Incompentado, scowling and looking like *Echidna* (the Greek's mythical half woman half snake, aka the "Mother of All Monsters") on a good day, had just asked General Sherman the same question, when the phone rang. She didn't have to check caller ID to know who it was.

"Good afternoon, Mr. President," she answered and watched General Sherman cringe.

"What the hell is good about it, Jane? What the hell *happened*?"

Damn, he's on a tear. When he gets like this there's nothing to do but take his abuse until he tires. "Well, sir, as it happens, General Sherman was about to tell me when you called."

"Put your phone on speaker."

"General Sherman, we're speaking with the President.

"Explain, in concise language, what went down in Mudford."

"Mr. President, it's an—"

"Cut the BS, Sherman. I wanna know what happened. How was your armed FEMA unit kicked outta of town and then outta state?"

Sherman gulped and looked at Incompentado, who sneered at him. "Mr. President, we were outgunned. The Alabama National Guard sent two mechanized companies of infantry and several tanks. The Guard officer told my commander the tanks had orders to destroy every FEMA vehicle, if one of them fired a shot. I was told they meant it."

"Are you telling me the vehicles you sent couldn't handle a few tanks?

"What the hell kind of general are you. You should have destroyed the damn tanks."

Shocked by the president's obvious lack of knowledge, Sherman was about to respond when Incompentado, touched his arm and shook her head. Getting the message, Sherman replied, "No excuse, Mr. President."

"What the hell does that mean ... *more military bullshit*?

"**JANE, GET YOURSELF A NEW GENERAL,**" the president roared and the line went dead.

Sherman decided being fired was a good thing and left.

Abomba's next call was to his secretary of defense. Haggler let the president rave until he had it out of his system, before attempting to explain FEMA didn't have anti-tank weapons, and a Bradley was no match for a M1A2 tank.

"Well, damn it, get 'em some better stuff ... get some of those, uh ... those uh, what did you call them? Yeah, those anti-tank things ... Yeah—and some damn tanks too."

Hearing the line go dead, Haggler shook his head in despair.

Nellie Balogni and her husband Hughbie had been watching the unfolding Alabama debacle since 9 a.m. Mudford was supposed to have set an example for enforcement of the pending federal gun regulations—but certainly not the example currently being set. As the morning events unfolded, Nellie became more and more frantic. The sight of her beloved FEMA Corps vehicles being escorted east on I-20 pushed her over the top and into a full-blown mental meltdown, forcing Hughbie to call 911.

Senator Finkelstein, blessed with a more stable personality, simply threw a temper tantrum.

Reporters on ABC, CBS, CNN, and NBC were struggling to report the rapidly occurring events in Mudford—events they didn't understand. Anticipating a gunfight in City Hall, NBC was caught by surprise when everyone rushed outside and departed. Sometime later, NBC's cameraman and reporter caught up with the action at the civilian barricade. Arriving in time to video Colonel Savage stomp to his Humvee and speed away, the news crew jumped back into their vans and followed the colonel to his vehicle lager. When the reporter attempted an ambush interview of Savage, the colonel lost it, and the cameraman videoed him shoving the reporter to the ground.

NBC remained with the FEMA Corps unit and covered their departure, but was unable to ascertain why they were leaving.

ABC, CBS and CNN attempted to keep up with events, reporting what they thought was happening, but mostly misreporting events. No one grasped the significance of Colonel Savage using binoculars to look at a distant hill, and thus none saw the tanks.

Only the FOX News reporter sought out Lieutenant Colonel Able and learned a sizable National Guard force was in the area. "Colonel, would the National Guard forces have fired on the FEMA Corps troops?" the reporter had asked.

"Guess we'll never know," Able replied, and then walked away smiling.

No White House representatives were available for Sunday news shows: neither was anyone from DOD or DHS, so the news shows interviewed the usual experts. One retired colonel made a futile attempt to change the subject to the Baghdad embassy investigation. On a different show, a retired general attempted to discuss the Chicago bombings, only to be overruled by the host. Mudford was that day's news. Who cared about yesterday? A former secretary of state's comment seemed to sum up the media's lack of interest, "What difference, at this point, does it make?"

Predictably, the following Monday Republicans in the House and Senate attempted to have committees investigate why FEMA had a FEMA Corps unit in Mudford, Alabama. And also predictably they were unsuccessful. Public opinion was split along racial and ideological lines, and normally soft-spoken conservatives were becoming more vocal.

States began to rebel, led by Kansas and Missouri whose legislators passed laws stating, "All federal acts, laws, orders, rules and regulations, past, present, or future, which infringe on the people's right to keep and bear arms, as guaranteed by the Second Amendment to the United States Constitution and similar provisions in their respective state constitutions, shall be invalid in this state, shall not be recognized by the state, shall be specifically rejected by the state, and shall be considered null and void and of no effect in this state." Missouri's legislation included provisions to make it a misdemeanor for federal agents to attempt to enforce *any* federal gun regulations that: "infringe on the people's right to keep and bear arms." The provision also applied to journalists who published any identifying information about gun owners.

As fall turned into winter, zero tolerance acts against perceived gun violations in schools became more numerous and parents' reactions more violent. Events were forcing law enforcement to choose sides—to either support the taxpaying parents or the school administration. Decisions were being made according to the political and ideological beliefs of department heads, and in a few instances ended in brutal confrontations.

Tax paying members of the population were finally beginning to notice reports of warrantless, no-knock police raids by masked SWAT units. Most troubling for many citizens were the number of incorrect addresses and the amount of out-of-date information being used. Wrong houses were being raided, resulting in several wrongful shootings by the police. Worse still, for the majority of the tax paying public, was the realization that non-taxpayers—people on welfare and illegal voters—were outvoting them. "We are paying for our own enslavement," became a popular lament.

Progressive-liberals continued to pour gasoline on the fire, by demanding repeal of "Stand Your Ground" laws—citing the Zimmerman and Puckett cases, and refusing to acknowledge both were clear acts of "Self Defense" not "Stand Your Ground." Attempting to discuss these issues with progressive-liberals was futile, and eventually various devices, such as baseball bats, fists, and tire irons, were used to keep argumentative progressive-liberals' attention focused on the facts. Arrests were made and demonstrations in support of both sides continued to grow increasingly violent.

The increased demand for guns grew to the point that every rifle, shotgun and pistol was sold before it left the manufacture's plant. The same was true for ammunition. By Christmas, the number of guns and ammo, wrapped in festive paper under the tree, could be used to arm an army—or a revolution.

Still the president and his party refused to accept they were out of touch with half the nation. As the New Year approached, those who correctly read the tealeaves either dug in or were leaving the country.

"A gun is like a parachute.
If you need one, and don't have one,
you may never need one again."
          – Anonymous

"To conquer a nation first disarm its citizens."
          – Adolph Hitler Poster

"All political power comes from the barrel of a gun.
The communist party must command all the guns, that
way, no guns can ever be used to command the party."
          – Mao Zedong, November 6, 1938

2016

Chapter 45

CENTCOM, MacDill AFB
January 1, 2016

General Beck was watching a football game in his quarters, but his thoughts were of his friend, John Ulrich. New Year's Eve festivities had been subdued and the usual good cheer was lacking. World and national events were partially responsible, but the real reason for everyone's low moral was the death of Brigadier General John Ulrich's wife, daughter and only grandson in an automobile accident on December 23rd. The general had planned to meet his family in Colorado Springs on Christmas Eve, and had a seat on an Air Force plane, departing MacDill and arriving at Peterson AFB at 1400 hours on 24 December. Tragically, a Colorado snowstorm changed his life forever when it caught up with his daughter, who was driving her Ford Fusion down a mountain on I-70 toward Denver. Visibility had dropped to thirty yards, and she most likely couldn't see the runaway eighteen-wheeler until it was on top of her. All occupants in the sedan were instantly killed, and the tractor-trailer driver was in critical condition.

Beck had seen the disastrous effect family tragedy had on other men and worried about how Ulrich would react. Lost in thought and annoyed that he'd missed seeing a touchdown pass, Beck realized he had to shake off his dark mood. *John's tough, he'll survive*, he told himself. *I'll be able to evaluate him during the funerals in Colorado Springs on Monday.* That settled, he concentrated on the game.

Sacramento, California
7:30 a.m., January 2, 2016

Governor Moonlight wasn't content to wait for the federal government to enforce its new gun laws. He was about to sign an order authorizing all state, county, city and local law enforcement personnel to immediately begin gun inspections and seizures authorized by new federal and state of California gun laws. Placing the pen he'd used to sign the order on the table, the governor looked up at the gaggle of reporters and six TV cameras covering the event, and proclaimed, "Today marks the beginning of a new era. Soon, almost all guns will be out of circulation and crime will quickly diminish. Within days, your news anchors will be able to report significant drops in armed robberies and shootings. Today is a great day for California."

The state's criminal population agreed.

Armed with lists of people who'd purchased ammunition, firearms, or applied for background checks, police began pounding on Californian's doors, demanding to enter and search the premises for illegal weapons. Searches went well in San Francisco, Oakland, and parts of Los Angeles; so much so, that by the end of the month almost all guns had been seized. However, for some inexplicable reason the crime rate had spiked to such an extent the line on the chart was almost vertical. "How can that be? What did we miss?" the governor and most of the legislators wondered. Finally they concluded there was only possible explanation. Guns were leaking into the state from Nevada. No worries, they decided, the feds would take care of the problem.

Gun and ammunition seizures may have started with no serious problems in the costal cities, but that changed as raids move inland. Citizens began resisting. Numerous firefights ensued, and soon hospitals were filled with gunshot victims, both police and civilians. Then retaliations began.

Overly aggressive SWAT units, accustomed to breaking down doors with no warning, began encountering real resistance—dynamite being the explosive attention-getter of choice. Men who'd fought to preserve the Constitution began keeping their oath to prevent it from being shredded. After several large explosions decimated entire SWAT teams, commanders began having second thoughts about warrantless, no-knock entries in the early morning hours.

Sheriffs, police chiefs, and mayors, who'd been vigorously enforcing the governor's orders, soon realized they'd become the hunted. Hunted by men and women who could reach out and touch them from great distances with high-powered rifles. After several mayors and police chiefs were killed, enthusiasm for conducting warrantless gun raids diminished.

Sometimes politicians require direct stimulus to consider facts contrary to their positions. Governor Moonlight's stimulus arrived in the form of a .416 caliber bullet, fired from 1,534 yards, which removed a hunk of his left ear. The week and a half he spent in hospital recuperating from ear surgery gave him plenty of time to consider the unintended consequences of his order. *How could things have gone so wrong?* he asked himself, waiting for his pain killing drugs to kick in. *Why is crime up ... when it should be down? Why are the people openly opposing a law designed to protect them? Could I have made a mistake?* The last thought shook Moonlight to his core. Fortunately, thanks to his pain meds, he slipped into a deep sleep, before having to further contemplate the horror of having been wrong.

Senators Boxnutter and Finkelstein weren't troubled by such trivial concerns. "Why did it matter?" they both raved, continuing to demand action and taking turns pounding the rostrum in Senate chambers.

On the House side, Nellie Balogni, the senior congresswoman from California and Speaker of the House, was chronically hysterical. Screaming and waving her arms on the House floor, she frequently hyperventilated and on two occasions passed out. Some feared she'd have a stroke, while others ... well they had different fears.

Sometimes getting what you wish for can greatly exceed your expectations. Such was the case when new federal gun laws went into effect on January 2nd, creating resistance in some states.

On February 17th federal agents entered Mississippi with orders to arrest anyone known to have firearms catches. In one incident, ATF agents attempted to burst into a farmhouse, triggering a shootout with the farmer. The agents were shocked when sheriff deputies arrested them. Learning of the arrests, Attorney General Helder filed suit against Mississippi.

Mississippi's attorney general ignored the lawsuit and did not appear at the hearing. Instead, a county sheriff accompanied by twenty deputies entered the hearing room in the federal courthouse. After informing the judge conducting the preliminary hearing the state didn't recognize his authority, the sheriff took the judge into custody and drove him to the state's northern border. Marching the furious judge to the state line, the sheriff used his large, right foot to boot him out of Mississippi.

Learning of the insult, Helder went ballistic.

Shortly thereafter, a meeting was held in the Oval Office.

The White House
Friday morning, February 19, 2016

Vickie Barrett and Jane Incompentado entered the Oval Office and found Edison Helder and Gene Haggler seated on a couch talking to the president, who as usual had propped his feet up on the famous Resolute desk—a gift from Queen Victoria to President Hayes in 1880. Abomba waved a greeting, pointed to a pair of chairs, and waited for them to close the door before snarling, "What the hell are we going to do about all this resistance by the goddamn gun crowd ... especially those sons-of-bitches in Mississippi?

"The fucking Governor allowed some red-neck sheriff to literally boot a federal judge out of the state.

"What the hell are we going to do about that?"

Well, so much for subtlety, Barrett inwardly groaned, wondering who was going to be impaled.

When no one answered, Abomba stuck his chin out and snapped, *"I asked a goddamn question!"*

Still no one spoke.

Glowering at his attorney general, Abomba said in a surly voice, *"Well?"*

"Uh, Barry ... we're uh, encountering more resistance than expected. Armed resistance ... all across the nation," Helder replied.

More resistance than expected? Barrett thought. *After Colorado and Alabama, what the hell did you think was going to happen? There wasn't a gun left for sale in any gun store on December 31st.*

"Governor Todd ordered his National Guard to engage our FEMA Corps unit, and he really meant engage. Think how it would have looked if our vehicles were destroyed on national television."

"Yeah Barry, uh ... perhaps we should, well, uh, back off the enforcement for awhile," Haggler suggested, and despite the president's scowling face hesitantly continued, "We've been booted out of Iraq and Afghanistan and communication with Israel is nonexistent. Egypt still has a smoldering civil war going on, and Russia has become the big dog in the Middle East. Even as we speak, they're establishing naval bases in Cuba and Venezuela—in our hemisphere." Haggler sat squirming in his seat, silently worrying, *And we—you—have cut our military to the point we can't go back to the Middle East or kick Russia out of Cuba even if we wanted to.*

"We're talking about *lawbreakers here,*" Abomba hissed, "We'll deal with the Middle East another day.

"I WANT THE DAMN GUNS CONFISCATED!" he boomed, swinging his feet off his desk and shaking his finger at Helder. "Our problem is trying to do the whole damn country at once ... and, damn it, it's not working ... so we'll do it one state at a time."

Abomba lifted his chin, posturing for the nonexistent cameras. "Yeah—that's what *I'll* do.

"JANE!" he stormed, so loud everyone flinched. "Have you replaced that *pussy-assed general* you put in charge of the Blue Shirts?"

"No, Mr. President," I haven't, but I'm evaluating candidates," Incompentado said, cutting her eyes at Barrett.

"WELL SHIT! ... That's no help. I want a real hard-ass. Yeah ... that's what I want, damn it. Someone who won't take shit off nobody."

Incompentado bit her upper lip. "You want someone who'll take on the locals—stand up to them?"

"*Yeah,* that's what I'm talking' about. A real ass-kicker."

Incompentado sighed, "Well, if you want a real ass-kicker then I'd suggest Colonel Savage."

"Didn't he get his own ass kicked in Alabama?"

"Uh, no, I wouldn't put it quite that way. The problem was he was totally outgunned—up against a bigger unit with heavy weapons and tanks. Under the circumstances, he did the only thing possible," she said with a shrug.

Fixing his gaze on Haggler, Abomba leaned forward and demanded, "Gene, what the hell have you done about this? Have you gotten them better ... er ... better—those anti-tank things?"

Haggler swallowed, "Yes, the Blue Shirts are training with anti-tank missiles. They still aren't capable of operating tanks."

"And why the hell *not* ... driving a tank can't be that hard to do?"

Haggler looked at the floor.

Turning to Barrett, the president softened his tone, "Vickie, so far you haven't had anything to say. What are your thoughts about this fuck up? What'd you hear from your bed buddy," Abomba leered.

"Well, I believe your question is, what will the military do, if you order them to suppress civilians—"

"*They damn well* better do what I tell them to do," Abomba exploded, rearing up in his chair. "Why else would I have wasted so much fuckin' time promoting generals loyal to me? They accepted my appointment and now those four star weenies have my logo tattooed on their asses."

Haggler realized what Barrett was attempting to say, and sitting forward on the couch interjected, "What Victoria means, Mr. President, is whether or not the military will accept your order as a *legal order*—"

"I'm their goddamn Commander in Chief. They goddamn well better follow my orders," Abomba growled, banging his fist on his desktop.

Haggler blanched and slouched back into the couch.

"And if they *don't?*" Barrett softly asked. "Barry, that is a possibility."

"That's what *you* were supposed to find out from your bed buddy."

Unperturbed, Barrett replied, "She hasn't found out because there is no answer. The consensus appears to be, wait for the order and then decide if it's legal."

"That's unacceptable. I'll, uh ... I'll, uh ... I'll ... what the hell do you call it? Oh yeah, I'll *prosecute* them."

"I believe you mean court-martial them," Haggler said, and for the first time seriously considered resigning. *Oh my god, he's losing it ... acting like a dictator.*

Seeing the need to get the discussion back on track, Incompentado suggested they begin the enforcement in the northeast, starting with Massachusetts, followed by New York and the surrounding states. "But," she cautioned, "Maine, New Hampshire and Vermont will be difficult."

The AG agreed.

The president stood and snarled, "They damn well better not be difficult. Now get out of here and make it happen."

Chapter 46

Southern Governors' Association Meeting
New Orleans, Louisiana
February 26 – 29, 2016

Billed as a conference on international trade, the Southern Governors' Association meeting provided a ready reason for governors from non-member states to attend. However it was the non-agenda item—federal gun laws—that attracted non-association governors and representatives. Quiet discussions on the issue began with casual meetings between governors and representatives at breakfast, in the bar, during breaks, in the halls, and later at private dinners and lunches.

On Monday evening a dinner meeting was held at a private club in Bay St. Louis. Governors from Maryland, Missouri and Virginia weren't invited because they favored gun seizure, however conservative representatives from those states were present. Conservative governors or representatives from non-association states were also in attendance.

Seceding from the union and forming a new confederacy was the initial topic, but it quickly became apparent many felt this was a desperation measure not yet called for. However, as the evening wore on, discussion quickly centered on protecting the Constitution. Foremost in most attendees' minds was how to deal with the federal government and its attempts to bypass the Constitution and grab the power reserved for the states.

Two states had already resorted to using their National Guards. Since no shots had been fired, the question was, what to do when—not if—it became necessary to engage federal troops. Forming a self-defense force was suggested, in effect creating the equivalent of a domestic NATO.

A couple of governors stated that such a move could split the nation, creating a nation within a nation, which prompted Colorado's representative to bring up the legality of the newly formed state of North Colorado. Washington hadn't recognized the newly formed state, because the Colorado legislature had yet to approve its formation. Stating there was no chance of that occurring with the current progressive dominated legislature, the representative hinted the northern counties were prepared to use force if necessary to complete their breakaway and legitimize their new state. After all, the representative reminded everyone, Thomas Jefferson left many wise sayings: one of which he quoted, *"I hold it that a little rebellion now and then is a good thing, and as necessary in the political world as storms in the physical."*

Before the evening ended, a gentlemen's agreement had been reached. States would back each other as required, if the federal government attempted to employ unconstitutional power. Each governor would employ his or her National Guard as needed. The issue of using force to support another state engaged in armed conflict with the federal government was left up to the individual governors. No one wanted to commit until forced to, yet all secretly feared it would become necessary at some point.

Upon returning to their respective states, the participants broached the subject with their state's National Guard commanders. Word quickly reached General Beck, who was being recognized as the go-to-general with the cool head. More than their civilian leaders, military commanders recognized the danger of a civil war—that it could mean the end of the United States. Worse still, it might well lead to the country being conquered by a foreign power.

The nation was divided along ideological lines.

Could a civil war be avoided?

As Federal and state gun law enforcement officers continued their efforts, in the New York state, they encountered several pockets of resistance in rural areas. Even though most guns had already been seized in cities and towns, and those few citizens still retaining firearms had met requirements by locking them in safes; there were separate incidents in which four men refused to surrender their weapons and were killed in firefights with SWAT officers.

Gun inspections in Connecticut and Massachusetts followed pretty much the same pattern. Independent Vermont was the first battleground state. Vermont, along with New Hampshire and Maine had skipped the Southern Governors' Association meeting, and hadn't engaged in any talks concerning mutually supporting each other.

Attorney General Helder received a call from the FBI director informing him that Vermont had refused to cooperate. Vermont State

Police had barred ATF and FBI agents from enforcing the new federal gun laws.

Helder called the president and then Incompentado. Vermont had just volunteered to be the administration's example. Something they would soon discover.

Chapter 47

Fort Indiantown Gap
Annville, PA
Friday, March 4, 2016

Lieutenant General Virgil Savage, commander of FEMA Corps' Blue Shirts, received a call from his boss, Jane Incompentado, at his headquarters on Fort Indiantown Gap (FTIG), near Annville, Pennsylvania. Known as "the Gap," FTIG's sprawling 18,000-acre military training installation had a history dating back to the mid 16th century and the French and Indian War. Established in 1755 by the colonial government, the Gap was one of the forts guarding the mountain passes, known as gaps; and now it was an ideal location for FEMA Corps' paramilitary Blue Shirt Corps.

"Yes, ma'am, I understand," Savage said, ending the call. Grinning, Savage was ecstatic—at last he was going to be allowed to kick some butt.

After General Sherman's departure, Secretary Incompentado had appointed Colonel Savage as the new FEMA Corp commander, but did not specify his rank, an oversight providing Savage the opportunity to promote himself to Lieutenant General.

With an ego expanded to match his new rank, Savage prepared to march on Vermont with a superior force. This was his opportunity to regain the face he'd lost in Colorado and Alabama.

Departing The Gap four days later, Lieutenant General (self-promoted) Savage led a column of ten buses, twenty Humvees and ten Bradley fighting vehicles on flatbed trailers north along I-81 through New York state to the I-88 intersection and proceeded to the northeast.

It wasn't long before Savage realized that, with the exception of Alaska, Incompentado couldn't have picked a worse state for him to start kicking butt. It was the month of March, and Vermont, largely rural with rugged terrain, had frigid temperatures and few large cities. The Blue Shirts were freezing their asses off.

Reaching the capital city, Montpelier, would be difficult. If the Vermont National Guard opposed him, his convoy would be exposed and easily attacked in the mountainous terrain. No, he decided, marching on the capital city was not a good idea. After conferring with the senior ATF agent, Savage decided Bennington, Vermont, located at the bottom of the state, would be his first target. From Bennington he could drive north on U.S. 7 or take State Road 9 east to Brattleboro, and then I-91 north toward the capital city. He decided to stage near Troy, New York, and then enter Vermont on State Road 9.

The long column of military-like vehicles driving north on I-81 quickly attracted attention. ABC was the first national television network to break the story. WNEP-TV Channel 16 in Scranton, PA, reported a column of FEMA Corps troops was on the move. Soon three TV vans and several reporters in automobiles were jockeying for position next to Savage's Humvee. "Where are you going?" was the question most often shouted at him.

Savage smiled and refused to answer.

The news media continued to shadow the column, taking advantage of every stop the Blue Shirts made in an attempt to learn their purpose and destination. Gradually the mission profile was revealed, and Vermont's governor, John Wilson, called the president to demand he put a stop to the madness—only to discover that President Abomba was en route to Hawaii for his monthly vacation. The governor's next call was to Vice President Blabberman, who assured him he'd look into the matter. The next morning, living up to his reputation, Blabberman confirmed, during a press conference, the column was heading to Vermont to support FBI and ATM agents in conducting inspections of homes and businesses for illegal guns.

After attempting to contact Secretary Incompentado and Secretary Haggler, neither of them would take his call, Governor Wilson realized the administration intended to make an example of him and his state.

"I should have gone to the New Orleans meeting," he muttered, waiting for his calls to the governors of Maine and New Hampshire to go through. Both governors expressed concern and promised to monitor events, but offered no assistance. *Don't they realize they're next?*

Resigned to his fate, the governor ordered his State Police to prevent the column from entering Vermont. *If they force their way past the police, I'll have a legal position,* he decided, but it failed to occur to him there might be shooting.

Known for its independence and free spirit, Texas was in turmoil.
The first and second "Come and Take It" events had exposed the problem,
but it still hadn't been widely recognized. Progressive-liberals fleeing taxes
and crime in northern states had moved to Texas to take advantage of its
lower taxes and climate. The new carpetbaggers slowly banded together,
and in addition to seeking and obtaining elected positions in local, state and
federal governments, began gaining control of the state's powerful news
media. Once in control, the progressives couldn't help themselves. They
began passing the same kind of laws and ordinances that ruined the states
they'd fled. Now the real Texicans were waking up. All they had to do was
look at events in Colorado to see where they were headed, and that wasn't
an acceptable destination.

Comments by politicians and news reporters pertaining to the
Alabama standoff with FEMA lit the fuse. A sarcastic commentary about
Colorado, Mississippi, and Alabama rednecks by Dallas TV news anchor
Paula Dunsforth-Frogmortin, a transplanted ultraliberal reporter from New
York City, triggered the first incident of the "No More Liberals"
movement.

Ms. Dunsforth-Frogmortin received a letter demanding an apology
for her comments, giving her two days to do so. Instead of apologizing, the
next evening she read the letter on her show, sneering at the ridiculous
demands of rednecks.

A week later, some unknown party pulled Dunsforth-Frogmortin into
a van inside the station's underground parking garage and drove off with
her. Police found her at five o'clock the next morning in front of the TV
station. Her head had been shaved, and she'd been tarred and feathered.

Outraged by the barbaric assault on one of their media darlings,
Dunsforth-Frogmortin's mewling, progressive-liberal sympathizers reacted
by demanding police protection for reporters and new laws against tarring
and feathering. Funded by a two million dollar donation by former Mayor
Goofyberg, the new carpetbaggers launched their anti-gun campaign—
aided by an endless list of like-minded celebrities. Dunsforth-Frogmortin's
leftist pals railed *ad nauseam* against crazy gun owners. "Guns are the root
of all evil," became the progressive-liberal's mantra.

Guns had to be taken away from the law-abiding. Apparently the libs
didn't want to pick a fight with cartels or gangs, since they were never
included in their tirades. After all, one had to be careful not to offend
people who retaliated with violent action. Apparently the libs failed to
equate Dunsforth-Frogmortin's tar-and-feathering incident to a violent
reprisal by Americans they called "gun-nuts."

Riled by what they perceived as an onerous assault on the Second Amendment, a group with the moniker "Texas for Texicans" took up the challenge of expelling liberals: thereby activating dormant liberal-conservative fault lines running through the state; and forcing law enforcement and elected politicians to choose sides. Texas had to decide whether it was a blue or a red state—purple was no longer an option. Since progressive-liberals were incapable of admitting mistakes, a mini civil war was brewing. The 21st Century carpetbaggers had to go.

The news media and thus the public had been ignoring the presidential primaries. Vice President Blabberman and Hilda Rodman were vying for the Democratic presidential nomination. It was a ho-hum campaign. Rodman would taunt the VP, and he would respond with another of his famous gaffs.

On the Republican side, the party was once again divided with ten assorted men and women seeking the nomination. The senior senator from Arizona was pushing a weak-kneed appeaser, no surprise there. Senator Crux had decided not to seek the nomination, because he was born in Canada with only one parent being a U.S. citizen. His father didn't become a citizen until 2005, thus the senator was not a "natural born citizen." Never mind that Abomba had gotten by with ignoring a similar problem. Colonel Alfred East was one of the Republican candidates, and appeared to be gaining traction with Constitutionalists, but the news media was doing everything in its power to discredit him.

Many Democrats and Republicans were seeking what was not available, a political party that represented old American values. Lifelong Democrats whose families had been with the party for generations couldn't contemplate becoming Republicans. In their minds the Tea Party was a branch of the Republican Party. Similar sentiments were true for many Republicans, who also considered the Tea Party an illegitimate stepchild.

President Abomba and his secret backers, The Obsidians, were aware of the splits and planned to take advantage of them. Funded with Islamic petrodollars, The Obsidians were led by a socialist billionaire who wanted to manage the world. Confident the master plan was about to be implemented, Abomba stood on the sidelines laughing at the fools competing in the primaries.

Other than Abomba and his wife, only five people knew the plan: Vickie Barrett, Edison Helder, the megalomaniac-socialist-billionaire-investor, a grand ayatollah, and an Arab king.

Abomba had no intention of leaving the White House and giving up his lifestyle. No, he wanted a civil war or insurrection so that he could declare martial law and remain president—president for life. *Once I gain control, why will I need Congress?* he smiled.

Chapter 48

New York – Vermont border
Thursday, March 10, 2016

Cɴɴ's **Walt Twister announced FEMA Corps** would be entering Vermont the next morning to support FBI and ATF agents inspecting houses and businesses for illegal guns, magazines and ammunition. Texicans and concerned citizens across the nation were glued to their TVs watching video of the FEMA Corps convoy, which was being led east on State Road 9 by a Humvee flying some sort of blue flag with three yellow stars. Ten miles ahead of the convoy, another TV channel showed two Vermont Highway Patrol cars blocking the road fifty yards inside Vermont's state line. Ten more patrol cars were parked in a line behind the roadblock. "Will there be a firefight?" one of the announcers wondered on an open mike.

Apparently the national networks didn't think so, because they returned to scheduled programming. If there was breaking news, they announced they would cut back to the live feed from helicopters. ABC's and CBS's helicopters stayed with the column, while NBC, FOX and CNN had vans stationed near the Vermont roadblock.

Watching the live video and growing increasingly concerned over the size of the FEMA force, Vermont's governor finally activated his National Guard. Unfortunately he'd waited too long. It would take time for the 86th Mountain Infantry Combat Team to mobilize and reach Bennington. Time they didn't have.

Over half of the Blue Shirts advancing on the Vermont roadblock had combat training, however, because of the selection criteria used, none could be considered leaders. The Blue Shirts would easily overwhelm police units, but how they would fare against a well-trained and disciplined Army unit was something Savage preferred not to dwell on.

The Bradleys mounted 25mm M242 Bushmaster main guns and M240C coaxial 7.26mm machine guns. Five Bradleys also mounted TOW

II anti-tank guided missile launchers capable of destroying any known tank. Each twenty-one foot long, twelve foot wide, twelve foot tall, thirty-three ton Bradley had a crew of three and carried six Blue Shirt soldiers.

Lieutenant General (self-promoted) Savage was ready to start a war.

Vermont highway patrol officer Lieutenant Alex Rydell watched the lead Humvee, flying an odd blue flag with three yellow stars, followed by the Bradleys, as the FEMA Corps' column crossed the state line and advance toward his position. Leaving the roadblock and walking down the center of the roadway toward the convoy, he held up his hand signaling for the vehicles to stop.

"What the hell does that jackass think he's doing?" Lieutenant General (self-promoted) Savage muttered, flinging open his Humvee's front passenger door and scowling as he got out and headed toward the highway patrolman.

Watching Savage approach, Rydell noted two things about him: first, he was swaggering; and second, he was wearing some kind of blue camouflage cap, with three stars pinned on its crown above the visor, and a matching camo uniform under a U.S. Army field jacket. *What the hell kind of uniform is that?* Rydell wondered. Having served two tours in Iraq, he'd seen many kinds of uniforms, but none like this one.

"Good morning, General, I'm Lieutenant Rydell, Vermont Highway Patrol. May I ask why you and your men are entering Vermont?" the patrolman said.

Savage sneered at the medium height man with the rank insignia of lieutenant. "Sonny, I'm the commander of FEMA Corps, and our mission is to make sure FBI and ATF agents do their job without interference from your men.

"Now, move your patrol cars out of the road so we can pass."

"I thought FEMA Corps was a civilian disaster assistance organization."

"Well, it is, at least part of it is. The other part is responsible for maintaining order.

"Seems your police force has interfered with federal agents, and we're here to make sure it doesn't happen again. So, move your patrol cars. This is the last time I'm gonna to tell you."

"General, *my orders* are to prevent you from entering Vermont. Now turn your vehicles around and leave."

Savage's eyes glistened—this was it. At last he could unleash his power.

Rydell watched the general's face morph into a wolfish grin. "Don't say I didn't warn you. What happens next is on you," Savage said, whirling around and leaving Rydell standing there, watching him stomp back to his Humvee.

What the hell is that arrogant bastard up to, Rydell wondered, watching the Humvee make a U-turn and pull in behind the first four Bradleys.

"Give me fuckin' orders to leave the state, will he? Well we'll damn well see about that," Savage scoffed, rearing back in his seat and keying his mike. "Eagle net ... this is Eagle-Six. Eagle's one, two, three, and four, advance and open fire on those patrol cars. *Take 'em out,*" he barked.

Two news helicopters from Albany, hovering north of the roadblock, were videoing the altercation. No one on board expected violence, as they watched the Bradleys form a line, four abreast, with their main guns pointing at the two patrol cars blocking the road. Only the reporter on board the CBS helicopter, who'd spent a month imbedded with troops in Afghanistan, realized what was about to happen. As soon as he contacted his producer, his video feed went live and was quickly picked up by the network.

A producer at ABC monitoring other stations saw CBS switch and quickly did the same. Both stations videoed and recorded what would later be compared to the first shot fired at Concord—the engagement that started the American Revolution.

Rydell watched in disbelief as four Bradleys pulled forward, forming a line. When the four began advancing, he understood. *The crazy general has ordered them to fire us.* "Son of a bitch," he muttered as he turned and ran screaming toward his two cruisers blocking the road, **"RUN—THEY'RE GOING TO FIRE."**

The four highway patrolmen manning the two cruisers saw Rydell running toward them and heard his voice, but couldn't make out what he was screaming. "What's he doing? one asked, when Rydell dived in a roadside ditch half way back.

"*Oh, my god,*" exclaimed one patrolman with combat experience. "THEY'RE GOING TO FIRE. TAKE COVER," he shouted, frantically running toward the ditch. He and two others made it, but the fourth wasn't so lucky. For rather than run, he'd stood mesmerized by the big guns and sadly perished when the first burst of 25mm explosive shells hit the two cars.

Vermont's Governor Wilson and the adjutant general were both in their offices watching the destruction of the roadblock on CBS. So were the governors of most of the lower forty-eight states, including New Hampshire and Maine. All had watched in stunned disbelief, unable to comprehend how the commander of a FEMA Corps unit—supposedly a civilian disaster assistance organization—would dare order his men to fire on state law enforcement personnel and vehicles. *Worse than that, they all thought, was how the commander, with no regard for human life, could callously order the Bradleys to advance two abreast, pushing the burning patrol cars off the road while continuing to fire on the remaining patrol cars.* What had happened to state sovereignty? Who would pay for this blatant disregard for human life?

The adjutant general didn't wait for the governor's call. Pushing the speed dial button for his commander, Colonel McGill, he issued terse orders, "Colonel, I'm ordering you to seek out—with prejudice—and destroy the FEMA Corps unit that has entered Vermont on State Road 9 near Bennington."

Colonel McGill was the commanding officer of the 86th Infantry Brigade Combat Team (Mountain), which had been known as the Green Mountain Boys since the revolutionary war. In 2006 the 86th was converted from a heavy infantry brigade to a light infantry brigade mountain, thereby losing its M1A2 tanks. Thus the 86th had no armor, which presented no problems for their commander since the terrain along State Road 9 was not suitable for armor, but very suitable for a light infantry specially trained for mountain fighting.

Shortly after speaking with the adjutant general and confirming his orders, Governor Wilson placed a call to the White House, only to learn the president was still in Hawaii. After being patched through to the president's vacation residence, Wilson was told the president was still asleep and would return his call after his morning golf game. Three hours later when the president awoke and was briefed on events in Vermont, his aide noticed he appeared pleased and wondered why.

Vickie Barrett was having grave doubts about the president's plan. Her sensitive political ear wasn't hearing what she'd hoped to hear. There was no doubt a revolution or civil war was brewing, but she was beginning to realize it might not be the war they were planning. *We may have started something that can blow up in our faces.*

Glenn Deck broke the Vermont roadblock story during the last few minutes of his morning radio show. Following Deck, Rusty Limbo picked up the ball and ran for the end zone.

FOX Evening News had an array of guests, retired military officers, former cabinet members or advisors and a few candidates. Later that evening Senator Crux was scheduled to be on the O'Rippley Quotient, and Colonel East would follow on Sean Haddley's show.

ABC, CBS, and NBC were attempting to put a good face on FEMA Corps' attack on the Vermont roadblock—something proving very difficult to pull off. CNN and MSNBC were making a valiant effort to justify killing five Vermont Highway Patrolmen and the destruction of twelve vehicles. None of the three networks had reported on the ongoing no-knock warrantless searches of homes in Bennington and confiscation of firearms by federal agents.

Enjoying the beach in Hawaii, the president refused to take calls from governors demanding explanations. Back home, calls for impeachment rose in House chambers; but, confident Senate President Realdick would never allow a trial, Speaker Balogni ignored them.

Many military commanders and senior enlisted began privately fearing they'd be called on to engage civilians and National Guard units. A number of generals and colonels quietly started drafting requests for retirement. In General Beck's office the phone continued to ring.

In Maine and New Hampshire the governors began to sweat. Would Vermont ask for help—and if they did, should they join the fight?

Colonel McGill met with his staff and decided the best way to stop FEMA Blue Shirts was to ambush their column on State Road 9, the Molly Stark Trail, near Woodford State Park. Op orders were issued immediately after the meeting, and McGill called the Highway Patrol commander to request he do everything possible to delay the FEMA Blue Shirts. "Keep them in the area as long as possible," McGill said, "I need time to move my troops and set up an ambush."

General Savage was about to experience civilian sabotage, something he'd failed to anticipate.

Chapter 49

The O'Rippley Quotient
8 p.m., Friday, March 11, 2016

William O'Rippley's talking points memo dealt with FEMA Corps' military component. After stressing the outpouring of public rage he'd been receiving in e-mail's and letters regarding the Corps' attack on Vermont's highway patrolmen, O'Rippley began his opening talking points memo. "It has recently become evident the Department of Homeland Security's civilian disaster relief arm, FEMA Corps, which has historically been comprised of eighteen to twenty-four-year-olds solely devoted to disaster preparedness, response, and recovery, has surreptitiously been used to mask nefarious activities. To be specific, we have learned FEMA Corps is now the current administration's hidden secret police force. The same police force Abomba called for in his first campaign. A paramilitary unit comprised of hardened, combat-trained troops, whose primary purpose is to assist FBI and ATF agents in enforcing federal laws. Commonly referred to by our military as 'Blue Shirts,' this new group of FEMA Corps enforcers is actually, in and of itself, a disaster … a *manmade* disaster we've most recently seen in the making in Vermont.

"We first saw the Blue Shirts in Golden, Colorado, and then again in Mudford, Alabama. Now it appears Blue Shirts have invaded one of our northeastern states, Vermont, to enforce the administration's unconstitutional gun laws. Here to join me this evening in the No Centrifugal Force Zone for a discussion on these recent events is my guest, Senator Crux. The senator is here at his own request and is anxious to share his views on what many are calling an invasion of one of the United States sovereign states."

After pulling back to show a view of Senator Crux sitting across the table from O'Rippley, the camera zoomed in on Crux, who began by saying, "Thank you for having me Bill, but while I'm pleased to be here I'm compelled to say I am deeply concerned by what's been happening in our country—particularly what occurred in Vermont. I couldn't believe my eyes when I saw those four FEMA armored vehicles open fire on

Vermont's highway patrol officers and their vehicles. I actually had to slap my face to make sure I was awake and not dreaming. Sure, this sort of thing could happen in Cuba, but in the United States? My God! President Abomba is acting like Castro—he's acting like *a dictator.*"

As Crux concluded, the camera zoomed in on a visibly shocked O'Rippley staring wide-eyed at his guest. Finally he said, "Now Senator, that's a pretty harsh statement, don't you think?"

"Bill, 'it' *is* what it *is* … to paraphrase a former president—and in this case *'it'* means dictator."

Frowning and looking perplexed, O'Rippley finally asked, "What happens if the Vermont's governor uses his National Guard like the governor of Alabama did?"

"Then we have the makings for a revolution. Maine and New Hampshire could join Vermont and secede. Actually, they could probably form a self-sustaining republic. Remember they have common borders with Canada, as well as lots of natural resources and a seaport."

O'Rippley sat quietly for several seconds, contemplating Crux's statement. "If they did, other states might follow," he said.

"Yes, and that could very well be the end of the United States as we know it."

After the station break, O'Rippley moved on to another subject. "Senator, in recent weeks media attention has been focused on gun control legislation; the Chicago bombings; the shootout in Golden, Colorado; the assassination of Reverend Dullston; the presence of the FEMA Corps paramilitary group in Mudford, Alabama; and now what appears to be the Department Homeland Security's invasion of Vermont.

"What's going on?"

"That's a very good question, Bill. While all of these things seem important and newsworthy, in reality they are diverting attention from our real problems.

"We have government controlled medical care, which is proving far worse than what it replaced, and becoming increasingly more complicated by a growing shortage of doctors and nurses. That's one thing.

"Another is rising unemployment. And still another—perhaps the worst—is the rising cost of electricity." Crux frowned. "In short, Bill, all of these examples are representative of our progressive-liberal leaders' meddling and the unintended consequences they have created.

"Environmental causes like the 'War on Coal,' 'Global Warming,' and 'Carbon Footprint Credits' are in reality nothing more than progressive hysteria … scams that are causing massive unemployment in coal producing states and making some progressives rich. Progressive-liberals demand changes that are having a huge impact on our economy and offer pie-in-the-sky fantasies as alternatives." Crux paused, and O'Rippley nodded.

"Look, Bill, let's take a minute to talk about electricity. In the United States, thirty-seven percent of our electricity is—or rather was—produced by coal-fired power plants. Natural gas power plants used to provide another thirty percent, along with nineteen percent from nuclear plants and seven percent from hydroelectric. Together they produce ninety-three percent of our electricity. A few power plants still use oil as fuel, about one percent. As things stand, all the so-called green energy sources combined produce less than six percent of our electrical power."

"*What?* Is it really that small a percentage?" O'Rippley asked.

"Yes, Bill, I'm sorry to say it is, and now—thanks to greenie-libs—we're reaping the unintended consequences. The reality is that coal-fired power plants are shutting down along with coal mining. We have currently lost over one-third of our coal fired electrical generating plants with no real replacement. This means a drastic increase in cost, coupled with a drastic reduction in available electrical power. When the last coal fired plant shuts down we will have lost thirty-seven percent of our electrical power generating capacity.

"And what are our liberal administration and Congress doing to solve the problem? The EPA is drafting regulations to reduce our carbon footprint by closing our natural gas and petroleum generating plants, knocking out another thirty-one percent of our electrical power generating capacity."

Blinking in consternation, O'Rippley shook his head, "Senator, I have to say I am completely *flummoxed*—which by the way is our Thesaurus word for the day. Don't you be flummoxed by the facts, folks," he said, raising an eyebrow and setting up his next sarcastic comment.

"How can this possibly be, when the President just told the nation green energy was our salvation, and America must set an example for the rest of the world. What say you?"

"Well, Bill, I hear what you're saying; and in response, *I'm sorry to say*, the only example we've been setting is how to destroy the greatest nation in the history of the world in seven years."

The Sean Haddley Show followed at ten o'clock, with former Congressman Colonel East as Sean's first guest. The camera shot opened on the show's usual set with Haddley and East sitting side by side on stools behind a tall interview counter. Haddley wasted no time getting to the main issue. "Colonel East, you are one of ten candidates for the Republican nomination for president; though if poles are any indication, there's no apparent clear-cut forerunner." Haddley pause, and then continued, "How do you see your chances of winning the nomination?"

"Well, Sean, the politically correct answer would be *good*, but then, as your viewers know, I'm not into politically correct answers."

Haddley chuckled.

"The truth is that once again the party is divided—so much so, that any one of the candidates will probably lose to former Secretary of State Hilda Rodman. All she has to do is sit back and let us destroy each other—just as we've done the last two elections."

Suppressing a grin, Haddley asked, "What about the Vice President? Secretary Rodman has to win the primary."

This time East chuckled, "Sean, she won the nomination when she declared her candidacy. Vice President Blabberman is nothing but a comic—a stage prop. He's her lightning rod. He attracts the hard questions, while she spoon-feeds the media pabulum."

"You don't seem very enthusiastic about your chances to win the nomination."

East took a deep breath and focused on the camera, "You're partially correct, Sean. I don't think I—or for that matter any Republican candidate—has a chance of winning the election."

East paused and sat blank-faced for three seconds, "That's why tonight I'm here to announce my formal withdrawal from the Republican Party primary and the Republican Party."

Prompted through his earphones by producers to zoom in on Haddley's face, the cameraman actually gave viewer's high theater. For in what inadvertently amounted to comic relief, the camera caught Haddley literally sitting with his mouth hanging open.

"And that's why, Sean," East said, his face morphing into a grin when the camera turned on him, "I'm pleased to make a second announcement tonight, "As of this afternoon, I've been named the nominee of the newly formed Constitutionalist Party. Our Founding Fathers were wise men, and I plan to lead the nation back to Constitutional values that made us great."

For several seconds Haddley continued gaping at East, until finally—prompted by his show's director cuing him, "*Say something,*" in his earbud, he jumped from his stool and reached out to shake East's hand. Then smiling broadly and looking into the camera, he said, with emotion, "Well, there you have it viewers. I can't tell you how touched I am, Colonel," he said turning to East, "that you have chosen to make this auspicious announcement on my show. I wish you all the success in the world, and may God bless you in your run for the presidency."

When word of East's announcement reached the president in Hawaii via a note delivered by his favorite aide, Abomba missed an easy putt and threw his club at the messenger.

Bennington, Vermont
Saturday, March 12, 2016

FBI and ATF agents began breaking into gun stores at dawn, only to discover empty shelves and gun racks. By noon, only fourteen boxes of .22 short cartridges, three boxes of .25 caliber pistol cartridges, and two boxes of specialty rifle ammunition had been seized. Frustrated and angry, the agents moved to residential areas and began banging on doors. Not surprisingly, no guns were found there either; however, agents did arrest several citizens who refused to answer question about rifles and pistols agents they were accused of having.

When Sunday turned into a repeat of Saturday, General Savage announced plans to depart Bennington for Brattleboro on Monday morning.

Although many Blue Shirts were ex-military, very few were interested in performing mundane duties such as sentry duty. It seemed as though men assigned to guard the FEMA vehicles found standing outside in the near sub-zero cold unpleasant, and somehow managed to find warmer locations inside where there were televisions.

As Sunday night became Monday morning, a group of men wearing dark cloths and ski masks slipped undetected into FEMA's vehicle compound, where they did their best to sabotage the Humvees and Bradleys. A task that proved more difficult than expected, but—on the plus side—accomplished just enough damage to delay departure until Tuesday, which gave Colonel McGill the additional day he needed.

Chapter 50

Colonel McGill completed a quick inspection of the ambush site. He'd received modified orders changing his mission from destroy to eject if possible, using whatever force required. This meant providing General Savage the option of retreating back down State Road 9 to New York, or turning south on State Road 8 leading to Massachusetts.

The terrain along parts of State Road 9 was mountainous and heavily forested, providing little maneuvering room for vehicles, which usually cut both ways—but this time, McGill had no tracked vehicles and the terrain was perfect for the 86th Infantry Brigade Combat Team (Mountain).

McGill decided on a close engagement—an ambush. Since the 86th no longer had heavy armor, the TOW II missiles on the FEMA Corps Bradleys wouldn't be a major concern, but the 25mm Chain Gun and M2 .50 caliber machine guns would. The 86th's M16s and SAWs wouldn't be effective against the armored Bradleys and Humvees, so the weapon of choice was the M136 AT4 84mm anti-tank rocket launcher, classified as a recoilless rifle.

Manufactured by Saab Bofors Dynamics, the AT4 replaced the Vietnam era M72 66mm Light Anti-tank Weapon, known as the LAW, with a 84mm projectile that had a 4 pound shaped charge warhead containing 1.73 pounds of Octol explosive, a very high-energy explosive mix of 70% HMX and 30% TNT. Both weapons are similar to the Russian RPG, in that they launch unguided projectiles—rockets; but unlike the RPG, neither the LAW nor AT4 can be reloaded, and neither has a sustainer rocket motor. In other words, the rocket motor completely burns out before the projectile leaves the launch tube, thus the recoilless rifle designation.

The next step up in anti-tank weapons are missile launchers, the difference being that missiles are guided and rockets aren't. And since they are guided, anti-tank missiles can engage targets at greater distances.

All the men and women assigned to the ambush had viewed video of the Bradleys chewing up the Highway Patrol roadblock. None had any intention of firing warning shots.

The ambush was staged along a curving section of State Road 9, with the anti-tank teams concealed in foxholes or behind natural barriers on high ground north of the road. Once the ambush was sprung, the missile teams had orders to take out any vehicle firing at them, but allow vehicles turning back without firing to depart.

An OP or observation point had been positioned two miles to the west near Molly Stark State Park, and the men and women of The Green Mountain Boys settled down and waited for the show to begin.

General Beck was in his home office when he received a phone call on his burner phone advising him of the ambush in Vermont. Quickly departing for the headquarters building, he mulled over the serious situation facing the nation. *The shit is about to hit the fan and it's going to be a shit storm ... wonder what the President will do ... order the military to attack a National Guard unit that's part of the 42nd Infantry? That would mean federalizing and ordering the Maine, New Hampshire, New York and Connecticut National Guards to attack Vermont's National Guard. I sure wouldn't want to be the commander of the 42nd Infantry Division Light— the Rainbow Division. What would I do, if I were in his chair? The 42nd is comprised of the Connecticut, Maine, Maryland, Massachusetts, New Hampshire, New Jersey, New York, Rhode Island, and Vermont National Guards. What if the governors of some of the other states order their National Guards to support Vermont? Damn, a mini-civil war in one command. Better start planning a course of action for CENTCOM. In a way I'm glad the vice commander retired and no replacement has been named, but, on the other hand, that places the ball in my court. Our commander won't have a clue. Then again, do I?*

Sergeant Wolfenberger watched the lead Humvee, displaying a blue flag with three yellow stars, pass Molly Stark State Park, round the curve where State Road 9 turned north, then curve back to the east, and then south; before hooking back to the north toward the horseshoe bend that swung the road back to the south. "Showtime," he whispered to Corporal Cooperjack, and then, keying his mike, he said, "Stag-Six, this is Crow-One, contact, repeat contact."

"Crow-One, contact understood. Out," Colonel McGill said, from his command post two miles to the east.

Every radio was tuned to the Stag network, and all heard the OP's report. Men and women moved into attack position. AT4s were armed and aimed toward the road. The fire order would be given when the lead Humvee reached the east end of the kill zone, leaving the other Humvees and Bradleys exposed along the road below. As the lead Humvee passed the first AT4 position—the position that would take out the last armored vehicle in the column—the gunner whispered, "It's gonna be a turkey shoot."

"Yeah, just like our police were at the roadblock," Julie-Anne acknowledged, standing ready to hand the gunner a second AT4.

The news media had tired of the Blue Shirts activities—or more to the point, the lack of activities—in Bennington, and moved on to other more interesting stories. FOX News, however, had received an anonymous tip. "Be sure to cover the FEMA Corps movement toward Brattleboro. If you don't, you're going to miss a great story," the caller had said.

The local station's helicopter, which had been quickly dispatched with a reporter and cameramen, was approaching Harriman Reservoir. "We should catch up with them any time now," the pilot commented, using the intercom. "The road is entering a remote area with lots of curves. Don't know what you expect to happen, but it's sure a good place to cause the Blue Shirts some trouble," he told Bob, the reporter. "There's the column about two miles ahead."

Bob saw the mile long convoy of vehicles approaching a horseshoe bend.

Reducing altitude, the pilot pointed to some military vehicles parked along two service roads north of State Road 9, and noted they wouldn't be visible from the road. *Something's up, that's for sure.* Next he saw men in military uniforms in among the trees north of the road. Having flown Blackhawks in Iraq, he recognized an ambush when he saw one. Pointing to the men scattered along a ridge north of the road, he keyed his mike on intercom, "Bob, Jim, I see men with rocket launchers on the ridge. I think they're going to ambush the FEMA Corps column."

Bob called his station manager and told him to get ready, "It looks like the FEMA Corps column is going to be ambushed and we can video it." The station manager told him to start videoing and they'd look at the feed.

Colonel McGill saw the news chopper and hoped it wouldn't spoil his party. Keying his mike, the said, "This is Stag-Six Actual. Hold your positions, do nothing to attract the attention of that chopper. The column is half way into the kill zone."

General Savage noted the helicopter and decided it was about time for his Blue Shirts to be back in the news. *Hope they stay with us, because we're gonna make a big splash when we get to Brattleboro.*

The ten FBI and ATF agents, riding in three black SUVs behind the last Humvee, had been griping ever since leaving Bennington about their lack of arrests.

None of the Humvee's gunners were standing behind their M2 .50 caliber machine guns. The Bradleys had all their hatches open, and their commanders were standing with their heads out of the top hatches. Bradley Blue Shirt crews were bitching about why the Brads were being driven rather than placed on the trailers—especially those crewmembers riding in the rear compartments. They all knew riding in heated buses beat the hell out of being in the cold, cramped Bradleys.

When the helicopter pilot saw men raising up and aiming rocket launchers at the column, he keyed his mike and said, "Get ready, it's about to start."

Bob notified his station manager, and a minute later viewers across the nation watched a Humvee being driven south along a service road somewhere in Vermont. Suddenly slowing and turning sideways to block the road, the Humvee came to a stop. Then the driver, dressed in a U.S. Army combat uniform, got out, walked to the middle of the road, and held up his hand to indicate the approaching FEMA column should stop.

First Lieutenant Appleman watched the lead vehicle in the column, a FEMA Humvee, flying a blue flag stop about ten yards in front of him. Walking toward the passenger side of the vehicle Appleton glanced at the blue flag with three yellow stars on it. *What the hell kind of general's flag is that?* He wondered, stopping by the vehicle's left bumper when a man with three stars on his blue camouflage uniform flung open the door got out. "What's your problem, Lieutenant?" the man demanded.

"Sir, I'm here to officially read you orders from Vermont's Governor and Adjacent General, who's commander of the Vermont National Guard," the lieutenant said, and holding up a slip of paper, began reading aloud, 'You are hereby ordered to turn around and depart the Freedom and Liberty State of Vermont. You have permission to exit on State Highway 9 without stopping in Bennington. Or you may turn south on State Road 8.' " Having delivered the orders, Appleton folded the paper, stuck it in his pants pocket and looked at Savage, who was leaning up against the Humvee sneering at him.

"Sir, in conclusion, I've been directed to tell you *we* have orders to stop you, if you refuse to turn around and depart the state."

"You do, do you? Well, just who the hell *are* you, sonny?"

"It just so happens, *we're* part of the Department of Homeland Security, and *we'll* go wherever the hell *we* want to. Your state police attempted to stop us once before. Didn't your people learn anything from that experience?"

"Yes, sir, we *most certainly did*. Now to answer you first question, we are the Green Mountain Boys, a military unit dating back to a time before the Revolutionary War."

Colonel McGill keyed his mike, and said, "This is Stag-Six, prepare to execute fire plan Alpha."

Rocket launch teams removed safety pins located at the rear of the weapon, freeing the firing rod. Next they uncovered the front and rear sights, allowing them to pop up. Grasping the firing rod cocking lever, gunners used it to cock the firing rod, which armed the AT4. Then, being careful to ensure the area behind the tube was clear—including both the gunner's and loader's legs, if in a prone position—the gunners assumed their firing positions and waited for the fire command.

All the Humvees and Bradleys were on the target list if they fired. Only the lead Humvee with the general's flag would be spared if the shooting started. SUVs transporting the FBI and ATF agents wouldn't be targeted unless they fired.

There had been a lot of heated discussion about ordering the FEMA Corps unit to turn around and exit the state. As it happened, the deciding argument for a "no warning engagement" centered on FEMA Corps having fired on the Highway Patrol roadblock with no warning. It was therefore concluded the Green Mountain Boys would return the favor. When FEMA first entered the state, the Highway Patrol had asked them to turn around, and this time they'd be given the same opportunity. Only this time if they fired, things would be decidedly different.

General Savage scowled at the tall lieutenant and said, "I'm only going to say this once. We are *not* leaving this state. Now, get the fuck out of my way, or I'll order my gunner to fire on you."

Obeying his orders, the lieutenant said nothing in return. Instead he turned, got in his Humvee and departed back up the service road.

Filled with rage as he stood watching the lieutenant depart, Savage spun around, ripped open the Humvee's door and got in. Then, keying his mike, he ordered his Bradleys to train their guns on the terrain on either side of the road and fire on anything suspicious.

So when the trigger-happy gunner in the third Bradley saw movement on the ridge north of the road and opened fire with his chain gun, the other Bradley's gunners joined in, firing into the tree line. Then, not to be out done, the machine gunners on the Humvees opened up with their .50 caliber M2s.

Colonel McGill had hoped it wouldn't come to this, but when the Bradleys fired, he keyed his mike and ordered, "This is Stag-Six. Execute, Repeat Execute."

Sighting in on the last Humvee, Sergeant Hollinger softly asked Julie-Anne, "Are your legs clear of the back blast area?"

"Yes"

Hollinger depressed the red safety lever and slid the red firing button forward with his right thumb, thereby releasing the cocked firing rod, which then struck the firing pin, igniting the rocket propellant. Once ignited, the propellant quickly decomposed into hot gases, which were expelled rearward through nozzles, blowing out the back seal of the launcher. At this point the projectile was no longer attached to the launcher, and the rocket motor propelled it forward. Forward thrust equaled rearward thrust, thus the designation recoilless. By the time the fin-stabilized projectile had cleared the launch tube, the rocket motor had burned out, and the 4-pound projectile was traveling at 985 feet per second on a ballistic path toward the last Humvee 200 meters distant. In less than a second, the projectile impacted, destroying the vehicle and killing its occupants.

"Holy cow," the helicopter pilot exclaimed, when he realized what was happening. "Oh my god, did you see those back blast clouds on the ridge, they're gonna take out the entire column. Did you get it on camera?"

Bob was attempting to explain why several vehicles in the column seemed to have been instantaneously destroyed, when he paused to listen to what the pilot was saying. "What'd you mean by back blast?" he asked, unaware his and the pilot's conversation was being heard by the entire FOX News network.

"If I'm right, we just saw a number of AT4 recoilless rifles fired. The weapon expels the rocket motor gases out the rear, and you don't want to be behind it. That's what caused the dust clouds."

"Oh. Thanks. What you're seeing, folks," Bob continued describing the scene below, "are destroyed FEMA Corps vehicles.

"No, wait a minute, not all the vehicles were destroyed. The lead Humvee with the blue flag is still intact. The rest are burning, some overturned and knocked off the road.

"Three black SUVs, several buses, and tractor trailers pulling flatbed trailers at the rear of the column haven't been damaged." Bob stopped reporting, attempting to regain his composure. "I don't know how to describe what just happened. You saw it. One minute there was a column of vehicles, the next second they were destroyed. I can't believe it."

"Looks like the Green Mountain Boys paid FEMA back for killing the Highway Patrolmen," the pilot muttered, forgetting he was still patched into the feed going to the station.

General Savage's first indication he was under attack was the concussion from the AT4 warhead destroying the Bradley behind his command vehicle. Jumping out of his Humvee, he stood staring in disbelief at the burning vehicles behind his—completely unable to process what his eyes and ears were telling him.

A couple of minutes later the same National Guard Humvee returned; but this time a husky colonel, dressed in the Army's new camo combat uniform, got out and walked up to the Blue Shirts' bewildered leader. "Are you the fool in charge?"

Incensed the colonel didn't salute or address him in the manner prescribed for addressing a senior officer, Savage instantly went on the defensive. "Colonel, I'm Lieutenant General Savage, and you have a lot of explaining to do. You just killed federal troops."

McGill sneered and said, "You're not a general in any army I know. Even so, I do know who you are. You're the fool who was going to machine gun civilians in Colorado, and then got kicked out of Alabama.

"Now, you're the same fool *I'm* kicking out of Vermont. I don't give a fuck who you think you are, but when you come into my state and machine gun our police, you're goddamn well gonna answer to me.

"Now ... turn around and get the hell out of Vermont—while you still can."

Destroyed or burning vehicles blocked the narrow road, making it nearly impossible for the busses and tractor-trailers to turn around. Several would be abandoned. National Guard medics began treating the wounded, and ambulances dispatched from Brattleboro and Bennington would soon encounter clogged roads.

More news helicopters arrived, interfering with National Guard and hospital helicopters attempting to remove the wounded.

Savage and his survivors were unable to comply with Colonel McGill's orders until late afternoon when the road cleared. Finally, the remnants of his once "mighty" FEMA column limped out of Vermont on State Road 8.

Chapter 51

Department of Homeland Security
Washington, DC
Tuesday, March 15, 2016

Secretary of Homeland Security Jane Incompentado glowered at the TV screen in her office, refusing to accept what she was seeing. FOX News had videoed the entire Vermont ambush, and now replays were up on every network. Even though Vickie Barrett had warned her a governor could order the state's National Guard to engage her Blue Shirts, she hadn't thought the possibility credible. *Hell, the only thing the governors of Alabama and Colorado did was threaten. Well, it sure as hell is credible now. I should have listened to Vickie. She's the real brains in the White House ... makes the hard decisions the President can't or won't make. I'm sure she prevented several raids on Osama bin-Laden, before the Secretary of State and the DCI authorized the final raid without her knowledge. I also think she handled the Benghazi affair correctly, after the President passed the ball to his Secretary of Defense. That damn fool was going to authorize the military to go into Libya, before Vickie put a stop to the nonsense. Hmmm... perhaps I should resign.*

Her thoughts interrupted by the phone ringing on her desk—the one only she answered—she checked caller ID. *Speak of the devil. It's the brains herself,* she smirked.

"WHAT THE HELL HAPPENED?" Barrett stormed. "The President's furious. He's in the White House, and there's no way for him to leave without encountering reporters. How's he going to explain this disaster?"

"Vickie, all I know is what's been broadcast by FOX."

"*Madam Secretary,* do you mean to tell me you haven't spoken with your kick-ass general?"

Hearing Barrett address her so formally told Incompentado she was in trouble. *Shit ... she's going to throw me under the bus,* she cringed; but then—buoyed by a random thought—smiled. *Oh, well, at least I'll have plenty of company.*

"Ms. Barrett, I'm attempting to contact General Savage, the FBI and ATF to see if they've heard from their agents."

"Don't bother, I've already called them. All they know is their agents need clean pants.

"Both Jay Schpinmeister and I need talking points. Reporters are clamoring for answers, and we can't suffer another epidemic of foot-in-the-mouth statements, damn it. Remember Benghazi?

"Get hold of Savage. Then get back to me … and when you do, you'd better have some answers."

"Bitch," Incompentado whispered, when the line went dead. Then, slamming down the receiver and reaching for her cell phone she redialed Savage's number—only to once more have her call bumped to his message box.

The White House
Late Tuesday morning, March 15, 2016

Tossing his favorite putter from hand to hand, President Abomba paced back and forth the length of his small private office. *How in hell do I explain this mess? Who's to blame? Who CAN I blame? Vickie's working the problem for me, and she always knows what to do. Sure hope she comes up with an answer soon. Damn, I hate being bothered with this crap. Jay's already been in here twice pestering me about what to tell the damn reporters … and I sure don't need the First Lady getting her panties in a wad—again.*

The Pentagon
Tuesday morning, March 15, 2016

"Good morning Mr. President," Secretary of Defense Gene Haggler's said, answering the ringing red phone on his desk.

"What's so fuckin' good about it?" a surprised Haggler heard Vickie Barrett say.

Damn! If she's calling from the president's desk, it means he's in panic mode. I can tell by her nasty tone she's spittin' mad, and for good reason. Shit! Now I'm going to get more politically stupid orders. "Yes, Vickie, you're correct, there's absolutely nothing good about this disaster. Remember, I warned the President this could happen.

"That damned idiot Savage fired on the Vermont Highway Patrol, killed some of them, and then went ripping into Bennington like an

invading army. What the hell did you nitwits *think* would happen?"
Haggler asked, disgust dripping off every word.

"That's past history. What are our options? There's no way we can
let Vermont get away with this. Hell, if we do we can kiss our gun
legislation good-bye. Probably our environmental regulations on coal as
well."

Yeah, and that might be a good thing, Haggler thought. *Your
healthcare plan turned to shit and you're still trying to weasel out of the
consequences. Coal fired power production plants started shutting down
last week. In about another month, generating capacity will be exceeded by
demand, and that's when under-informed voters'll wake up. No electric
stove, no heat, no lights, and no water.* Haggler chuckled. *If Abomba thinks
the Vermont fuck-up was a problem, wait until that happens.*

"What the hell's so *funny,* Gene?" Barrett snapped.

Haggler realized he'd laughed out loud and attempted to cover.
"Nothing, Vicki—sorry. I just had a vision of that phony general hauling
ass out of Vermont with his tail between his legs."

Vickie chuckled, "Yeah, I get the picture."

Becoming serious, Haggler asked, "I'm not sure what you want.
Vermont's governor activated his National Guard and told them to eject
Savage and his Blue Shirts. I've watched the video, as have the Joint
Chiefs. We've all concluded one of FEMA Corps' Bradleys opened fire
first, followed by the rest of the Bradleys and Humvees—*damn trigger-
happy fools.* Look, Vickie, the National Guard only took out the armored
vehicles. The fact that FEMA shot first is what we need to remember."

"Well, that's no excuse. The Guard's sneak attack on federal forces is
unacceptable. We have to make an example.

"We can have the AG issue arrest warrants for the governor and
commanding officer." Barrett suggested.

Fool! Do that and you'll become the example. "If you do, who's
going to serve the warrants? Do you want more killing?"

"Do you really think the National Guard would interfere with federal
agents?"

Finally realizing how out of touch progressive-liberals like Barrett
really were, Haggler wanted to pound his head on his desk. "Vickie, if the
Guard destroyed a column of FEMA Corps vehicles, do you honestly think
they'll let your federal agents come in and arrest their governor? By
invading Vermont you've started a war. *Back off* … before it goes any
further. Fire somebody and have the President apologize to the governor."

"WHAT? *APOLOGIZE?* Are you nuts? Look, I did some checking. You have the 42nd Infantry Division at Troy, New York. Order the commander to put an end to this Vermont rebellion." Barrett paused to think about what she'd just said. "Rebellion ... *Yeah,* that's what this is—a rebellion."

Now Haggler really had to restrain himself from banging his head on his desktop. "Vickie," he said clinching his jaw, "the 42nd Infantry Division is made up of Connecticut, Maine, Maryland, Massachusetts, New Hampshire, New Jersey, New York, Rhode Island, and *Vermont* National Guards. The President will have to federalize all of these National Guards, and then order the commander to take action."

"There are several problems associated with your suggestion."

"What problems?"

"First, one or more of the governors could counter the President's orders, just like the Alabama governor did.

"Secondly, it's conceivable that one or more of the governors might order their state's National Guard to support Vermont. If the President pushes this ... well, it could get *very* nasty."

After a long pause, Barrett asked, "Do you think that could really happen ... governors going against the President, I mean?"

"I don't know, Vickie ... and I don't want to find out. Do you?"

"Let me think about this. I'll call you back."

CENTCOM
Tuesday morning, 15 March 2016

General Beck had asked the entire staff to assemble in the main conference room to watch FOX News on WTVT, Channel 13. Everyone was patiently waiting through a string of commercials and news trivia for whatever they were supposed to watch. All of them were wondering why they were there, and as usual Beck wasn't saying anything. Colonel Collins had managed to sit in the chair across the table from him, so that she could study his expression. *He always knows more than he lets on. Why has he called us in to watch FOX? What's so important? It's mostly local news,* she wondered. She, along with everyone else, soon found out when a Breaking News banner flashed on the screen.

Watching in earnest, they heard the national anchor say, "We interrupt our regularly scheduled programming for a FOX News Alert. Earlier in the hour, one of our Fox affiliate stations in Vermont received a tip suggesting its news helicopter should follow a FEMA Corps column departing Bennington, Vermont for Brattleboro. Our helicopter caught up with the column on State Road 9, and we've been monitoring the feed for the past few minutes. What you're viewing is live coverage from the area."

Conversations ceased and all eyes watched the large screen showing a ridge above a two-lane rural road, where men and women, wearing camouflage uniforms, were taking up positions—some holding rocket launchers.

"Ambush," General Roberts muttered.

No one disagreed, as most sat intently watching. All that is, but John Ulrich, whom Beck happened to notice sitting off to the side by himself. *Everyone but John is actively showing interest in what's happening,* Beck observed studying his friend's emotionless face. *Poor brokenhearted soul is still grieving over the death of his loved ones. I need to come up with something for him to do that'll help him live with his loss.*

Realizing General Doughberry wasn't in the room, Collins used her cell phone to call him, "Sam, you'd better watch FOX News, Channel 13 … No, just watch. I'm watching in the main conference room."

Beck had seen Collins pull out her phone and figured she was calling Doughberry. *Good, let him watch. It'll do him good to see what's coming down the pike,* Beck decided, watching his staff members' reactions. When the National Guard lieutenant got out of his Humvee and spoke to General Savage, he could hear the group quietly murmuring, speculating over what the two men were saying. But when the lieutenant's Humvee departed and General Savage stomped back to his Humvee, everyone quieted down and sat forward in their seats.

"Oh, God, look," someone gasped, when they saw the lead Bradley's turret suddenly swing to the north.

"That Blue-Shirt bastard's ordered them to fire on the Guard," someone else exclaimed. A second later the gunner began firing at the ridge.

"Jesus, they're all firing," another cried, when the other Bradleys joined in and the Humvees' machine gunners began firing to the north and south.

After dust clouds appeared on the ridgeline, and the rockets struck FEMA Corps Bradleys and Humvees, the conference room exploded with comments.

"Damn!" "Oh my god!" "Holy shit!" "Crap," were but a few words shouted to express the staff's surprise; for in the blink of an eye they'd witnessed Vermont's National Guard forces conduct a perfect ambush that completely wiped out part of the FEMA column.

Whispering *"Shit,"* Beck ground his teeth, knowing it had finally hit the fan.

Collins wouldn't be able to remember what if anything she'd said.

"WHAT THE HELL JUST HAPPENED," General Doughberry shouted, storming into the room.

Nobody responded, because—beyond the obvious destruction—no one knew.

"WHAT'S THIS ALL ABOUT?" Doughberry demanded, looking at Beck for an explanation.

"Sir, I assume you know the Blue Shirts from FEMA Corps fired on the Vermont Highway Patrol, killing several men and destroying ten or twelve vehicles. Then they entered the town of Bennington with federal agents and proceeded to raid businesses and houses for firearms." Doughberry nodded and Beck continued.

"Vermont's Governor sent his National Guard to put a stop to FEMA Corps and eject them from the state. What we just saw was the National Guard stopping FEMA Corps."

It was obvious Doughberry was oblivious to the seriousness of the situation. "Are you telling me a National Guard unit just destroyed a column of federal ... federal ... *What the hell were they?*"

"Sir they are part of the military wing of FEMA Corps: our men call them Blue Shirts. The man in command was Colonel Savage. If you remember, he was involved in dustups at Golden, Colorado and later at Mudford, Alabama. Apparently someone promoted him to Lieutenant General, or perhaps he promoted himself."

Doughberry collapsed onto an empty chair—for once forgetting about posturing. Shaking his head, he muttered, "This is the first time a state military unit has engaged a federal military unit since the Civil War." After pausing to think, he added, "The President will not stand for this. I expect we'll receive orders, so we'd better start planning."

"Planning for *what,* Sir?" Ulrich asked.

Everyone in the room scrutinized their commander, waiting for his reply.

Doughberry's eyes swept the room. Instead of seeing excitement over taking action, he saw confusion. "Well ... to answer your question, we may be ordered to take down the National Guard unit and occupy Vermont."

What Doughberry saw next was shock and disbelief. Confused and not understanding their reaction, he turned to Beck and said. "General, you and your staff appear to disagree with me."

"Sir, if we, or any other military command receives and follows such an order. Then one of us will have started the Second Civil War."

"You *can't* be serious."

"Sir, I'm *very* serious."

Stepping forward to support Beck, Ulrich said, "Sir, I agree with General Beck"—a comment prompting others in the room to make similar statements.

Saying nothing in response, General Doughberry stood, shook his head and left the room. Shocked by what had just happened and by his staff's comments, he returned to his office wondering how widespread their sentiments actually were.

By the time the informal staff meeting broke up and everyone was leaving, Beck had come to a decision about helping Ulrich. Tapping his friend on the shoulder, he asked him to walk with him to his office. Once there with the door closed, Beck brought up the subject he'd been thinking about earlier.

"Have a seat John," he said nodding to the chair in front of his desk. "As your friend as well as your boss I'm concerned about you. I think you need a change of scenery. I want to send you TDY to Langley AFB, so you can do some flying. Get yourself checked out on the F22A. While you're there, visit the SEALS. You know Captain Hazzard. He'll take you fishing. You'll have a great time out on the water—plus having a delicious fresh fish dinner."

Giving Beck a wounded look and swallowing hard, Ulrich lowered his head, fighting to control his emotions. He knew what his friend was doing and why. "Thanks, Tony, perhaps some flying will help me," he said looking up at Beck. "My quarters feel … well they're awfully empty," he muttered, looking down again.

"I'm sure they do feel empty, and that's why I think you need some time away to get a fresh perspective."

"Has my work been slipping?" Ulrich asked, searching Beck's face for any indication he's job performance was down.

"No, not at all, but you have become moody, which is understandable. I was hoping you'd take some personal time off to adjust, but you haven't. So I'm going to see to it that you do. I'll make arrangements today and have orders cut."

"Thank you again, my friend," Ulrich said, standing and reaching out to shake Beck's hand. "I'm looking forward getting back in the cockpit."

The *Washington Times* rushed an afternoon edition that hit the streets at four p.m. The headline read, "BIG MAMA GET'S HER BUTT KICKED—AGAIN."

FOX and Drudge picked up the headline, followed by talk radio stations, bloggers and Internet news sites. By the time the evening TV news aired, the nation was divided and angry.

William O'Rippley, Sean Haddley, Glenn Deck and their guests all talked about a federal invasion of a sovereign state.

News anchors and bloviators on CNN, MSNBC, ABC, CBS, and NBC placed the blame, to varying degrees, on Vermont for preventing federal agents from enforcing new gun laws. They blew off the Second Amendment argument, which only encouraged clashes across the nation between progressive-liberals, with their "living Constitution," and Constitutionalists—the name being used to identify a diehard group of patriots once referred to as conservatives.

While Constitutionalists cheered Vermont's leaders for standing up to the "Federal Nazis," progressive-liberals branded the state an outlaw, and demanded the federal government take it over and prosecute those responsible for "massacring federal agents."

In Washington, the Senate President and the Speaker of the House blocked Republican's demands for public hearings on FEMA Corps. Progressive-liberals cheered and Second Amendment supporters smoldered.

The more vigorously police and SWAT units enforced federal, state, and local gun regulations, the more Constitutionalists screamed for Second Amendment rights. Gun battles erupted in many locations between police, attempting to enforce gun laws, and resistant citizens. In one instance, federal agents, using armored SUVs to conduct a raid on a farm, found themselves trapped when three large bulldozers arrived on flatbeds and proceeded to build an earthen berm blocking their exit. A local TV station videoed one of the SUVs overturning and rolling back down the steep incline, when the driver attempted to drive up and over the huge earthen wall. After waiting several hours for help from local police, the feebees gave up and walked to the nearest community some ten miles away. FOX and ABC picked up the story, complete with pictures of bedraggled, dust covered, sweaty men limping into a small town.

The number of school principals and school board members encountering enraged parents of children expelled for violating no-tolerance gun policy rules continued to increase. Progressive-liberals were discovering issuing rules banning guns was much easier than enforcing them. Angry parents began routinely interrupting school board meetings and demanding major changes—such as requiring students to stand and recite the Pledge of Allegiance at the start of the school day. Progressive-liberals objected on the grounds that reciting the pledge could offend someone. At one school board meeting, an angry veteran grabbed a whiner and said, "If pledging their faith to the flag of this nation offends them, tell them to get used to it—or get the hell out." The encounter ended with the veteran and several others ejecting the whining man by booting him out the building's front door.

Encounters increased and became more violent. One especially dogmatic school board member was shot. A few days later, two elementary school principals suffered the same fate. And, there again, progressive-liberals were learning zero tolerance has two sides, and the second side was zero tolerance for them.

Overly opinionated news reporters also became targets. It was finally beginning to dawn on some progressive-liberals their words and deeds could cause them bodily harm, and they toned down their rhetoric.

President Abomba's progressive-liberal base was verbally stoning him for not interceding when the National Guard attacked FEMA. He knew he had to do something. So, in a fit of pique, he issued an executive order declaring federal sanctions against Vermont and ordered Jay Schpinmeister to announce that: all federal aid to the state would be cut off, and federal highways leading into the state would be closed—effective immediately. An action many in the northeast found laughable, because even if surrounding states agreed to support the highway closures, there were numerous state roads leading into Vermont: making it doubtful that this punitive action would accomplish anything. Sanctions didn't work against Iran and North Korea and they wouldn't work against Vermont.

New Hampshire's legislators passed a resolution condemning the president's plan, and the governor sent a letter to the president telling him to keep his roadblocks out of New Hampshire. Adding insult to injury, Canada announced they would welcome Vermont as a new province, and Vermont replied it was considering the offer.

Chapter 52

The White House
Thursday, March 17, 2016

The president sat brooding in his small private office. His party was actually criticizing him—a new experience for him, and one he didn't like. *Damn, Vermont is responsible. They're to blame, not me. Everybody knows that ... what the hell's wrong with all of them? Shit, my golf game's off because of all these distractions. I need a vacation. Yep, that's exactly what I need—a vacation. Haven't been to Jamaica for a while. Sandals Resort has great entertainment programs that'll keep the First Lady and the kids busy ... yeah, and a world-class golf course too,* he snickered, suddenly feeling better. *I'll talk to Vickie. See what she recommends.* Picking up the receiver, he punched the button for Barrett's extension, and with no preliminaries, said when she answered, "Vickie, need to talk to you ... in my private office," and hung up.

Barrett had been waiting for Abomba's summons. *Guess the heat's finally gotten to him—I'll let him stew awhile longer. I've got a lot to sort out, and I have to demonstrate I'm not at his beck and call. His progressive-liberal base is demanding confiscation of all guns. The riff between progressive-liberals and people calling themselves Constitutionalists is growing. What's troubling though are the numbers of Democrats who are beginning to consider themselves Constitutionalists.*

An early morning call from the megalomaniac investor had awakened her. In his usual abrupt manner, he'd told her the Obsidians were concerned. Obama's actions and loss of popular support was threatening their plan to keep him president. Barrett remembered the investor's last cryptic words, "It's your job to handle him ... put some steel in his spine."

Barrett felt uneasy after the call and had spent the morning evaluating the situation. Nationwide marches demanding repeal of federal gun laws were planned for May. Groups calling themselves Second Amendment Supporters had announced demonstrations that would be backed up with bullets if necessary.

The Occupy movement planned to block Second Amendment marches, and then occupy city centers. For the most part, Barrett was pleased with the situation. *All the pieces are in place. Major confrontations are going to occur, and they'll provide the situation I've been working to create: one where the President can declare a national emergency, order martial law, and suspend elections. Now, all I have to do is keep him from fucking up again,* Barrett resolved, as she stood and picked up her briefcase.

Walking through the Oval Office, Barrett entered the president's private office without knocking, closed the door and found the president sitting at his desk with a hangdog look. "Good morning, Barry," she cheerfully said.

"Yeah ... maybe, but this Vermont stuff won't go away. Worse still, the media and some of my base are blaming me ... *ME!*" he whined, hanging his head and slowly shaking it. "I gotta *do* something, Vickie. You always have good ideas, what'd you suggest?"

"Well, Barry ... Gene Haggler's suggestion would certainly *solve* the problem," she said in a soothing tone of voice.

"WHAT? he exclaimed, springing forward in his chair. "You mean I should *apologize*? NO WAY! That would mean *I'd* made a mistake. "Nah ... in fact, Haggler's the one who's not cutting it. Time for *him* to go."

Barrett mentally sighed. *It's like dealing with a spoiled five year old.* "Barry, firing him wouldn't look good ... but firing Savage might work."

Abomba propped his feet up on his desk, stuck his lips out in a pout and frowned, "Yeah ... but that would put Jane's knickers in a knot. I've got enough trouble with the First Lady goin' on at me. *No,* that's appeasement." Nodding decisively, he added, "Appeasement's okay for our Muslim friends—not the damn conservatives. No, I want to make an example of Vermont."

Not a good idea. Nope—way too soon. "Barry," she said leaning forward and using her wheedling voice, "Vermont is a minor glitch in our plans. The major demonstrations planned for May will turn into major confrontations, and that's when you'll act.

"If you turn Vermont into a major crisis it can fuck up plans to keep you president," she concluded, frowning.

"You think?" Abomba said, swinging his feet off the desktop. "The media's callin' me weak and indecisive."

"I understand how these personal attacks hurt you, but it's part of the job. Keep being the cool, levelheaded leader I know you are, and you'll win the support of the people. Then the media will rally to support you."

"You think so? I was thinking of going to Jamaica next week."

"Yes, I think you can win the peoples' support, but going to Jamaica right now may not be a good idea. It would be better if you called a meeting with your key advisors and supporters in Congress to formulate a response to the Vermont ... uh," Barrett caught herself before she said catastrophe, "the unfortunate events in Vermont.

"Camp David is the perfect place for the meeting."

Abomba rubbed his chin, mulling over Barrett's suggestion. "Yeah ... that just might work," he added, grinning deviously. "That way I can establish who's to blame. How 'bout you prepare a list for me of those who should be invited?"

Barrett considered handing him the list she'd already prepared, but decided to come back with it after lunch. That would give Abomba time to get the First Lady's blessing.

"I will. After the meeting you can hold a press conference and announce your decision. Once you've done that, there's nothing to prevent your Jamaican vacation."

Camp David, Maryland
Saturday morning, March 19, 2016

Helicopters and SUVs began delivering men and women summoned by the president. Most invitees were unhappy to have their weekend plans cancelled, but they were not alone. One person in particular, Vice President Blabberman, who hadn't been invited, wasn't just unhappy, he was hoppin' mad. Calling Abomba at the White House to complain, he only grew angrier when told the president's calls were being held and he'd have to leave a message. The vice president's opponent in the upcoming presidential race, former Secretary of State, Hilda Rodman, was also vexed that the VP hadn't been invited. Why? Because she was preparing to connect Blabberman to the Vermont mess and embarrass him during the next debate by mentioning his presence at the meeting with Abomba's other cronies. His name being left off the invitation list caused her to wonder what Abomba was up to.

Senate President Harold Realdick, Speaker Nellie Balogni, Senator Dana Finkelstein, Attorney General Edison Helder, Secretary of Defense Gene Haggler, Secretary of Homeland Security Jane Incompentado, and chairman of the Joint Chiefs General Robert Dumpsterson stood when President Abomba entered the lodge: Special

Assistant Vickie Barrett, National Security Advisor Sandra Wheat, and Press Secretary Jay Schpinmeister followed. The president took the empty seat at the head of a long table, with Barrett to his immediate right. Wheat and Schpinmeister took the last two empty chairs next to Barrett.

As soon as everyone was seated, Barrett stood and opened the meeting. "The President has invited you here to discuss the situation in Vermont, and to determine the best way to put it to bed.

"Sanctions have only made the situation worse, because now Vermont has become the rallying cry for the Second Amendment gun-nuts. The issue must be resolved or it will disrupt our plans to enforce the new gun laws. The President is seeking your suggestions for a solution."

Barrett sat and waited to see who would speak first. When Nellie Balogni spoke, Barrett suppressed a smile, for she'd just won a bet with herself. *I knew she couldn't keep her mouth out of it.*

"We can't let Governor Wilson get away with this … this … this thumbing his nose at our authority. No—drastic action is called for."

Looking at the attorney general, Nellie continued, "Ed should charge Governor Wilson and the military commander with murder and send agents to arrest them—"

Finkelstein realized Nellie was working herself up for a tirade and interrupted, "That could make matters worse, Nellie."

"How can things get any worse?" Balogni shot back.

"Well, the agents could be arrested or shot by Vermont police. That's one way."

Helder jumped in, "If we attempt to arrest Governor Wilson, two things could happen: first, he'll order the state attorney general to challenge the warrant on Constitutional grounds and tie the issue up in the courts for years; or, second, Vermont could secede and join Canada.

Barrett felt Abomba tense and put her hand on his arm. Abomba slowly deflated and said, "Anyone have a practical answer?"

No one spoke, so the president stared at his National Security Advisor and said, "Sandra."

"Mr. President, I think we need to cool the issue down, not heat it up. I agree with Secretary Haggler, fire someone and apologize."

"I WILL NOT APOLOGIZE," Abomba stormed.

Sandra Wheat, who owed the president big time for saving her career after her African screw up, offered a suggestion, "Mr. President, I can take responsibility and apologize. You don't have to know anything about my actions. I can say I misunderstood your orders and take responsibility for the results."

Abomba, who could care less about anyone who worked for him, sat quietly considering her idea. *It would work, but it still makes it appear I'm not on top of what my people are doing. Haggler wanted to fire Savage. Hmmm, yeah, I could say Savage exceeded his instructions ... yeah, that sounds better. That way I'm not to blame.*

Jane Incompentado read the president's expression and guessed what he was thinking. *I need Savage ... don't have anyone else as mean who'll follow my orders without questions.* "I like the Sandra's idea, but let me take responsibility. I can say it as a mix up in communications. My instructions weren't properly transmitted. General Savage followed the orders he received, however the orders accidentally left out some words." Incompentado paused to think, and then continued. "Yes, the orders should have read 'do not engage' but as transmitted, they read 'engage.' "

General Robert Dumpsterson thought it a childish ploy that wouldn't fly, but he never shared his private thoughts in a meeting unless forced to do so.

Haggler was elated, because if the president bought it, he'd be off the hook.

Barrett knew the opposition would have a field day with the ploy, but it would keep them busy and their minds off the real issue. In fact, allowing it to absorb the media's attention was brilliant. *Now, how do I keep Abomba out of trouble until it's time to act?*

Jay Schpinmeister provided the answer.

"Mr. President, I can sell Secretary Incompentado's idea. It'll work.

"I suggest you schedule a news conference, announce the results of your investigation, and then leave. I'll handle the press."

Abomba liked the idea—especially the leaving part. Someone else was to blame, and he could go to Jamaica. He was getting ready to end the meeting when Haggler spoke.

"Mr. President, now that our number one problem is solved, I would like to bring up another matter for discussion."

Abomba scowled. "What matter?"

"Troop morale, Mr. President."

"What's wrong with their morale?"

"Mr. President, the men and women are starting to complain about you—specifically, our lack of action in Iraq, after the embassy was destroyed."

"Why does that concern them? Hell, they should be happy I haven't sent them over there to get killed."

General Dumpsterson found a very interesting coffee ring on the tabletop to study.

Barrett realized this could be trouble. *Abomba considers the military his servants. And servants don't have morale problems. On the other hand, Rebecca has mentioned the problem, said it was serious. And, I do need to find something to keep him busy until May.* "Mr. President, this is a perfect opportunity for you to demonstrate your leadership abilities. Visit some military bases and give one of your resounding speeches. That'll boost morale, and you'll get great press coverage." Barrett smiled, "And it will take the media's attention off Vermont."

Abomba sat contemplating Vickie's suggestion. *Damn good idea. I love standing up in front of a bunch of men and women in uniform. Boosts my presidential image. Yeah, I haven't visited a military base in over a year. The weather's breaking, so it'll be a good trip ... and most of the installations have pretty decent golf courses.* "That's a great idea, Vickie.

"Make it so, General," he said, grinning when Dumpsterson looked up at him.

"Anything else ... No? Well then, enjoy your weekend," he said, jumping to his feet and walking out the door.

Chapter 53

Occupy America Movement
April 1, 2016

*A*DCRUSHER **Magazine sent an announcement** to its worldwide email list that occupyamerica.org was up.

Based in British Columbia, *ADCRUSHER*, a not-for-profit, reader-supported, 110,000-circulation magazine is concerned about the erosion of our physical and cultural environment by commercial forces. Part of a worldwide media network, *ADCRUSHER'S* espoused the following statement of purpose: "We are a global network of artists, activists, writers, students, educators, pranksters, and entrepreneurs, who want to advance the new social activist movement of the information age. Our aim is to topple existing power structures and forge a major shift in the way we live in the 21st century."

Vladimir Lenin and Carl Marx would have been proud of them.

News of the Occupy America movement spread like a California wildfire. Idealistic students, educated on revised and sanitized history taught by progressive-liberal teachers and professors, began preparations to occupy one or more of occupyamerica.org's target cities listed on their website. Dates for occupying the cities were spaced two weeks apart. First on the list came Boston, where they knew they'd receive a friendly reception. Denver followed with Montpelier, Vermont coming toward the end of the list.

Young men and women in the Occupy movement, on an idealistic crusade to change the world to socialism, were unable to understand that because socialism is incompatible with human nature it cannot work—a fact easily proven by examining the number of healthy men and women living on welfare in America. While some people willingly work to produce products, others sit and watch, expecting to receive their share of whatever products are produced.

President Abomba promised to change America and Occupiers were determined to help him: even though they had no idea of what to change America into, or how to do it. History has shown dictators tended to follow such movements, but unfortunately that minor detail had been sanitized from history texts Occupiers studied.

YES-UM! Magazine quickly joined the movement and began publishing glowing articles about the wonderful new America waiting for them over the horizon.

Socialist entrepreneurs quickly responded by marketing T-shirts and black anarchy flags bearing a red "A" logo. By using a pull down menu on several websites, customers could select one of the following messages: Occupy America, Occupy (pick your city from a second pull down menu), No More Guns, No More Guns—No More Crime, Remember Trayvon, Remember Artavius, Remember Scandale, and No More 2nd Amendment.

Grand Ayatollah Hamid Khomeini was so elated when he learned of the Occupy America movement he arranged to have several million dollars donated to the cause. After further thought, he realized Occupy events provided an ideal opportunity to use some of his sleeper cells to guarantee the demonstrations turned bloody. *Truly, Allah has provided this opportunity. I will instruct Quds Force to prepare and implement a plan.*

Ayman al-Zawahiri had similar thoughts and implemented a similar plan, but made no monetary donations to the cause. His plan was based upon stirring up racial hatred in black communities in order to precipitate violent confrontations.

The king of Saudi Arabia, however, was in a generous mood and contributed several millions to the cause.

Fort Bragg, North Carolina
Friday morning, April 1, 2016

It was a warm spring North Carolina morning. The sky held a few puffy white clouds and a light breeze blew from the east. President Abomba, wearing a navy blue suit with a purple tie, stood on the reviewing platform gazing out over the 82nd Airborne Division standing before him at parade rest. Abomba was posturing for the TV cameras: some showing him silhouetted against the blue sky with his Mussolini-like jaw jutting out; others showing him from the rear, facing the formation. NBC chose to position their camera at the rear of the formation with the reviewing stand a speck in the distance, and then slowly zoom in on the president.

Basking in his own glow and puffed up by the division commander's introduction, Abomba was oblivious to the somber expressions of the men and women facing him. However once he took the rostrum he wondered why no one was looking at him. Not understanding why they all looked so serious, he set about trying to wow them with his masterful speaking skills. After all, since he was honoring them by being there, his very presence should make them happy.

Beginning with his usual pandering remarks about how delighted he was to be there with the men and women in the military, he threw in a quip he thought would surely prompt some laugher, "You know, I've always said I admire men and women who jump out of perfectly good airplanes."

But for some reason there was no response. The men and women standing at parade rest remained silent, staring straight ahead. *What the hell's wrong with these jackasses?* Abomba wondered, unaware the division's commander assumed the president, the Commander in Chief, knew he should issue the "Stand at Ease" command. Or perhaps the general was testing his CINC, who should have known—well shouldn't he?

Still getting no response, Abomba rambled on about ending the war in Afghanistan and Iraq: neglecting, however, to mention the attack on the Baghdad embassy; the continuing green on blue killings in Afghanistan; or the civil war in Egypt. Yemen and Syria were definitely off the table.

As the president continued his animated gesturing, the producers at major networks realized his typical speech technique was falling flat, but had no clue why. One after another, major network's TV directors switched to regular programming.

Thousands of former and retired military men and women, watching the president on their TV screens attempting to elicit a response from troops standing at parade rest, were howling with laughter. Finally Abomba saw the "cut" symbol on his teleprompter and ended his speech.

Only FOX continued broadcasting the president's embarrassing attempt to bond with his military.

Since none of his aides and advisors had any military experience, they were at a loss to explain the lack of response from the 82nd. Two Secret Service men knew, but no one asked them. Annoyed, the president boarded Marine One and flew to Hilton Head. He needed to recover from his traumatic experience and get in a round of golf.

Monday morning the president boarded Marine One for a short hop to Paris Island, and then on to Camp Lejeune before heading back to Washington. This time the president would be addressing troops seated in hangers or auditoriums, where his handlers thought he would be more warmly received. Paris Island recruits gave him a rousing ovation. At Camp Lejeune, however, the Marines took umbrage at his failure to mention either the attack on America's embassy in Baghdad or events in Vermont, and gave him a cold and formal reception.

The president's last visit was scheduled for the following week at Fort Hood, where once more the president received a cold, formal reception. *Why don't they love me?* he pouted.

Other than an opportunity for the president to play on several new golf courses, his visits to military installations accomplished little—but did keep him occupied for the remainder of the month.

Chapter 54
May 2016

Capitol Building
Washington, DC

Interest in the president's boondoggles and vacations melted like snow on a hot August day in Death Valley. Demand for electricity had exceeded domestic production by twenty percent, brownouts were rolling across the nation, and the hot summer months lay ahead. Canada had long anticipated major demands for electrical power from America, and built several large CANDU nuclear power plants in the 1980s, but the American demand failed to materialize. Canadian growth gradually absorbed the excess capacity, and now that American demand had finally materialized, Canada had limited ability to fill it.

◆ ◆ ◆

CANDU is the acronym for CANada Deuterium Uranium reactor, a heavy water reactor that uses natural uranium fuel. One of the unique features of the CANDU design is its ability to be refueled while on line, while other types of reactors must be shut down for long periods of time for refueling.

◆ ◆ ◆

Angry citizens calling their Congressional representatives to demand electric power were not interested in Canada's CANDU plants. No, they just wanted electricity. They wanted their lights to come on, their electric range to heat, and as summer approached their air conditioner to cool. Green energy sounded so amazing, saving the planet so noble, and reducing carbon footprints so attractive. All these causes were worthwhile—as long as their electric appliances worked—only now they didn't.

"I don't give a shit about your carbon credits, I want my goddamn lights to come on when I throw the switch. Take your goddamn windmills and solar panels and *shove 'em up your ass*," one irate constituent told a congresswoman when she started explaining why everyone had to sacrifice to save the planet. Stunned by the caller's comments, the congresswoman was devastated, for not only had the caller been her largest campaign contributor; it seemed the call was typical of calls, letters, faxes and e-mails her fellow Democrats and a few Republicans were receiving.

When angry consumers learned it took years to approve a power plant's license, they began demanding the EPA be abolished—the DOT and NRC too. Having to cook meals on the charcoal grill and use candles to see at night had succeeded in waking up the population.

There was also the problem of water availability. Pumps were electrically powered devices, and no electricity meant no water. Candles, bags of charcoal, and LP gas tanks became scarce and their prices soared out of sight. A liter bottle of water cost the same as a liter of Grey Goose Vodka. And this was just the beginning.

Lack of electric power forced all types of business to shut down and caused lay offs of both blue and white collar employees.

It didn't take very long for unhappy citizens, especially those recently unemployed, to identify with the Second Amendment groups, and the newly formed Constitutionalists Party. Out of work coal miners and electric power plant workers, most who were members of unions quickly joined the Constitutionalists, and their unions, who were masters at organizing demonstrations, put those skills to work. Massive marches on Washington were being organized, and politically correct legislators were about to meet pissed-off voters.

John E. Amos Power Plant
Winfield, West Virginia
May 4, 2016

It was 4 o'clock in the morning and the chief engineer of the shuttered local power plant, as well as the plant's engineers and technicians, was awakened by angry, former power plant workers pounding on their doors. Two hours earlier a group of laid-off plant employees and a number of local citizens had held a meeting and decided—EPA be damned—they were going to bring the plant back on line. While the sleepy men were being rousted out of bed, a large number of locals and laid off workers cut the chain on the plant's gate, entered, and set about bringing the huge power plant to life. Some lit the oil-fired boiler while others prepared the coal-fired furnaces for lighting.

Tipped off anonymously to trespassers on the plant's property, local and state police arrived to find several hundred citizens forming human blockade at the plant's gate. Outnumbered and prevented from entering the plant, local law enforcement was powerless, and not very enthusiastic about, ejecting former employees who were busily going about their jobs. A citizen's spokesperson at the blockade told a local TV reporter that workers at the plant were determined to bring it back on line. In addition he said, "It is our hope that other laid-off workers from shuttered power plants across the country will do the same."

The citizens' blockade was still in affect later that day, when a vice president from Appalachian Power arrival. Confronting the spokesperson, the VP declared, "Operating this plant is a violation of federal EPA regulations. Inform workers inside they are hereby ordered to shut down this plant immediately and leave the premises." In turn, the spokesperson replied, "If Appalachian Power isn't going to operate this plant, they are in breach of the utility contract with this county. Therefore the plant is legally forfeited and the property of the citizens of the county who intend to see that it *remains* on line." The TV station's cameraman had videoed the exchange, and when the reporter asked for a comment on EPA enforcement, the spokesperson caustically replied, "Hunting season for federal inspectors is now open."

By the following day the plant was producing power, and the lights in Charlestown stayed on. Success always attracts followers and soon other coal-fired power plants began operation.

Attorney General Helder filed lawsuits against the power companies, who responded that they were not operating the plants—the workers were. Several attempts were made to serve workers with lawsuits. None ended well for the servers.

When the job of shutting down the rogue power plants was given to Homeland Security, numerous firefights ensued. Several power plants suffered major damage, and workers were killed. Ranks of the Constitutionalists Party and Second Amendment groups swelled.

Nellie Balogni and Betty Boxnutter took the floor in the House and Senate respectively and ranted and raved for over an hour each. Guns were to blame. If the West Virginia hicks had no guns, the evil CO_2 emitting power plants would not be destroying the planet. Guns must be confiscated now.

In response, West Virginia coal miners began organizing a May 27th protest march on Washington. They were quickly joined by Constitutionalists, Second Amendment supporters, and pissed-off citizens. Laid-off workers in Ohio and coal miners in Pennsylvania also decided to join the march; as did unemployed and disgruntled citizens from other states.

Occupyamerica.org quickly reacted to the coal miners' planned marches by declaring Occupy Washington, DC the movement's top priority. Washington DC would be occupied on May 27th.

Al-Qaeda operators based in suburban Washington, DC mosques began agitating in black communities, encouraging support for the Occupiers and advocating violence against the redneck coal miners who wanted to destroy the planet. For bored homeboys, this sounded like fun.

Hezbollah, acting on orders from the Quds Force commander, planned to incite violence during the Occupy Denver event scheduled for May 7th and 8th.

Chapter 55

Denver, Colorado
Saturday morning, May 7, 2016

Enforcement actions of the Abomba administration's green energy policy and EPA regulations were shutting down coal burning plants, which in turn eliminated the need for coalmines. Colorado's coal mining operations had employed 3,000 workers and provided the energy for over seventy percent of the state's electrical power. Coalmine closings had delivered a devastating blow to the state's economy, and unhappy citizens were in no mood to put up with raucous, destructive Occupiers. Trouble began as soon as the Occupiers took over Denver's City Park.

By Sunday morning, the park belonged to the Occupiers and the beleaguered, resident Canadian geese. Trash mixed with droppings from frightened geese littered most of the park's 330 acres. Like Mudford, the park's bathrooms had been trashed and closed, so both Ferril and Duck lakes were being used as toilets.

Governor Hickengooper, standing at the park's edge with the manager of parks and recreation, the mayor, and the police chief, was appalled by what he was being told and the chaos and filth he saw. Unable to deal with the multitude of Occupiers who'd moved in and squatted, the park's manager had pulled out the park rangers, who'd been verbally abused and physically assaulted with human waste.

The four dignitaries stood looking into the park at a large group of raucous University of Colorado students camped around a huge, black flag, with a large red "A" for anarchy in its center. Observing how the students were gyrating and whooping it up to rap music blaring from numerous boomboxes, it was obvious they were either drunk or high on weed.

Disturbed by the noise and being chased, pestered, poked and prodded by Occupiers, the normally gregarious park geese were loudly protesting and pooping, while either running or flying from one park location to another. In short the den emanating from the park could be heard for miles around.

Citizens from all over the Denver area were driving by to gawk, many blowing their horns and shouting insults. Local residents, used to enjoying daily visits to the park, had gathered around the VIPs, waiting for them to do something—anything. Finally one older lady using a walking cane approached the mayor and accosted him.

"Mr. Mayor, when you ran for office, you pledged to protect the rights of *Denver's* citizens and maintain the City Beautiful. Well I can tell you right now you'll never get my vote again. I demand that something be done immediately to expel these filthy scallywags."

After listening to the mayor's lame explanation about not violating the young peoples' rights, the woman raised her cane in a threatening manner, hissed, "Spineless Democrat," to his face, and turning on her heel hobbled away.

By early Sunday afternoon the Occupiers had become restless. They wanted action, a confrontation. Which was exactly what Marwan the Palestinian had been waiting for. A student at Bolder, and an active member of the Islamic Student Association and leader of a secret Hezbollah cell, Marwan and his six followers approached the Occupiers' leader and suggested a march through the business district. Breaking store windows was always fun, and a little looting was a good thing. Besides it would bring out the police.

An hour later the Occupiers began spilling out of the 17th street park exit, heading west toward the business district. Caught off guard, the police attempted to get ahead of the mob by establishing a barricade at 17th and Broadway, and that's where the first confrontation occurred. Undeterred by tear gas, the mob blew through the barricade, surged into the downtown area, and began smashing storefront windows and looting. Finally forced to act, the mayor turned the police, backed up by sheriff's deputies, loose on the Occupiers.

Riot control units arrived, formed lines with shields and batons, and began firing CS shells and rubber bullets from shotguns at the Occupiers. Soon tear gas floated on the breeze throughout the business district, ending commercial business for merchants, and providing evening work for insurance adjustors. As the sun began setting, combined police and sheriff forces' drove the Occupiers back toward City Park. Several injured police and a number of demonstrators were taken to nearby hospitals. It had been a long day and tempers were short.

Marwan knew the downtown party was over, so he and his fellow cell member, Ibrahim, beat a hasty retreat back to the park, retrieved their hidden weapons, and set up an ambush for the police.

The sun had almost disappeared behind the mountains when lines of police, continuing to fire CS shells and rubber bullets, drove the last Occupiers into the park where Marwan and Ibrahim waited. When the last Occupier rushed by them, both shouted *Allahu'Akbar* and opened fire with their AK-47s. Firing short bursts into the police line, they killed three police officers and wounded four others. As soon as the police commander heard automatic weapons firing, he ordered his men to withdraw. Someone further up the pay scale would have to decide what to do next.

Prior to the rioting, Marwan had identified several radical student extremists—young men and women who wanted to draw blood. After the police withdrew and things quieted down, Marwan hunkered down with the radicals' leaders. By the end of an hour-long planning session, he'd decided not only to provide them with a few pistols and AK-47s, but also some basic training in how to use them. He didn't think police would take any more action until morning, when he expected them to move in and force the Occupiers out. Now that he'd armed a few students, they would add to the confusion and increase the cell's chances of avoiding detection.

While ABC, CBS, CNN, FOX and NBC broadcast the rioting, looting and violent confrontations, progressive-liberals cheered, Constitutionalists cursed, and Governor Hickengrooper began wishing he'd lost the recall election. Now everyone was waiting for him to decide what to do, and using force against protesters wasn't something he could bring himself to think about, much less order.

Colonel Bob and his fellow militiaman, Lee Jenkins, were watching TV coverage of the melee at the Colorado Militia's camp deep in the Rocky Mountains. Neither were surprised that live ammunition had been fired, but neither knew Hezbollah cell members were doing the shooting—for that matter, nor did the police or any other government agency.

Governor Hickengrooper was beside himself. If he sent in the National Guard, he'd again be demonstrating his inability to lead the state. On the other hand, allowing law enforcement officers to be shot or killed was unthinkable. *What to do? What to do*, he worried.

Colonel Bob and Lee Jenkins were also beside themselves—but for different reasons. After spending the better part of the day watching TV news coverage of the Occupiers rampage and the continuing melee in City Park, Bob looked at Lee and said, "Somebody has to put an end to this anarchy—the Colorado Militia has a mission. It's time to draw weapons, mount up, and clean the vermin out of City Park."

"Yeah. It's too bad Arthur and Orville can't join us."

"Yeah, but they're on probation," Bob agreed, and then an idea struck him. "But, there's no reason they can't watch." Opening a burner phone he speed-dialed the brother's number.

"Hey Buddy," Bob said with a wide grin when Arthur answered. "I know how Rex loves sniffing up all that goose poop around City Park. How 'bout you and Orville take him there for an early morning outing? Zero-dark hundred along East 17th Street would be a great time for a stroll."

General Morrison, who had three infantry companies on standby, had also been keeping up with TV reports on the Occupiers. Governor Hickengooper hadn't called, but Morrison expected he would when things got worse. *So far FEMA Corps hasn't shown up, and that's a good thing,* he thought, which led him to wonder what the Colorado Militia was doing—or about to do? *Orville and Arthur know how to contact them. Perhaps I should ask them to find out ... or, if they can, put me in contact with their commander. I'll call them in the morning.*

Chapter 56

Denver, Colorado
2:15 a.m., Monday morning, May 9, 2016

The Colorado Militia's convoy rolled down the mountains west of Denver on I-70, turned south on Colorado Boulevard, and then east on 23rd Avenue; where their vehicles pulled onto the ballfields, and the militiamen dismounted and formed up in platoons.

The southwest corner of the ballfields opened onto the grounds in front of the Denver Museum of Nature and Science, which faced the east end of City Park's Ferril Lake. After clearing Occupiers from the museum grounds, the plan called for holding the fifth platoon in reserve, while two platoons advanced around the north side of Ferril Lake, and two more advanced around the south side—ultimately driving the Occupiers out of the park.

Colonel Bob stood before the five assembled platoons and announced their orders, "Lock and load. Fix bayonets. Fire if fired upon. Run the damn anarchists out. Burn their camps—and *don't* be gentle."

At 0500, the Colorado Militia advanced onto the museum grounds and all hell broke loose. Trash and geese droppings covered the grounds, which now looked more like a garbage dump than a city park. Covered in geese droppings, young men, women, and some of indeterminate gender lay sprawled out; either on the bare ground, or, in some cases, on sleeping bags. All appeared either high or drunk.

"God a'mighty they stink," Sergeant Gonzales muttered as he used his bayonet to poke what appeared to be a man's buttocks. "GET UP, PUNK ..." Gonzales yelled, nearly retching from the smell, "TIME TO LEAVE!"

Grabbing his butt and rolling over, the Occupier, Tom from Oakland, California, squinted at the silhouette of a man standing over him holding something in his hands.

"FUCK OFF PIG," Tom screamed, trying to squirm away from a man he thought was a police officer. His efforts were rewarded by yet another painful poke from Sergeant Gonzales' bayonet—this one in the abdomen. Totally pissed then, Tom jumped to his feet and bellowed, **"THE FUCKING PIG STUCK ME."**

Gonzales grinned, "Now you've gone and made my day, asshole. I'm not a pig, but you smell like one," he said, emphasizing his words with a butt stroke to Tom's jaw.

Alerted by shouts and screams from the museum grounds, Marwan roused his Palestinian cell members and told them to arm themselves. Marwan ordered his wanna-be-martyrs to, "Follow me," and started around the south side of the Ferril Lake toward the museum. They hadn't gone far before they encountered a screaming throng of Occupiers fleeing toward them, like a herd of stampeding cattle. Jostled and shoved out of the way, two of Marwan's men with AK-47s were knocked down and trampled. Once the stampede had passed, the cell members reassembled, but they were unable to find one of their AK-47s.

Marwan was just about to order his young jihadis to continue toward the museum, when he spotted a line of men holding rifles with fixed bayonets advancing toward them. **"KILL THE INFIDELS,"** Marwan screamed, firing a burst from his AK-47 toward the advancing men. Three fell and the others scattered, found cover and returned fire.

When a bullet whizzed past his left ear, Marwan, realizing he was dealing with trained soldiers, dove behind some bushes. Calling out his men's names, he counted his remaining forces. Two didn't answer, but when Ibrahim did, Marwan silently praised Allah and screamed, **"IBRAHIM, COVER ME."**

Ibrahim opened up with his AK-47 on full auto, firing bursts toward the militia's hiding places.

Billy Bob Taskell saw Ibrahim's muzzle flash and carefully sighted his old BAR. "Fire again, sucker, and your ass is mine," he muttered.

Allah must have decided it was time for Ibrahim to join Him, because as soon as he rose and fired another burst, he found himself on the way to jihadi paradise—at least that's where he thought he was headed.

With Ibrahim gone, Marwan realized he was out-gunned and decided to pull back—which is another way of saying he ran for his life.

Two of Marwan's female radicals with AK-47s were on the north shore of Lake Ferril. Sondra, a real in-your-face radical feminist, grabbed her weapon, and remembering to take the safety off, pointed it at the vague shapes coming toward her. Afraid of guns, and having no idea what would happen when an AK-47 is fired on full auto, Sondra was barely holding the weapon. So when she pulled the trigger, the AK-47 jumped out of her left hand and continued firing a stream of bullets as it climbed upward. Her first three bullets had passed between two militiamen before the stream climbed into a nearby tree—terrorizing two squirrels and clipping the tail feathers of an endangered owl. As soon as the rifle pulled itself out of her right hand, it stopped firing and fell to the ground.

Sondra's friend, who'd made no attempt to fire her AK-47, peed herself. Then, flinging her weapon toward the men, she grabbed Sondra's hand and the two of them ran screaming into the night.

Chapter 57

Orville and Arthur were walking East 17th Avenue. They'd just passed Adams Street, when Rex's ears perked up, and he started growling toward the northeast. "Easy boy," Arthur said, patting the dog's head.

Both men stopped and gazed into the park toward the east end of Ferril Lake. "Yeah, Rex's ears are up. He hears something. I'll bet the party's about to start," Orville said. "Damn nice of Bob to tip us off."

A few minutes later when they heard shouting and screaming, Rex growled, bared his teeth and began lunging on his leash. "No … sorry boy," Arthur said, restraining the dog and stroking his back in an attempt to calm him. "We can't let you join in the fun, but if one of those lowlifes comes our way, I just might not be able to hold on to you."

"Don't know what's going on, but whatever it is, it's coming our way," Orville said.

Soon they heard more screaming and shouting from people running inside the park grounds toward the main entrance at East 17th and City Park Esplanade. "I hear a lot of splashing over there ahead of us. Sounds like some of them are running through the shallows of that little pond on the southeast side of Lake Ferril. Guess they got their eviction notices," Orville grunted, struggling to hold on to Rex, who continued barking and lunging on his leash.

"Whoa … bet I know who that is," Orville said, feeling his burner phone vibrating in his pocket and pulling it out. "Yep, just as I suspected—it's Bob," he said, after checking caller ID and pressing the speakerphone button.

"Where are you?" Bob said.

"Right where you suggested."

"Good—enjoying the show?"

"Yeah … we sure are, and Rex is raring to join in. So are we."

"I know, but you can't. Stay where you are, but don't dilly-dally. Talk to you soon … gotta go."

A couple of minutes later, the brothers did a double-take. Looking at one another in surprise, they couldn't believe what they were hearing—a sound from the past neither brother would ever forget—the sound of an AK-47 firing on full auto.

The sharp crack of rifles followed, accompanied by more AK-47 bursts. After that, things quieted down for few seconds. Then they heard another long burst from an AK-47—this one being stepped on by reports from a .30 caliber firing on full auto. "Damn, that was a machine gun. Sounded like a Browning," Orville exclaimed.

"Yeah ... sounded like one of the Militia's M1919s, or it could have been a BAR," Arthur replied.

"Uh-oh, somebody's dialed 911," Orville said when they heard sirens approaching. "Guess that signals the end of the militia's foray in City Park."

"Yeah, it looks like Colonel Bob's done a fine job of running off the stinking riffraff, but I think it's time for him to skedaddle," Arthur said as he, Orville and Rex watched patrol cars, fire trucks and ambulances streaming past.

The sound of wailing sirens and caterwauling geese, plus the putrid smell of their poop burning in numerous fires throughout the park had Rex in a frenzy. Yelping with his ears pinned slightly back and sniffing the air, the big dog lowered his head and began pawing his nose and eyes. "Yeah, I know it stinks and burns your eyes. It's time to go home," Orville said, patting the dog's head and tugging on his leash. Let's head down Madison Street to 16th Avenue."

"Good idea. Then we can head back west to our truck."

The brothers and Rex had walked a short distance down Madison Street when lights began coming on in the houses and apartments on both sides of the street. People wearing pajamas and robes quickly poured out onto the sidewalk asking them what was happening?

"There's been a shooting in the park. We just left that area because it's dangerous. Don't go there," Arthur said over his shoulder, as they hurried along. Of course some ignored the warning and ran toward the park to see for themselves.

Standing on the Museum grounds, Colonel Bob had been surprised to hear the distinct sharp popping sound of AK-47s, followed by the militiamen's return fire. After receiving a report they'd encountered AK-47s from the sergeant leading the squad, Bob ordered his men to continue with their mission for another ten minutes, and then return to their trucks. It would be wise to clear out of the area before the police got organized. Taking their wounded with them, each vehicle's driver would proceed along a different, circuitous route back to their camp. The Colorado Militia had many supporters; among them physicians and nurses, who would treat the wounded men in private offices and clinics.

In the hours before the Militia arrived, three police cruisers had been stationed around the park, and officers manning them were tired and sleepy; tired of blaring, nerve-wracking rap music, foul language, insults, and having human feces hurled at them by the Occupiers. Having served extended shifts, the officers were bored and disgusted with doing nothing while the Occupiers were destroying City Park.

Two officers in a cruiser parked in a cruiser on East 17th Street near the park's East 17th Street and Esplanade entrance were glad the blaring rap music had finally stopped. "I was wondering if they were ever gonna go to sleep?" the driver said. Glancing at his watch he saw it was 5:03 a.m.

"Wish we could go in and break some heads," his partner groused.

An hour later the drowsy officer in the passenger seat noticed two men walking east with a dog. "They're up early," he commented.

"Yeah, guess if your dog's gotta go, *you* gotta go," the driver quipped.

Both officers continued fighting sleep, until sounds of screaming and shouting coming from the east end of the park jarred them awake. "It sounds like the ruckus is coming from the museum grounds, and it's getting worse," the driver said, deciding to make a U turn and drive east toward the disturbance. "Better call this in," he told his partner.

They hadn't gone far when they spotted the two men they'd seen earlier standing with what they could now see was a large German Shepherd. Both the men and the dog were looking into the park toward where the screams and shouts were emanating.

"What the hell's goin' on," the driver said lowering the cruiser's windows. "Sounds like they're runnin' toward the Esplanade entrance we just left. Wonder what's got 'em so spooked," he said, making a U-turn. "*Shit!* Did ya hear that?" he asked his partner when the sound of automatic weapon fire echoed through the night.

"Yeah, I heard it … that and a lot more gun fire besides. Something bad's goin' down," his partner said, grabbing the mike. "Dispatch, Unit five. Gunshots, Eastern end of park near museum. Automatic weapons fire. Occupiers fleein' toward the Esplanade entrance."

When the police chief was informed of a second similar report a few seconds later from a cruiser at East 23rd Avenue and St. Paul on the north side of the park, he issued the mobilization order.

All around the park, disoriented young men and women—most half-dressed and high, ran or staggered out onto surrounding streets and avenues. A few were bleeding from being jabbed with bayonets, and most had fallen and rolled in the plentiful geese droppings. Stinking and sorely in need of a shower, they'd been roughly roused and experienced a night unlike any they'd ever known. The sounds of gunshots and screaming wounded men had terrified them.

Much to the distress of residents, dawn's early light revealed hundreds of filthy young men and women wandering through neighborhoods near the park. As police began rounding them up, health department officials were called in to advise authorities on how to handle the situation. The first order of business was cleaning up the Occupiers. In their current condition they presented a health hazard. Since using cattle hauling trucks to move them to holding areas was considered too extreme, the fire department solved the showering problem with fire hoses.

The rising sun allowed TV cameras to video the extent of the damage. Two men, assumed to be Occupiers, had been found shot to death, with AK-47s lying next to their blood soaked bodies. Several others with head injuries from being butt stroked by militiamen were found sprawled on the ground. Burning piles of debris were found—sleeping bags, ghetto blasters, tents, and clothes—doused with diesel fuel and set on fire by the militia as they withdrew. Four AK-47s were discovered along the north shore of the lake, one had been fired. Several dead geese lay scattered throughout the park, either killed during the shootout or trampled by fleeing Occupiers.

Governor Hickengooper, a bandana tied over his nose and escorted by the police chief, toured the damaged park; and then visited holding areas where the dripping wet Occupiers had been corralled. Most had left their belongings, including IDs and money, in the park where the objects smoldered along with other refuse never to be recovered.

Looking at the bedraggled Occupiers, Hickengooper realized he had to get them out of Denver, but doing so would require purchasing clothes, airplane, train or bus tickets, and providing funds for food. The problem was he had no budget for such expenses. Unable to contemplate he was to blame for allowing Occupiers to occupy in the first place, he fretted, *What to do? What to do?*

Later, Orville and Arthur were enjoying a cold beer on their patio behind their house when they heard an automobile's horn honking in front of their house. Rex, who'd been lying at Arthur's feet gnawing on a chew treat, immediately went on guard and charged around the house. Wondering who was visiting, Orville and Arthur followed him and smiled when they saw a National Guard sedan stopped at the entrance to their drive way.

Waving for the car to come through the gate," the brother's laughed when Rex suddenly galloped toward the sedan with his tail wagging. "I think he knows the general's car when he sees it," Oliver said, watching the dog yipping a greeting and running along side the car.

Getting out and bending over to rub Rex's head and receive a big doggie kiss, Morrison warmly greeted the dog, before following him to where the brothers waited. "Good afternoon, Orville, Arthur," he said, reaching out to shake their hands. "Looks like Rex is in good health and happy to be home."

"Good afternoon, sir. Yes and we're glad to have him back. Thank you again for taking such good care of him," Arthur said. "We're sitting out back. Will you join us in a beer?" he asked, leading the way around the side of the house.

"Thank you, I will."

Taking the beer Arthur had retrieved from an ice chest and sitting at the outdoor table on the patio, Morrison rubbed Rex head and looked around, "You've done a great job of restoring your house,"

"Thank you, sir," Arthur replied.

After a few minutes of idle chitchat about how they were getting along—during which the brother's kept wondering why he was there—Morrison got to reason for his visit.

"Other than visiting Rex," Morrison said with a grin, "I'm here to ask you to relay a message to the commander of the Colorado Militia. I believe his name is Bob."

Arthur and Orville looked at each other.

Morrison grunted. "I know you're both militia members. And I also know that while you match the description of two men walking a large German Shepherd before dawn near City Park, you weren't involved in what went on there.

"So when you can, please tell Bob to stand down and contact me before any new missions. The contact can be informal ... one of you can relay the message." Morrison grunted. "Let's just say this morning's raid has caused a real flap, and I don't need any more surprises."

Morrison stood and the brothers jumped to their feet. "Sir, we'll do our best to follow your orders."

"I have no doubt you will, but it was a *request* not an order. Thanks for offering to help and the cold beer. I'd like to stay and visit, but duty calls, and I must be going."

Rex seemed to know the general was leaving and led the three men around the house. After a final pat on the dog's head, Morrison said goodbye and got in the car.

Rex ran along beside the car all the way to the gate, and then dutifully returned to the house on hearing Arthur's whistle.

Chapter 58

Fort Belvoir, Virginia
Monday morning, 9 May 2016

The head of President Abomba's Secret Service detail answered his cell phone, listened to the caller, and then walked toward the president, who was setting up a 152 yard shot toward the fourth green. Knowing the consequences of interrupting POTUS when he was about to drive the ball, the agent waited until it had landed on the distant green. "Nice shot, Mr. President. Sir, you have a call from the situation room—trouble in Denver."

"Why the hell are they bothering me. They're supposed to take care of problems. Give me the damn phone."

The agent handed the president his cell phone, and Abomba said, "What's the problem? Why are you bothering me?"

"Mr. President, A major incident of parkplace violence has taken place in Denver's City Park. A local militia stormed the park at dawn, killing two Occupiers and ejecting the rest.

"Mr. President, there were ten Palestinian students among the Occupiers. Six were armed with AK-47s—including the four injured and two who were killed. Initial reports indicate the two dead were members of Hezbollah."

Ignoring the agent's comment regarding Hezbollah, Abomba wondered, *What's an AK-47? Oh, yeah, it's an assault rifle.* "Find out where they bought the assault rifles and arrest the seller.

"Inform Secretary Incompentado and tell her to take care of it. I don't want any talk about Muslims or Islam. Tell her to put a lid on it, and then find out where the, uh … the assault rifles came from."

CENTCOM
Monday afternoon, 9 May 2015

General Doughberry and his staff were watching news programs in the main conference room. News of the Denver, Colorado City Park shootout broke at nine a.m. on the major TV networks. Throughout the morning and well into the afternoon, the world watched videos of scantly clad, filthy young men and women being washed down by fire hoses. Aerial views followed of Denver's large city park, where numerous smocking piles of rubbish burned and trash littered the landscape. The park's notorious pooping Canadian geese were clustered in the center of Duck and Ferril lakes, noisily honking their displeasure.

"Does anyone have any idea what happened to these people?" General Doughberry asked.

When no one responded, Doughberry gave Beck a look that demanded an answer.

"Sir, I can only offer an opinion. I suspect it was the Colorado Militia."

Doughberry stared at Beck, apparently having trouble accepting his statement. "Are you saying a bunch of armed civilians, pretending to be soldiers, went into a public park and shot men and women exercising their constitutional rights to protest?"

"No, sir, that is *not* what I said.

"Six of the Occupiers—the men and women you just mentioned—were armed with AK-47s and they fired first."

Doughberry's knitted eyebrows clearly indicated he was perplexed. "Armed with AK-47s you say? I haven't heard anything about that on the news."

"No, sir, you haven't. I received a call from a friend in Denver who told me. Worse still is the information that at least two of the shooters were Palestinians—students attending the university and suspected members of Hezbollah."

Beck's last statement got Colonel Collins' attention. *Hezbollah? Hezbollah is Shi'a—that means Iran. Damn.*

"Hezbollah is Iran's terrorist organization," Roberts commented. "We let Iran get by with destroying our embassy and killing military and civilians, so their assumption we're weak makes sense. Sure, why not bring violence to the good old USA? That's the way they think."

Doughberry looked at General Roberts like he had BO. "Surely not. President Abomba and Secretary Heinz are making progress with the Iran's president. Iran wouldn't do anything to endanger the talks."

No one commented.

Beck decided to move on before someone said something they shouldn't. "I think we should be considering what will happen if the same thing occurs at the next Occupy rally, which I believe is in Tulsa.

Glenn Deck spent most of his three-hour radio show talking about the Occupiers' destruction of private property, and their forcible removal by a group of armed men, later identified as the Colorado Militia. He mentioned shots had been fired, but neither he nor any of his callers had details.

Rusty Limbo followed and near the end of his three-hour show, a Denver caller reported details of the Colorado Militia's raid, including the yet unreported fact that the Occupiers had AK-47s and had fired the first shots.

Sean Haddley opened his show by playing a recording of Homeland Security Secretary Incompentado's newly released statement.

"In the early hours this morning, men identified as the Colorado Militia stormed Denver's City Park and drove out peaceful men and women demonstrating their right of free speech. Shots were fired and two students who were part of the Occupy movement were killed. The actions of these so-called militiamen are a disgrace and will not be tolerated. The shooters will be tracked down and arrested. Another demonstration, Occupy Tulsa, will begin on May 21st. Homeland Security will ensure there is no reoccurrence of today's parkplace violence."

"Can you believe this boloney ... parkplace violence?" Sean said. "*Get real!* I have unconfirmed reports there were six Muslim students among the Occupiers in the park. All six were armed with AK-47s, and two were killed while firing at the militiamen. Four more AK-47s were found in a different part of the park.

"I have no reports of any militiamen being wounded or killed.

"But I have watched video shot from helicopters and on the street. What I saw were filthy young men and women who'd totally trashed the park." Haddley chuckled, "They were so dirty the city wouldn't even put them in cattle hauling trucks, so Denver's fire department was called to hose them down."

Capitol Building
Oklahoma City, Oklahoma
2:30 p.m., Monday, May 9, 2016

Oklahoma's Speaker of the House, Tom McCann, barged into the Senate President Jim Hill's office, closed the door and excitedly asked, "Jim, have you been watching TV?"

"Good afternoon to you, too, Tom," the startled Speaker said, taken aback by the Hill's abrupt entrance. "Are you referring to what's happened in Denver?"

"Yes, and the no-good SOBs are on their way *here*—coming here to Occupy Tulsa." McCann struck the palm of his left hand with his right fist, "Like hell they will."

"Cool down, Tom, and have a seat. I agree. I've had enough of federal meddling in our business. Our citizens passed a Constitutional Amendment to ban Shariah Law and a damned federal judge struck it down. Yeah, I've had enough, and so have most of the senators."

McCann, who'd settled in one of the Speaker's plush leather chairs, was ready to do business. "Same thing's true in the House. I have my staff working with Larry Metz, our best legal mind, drafting a bill to require a special permit to "Occupy" any state, county, or city property. Such a permit will have to be applied for three months before the event," Hill gave McCann a sly smile, "and approved by the governor. Metz plans to introduce it Wednesday morning and I'll bring it directly to the floor for a vote."

"Great," Jim said, nodding his head, "Ask Larry to coordinate with Alan Hays and I'll do the same in the Senate. That way we'll have passed identical bills, which, once combined, can be sent directly to the governor for signature."

"I'll do it. The bill should be on the governors' desk with an effective when-signed clause by four o'clock Friday afternoon."

"You know Judge LeGrunge will issue a stay ... but that'll take time," Tom noted, with a sly grin. "In the mean time there'll be no Occupy Tulsa."

Jim nodded in agreement and both men laughed.

The White House
Monday afternoon, May 9, 2016

President Abomba found Vickie Barrett waiting for him when he entered the Oval Office.

"Good afternoon, Barry. How was your game?"

"I was under par for the first three holes, but then I got the news about Denver and my game went to shit. I've had enough of these damn gun-nuts screwing up my plans."

"Yes, it's terrible," Barrett said, placating his bruised ego. *Poor baby.*

"And that's why I'm here. It's time to replace the commander of Northern Command. I don't think he'll go along with your plans for martial law based on declaring an extreme national emergency."

"Who've you got in mind … that other general we considered before picking Doughberry?"

"Yes, Lieutenant General Garry Lackiemann."

"Why a lieutenant general? Isn't a major general higher? I know a major outranks a lieutenant."

"No, a lieutenant general is higher. I know it's confusing, but that's the way it is. Anyway, I'd like you to nominate Lieutenant General Lackiemann as the next commander of U.S. Northern Command. Harry guarantees approval within three days. Secretary Haggler is ready to announce the current commander's retirement as soon as you approve."

"What's this Lackiemann fellow doing now?"

"He's working at the Pentagon for the Air Force Chief of Staff on something having to do with base housing. Don't you remember? He and Doughberry were the only two of the last five lieutenant generals interviewed who had no problem ordering troops to fire on civilians. You've already replaced four of the major combatant commanders— CENTCOM, EUCOM, AFRICOM and SOCOM—with men who will follow your orders. Now it's time to do the same at NORTHCOM."

Abomba postured, jutting out his Mussolini-like jaw, "Yeah, and now they *all* have my logo tattooed on their asses." *And what you don't know, Vickie, is that I plan to proclaim a national emergency in the next thirty days.*

"Yes, I approve. Have Haggler announce it in the morning."

Pleased she had him focused, it was time to move on to the next and most important item on her agenda. "Barry, your base is very upset … upset with *you.*"

"They are? About what?"

"Well, we all know how busy you are, having to deal with all the problems and making the hard decisions; but, I'm afraid, your base thinks you've let enforcement of gun laws slip to the back burner."

"They do? Hmmm ... perhaps I have been a little too occupied with other matters."

"I'm afraid you have. This mess in Denver has the base screaming, 'More gun violence,' and 'if federal laws had been enforced there wouldn't have been any AK-47s for the Colorado militia to buy.' As it is, the militia left a bunch of them lying around in the park to make it look like the peaceful Occupiers had them."

"Yeah, that's true. You're right. It's time to act. Do you have the draft executive order?"

"Yes," Barrett said, removing a folder from her briefcase and taking the document out to hand it to the president. "It has all the changes you requested. I thought you might want it, so I printed it with today's date."

"Good," the president said using a pen lying on his desk to sign it.

"I'll give it to Jay. This will make your base happy." *And take the peoples' minds off the electric power problem,* Barrett sighed, as she left the president. After making copies of the executive order, she planned to distribute it through proper channels to all affected agencies, and then visit Jay Schpinmeister to gave him a copy for release.

Schpinmeister read the release and whistled. "Boy, this will start a fire storm." He had no idea how prophetic his comment was. Later that afternoon he announced the president's executive order and handed out copies of EO 13978.

The White House

Office of the Press Secretary

For Immediate Release   May 10, 2016

Executive Order -- Authorizing the Implementation of provisions of the Firearms Acts of 2014 as listed below.

By the authority vested in me as President by the Constitution and the laws of the United States of America, including the National Emergencies Act, the Comprehensive Firearms Registration and Storage Act, the Fix Gun Checks Act, the Ammunition Background Check Act, the Gun Owner Licensing Act, the Buyback Our Safety Act, the Handgun Licensing and Registration Act, the Support Assault Firearms Elimination and Reduction for our Streets Act, the Firearm Safety and Public Health Research Act, the Large Capacity Ammunition Feeding Device Act, the Stop Online Ammunition Sales Act, the Assault Weapons Ban Act, the Firearm Safety and Buyback Grant Act, the Firearm Risk Protection Act, the Gun Owner Licensing Act, the Equal Access to Justice for Victims of Gun Violence Act, the To Prohibit the Possession or Transfer of Junk Guns Act, and the Explosive Materials Background Check Act.

I, BARRINGTON ABOMBA, President of the United States of America, hereby order:

Section 1. (a) The Secretary of Homeland Security, in consultation with the Secretary of Defense and the Attorney General, is hereby authorized to impose all provisions of the laws and acts listed below, on or after the effective date of this order:
The Comprehensive Firearms Registration and Storage Act, the Fix Gun Checks Act, the Ammunition Background Check Act, the Gun Owner Licensing Act, the Buyback Our Safety Act, the Handgun Licensing and Registration Act, the Support Assault Firearms Elimination and Reduction for our Streets Act, the Firearm Safety and Public Health Research Act, the Large Capacity Ammunition Feeding Device Act, the Stop Online Ammunition Sales Act, the Assault Weapons Ban Act, the Firearm Safety and Buyback Grant Act, the Firearm Risk Protection Act, the Gun Owner Licensing Act, the Equal Access to Justice for Victims of Gun Violence Act, the To Prohibit the Possession or Transfer of Junk Guns Act, and the Explosive Materials Background Check Act.

(b) With respect to interference by state and local authorities, the Secretary of Homeland Security is authorized to overcome such interference and may employ law enforcement officers of:
(i) The Bureau of Alcohol Tobacco, Firearms and Explosives;
(ii) The Federal Police;
(iii) Immigration and Customs Enforcement (ICE);
(iv) FEMA Corps.

Section 2. The Attorney General is authorized and ordered to provide:
(i) All legal support required, including but not limited to lawsuits;
(ii) Arrest and prosecution of any state official or employee attempting to interfere with government employees carrying out his order.

Section 3. The Secretary of Defense is authorized to provide support as requested by the Secretary of Homeland Security.

Section 4. (a.) Civil Unrest. The Secretary of Homeland Security, assisted by the Secretary of Defense will control civil unrest, rebellious acts, and massive civil disobedience.

(b.) Rebellion. The Secretary of Homeland Security is authorized to arrest and confine rebellious men and women under provisions of the Patriot Act.

(c.) Domestic Terrorism. The Secretary of Homeland Security, assisted as required by the Secretary of Defense, shall use such force as required to stop acts of terrorism and to control and confine persons deemed domestic terrorists.

Section 5. This order is effective at 12:01 a.m. eastern daylight time on May 16, 2016.

BARRINGTON ABOMBA

Chapter 59

Capitol Building
Oklahoma City, Oklahoma
4:30 p.m., Thursday, May 12, 2016

The Speaker of the House banged his gavel and declared House Bill 819 had passed with 99 Yeas and 2 Nays.

Twenty minutes later Senate Bill 498, an identical bill to HB 819, was put to a vote. Five minutes later the Speaker reported the vote: 47 Yeas and 1 Nay.

The governor signed the Prevention of Occupation of Public Property Act of 2016 at 6:45 p.m. and the bill became law: a law with harsh provisions for violators.

Governors of other states on the Occupy list watched and some immediately requested copies of the legislation.

Nellie Balogni and her husband Hughbie learned of the new Oklahoma law while watching *Hardball*.

"I don't believe it," Nellie wailed after hearing the reporters' action news alert. "How dare they interfere with the rights of those peaceful demonstrators? What the militiamen did in Denver was *ghastly ... just ghastly. I tell you ..."* she gasped, pausing in her harangue to catch her breath.

"Now—Now look what's happened. OOOOH ..."

"Now, Nellie, calm yourself, dearest," Hughbie said, patting her on her knee, while reaching under the sofa for a large brown paper bag he kept hidden there.

"Calm myself ... Are you mad?" Nellie screeched, "Don't you get it you *dunderhead*? Instead of providing adequate protection for the Occupiers, they've ... *Oh!* They've passed a law *violating* their constitutional rights. *How dare they ... "* she ranted, jumping to her feet and chopping the air with both hands.

"Sit down Nellie, you know what happens when you get riled up," Hughbie said trying to avert the inevitable; but unable to do so, watched as she passed out and fell back on the sofa.

Continuing to feel around under the sofa, he finally retrieved the paper bag an EMT had shown him how to use to end her hyperventilating. Easing Nellie forward and slipping the bag over her head, he used both hands to crush the sides of it up around her throat to seal it. After years of living together and witnessing so many manic attacks, Hughbie was quite adept at bringing his wife around. Although there were times, like today, when he'd ask himself if putting up with the bitch was worth it. Sorely tempted do something more than simply hold the bag over her head, Hughbie fantasized about using a plastic bag instead. *I could end it all and no one would be the wiser. Though if I did, how would I continue to add to the fortune I've amassed in green energy contracts,* he sighed as he finally felt her stir and start muttering. *Oh, well, there's always tomorrow,* he chuckled, and whipping the bag off her head, quickly stuffed it back under the sofa and sat staring at her.

"What the hell are you looking at Hughbie? Get me my damn phone. I have to call Speaker Realdick."

"Harold, what the hell are we going to do about Oklahoma?" she said when Realdick answered. "Those assholes just passed a damn law preventing the Occupy Tulsa demonstration. We have to—"

"Nellie, calm down. We *can't* do anything. President Abomba or Attorney General Helder will have to take action. I think the presidents' executive order provides authority for the AG or DHS to intervene."

"Are you sure?"

"Nellie, we'll have to wait and see what President Abomba does. It's not our call."

"Well, okay … if you say so."

U.S. District Court
Oklahoma City, Oklahoma
Judge LeGrunge's Chambers
8:30 a.m. Friday, May 13, 2016

Chief Judge Veronica LeGrunge finished reading CAIR's motion for a stay of the Prevention of Occupation of Public Property Act of 2016, looked up at Allan Sowash and nodded. Turning to the other man in her chambers, Ryan Kunkle, she said, "I understand the ACLU has a similar motion."

"Yes, your Honor. Here it is," Kunkle said, handing LeGrunge the ACLU'S motion.

Since it was almost identical to the one she'd just read, LeGrunge skimmed through the six-page motion. Looking up, she said, "Gentlemen, you both offer compelling arguments. It's abundantly clear the Act's primary purpose is specifically targeted at a group known as the 'Occupiers.'

"I'll immediately issue an order to block implementation of the law."

This wasn't the first time the U.S. District Court for the Western District of Oklahoma had ruled Oklahoma laws or constitutional amendments violated the U.S. Constitution. In 2013, the District Court struck down an Oklahoma state constitutional amendment prohibiting Shariah law by stating: "the law [is] in violation of the U.S. Constitution's Establishment Clause." A ruling that angered the majority of the state's citizens.

Judge LeGrunge wasted no time in announcing her decision, and local TV channels broke the story at noon.

LeGrunge's decision was not well received. Citizen reaction was swift. Within minutes of the news airing, a large group of angry Oklahomans began gathering in front of the Court House on NW 4th Street. Soon the crowd had swelled to over two hundred, with more men and women arriving every minute.

The U.S. Marshal Service's Office of Security Systems (OSS) is responsible for protecting ninety-four federal judicial districts, 2,000 sitting judges, and many more court officials at over 400 locations. OSS contracts for over 3,800 court security officers (CSOs), who provide personnel to guard court buildings and their entrances. Now ten CSO officers were facing an increasingly agitated throng milling around in front of Judge LeGrunge's District Court building, and shouting expletives and epithets at her.

Outside on the sidewalk several men arrived carrying a large Gadsden "Don't Tread on Me" flag on a pole, and began passing out smaller versions of it. When someone in the crowd began yelling, "WE WANT LEGRUNGE," others picked up the chant.

Fearing the worst—a violent flash mob breaking into the building—the senior CSO officer in charge of guarding the courthouse's entrances called his company's manager, who called his OSS contact for instructions—who, in turn, contacted the city police and the FBI office to request assistance.

By the time the first FBI agent arrived, traffic was at a stand still, and the streets and sidewalks around the building were overflowing with angry men and women chanting, "WE WANT LAGRUNGE," loud enough to make the building's windows vibrate.

Chief District Judge LeGrunge stared down at the chanting crowd from the top floor office window of her chambers and seethed. *How dare they challenge my order? It's time to end this resistance to authority ... this constitutional fundamentalism. I won't stand for this rebellion. I'm going down there and set them straight,* she decided, and jerking open her office door, almost ran into a CSO officer blocking her path. "Your Honor, we're here to ensure your safety, please stay in side," he told her.

"Do as he requests ma'am," added an FBI special agent standing beside the CSO officer. "The Marshal Service has deputies on the way. As soon as we have enough men, we'll escort you out of the building and take you to a safe location."

"Are you implying the crowd would dare to attack me?"

"Your Honor, to put it bluntly," the agent replied, "They're likely to tear you limb from limb. Your order has ... er ... obviously not been well received. We need to get you out of here."

TV vans had finally arrived, after making their way through the snarled traffic—mostly by driving on sidewalks—and parked in the center of the street. While helicopters hovering overhead videoed the courthouse action below, cameramen and reporters fanned out to interview outraged demonstrators.

After making their way through the mob to the front of the building, one cameraman and a reporter encountered a large group of men wearing business suits who'd joined in the chant to get LeGrunge.

"Excuse me, sir, can you tell me why you're here and what you'll do if you do get hold of Judge LeGrunge," the reporter asked, sticking his microphone in one well-dressed man's face.

"Yeah, I'll be glad to tell you why we're here. We're lawyers who believe in upholding the Constitution, and we're fed up with judges who write their own laws.

"As for what we'd do if we did get hold of her, the answer is obvious—we'd boot her sorry liberal ass out of Oklahoma ... maybe even tar and feather her first."

Turning away from the angry lawyer and surveying the crowd around him, the reporter couldn't help but relate what was happening to a college lecture he'd attended on the Law of Unintended Consequences. According to his sociology professor, American sociologist and 1994 Medal of Science winner, Robert K. Merton had developed the unintended consequences theory along with the term self-fulfilling-prophesy. *The citizen's reaction to LeGrunge's ruling is a perfect example of an unintended consequence, which I predict is only the first of many more detrimental occurrences to strike the city,* the reporter concluded, looking for another demonstrator who'd be willing to have a microphone stuck in his or her face. He would not learn how prophetic his musing was for several hours.

Off duty and reserve police officers had been called in for duty and ordered to backup officers at the Court House. And like the bombings in Chicago, when all the police are at one location, opportunities for mischief are created at other locations. Such would be the case today. Fed up Constitutionalists recognized the opportunity. Cell phone calls were made and plans quickly developed and implemented.

Some distance north of the courthouse, two pickup trucks full of opportunistic mischief-makers, parked on 29th Street half a block from Paseo Drive and four men got out. While three of them walked toward the ACLU building on the corner of Paseo and 29th, the fourth, their leader, grabbed a cardboard box out of his truck's cargo area and hurried to join the others outside the building's entrance. Setting the box down near the door and pulling down his black balaclava facemask, the leader nodded to the others to do the same and eased open the door. Then, quietly stepping inside to check out the layout, he counted three men and a woman working at desks and tables in a large open room. Against the far wall, stood two old file cabinets, their drawers open. Bulging file boxes were stacked everywhere. Reopening the door and gesturing for the others to bring the box and enter, the leader walked toward the man working at the desk nearest the door.

Richard Kunkle, who'd been so busy texting on his cell phone he hadn't heard the door open, finally looked up in shock to find four masked men standing before his desk looking down at him.

"W-what do you want?" Kunkle sputtered, his eyes bulging and voice quaking.

"You have one minute to get out of this building, and twenty-four hours to get out of Oklahoma," Kunkel heard the leader hiss and gasped at the sight of the other three masked men removing Molotov cocktails from a cardboard box and lighting the rag-wicks.

"You're wasting time gawking," the leader warned, turning his head to look at the other workers in the room.

"GET OUT ... OR YOU'LL BE CHARBROILED," he shouted.

Yelling for his people to run, Kunkle—closely followed by the rest of the ACLU staff—bolted for the door, while the four masked men created an instant inferno by throwing their Molotov cocktails into various parts of the room.

Quickly leaving the building, the four masked men encountered Kunkle and the others standing in the street staring at them with expressions of shock and disbelief etched on their faces.

"You *still* here?" the masked leader asked, standing near the building's entrance.

"You'd damn well better run," he declared holding up the last Molotov cocktail with its wick lit. "RUN, DAMN IT!"

Needing no further encouragement, Kunkle and his coworkers took off running like the hounds of hell were after them down Pasco Drive.

Grinning under his mask and pointing toward their trucks, the leader told his men, "Time to go. I'll catch up with you at the trucks." As soon as his three associates started running toward their trucks, he opened the entry door and tossed the last firebomb inside. *One more thing to do, then I'll skedaddle.* Picking up a loose brick from the sidewalk he hurled it through the building's front window, causing a mini-explosion as air rushed in. "BURN BABY BURN," he yelled as he ran to catch up with his men.

Witnesses later reported both trucks' license tags were covered and there were no identifying marks other than their color and make—one black Ford and one dark green Toyota.

By the time the fire department arrived, the contents of the building were a total loss.

Meanwhile in another part of the city, eight men had entered a large office condo building on United Founders Boulevard and converged on a first floor suite. Pulling down their balaclava facemasks, the men burst through the Council on American Islamic Relation's, CAIR's office door and found two men wearing prayer caps. One swarthy and bearded, with the dark complexion of a Middle Easterner, sat at a desk writing something in Arabic on a poster board. The other, with light complexion and apparently Caucasian, sat reading a Qur'an and nervously fingering prayer beads. Looking up in consternation at the eight masked men, the two CAIR operatives blinked when their visitors simultaneously snapped open their telescoping metal batons.

"Up against the wall," the apparent leader ordered. "We've had enough of CAIR's whining, griping and interference.

"If you don't like our laws and constitutions, why are you here? This is America. When you come here you must obey *our* laws. If you can't, then leave.

"I understand some of you Muslims believe your Qur'an is above manmade laws. Well, your unholy Qur'an isn't above our Constitution or our laws.

"Understand this, and understand it well. This is the only time you'll be told. Obey our laws or leave. If you don't you'll be killed. Make sure everyone in your Muslim Brotherhood front organizations gets our message."

While the leader was speaking to the two Muslims, his companions were busy removing hard drives from computers and picking through documents. Telephones and computer wires were ripped out of the walls, and cell phones and interesting documents placed in bags.

So far, everything was going according to plan. Torching the office wasn't an option, because it was one suite in a large building. As the visitors began to leave, the swarthy Muslim took the opportunity to spit on the leader's facemask. A decision that earned him a blow from a baton that broke his jaw and knocked him to the floor.

"*Nooo!* Don't hurt me," the young Caucasian pleaded, cringing in fear. "I'm an American citizen. I attend the local university."

"Bullshit! Don't give us that crap. You may be a citizen but you *are not* an American. A traitor is closer to the truth. You've made a bad choice, young man; and if you continue on your current path, you'll most likely discover it was a life-ending choice."

Turning to the Muslim who lay on the floor glaring up at him, the leader used his baton to deliver a second vicious blow below the man's rib cage. Glaring down at the groaning man, he said, "This country was built by immigrants who came to join our culture and enjoy our freedoms. You Muslims come to force your backward, stone-age, political-religious ideology on us. I killed your kind in Iraq and Afghanistan, and if I ever lay eyes on you again in America, *I'll kill you too.*"

Oklahoma's governor and members of the legislator were shocked: first by Judge LeGrunge issuing a stay order within hours of the bill being signed; and second, even more shocked by the public's reaction to the judge's order.

Seated at his desk the governor stared at the stacks of constituents' messages heaped up in front of him. *What the hell do I do about all these?* he sighed when his intercom buzzed.

"Yes, what is it?"

"Sir, I know you asked me to hold your calls, but the Secretary of Homeland Security is on the phone. Line three."

"Oh, hell!" the governor muttered, and knowing it wasn't a social call, jabbed the blinking button on his phone. "What can I do for you *Madam Secretary?*"

"Governor, I assume you're aware of the ruckus going on at the Federal Court House. What are you doing to end this mob violence?"

"For God's sake, Madam Secretary!" the governor snapped, having had more than enough of Washington's interference. "Don't you have enough to do protecting our homeland and guarding our borders? Why don't you concentrate on doing your job and keep your nose out of our state's business? If your damn federal judge had kept her nose out of our state's business there would be no, as you call it, *'ruckus.'*

"Our city police are on the scene and will take care of the problem."

"That's not good enough, Governor," Incompentado snapped back.

"Well in that case, Madam Secretary—that's just *too damn bad.*"

"Governor, how dare you? I won't stand for being spoken to like that. It's obvious you're incapable of handling the situation, so I'm sending federal officers and FEMA Corps to restore order."

"Do that and you'll have another Vermont on your hands, because I'll order my National Guard to treat them as invaders."

"You can't be serious?"

"Send them and find out." The governor hung up the phone.

The occupytulsa.com website announced Tulsa would be occupied on Saturday, May 21, 2016.

Chapter 60

Monday, May 16, 2016

Pᴿᴇˢᴵᴰᴱᴺᵀ Abomba's EO 13978 went into effect at 12:01 a.m. eastern daylight time, resulting in more unintended consequences. As the clock struck midnight, gun control fanatics in several blue states were ready to pounce on their states' gun-nuts. Assuming the feds would take their time before beginning enforcement, some state, county and city police and a few sheriffs sallied forth to implement the order. As is often the case, haste makes waste, and in this instance it made for several wrong addresses. Terrified citizens, who'd neither owned guns nor supported gun ownership, were being awakened by having their front doors kicked in, and then held at gunpoint by armed, masked men who'd burst into their bedrooms and ransacked their houses. Those few who vigorously objected were either tased or sprayed with mace. One overly opinionated man was shot. For once progressive-liberals were finding themselves on the receiving end of their sacred anti-gun laws, and they weren't enjoying the experience.

Second Amendment supporters and Constitutionalists didn't like it either, and were surprised when a few progressive-liberals joined them at protests in front of city halls and police headquarters. It seems the elitists had experienced a taste of how life would be in a police state: the very kind of state they were working so hard to create; and it wasn't going to be the utopia they'd envisioned.

Because, every household authorities suspected of harboring a gun could not be raided on the first day, firefights erupted across the nation in the days that followed. In-your-face, anti-gun demonstrators found out they were no longer tolerated, and verbal insults and flag burnings resulted in severe bodily injuries and in some cases death. Progressive-liberal and conservative cultures were clashing—clashing in the streets across America. Citizens in northern and central California were resisting with force, as were eastern Oregonians and Washingtonians—to the amazement of costal progressive-liberals.

A few days after federal marshals placed Judge LeGrunge in a safe house, she'd learned her Oklahoma City residence had burned to the ground. Federal and state law enforcement alike advised her that given the number of death threats she'd received, it would be prudent to leave Oklahoma.

All political movements have extremists, and conservatives, Constitutionalists and Second Amendment movements were no exception. As unrest swept through the nation, extremists seized on opportunities the chaos provided to begin settling old scores—plus a few new ones. Murders and assassinations increased and law enforcement authorities were overwhelmed. In addition to whacking activists, elected officials, government employees, prosecutors and ultra-liberal judges were also targeted.

The chief justice and two justices of the New Mexico's Supreme Court were assassinated. When an unsigned letter to a local TV station stated, "The people executed these judges because they intentionally used their court to alter the meaning of the Constitution," judges responsible for similar rulings got busy finding a hole big enough to hide in. Unfortunately, three federal justices on the Ninth Circuit Court failed to heed the warning signs and fell victim to snipers.

After three ultra liberal news show personalities were shot, members of the news media realized they too were targeted, and reporting suddenly became factual and balanced.

Approximately one hundred Occupiers arrived in Tulsa on Friday and were run—literally run—out of town.

The revolution had begun.

Chapter 61

Washington, DC
Friday, May 20, 2016

Wall **Street and foreign investors had finally realized** the extent of the divide in the U.S., causing all the American markets to go into free fall at the opening bells. By 9:50 a.m., the NY Stock Exchange suspended trading after falling over 1,500 points. The S&P and NASDAQ followed. Traders dumping stocks turned to gold, which by 4:30 p.m. was trading at $5,041 per ounce. Capital was fleeing the U.S. at a staggering rate.

In the nations' capital, the elite finally got it—the message that hundreds of thousands of citizens would be marching on Washington, DC the following week. In a massive demonstration of public displeasure, citizens were coming to the nation's Capital for answers and change. They were coming to take back America.

The inside the beltway crowd quickly rationalized the number of people coming exceeded the District of Columbia's ability to accommodate, so they decided to leave town in order to provided more room for the demonstrators. Congressional representatives and staffers booked flights or packed vehicles. It was time, as the 'ins' were privately saying, "To get out of Dodge."

Friday afternoon the exodus began, with many headed for foreign destinations. Friday evening found Reagan, Dulles and BWI international airports clogged with fleeing congresspersons, senators, staffers, and lobbyists.

Saturday morning the Secret Service advised President Abomba to play golf at Joint Base Andrews or at Fort Belvoir. True to form, POTUS objected, stating he already had a golf date at the Army-Navy Club. When his Secret Service detail was finally forced to tell him they couldn't protect him there, POTUS threw a fit.

It required FLOTUS to persuade him to follow the Secret Service's advice. After all, she liked her current life style. While POTUS pouted,

FLOTUS ordered the Secret Service to collect his golfing buddies and take them to the golf course at Joint Base Andrews. For once, the agents were please by her interference.

Before departing on Marine One, POTUS told his aide to have Haggler, Helder, and Incompentado waiting to meet with him when he returned, and then, as an afterthought, added, "Ask Ms. Barrett to attend also."

Marine One landed at a remote location on Joint Base Andrews in order to avoid the swarm of reporters awaiting the president.

When Marine One returned POTUS to the White House at 1:12 p.m., he disembarked, blew through the reporters, and headed to his private quarters for a late lunch and a shower. Those reporters who'd had been waiting for the president since noon were furious.

"Ask Ms. Barrett to join me for lunch," Abomba told one of his Secret Service detachment members as he entered the White House."

"Mr. President, the Attorney General and Secretaries Incompentado and Haggler are waiting for you in the Oval Office," an aide reminded him.

"Tell them I'll be down after I eat."

President Abomba and Special Assistant to the President Vickie Barrett entered the Oval Office 3:44 p.m. Haggler, Helder, and Incompentado stood, suppressing their anger at being left cooling their heels for two and a half hours. Choosing to sit at his desk and assuming his classical Mussolini pose, Abomba looked down his nose at them while they returned to their seats.

"All right ... *What the hell's going on?*" he growled. "My golfing partners said the stock markets tanked, and Washington is about to be overrun by gun-nuts, Second Amendment nuts, and Constitutionalists.

"I thought the Occupiers were going to occupy DC next week? Now I have to learn—*on the golf course* no less—there's a bunch of whiners coming to bitch about *my* government.

"Why haven't I heard about this before?"

When no one answered, Abomba scowled and demanded, *"Well?"*

Helder attempted to explain, "Mr. President, a number of your ... uh, of the country's right-wing, opposition groups have decided to bring their grievances here. Our best guess is that as many as five hundred thousand people will be here by Saturday morning. That includes, uh ... coal miners, power plant workers, unhappy citizens, and as you just said, uh ... gun-nuts, Second Amendment nuts, and uh—of course, the Constitutionalists.

"There've also been reports of plans to burn the EPA, HHS, and Energy Department buildings. Some protesters have threatened to physically punish members of Congress and the Supreme Court," Helder added, deliberately omitting the president's name to avoid a tongue-lashing.

"If the Occupiers show up, we expect wholesale violence," he continued.

"*What?* Are you telling me that five hundred thousand people are coming here to oppose *me* and *my* programs?*

"Sir, I uh—"

"*You, what* ... what the hell were you going to say?

"You above everybody else should know I don't want a bunch of fuckin' troublemakers coming to Washington to oppose *me.*

"I WON'T STAND FOR IT!" the president suddenly yelled, glaring wild-eyed at Helder.

"DO YOU HEAR ME?

"DO WHATEVER IT TAKES ... DAMN IT—*STOP THEM!*"

"Mr. President ... uh, that's going to be very difficult, sir," Haggler replied, looking down at the rug.

"DON'T TELL ME THAT ... I DON'T WANNA HEAR IT," Abomba raged, jumping up from his chair so violently it rolled back against the wall. "YOU SNIVELING IDIOT," he roared, raking papers off his desk, and stomping around his desk to glare down at the secretary of defense. "THAT'S WHAT MY GODDAMN ARMY IS FOR. They're my servants.

"Gene ... *Gene! GENE are you listening to me? GODDAMNIT,* I'm only gonna tell you this once. Order those army shitheads to get up off their sorry, lazy asses and stop those ... those *revolutionaries* ... those *terrorists.* SHOOT THEM! I don't give a shit how many die. *Just stop 'em.*

"YOU TOO JANE ... *You'd damn well better listen too,*" Abomba snarled, leaning over Incompentado and shaking his finger in her face. "Order those bumbling FEMA Corps fuckers you're so proud of to protect me and enforce my orders. What the hell did we train 'em for in the first place? It was your bright idea to form the Corps.

"I expect them to *jump* when I tell them to, damn it. *Remember this bitch,* just because you have a title in front of your name, you're no better than they are.

"*UNDERSTAND THIS* ... Not one of those damn SOB demonstrators is to enter this city, or I'll have both you shot. GOT IT?" Without saying another word Abomba stalked out of the Oval Office.

White faced and shaken Haggler and Incompentado gaped at each, astounded by the president's threat and out of control behavior.

Helder, who'd been Abomba's life long friend, realized he'd just ordered the wholesale slaughter of American citizens. *I'll never be able to cover this one up. If the Army or the Blue Shirts fire on civilians, we're all toast. Think it's time to move on. I need a change of scenery.*

Barrett too was astonished by Abomba's order and maniacal threats against Haggler and Incompentado. *Oh my god, he's started believing his own bullshit. He's not going to wait for the right time to declare marshal law. He thinks he's already the dictator. I've worried about being able to control his ego when we made him president for life. Now I realize we can't. He's driving events faster than our timetable called for, and he's going to blow it. I'd better advise the Obsidians.*

Haggler finally recovered his composure and asked in a quaking voice, "Did I just receive an order from the President to order the military to fire on the demonstrators? I want to make sure I heard his order correctly."

Jane Incompentado nodded, her expression still one of disbelief. "Yes, Gene, that's what I heard him tell both of us to do. Guess I'd better get FEMA Corps moving."

Helder looked at his fellow cabinet members and came to a conclusion. Blood was going to be spilt, and now his main concern was that it did not include his. The time had come to follow Congress' example and get the hell out of Dodge too. Shaking his head, he stood and departed.

Barrett, who'd chosen to say nothing throughout the meeting, remained silent as she also rose and left the Oval Office. Heading for her office to collect her personal effects, she discretely departed for her condo to make several unpleasant phone calls. Driving across the 14th Street Bridge, a thought struck her, *I wonder if today was my last day at the White House?*

Still sitting in the Oval Office contemplating the consequences of Abomba's orders, Haggler finally found the strength to get up and leave. Gesturing a limp-wristed good-bye to Incompentado, who seemed stuck on hold, he trudged along through the servant's corridors and snuck out a back exit of the White House. *How in hell am I going to implement my orders? Will the military follow the President's orders?* he worried, as he drove to the Pentagon. "Oh, how I wish I'd resigned," he groaned, reaching for his cell phone to summon the Joint Chiefs of Staff to his office.

Mentally at sea over what just happened and also wishing she'd resigned, Incompentado was the last person to leave the Oval Office. Still in a mental fog, she returned to her office in the DHS building.

Pouring a glass of wine, Barrett kicked off her platform heels, flopped in her desk chair, and stared out her Arlington condo's window at Washington's skyline. *Who the hell do I call first?* she wondered, resting her elbows on the desk and rubbing her aching temples. *Probably need to get as much information as I can before calling the Obsidians,* she decided, pressing Rebecca's speed dial number.

"Hello, lover. Been thinking about you, looking forward to seeing you next week," Colonel Collins said when she answered.

"I am too, but we may have to cancel. Things are getting a little tense here."

"Yeah, here too. All of CENTCOM is nervous. You can feel the tension in the air."

"How's your Doughboy doing?" Barrett asked and heard Collins chuckle.

"Same old, same old. General Beck's the one who's uptight."

"Vickie, what's going on? The stock markets tanked. Thank God I only had a few stocks, however I heard Beck say his gold SPDR had gone through the roof."

"Rebecca, that's why I'm calling," Barrett said, taking a sip of wine.

"Remember when I asked you about the military following orders to suppress civilians?"

"Yeah ... Oh! Are we going to get such an order?"

"Maybe ... I'm not sure. It's estimated that five hundred thousand or more demonstrators will be coming to Washington on Friday. That's in addition to the Occupiers. The President doesn't want demonstrators in the city—unfriendly demonstrators that is. None are to enter the city.

"If the military is ordered to block the demonstrators, I need to know if the order will be followed."

Barrett, heard Collins sigh before responding, "I think a better way to put it is ..." Collins sighed again, "Who will follow the order?

"General Doughberry will, but if your question is, how many officers—and for that matter, enlisted—will follow his orders? I don't think we'll know until the orders are given."

"Yes ... that's what I'm afraid of."

"Vickie, are we going to get such an order?" Collins asked again, now intently listening.

"I'll do my best to prevent it, but I just don't know. Let me know if you learn anything else. This is *extremely* important."

"Of course. Thanks for the heads up."

"Yeah, talk to you later," Barrett said ending the call, and then, finishing off her glass of wine, smiled. *So, according to Rebecca, Beck's worried, but his gold SPDR's up. Well, so's mine ... up 300 percent as of this afternoon, and my gold stocks were doing even better,* she chuckled, pouring another glass of wine.

Three-quarters of a bottle of Cabernet Sauvignon later, after weighing numerous pros and cons, she decided to make one more attempt to calm Abomba down and dialed his private number. One of his Secret Service detail answered and told her the President had left orders not to be disturbed for any reason.

"Well that settles that, now it's time to beard the lion in his den," she muttered, ending the call. Fifteen minutes later, after learning the billionaire investor had already correctly accessed the situation, as well as Abomba's mental state, she listened carefully to his final statement.

"I'll notify the others," he said. "We'll sit tight and see if he wins this skirmish—which I doubt. If he does we'll implement a plan to regain control over him. If we can't, or if he doesn't win, we'll cut our losses and move on. Keep in touch," he said, ending the call.

Okay, the lion has roared, and I guess it's tough decisions like this that made him a billionaire. So now I think I'd better do what he suggests, and cut my losses and move on.

With that thought in mind, she called her travel agent and booked a flight departing Philadelphia on May 30th to Rio de Janeiro, Brazil.

Chapter 62

MacDill AFB, Tampa, Florida
Colonel Rebecca Collins' quarters
Saturday afternoon, 21 May 2016

Colonel Collins placed her cell phone in her purse and sat, reviewing her conversation with Vickie Barrett. She realized a crisis approached: a crisis that could end the Founding Fathers' great experiment. For the first time she fully realized the country, the Republic she'd grown up in could violently end. A country born from revolution could die in revolution. Collins started to pick up her glass of water and realized her hand was shaking. *I need to have a private talk with General Beck. It can't wait.*

Tony Beck and his wife were almost to the front door when his cell phone vibrated in his pocket. Removing it he was surprised when he saw COLLINS, R on the screen. "Hello, Rebecca, what can I do for you?"

"Sir, uh … Tony, I need to talk with you ASAP. I just had a call from my girlfriend in Washington … sir, it's serious."

"We're on our way to a dinner party. Should be back by 2100. Can it wait until then?"

"Yes, sir."

"Good, I'll be expecting you at 2100."

"Thanks, Tony. I'll be there."

"What was that all about?" Mrs. Beck asked.

"Don't know. I'll find out when she gets here."

The Pentagon
Saturday evening, 21 May 2016

Secretary of Defense Haggler did his best to remain impassive while the Air Force Chief of Staff, the last chief to arrive found a seat. "Gentlemen, as we all know, several hundred thousand unhappy citizens are coming to Washington on Friday. All the roads leading into the city will be jammed with demonstrators. Most will be coming to protest new laws.

"Adding to that problem, Occupy Washington demonstrators will be in the city or still arriving. The two groups don't get along and there will be violent confrontations."

The chiefs sat quietly, for they were well aware of these problems.

Haggler waited to see if anyone would comment. When no one did, he continued, "I met with the President this afternoon." Haggler paused for effect before continuing.

"The President is not pleased with the spectacle of violent clashes."

The chiefs sat stone faced, offering no comment.

"The President has ordered us, the military, to prevent the demonstrators from entering Washington. What is your advice?"

When the chairman remained silent, the commandant of the Marine Corps asked, "Mr. Secretary, what does 'prevent from entering mean'? What are the ROEs?"

"Determining the rules of engagement is one of the reasons you are here," Haggler replied.

◆ ◆ ◆

During WWII, the chairman of the Joint Chiefs, and the chiefs of the Army and Navy were in the chain of command leading from the Commander in Chief to the secretary of war, to the secretaries of the Army and Navy, to the admiral or general commanding major areas: Generals McArthur and Eisenhower, and Admiral Nimitz for example. That made the chairman the most senior military officer in all services.

All that changed with the Goldwater-Nichols Act of 1986. The Joint Chiefs of Staff no longer had operational command authority. Now the chain of command goes from POTUS to the secretary of defense to the combatant commands, CENTCOM for example. The Chairman of the Joints Chiefs of Staff is now the principal military advisor to the secretary of defense.

◆ ◆ ◆

Admiral, what are your thoughts?" General Dumpsterson asked

Damn him, he would start with me, the chief of Naval Operation silently winced. "Sir, with the exception of the special unit assigned to NORTHCOM, our men and women aren't equipped for, or trained to handle civilians. If we're dealing with hundreds of thousands of angry civilians … well … things can get out of hand."

"Mr. Secretary, if civilians force past our check points, the only way to stop them will be to fire on them. Is that what you're suggesting?" the Army chief of staff asked, leaning forward.

"I'm not suggesting anything. I'm asking for opinions. Are you saying the only way to stop them would be with live ammunition?"

"Yes, Mr. Secretary, if we are dealing with hundreds of thousands that is the only way to stop them."

Haggler felt a dark cloud descending on the room. He had hoped that somehow there would be another answer. "Does anyone have a better solution to the problem?"

None of the men in the room answered, and that was the answer.

"Mr. Secretary, does the President realize what his order means. That the military will have to fire on civilians, our citizens?"

Haggler was wondering the same thing. "I will make sure he does before relaying his orders to the combatant commands."

"The real question is, will the commands follow his orders?" the commandant of the Marine Corps said, catching himself before adding, I won't.

"Any other comments, questions or ideas?"

When no one replied, Haggler said, "Well that means the ROEs will be: use whatever force is necessary to turn back demonstrators.

"But before issuing that order, I'll make sure the President knows exactly what the orders means. Thank you for coming."

MacDill AFB, Tampa, Florida
Major General Beck's quarters
2100 hours, Saturday, 21 May 2016

General Beck opened the door and greeted Colonel Collins, "Good evening, Rebecca. Please come in." Leading her past the kitchen on the way to his study, he asked, "Would you like a cup of coffee?

"No, sir. I've had too much coffee already."

Once seated with the door closed, Beck asked, "Okay, what's so important it can't wait until Monday morning?"

"Sir, I received a disturbing call from my friend in the White House." Collins paused, trying to find a good way to approach the subject. "There was a meeting this afternoon ... a meeting with the President ... a meeting about the large number of protesters planning to march on Washington next weekend."

Beck had feared that was why Collins was concerned. *In spite of being Doughberry's mistress, she is a fine officer. The fact she's here confirms that. Time to find out whose side she's on—that is if she knows.* "What did your friend hear about what went on in the meeting?"

Collins realized the question trapped her. *I wonder how much he already knows? It's time to put all the cards on the table.* "Sir, she was in the meeting. The President met with Secretaries Haggler and Incompentado. The attorney general was also present."

Beck nodded, for he'd received a report of the meeting, but not the substance. He also knew the Joint Chiefs had been summoned to meet with Haggler earlier in the evening, and the subject of that meeting was ROEs. "And what did your friend tell you about the subject of the meeting?"

Collins looked up, grimaced, and then looked into Beck eyes. "Sir, the subject was the angry demonstrators march on Washington scheduled for next Friday." Collins grimaced again. "Sir, the President ordered the military to turn back the demonstrators. Not to allow them to enter the city."

"And Ms. Barrett asked you to find out how the orders will be received?"

Beck's reference to Barrett shocked her. *He's been watching me. He's always one move ahead of everyone else. Isn't that why I'm here? Time to choose sides, and I'm not going to have any part of turning this country into a dictatorship.* After recovering her composure she answered, "Yes, sir. But I'm not here for the answer, I'm here to give you a heads up on the pending orders"

Beck smiled. "Good. How about a brandy to take the edge off your coffee nerves." Without waiting for her answer, he stood, poured two snifters of VSOP brandy and handed her one.

Collins accepted the snifter, realizing it was his way of telling her he believed her.

"Rebecca, I've been concerned events would force the military into having to decide if an order is legal," Beck said, returning to his chair.

"As for your friend's question, there's no black and white answer. Some will obey ... and some will not. The real question is, will some of our units engage others? Beck paused to look at his snifter, sighed, and looking directly into Collins' eyes completed his statement, "I dearly wish I knew the answer."

"I told Vickie there was no answer. Told her most of what you just said. She's going to try to get the President to change his mind."

"Do you think she can?"

"No."

"Neither do I," Beck said standing. "Thank you for coming to me with this information. Our duty is to the Constitution, to protect it. You're a fine officer, and there are thousands more officers and senior enlisted who feel the same way. My prayer is that when the time comes they'll stand by their principals and refuse to obey an illegal order.

"Now, in so much as we both must be alert tomorrow, I'll ask you to join me in a toast before you go and get some rest," Beck said, raising his snifter.

"To the Constitution of United States of America."

Taking a deep breath, "Collins stood, touched her snifter to Beck's and they both drained their snifters.

Beck walked Collins to the front door. "Again, thanks for trusting me, Rebecca. I'll keep you informed, and please do the same for me."

"Yes, sir. I will. Thank you and goodnight."

"Good night."

After closing the door and turning out the porch light, a worried Beck returned to his study, opened his burner cell phone and began making calls.

Chapter 63

Secretary of Defense Haggler was waiting for the president to see him. He was sure the president knew why he was there, but didn't want to be bothered. *Should I offer my resignation? But if I do, I'll dump the problem into my deputy's lap, and she doesn't have a clue about what's going on. I've had plenty of opportunities to get out. Now it's too late. It's time to man up.*

An hour later he was told the president could see him for five minutes. Entering the Oval Office, he found Abomba in golf attire using a putter to hit golf balls into a glass with the presidential seal.

"What's so important you had to interrupt me?" Abomba asked as he neatly directed a ball across the carpet into the glass.

"Mr. President, I must review my instructions with you before issuing orders."

"Are you referring to stopping demonstrators? The hicks that don't understand my grand achievements … what I've done for them?" the president asked, lining up his next putt.

"Yes Mr. President. I met with the Joint Chiefs to discuss how to accomplish your orders."

Abomba hit another golf ball into the glass.

"Mr. President, they all agree the only way to stop the protesters is by force. Mr. President, it may be necessary to fire on them."

Abomba looked up from his next put and asked, "So what's the problem."

Shaken by the president's attitude, Haggler said, "Mr. President, that means I'll be ordering our military to fire on our citizens. Are you sure you want to give such an order?"

Enraged, Abomba threw his putter against the wall and snarled, *"They're coming to oppose my plans.* They're opposing *me.* That makes them revolutionaries. *Damn right!* Fire on them! They need a lesson. They need to know I'm the boss.

"Now, *get out!* Follow my orders, or I'll find someone who will."

Haggler left the Oval Office and wandered trance-like toward the entrance. Vickie Barrett was waiting for him in hall, "Gene, How did it go? Were you able to get him to change his order?"

"No, God help us, I wasn't."

Barrett nodded, for there was nothing left to say. After watching Haggler slowly continue down the hall, she came to a decision and returned to her office. Closing her office door and frowning, she dialed a number in New York City—one she knew would be forwarded through several other phones—and waited. After several rings, a familiar voice answered. "The order stands," she said, and hung up.

Then, using her notebook computer, she logged onto the airline's website and changed her May 30th flight to Rio de Janeiro, Brazil to one departing on Wednesday morning, May 25th. It was time to get out of Dodge. *Should I call Rebecca and ask her to come? No, I need to make a clean break ... and the girls from Ipanema are luscious. I'll tell Barry I need to take Wednesday off and drive up to Phili after work on Tuesday.* Barrett spent the remainder of the day making plans, transferring her broker accounts to Rio de Janeiro, and confirming her purchase of a villa.

Secretary Haggler returned to his office and summoned General Dumpsterson. When he arrived Haggler said, "The President confirmed his order. I'm going to issue the order with NORTHCOM as the lead, supported by CENTCOM and SOUTHCOM.

"Order them to report to me at 0700 tomorrow."

Still standing, Dumpsterson said, "Yes, Mr. Secretary, I understand. Is there anything else?"

"No."

Returning to his office, Dumpsterson placed calls to Generals Lackiemann and Doughberry and relayed secretary of defense's orders to report to him at 0700 the next day. SOUTHCOM's commander was in Argentina and would not be able to attend the morning meeting.

The following morning, Generals Doughberry and Lackiemann entered the secretary of defense's secure conference room at 0708 hours and found Secretary Haggler waiting for them, along with the assistant deputy secretary for human rights, General Dumpsterson and two colonels, with JAG insignias on their uniforms. As soon as Lackiemann and Doughberry were seated, the assistant deputy secretary for human rights began, "I'm sure you're aware that numerous conservative protests are scheduled for this weekend in state capitols." Lackiemann and Doughberry nodded.

"There has been a drastic increase in violent protests by extremists. Some attribute this increase to opposition to new gun laws.

"The President, our Commander in Chief, considers extremist revolutionaries the primary source of this social unrest—along with other sources attributable to racists and Islamophobes.

"DOD's policy defines extremists as persons who advocate the use of force or violence; advocate supremacist causes based on race, ethnicity, religion, gender, or national origin; or otherwise advocate engaging in illegal activities that deprive individuals or groups of their civil rights.

"Conservatives, Constitutionalists, Second Amendment supporters, Tea Party members, even members of the American Legion are people who embrace 'individual liberties' and honor 'states rights'—these people are extremists."

Lackiemann and Doughberry sat nodding their heads.

Secretary Haggler took over the meeting, "It's estimated that five hundred thousand extremists are planning to march on Washington on Friday. Among their stated intentions are: burning down the EPA; throwing liberal Senators and Congresspersons out of the Capitol building and Justices out of the Supreme Court building. However, most disturbing of all is their announced intention to eject our President from the White House.

"This action will not be tolerated."

Again Lackiemann and Doughberry nodded their heads. Both were beginning to fear what was coming next.

"Good. General Lackiemann, you are ordered to use all necessary force to prevent the extremist demonstrators from entering the District of Columbia.

"General Doughberry, you will provide NORTHCOM all available support and assist General Lackiemann in carrying out his orders. Both of you are authorized to draw on SOCOM assets as required."

After a full minute of silence while the two generals considered their orders, Lackiemann asked, "Mr. Secretary, do my orders include preventing the Occupiers from entering?

The Assistant Deputy Secretary for Human Rights answered, "Occupiers are not extremists. Any more questions?"

"No, sir," both generals answered in unison.

"Good, then carry out my orders," Haggler said, standing.

As soon as the meeting was over and Doolittle and Doughberry boarded a helicopter for the short hop to Joint Base Andrews where their aircrafts were waiting and ready for takeoff.

Chapter 64

CENTCOM
0835 Tuesday, 24 May 2016

Major General Beck had just received a call on his burner phone from a master sergeant at the Pentagon informing him of the gist of SecDef's orders. After ending the call, Beck sat staring at the wall. *It's really going to happen. Our President is going to start a revolution. No, he's already started a revolution, now he's about to start a civil war. God help us.*

An hour later Beck received a call from his boss who was en route to MacDill AFB. After informing Beck his ETA was 1115 hours, Doughberry instructed him to have the entire staff assembled when he arrived. When Beck asked about the subject of the meeting, Doughberry replied, "I've received direct orders from the Secretary of Defense, which I will relay to the staff when I arrive. We will then prepare plans for immediate implementation."

General Doughberry entered the main conference room at 1126, waddled to his chair at the head of the table and muttered, "Please be seated.

"Yesterday evening, I was summoned to the Pentagon and told to attend an 0700 meeting this morning with the Secretary of Defense. General Lackiemann was also summoned. The President and SecDef are concerned about the large number of extremists preparing to march on Washington on Friday. More to the point, these marchers are considered revolutionaries and violence is expected.

"NORTHCOM, supported by CENTCOM, has been ordered to prevent these extremist marchers from entering the District of Columbia.

"NORTHCOM has been given authority to requisition required forces from other commands, including us and SOCOM."

"Any questions?" Doughberry asked, keenly aware from his staff's somber expressions they were deeply disturbed by what they'd just heard.

"Yes, sir," Brigadier General Roberts said, frowning and leaning forward in his chair to stare at Doughberry. "How can we stop civilians from using public highways?"

"Block the roads with vehicles."

"Sir ... that won't prevent civilians from going around roadblocks or taking alternate roads.

"Access to the city from the southeast and southwest quadrants—90° to 180°—might be prevented by setting up roadblocks at bridges over the Potomac and Anacostia Rivers," Roberts said. "But there is no easy way to block entrance from northeast and northwest quadrants—180° to 90°."

"FEMA Corps will coordinate with NORTHCOM and us. I spoke with General Savage while en route here. He plans to concentrate on blocking interstate highways and major roads at their junctions with the Washington beltway."

Roberts persisted, "Sir, I don't think roadblocks will stop the marchers. They'll simply flow around our roadblocks ... and sir, I don't consider them extremists or revolutionaries."

Doughberry stood and glared at Roberts. "Are you saying you'll disobey a direct order?"

Before Roberts could answer, Beck intervened by saying, "Sir, I believe General Roberts is asking about the rules of engagement for dealing with the marchers."

Doughberry harrumphed and continued glaring at Roberts, prompting Colonel Collins to inwardly cringe. Everyone in the room knew Doughberry was being deliberately obtuse, and she knew Roberts was rapidly approaching his boiling point. The problem was she had no idea how to prevent it.

Finally addressing Roberts directly, Doughberry snarled, "Exactly what are you questioning General? Are you asking what kind of force is authorized for use in turning back the extremists?"

Roberts face flushed. Fighting to control his fury, he managed to reply, "Yes, *sir.* That *is* my question."

Doughberry leaned back in his chair and sneered, delighted he was intimidating this upstart Marine—at least he thought he was intimidating him. "I see ... well General the answer quite simply is—use whatever force required to meet you mission objective."

Roberts jumped to his feet, "General, are you telling me to use *live ammunition* to fire on U.S. citizens?"

Slamming his fist down on the table, Doughberry sneered at Roberts and barked, *"That's exactly what I'm telling you.* IS THAT A PROBLEM?"

Before Roberts could reply, Beck stood. "Yes, sir," he said, the tone of his voice like steel. "That *is* a problem ... and it is a problem because it's an *illegal order."*

"HOW DARE YOU CHALLENGE ME? Doughberry stormed, "YOU ARE RELIEVED."

Without batting an eye, Beck remained standing, and looking his boss straight in the eye asked, "General Doughberry, do you remember the oath you took when you were commissioned? Part of that oath was, 'I solemnly swear to protect the Constitution of the United States of America against all enemies, foreign and domestic.'

"We did not swear to protect the President, Congress or the Supreme Court. No, sir, we swore to protect the Constitution.

"Sir, the actions of the current administration and the orders you just relayed are unconstitutional. Many of the men under your command have joined Oath Keepers, an organization of men and women who have reaffirmed that sacred oath. While I haven't joined myself, I support the organization's purpose.

"Sir, I respectfully request that you inform the Secretary of Defense you cannot obey his order, because it is an illegal order."

"I'll do no such thing.

"SERGEANT MAJOR," Doughberry called toward the conference room's entry door.

As second later Sergeant Major Osborne entered the room.

"Sergeant Major Osborne, place both Major General Beck and Brigadier General Roberts under arrest."

Sergeant Major Osborne stood at attention and said nothing.

"Sergeant Major Osborne, I just gave you a direct order. NOW, CARRY IT OUT!"

Everyone in the room sat frozen in their seats watching the drama playing out.

While Osborne remained standing at attention, Doughberry searched the faces of the others in the room looking for support. Shocked and furious that no one had risen to back him up, he finally turned to Collins and sputtered in anger, "Colonel Collins, summon the MPs."

Collins closed her eyes and grimaced. After a few seconds, she replied in a near whisper, "No, sir. I will not. You're *wrong* ... the order is *illegal* ... and it's *wrong."*

Looking at Collins in amazement, Doughberry stood there for what seemed like an eternity. Finally, slouching forward and resting his hands on the tabletop, he bowed his head so low his chin was nearly touching his chest.

Beck stood, shaking his head at what Doughberry had just done, and what he was about to do. "Sergeant Major Osborne, place General Doughberry under house arrest. He is to have absolutely no communication with anyone."

"Yes, sir.

"General Doughberry, please come with me ... and by the way sir, I'm an Oath Keeper, as are most on the men and women in CENTCOM."

Once General Doughberry had departed, Beck addressed the others in the room. "That was unfortunate. I have no way of telling you what the fallout from my actions will be. But I cannot simply stand by and be a party to shooting U. S. citizens.

"If anyone disagrees with my action please return to your quarters and place yourself under house arrest. That way you won't be held responsible for my actions."

No one moved.

"Thank you. CENTCOM should never have been placed in this position ... but regrettably we have been," Beck said, profoundly disturbed by what he'd been forced to do. "Through no fault of our own, our military finds itself facing a Constitutional crisis. Hopefully, we'll be able to stay on the sidelines and not become involved.

"Hope is a wonderful thing, but we all know you must plan for the worst and hope for the best. And that's exactly what we must now do.

"If some commanders follow the President's order and fire on civilians, the civilians will probably return fire. If this occurs it could start a civil war.

"I'm going to start calling other commanders to discuss the consequences of carrying out the order, and the possibility of doing so triggering a civil war.

"I want each of you to consider is what CENTCOM should do if a U.S. military unit fires on our citizens.

"We'll meet here tomorrow at 0600 to discuss our options. Please be ready to present your thoughts at that time."

Beck returned to his office and began making phone calls. The pot was about to boil over.

Chapter 65

NORTHCOM
Peterson AFB, Colorado
Tuesday afternoon, 24 May 2016

Arriving at NORTHCOM headquarters, General Lackiemann did what General Doughberry had done, published his orders and encountered a similar reception. "So that's the situation," he told his staff after explaining President Abomba and SecDef have no intention of allowing these extremist to enter the city and disrupt the government. "NORTHCOM, supported by CENTCOM, has been ordered to prevent these extremist marchers from entering the District of Columbia. In addition NORTHCOM has been given authority to request forces from SOCOM and all other commands," he said surveying the hostile faces in front of him.

Used to having his staff looking at him with thinly veiled resentment and disrespect, this time he detected something different—something closer to rebellious hostility and anger. He knew they'd never really accepted him after the way the president appointed him without warning on the heels of relieving his predecessor. *I had nothing to do with the President's press secretary announcing my appointment before General Craig had been told he'd been reassigned. Anyway, being liked isn't my job, following the Secretary's orders is.*

For several seconds everyone in the conference room sat gravely looking at him in silence.

Finally Brigadier General Bedford, commander of Joint Task Force North asked, "Sir, what are the rules of engagement?"

When Lackiemann answered, "Use whatever force necessary," staff members started squirming in their seats and looking at each other in astonishment.

"It *is* what it *is* ladies and gentlemen," Lackiemann said, standing erect and squaring his shoulders, "I have authority to commandeer all needed resources and assets. I want plans to implement the Secretary's order on my desk by noon tomorrow. That will be all. Dismissed."

A divided staff left Lackiemann's briefing, some would follow orders and some wouldn't. Two senior officers knew what had occurred at CENTCOM and were considering doing the same.

An hour after the staff meeting ended, two brigadier generals requested a meeting with General Lackiemann. When they entered his office, both submitted their resignations and retirement requests. Their reason—they could not follow an illegal order. Lackiemann was enraged.

◆ ◆ ◆

United States Northern Command (USNORTHCOM) is a Unified Combatant Command of the U.S. military tasked with providing military support for civil authorities in the U.S., and protecting the territory and national interests of the U.S. within the contiguous United States, Alaska, Canada, Mexico (and air, land and sea approaches to these areas). USNORTHCOM was created on April 25, 2002, following the September 11 attacks, when President George W. Bush approved a new Unified Command Plan.

NORTHCOM's mission is to: (1) conduct operations to deter, prevent, and defeat threats and aggression aimed at the United States, its territories, and interests within the assigned area of responsibility; and (2) provide military assistance to civil authorities including consequence management operations, as directed by the president or secretary of defense.

◆ ◆ ◆

The Morning Drive Radio Talk Show
WPTF 680AM, Raleigh, North Carolina
7:36 a.m., Wednesday, 25 May 2016

Radio Talk show host Doug Kellett and his producer Ron opened the show discussing the May 27th march on Washington by the Take Back America advocates. About five minutes into the show, John, who said he was a regular listener, phoned in from Fayetteville, NC.

"Doug, the President has ordered the military to use force to stop the marchers from entering Washington. The order was issued yesterday."

"What? You have to be kidding me," Doug responded. "I don't think the President can order the military to interfere with a citizen protest."

"It doesn't matter what you think, the President has ordered use of whatever force necessary against marchers. It looks like he plans to declare martial law."

"Are you sure? John, this is nothing to joke about. If this is true, we have a Constitutional crisis."

"Yeah, that's exactly what we have. If the military uses force to stop the Take Back America marchers, the stage is set for Abomba to become a dictator."

"That's a very strong statement."

"Yeah, I'm aware of that, but are you aware that senior officers at CENTCOM relieved their commanding officer yesterday for giving an illegal order—the President's illegal order?" John hung up. He'd said enough. *That ought'a get the ball rolling,* Rocky Rockford grinned, pleased his call had gotten the reaction he'd sought.

Shortly thereafter FOX News picked up the story of the president's illegal order and CENTCOM's commander being relieved. Soon each congressperson's email box was filled and their phone and fax machine lines jammed. Angry voters learned that many of their representatives were out of town or out of the country on junkets.

Next came calls to the White House, which sent President Abomba into a rage, causing Jay Schpinmeister to invent several new dance steps.

The clock in General Lackiemann's office reached 1200 hours. Only one plan rested on his desk and he was seeing red. Picking up his phone he dialed the first task force commander whose plan was missing and proceeded to give him a first class ass-chewing: a procedure he repeated for each of the other staff members with missing plans. To a man, they all said they were still attempting to prepare a workable plan without using the words, "whatever force necessary that would stop U.S. citizens from entering their capital city."

When it was his turn, Brigadier General Bedford said, "Sir, using whatever force necessary against citizen exercising their Constitutional rights is a violation of our oath to defend the Constitution. Sir, so far my staff and I have found no way to follow your order without violating our oath."

"Damn it, Bedford, I gave you an order. You will obey it or be court-martialed. Let me worry about the oath."

"No, sir. *I took the oath.* You didn't take it for me. It's *my* oath and *I will honor it.*"

General Lackiemann soon discovered most of his senior staff and the men and women under his command agreed with General Bedford. While he was formulating plans to court-martial his staff for mutiny, he learned that General Doughberry's chief of staff had relieved him.

A quick call to the secretary of defense resulted in more confusing orders. After completing the call, Lackiemann, overcome by the realization the chain of command had broken down, sat quietly in his office. *SecDef has no idea what to do, and the Commander in Chief is issuing more orders that clearly violate the Constitution.*

An hour later, having prepared proper forms and written a letter to his superior, General Lackiemann notified the Pentagon of his intention to resign his position and immediately retire.

Berating the military and saying he had to do everything, President Abomba fired Haggler and began placing personal calls to military commanders, ordering them to protect the capital city from revolutionaries and terrorists. Some accepted the order without question and ordered their units to proceed to Washington, DC.

The first wave of Take Back America marchers began arriving Wednesday afternoon. Traffic jams filled the highways, blocking all major roads leading to Washington. Tent cities sprang up on any available location—farm fields, shopping center parking lots, and along highways. By nightfall, Take Back America camps ringed Washington, D.C., and the main wave of marchers was expected to arrive the next day.

Chapter 66

Washington, DC Area
Thursday, May 26, 2016

News helicopters were providing nonstop video of the Take Back America camps and the roads leading to the city—roads clogged with RVs, camper trailers, busses, trucks, automobiles and motorcycles transporting men and women marchers. New arrivals swelled the tent cities and created new ones. Maryland's and Virginia's state and local police were at a loss as to how to handle the crowds. Yet, even though most marchers were armed, there was little to no violence. Spokespersons told reporters they were there to, "Take Back America."

American flags with "Take Back America" printed on them in bold letters flew alongside Yellow Gadsden flags; flags with words proclaiming "We've Come To Take It Back;" and flags with a rattlesnake and the words "Don't Tread Upon Me" superimposed on a field of Red and White stripes. Men and women wore patriotic shirts and hats. Constitutionalists, Second Amendment and Tea Party organizations, along with state militias and just plain concerned citizens were there to take back their country, and planned to do so in the morning.

Text messages between Take Back America leaders filled the ether. Coal miners would concentrate on the EPA and DOE. Second Amendment marchers would go for the Department of Justice, Health and Human Services, and Homeland Security. Constitutionalists would march on the Supreme Court and the Capitol building. Marchers not directly affiliated with one of these movements would follow whichever group was ahead of them. The White House would be the afternoon target.

By the end of the day, they hoped to have taken back America.

Military roadblocks were established on the bridges and on major roads leading into the city from the south, which prevented both Take Back America marchers and government employees from entering the city. America's military is an all-volunteer force employing sophisticated weapons, electronics and vehicles. Consequently, the men and women serving in America's armed forces must be capable of operating their complicated equipment, which means a minimum of a high school education with many holding college degrees. Private Beetle Bailey, a lazy WWII era comic strip character, modeled on a college drop out, who usually napped and avoided work, no longer represented the new enlisted man and woman. Now privates were better educated and capable of thinking for themselves. So it should have come as no surprise when they began questioning orders to fire on civilians. Company grade officers and a many field grade officers were also questioning their orders. Rumors were rampant: "The CENTCOM commander had been removed," "The 82nd and 101st Air Borne divisions had received deployment orders but hadn't left their barracks."

Tomorrow America's military would be forced to make their decisions—to fire or not to fire on their fellow countrymen.

Colonel Collins was not only conflicted over the orders CENTCOM had received and her boss being relieved from duty, she was also concerned over not being able to reach her lover. She'd placed several calls to Vickie Barrett's office, only to learn Barrett had taken a personal day leave. When Collins called Barrett's condo, the answering machine greeted her. After leaving six messages, Collins realized Vickie wasn't going to answer. *If she's not in the White House advising the President, where is she?* Collins wouldn't learn the answer to her question for many years.

The White House
8 p.m., Thursday, May 26, 2016

President Abomba had been pacing back and forth in his private quarters for over an hour. The First Lady and his children were on vacation in Hawaii. *Things have gone to hell in a handbasket and I have no one to talk to. Where is Vickie? The damn marchers are surrounding the city and I need her advice. No one knows where she is. Damn her. How can she be so inconsiderate? Taking a personal day when I need her? Damn her.* Now in panic mode, he turned to his aide, pointed at the phone and stormed, *"Get General Dumpsterson on the phone."*

Too agitated to wait for his aide to tell him Dumpsterson was on the line, Abomba grabbed the handset and stood rocking back and forth waiting for the general to answer. As soon as he did, Abomba demanded, "What the hell's going on with the damn roads? Are they blocked? I don't want even one of those damn marchers to set foot into the city."

"Yes, Mr. President, the roads are blocked." The general responded, but refrained from voicing his fear the marchers wouldn't be stopped. In fact, he'd been reviewing his retirement papers when the president called.

While the president stewed over the roadblocks being in place, the Secret Service worried about protecting him if the marchers did enter the city.

Al-Qaeda cells operating out of mosques in Virginia and Maryland had been busy. While Reverend Scoundrell was organizing his morning march on the Capitol building, cell members had been busy meeting with gang leaders and bored young black men in the rundown areas of Washington, DC, which as it happened encompassed a major portion of the city. After being promised weapons and cocaine, gang leaders eagerly agreed to participate in rioting. Early tomorrow morning they'd be able to create havoc, break widows, loot, and kill white crackers—best of all, they were getting paid for doing what they desired most to do.

Unlike the military, General Savage and his Blue Shirts were undeterred by the prospect of killing citizens. In fact, they were looking forward to opening fire on arrogant, lazy civilians. It was time to teach them who was boss. Teach them to obey orders and do so quickly. Most of Savage's men had never heard of *Der Führer,* Adolf Hitler, or the *Waffen-SS*—the armed wing of the Nazi Party's *Schutzstaffel,* Protective Squadron—nor that Nazis stood for a form of fascism that incorporated biological racism and anti-Semitism. Even so, if FEMA Corps' forces prevailed, they were about to become America's version of the SS.

Sean Haddley Show
10 p.m. Thursday May 26, 2016

"Good evening, America ... " Haddley frowned, "or is it? I regret to tell you that FOX has just confirmed President Abomba has issued an executive ordered directing the military to use whatever force required to prevent Take Back America demonstrators from entering the capital city tomorrow morning. In addition, I can confirm that hundreds of thousands of those demonstrators are camped in every available location around Washington preparing for their morning march into city.

"Will the military follow the President's orders? No one knows, but we're certain to find out in the morning. However, I do have reports several commanders have refused to follow the order.

"The President's Constitutional authority to use military force against American civilians is the subject of tonight's show. My two guests this evening will offer their views and opinions. Please welcome Senator Crux and former congressman and now presidential candidate, Colonel Albert East.

"Senator, let's begin with President Abomba and the Constitution."

Wearing a somber expression, Crux looked into the camera and said, "Thank you for inviting me Sean. America is facing the worst Constitutional crisis in its history. Tomorrow will determine the course of the nation. Will America remain a Constitutional Republic governed by its Constitution and the Founding Fathers' wisdom," Crux paused, and his expression hardened as did his voice, "or will it become a Socialist state with a dictator. A state resembling the Soviet Union."

"Are those really the only two choices left?" Haddley asked.

"I fear they are," Crux answered.

Haddley turned to Colonel East, "Do you agree?"

East stared at Haddley, "Yes, Sean, I do. However, I'm hopeful we'll chose to remain a Constitutional Republic.

"I have good reason to believe the military will remain loyal to the Constitution, not the President."

Haddley leaned forward, "Do you really think that's what's happening? Is it really the President versus the Constitution?"

"Yes. Forget all the rhetoric, talking points and hype. We're past all that. As Senator Crux just said, tomorrow we decided if we are to remain a Constitutional Republic.

"President Abomba ordered Secretary of Defense Haggler to use whatever force required to prevent Take Back America marchers from entering the city. Secretary Haggler met with the commanders of U.S. Northern Command, NORTHCOM, and U.S. Central Command, CENTCOM, and gave them direct orders to prevent the marchers from entering Washington.

"CENTCOM's officers and enlisted refused the order because it was illegal, and CENTCOM's chief of staff relieved the commander.

"After learning of the situation at CENTCOM, NORTHCOM's commander resigned and submitted his retirement papers.

"Other commanders have ignored their orders."

"So you don't think the military will use force against the Take Back America citizens?"

"I can't be one hundred percent sure. Some may. We'll find out tomorrow.

"The Blue Shirts are another matter altogether. I fear they won't hesitate to fire."

Senator Crux interjected, "If serious firefights break out, the Blue Shirts can cause a civil war. Skirmishes are already occurring across the nation. Four progressive-liberal college professors who denigrated the Constitution and classified the Founding Fathers as extremists have been shot in their classrooms by students."

"As have three student activists burning a flag," East added. "Progressive-liberals have pushed the envelope too far and won't back down. Liberal judges have rewritten parts of the Constitution, interfered with states' rights, and created laws from the bench to suit their beliefs. People have had enough. Since judges have lifetime appointments and liberals in Congress approve of their actions, there's only one practical way to remove them."

Haddley was obviously shaken by East's statement. "Are you referring to the assassinations of federal judges?"

"Yes. Congress failed to impeach judges for overstepping their authority, so now citizens are applying the only remedy available to them."

"Senator, do you agree?"

"I agree with Colonel East's description of events, but I do not agree with assassinations."

"Nor do I," East added.

"Is there a non-violent solution?" Haddley asked.

"If we survive tomorrow, a general recall election is the only solution I can see," Crux replied.

"Do you mean reelecting everyone, the House, Senate and president?"

Crux replied, "Exactly, new elections for every office."

"I agree," East added. "We can follow the procedure developed by the Founding Fathers for the first election, elect senators to staggered terms."

After watching the Sean Haddley show, General Beck decided to place CENTCOM on alert. The chaos in America invited mischief by others, especially jihadis and Iran.

Chapter 67

Rioting began at 1:35 a.m. and quickly spread into the downtown area, where large department stores and upscale shops were the first targets. By dawn, stores had been looted, banks broken into and fires stretched along 16th Street and Connecticut Avenue. Gangs marauded through Georgetown, breaking into townhouses belonging to Washington elitists, doing what they did best—robbing, raping, and killing. According to "Responding to Gang, Crew and Youth Violence in the District of Columbia," a report, commissioned by the D.C. Council in 2009, the District of Columbia was at that time home to about 130 criminal street gangs and smaller crews, whose members are involved in a disproportionate number of the city's homicides. Gang members made up more than sixty percent of the city's homicide suspects and four in every ten of the victims. Now some gang members were armed with al-Qaeda's automatic weapons and police and riot control squads were being outgunned and slaughtered. Needless to say those few gang members who were arrested had no carry permits for their unregistered guns. Federal police surrounded the White House and government buildings; however, gangs had no interest in any of these buildings. No, they were out after loot and killing Crackers.

The first encounter between Take Back America marchers and the military occurred at Chain Bridge. Marchers who'd camped in Fort Marcy Park in Virginia reached the bridge at seven a.m. As the lead vehicle, a truck flying a large Gadsden Flag, approached the bridge, it encountered two army Humvees parked sideways across the road, effectively blocking passage to the bridge. Pulling to a stop before an MP standing in front of the Humvees holding up his hand, the driver of the truck stuck his head out the window and asked, "Is there a problem with the bridge?"

"No sir, the bridge is closed. You'll have to turn around," the young MP responded, suddenly feeling ill at ease when a passenger in the truck, an older, husky looking man, stepped out and walked toward him. Studying the man in detail, the MP saw the older man was wearing: a dark blue NRA Stand and Fight ball cap; a white T-Shirt with a coiled rattlesnake and the words "Don't Tread On Me" printed on it; camo pants and military style boots; and a M1911 .45 caliber pistol in a holster on his right hip.

Coming to a halt in front of the MP, the man asked, "Private, why is this bridge closed?"

"Sir, I don't know. Our orders are to block the bridge."

"Private, I'm a retired master sergeant, so don't bullshit me. By whose order is this bridge closed?"

"Sir, er ... Master Sergeant, I honestly don't know."

"Well, let's both find out. Go get your commanding officer."

Turning toward the Humvees, the MP waved, and a few seconds later a sergeant appeared from around the far side of one of the vehicles.

"What's the problem?" the sergeant asked, walking toward the young MP and giving the civilian standing with him the once over. But before the young man could speak, the older man answered for him.

"No problem ... just a question. Why is this bridge blocked, Sergeant Cramer?" the sergeant major asked, having identified the man by reading his nametag.

"Orders, sir."

"No need to call me 'sir.' I'm retired—a master sergeant, Special Forces; however, the man sitting in the truck behind ours ... well, you'd do well to call him 'sir' ... he's a retired two star.

"Now, back to my question ... why is this bridge closed?"

"As I said, Master Sergeant, orders."

"Fine, I understand, so who's in command?"

"Second Lieutenant Vincent."

"Very well, please get him, if you'd be so kind."

If I'd be so kind, Cramer gritted his teeth ... *he's a sarcastic bastard, but he was also a master sergeant and Special Forces ... better do what he says. Anyway, I don't have the foggiest idea as to why this friggin' bridge is closed. This is the LT's problem.* "I'll get the LT," Cramer said started back toward the Humvees blocking the road.

When Cramer returned with Lieutenant Vincent, the sergeant saw a large group of men wearing camo pants and military style boots—most of them openly carrying side arms—had gathered around the marcher's lead truck.

Lieutenant Vincent also noticed the group's size and began feeling unsure about confronting so many determined looking men. But summoning his courage and feigning a confidence he didn't have, he marched toward the marchers and announced, "THIS BRIDGE IS CLOSED. I'm ordering all of you to turn around and leave."

"*SON*," the retired two star said, the tone of his voice so stern the lieutenant stopped dead in his tracks, "You're not authorized to order U.S. citizens in America to do anything. Now, clear the bridge. *We're coming through.*"

Vincent was about to repeat his order, but after considering the manner in which he'd been addressed, decided he might be speaking to a senior officer. "Sir, we have been ordered to close the bridge. My orders come from the Commander in Chief."

"And what will you do if we refuse to leave and remove your illegal roadblock?" another man in the group asked.

Surrounded by a group of determined looking, armed men, Vincent realized he was in over his head. These men intended to force the roadblock, and they were citizens—probably former military. "Sir, I have orders to fire if necessary."

"You have orders *to fire on civilians* ... on American citizens? Are you serious?" the two star asked.

The lieutenant's statement shocked Sergeant Cramer, who suddenly realized what was at stake. This was the first he'd heard about firing on civilians.

Vincent swallowed, "Sir, ... those are my orders."

"Lieutenant, are you aware you are prohibited from following an illegal order?

"Do you remember the oath you took when you were sworn in as an officer? Part of your oath was to protect the Constitution against all enemies, foreign and domestic. Do you remember saying those words?"

Vincent's confusion was obvious to everyone. "Lieutenant, he is correct. I swore the same oath," Sergeant Cramer said. "I'm an Oath Keeper, and I will not fire on fellow Americans.

"Sir, I respectfully suggest we get the hell out of here."

Vincent didn't know what to do, but he did know he wouldn't order his men to fire on civilians. Without saying another word, he turned, started back toward his vehicles and called out, "MOVE OUT. WE'RE LEAVING."

Within minutes, the column of the Take Back America marchers' vehicles, all flying different flags, streamed across Chain Bridge and turned southeast on Canal Road toward Georgetown.

Similar encounters occurred at the other bridges. One lieutenant ordered his men to fire, but his sergeant refused to obey.

Marchers crossing Key Bridge from Rosslyn were joined by the marchers from Chain Bridge, and quickly encountered police roadblocks preventing them from entering Georgetown. When asked why the roads were blocked, police told Take Back America leaders it was too dangerous for them to precede into the area. Numerous shots had been fired and gangs were still rampaging throughout the neighborhood. "Well," one of the leaders said, "I think we've found our first target."

Pickup trucks with men armed with a variety of rifles and shotguns sped around the surprised policemen and headed north on Wisconsin Avenue. Peeling off into the residential streets, they quickly found gang members looting townhouses. Firefights broke out, and the gangs quickly learned that exchanging fire with experienced men and women, who consistently hit their targets, was nowhere near as much fun as shooting at unarmed, wimpy, progressive-liberals.

Marchers entering the District of Columbia over the 14th Street and East Capitol Street bridges encountered different gangs and immediately engaged them.

Surviving gang members retreated back toward the center of the city where a different type of culture clash occurred. When the remnants of one gang encountered Reverend Scoundrell's marchers, and two hundred Occupiers flying black flags with a large red "A," a violent confrontation occurred. Later, the good reverend's bloody corpse was found along with those of twenty-six white Occupiers who'd been murdered at various locations throughout the Circle's grounds. Scoundrell had been stabbed repeatedly and robbed.

FEMA Corps had used the night to move into blocking positions along I-495, I-95, US-1, MD-295 and US-50—all were major routes leading into the northeast corner of Washington. When Take Back America marchers attempted to force the FEMA roadblocks, they took fire from M2 machine guns. While an ABC helicopter videoed the slaughter at the U.S.

Highway 50 roadblock, NBC and CBS's helicopters quickly moved to cover other FEMA roadblocks and recorded similar scenes.

General Beck's phone rang. It was the Governor of Maryland. "General, are those your men shooting civilians on the Washington beltway?" the governor angrily demanded.

"No, Governor. They are the paramilitary unit from FEMA."

"The same bunch that shot up Vermont?"

"Yes, Governor."

"Can you stop them?"

Beck, who'd expected the call, answered, "Governor, I could if I have any units in striking distance. However, if you release the 104th Fighter Squadron to me, I can use them to put an end to the Blue Shirts— that's what we call them. The 104th is stationed at Warfield Air National Guard Base, Middle River."

Sighing heavily and pausing for several seconds, the governor finally responded, "General, I'll contact my Adjutant General and order him to release the squadron to you. Stop the killing, General ... *Please!*" he pleaded.

"Governor, I'll do so as quickly as possible."

While Beck waited for the transfer orders to be issued, he called the 104th's squadron commander, Lieutenant Colonel Davidson, told him to expect orders placing him under his command, and asked him to arm his A-10s with cluster bombs and rockets for ground attack. Next he told Colonel Collins to contact air traffic control and have the news helicopters pulled back. He didn't want one of their helicopters accidently shot down or to have one collide with an A-10.

Beck's next call was to John Ulrich at Langley AFB, where he learned that General Ulrich was flying an F-22, one of the new stealth fighters invisible to radar, until it opened one of its internal weapons' bays. Beck requested to be patched through to Ulrich.

General Ulrich heard his controller's voice, "Lone Eagle, you have a call from General Beck."

"Acknowledge. Patch him through."

"Lone Eagle, sir. What's up?"

"Lone Eagle, is your bird armed?"

"Yes, air to air. Wanted to be prepared in case we encountered unexpected visitors."

"Good idea. However, you won't be able to assist the A-10s engaging the Blue Shirts—Stay frosty."

Beck had just ended the call when his aide informed him the 104th's squadron commander was on the line.

Punching the blinking button, he answered, "General Beck."

"Sir, I'm under your command, and I have the coordinates for the Blue Shirts. What are your orders?"

"Destroy them with extreme prejudice. Avoid collateral damage if possible, but finish them off. Look for a Humvee flying a flag with three stars. Make sure you get it."

"Yes, sir. Glad to oblige. The Governor is on all local radio channels asking marchers to pull back from the roadblocks."

Chapter 68

Calls to the White House from the major networks and the AP demanding an explanation went unanswered. After several attempts by the president's White House advisers to make him aware of the dangerous situation in Washington, the senior agent of President Abomba's Secret Service detail told the president, "Mr. President it is imperative you leave Washington now—not a moment later."

When Abomba smiled at him and asked why, the exasperated agent said in desperation, "Mr. President, the marchers have broken through, they're in the city. After the slaughter of civilians by FEMA Corps, the marchers are on their way here—to the White House. They will hang you if they catch you. There are too many of them and they're armed. We won't be able to stop them."

"Huh? Marchers? What slaughter?"

"I'll explain later. Marine One is outside and Air Force One is warmed up and ready to take off. I suggest you come with me and board the helicopter before the marchers get here and it's too late."

"Right now?"

"*Yes,* Mr. President, *right now.* Let's go."

Abomba stood, looking around, attempting to process the agent's report. *What about my morning golf game? ... Where should I go?*

"Mr. President, we have to go. *Now,* sir!"

"Oh, all right," Abomba said in disgust. "I don't see any reason to hurry. My Army and FEMA Corps can handle those rebels. But if you insist I have to leave, I'll go to Hawaii earlier than I planned and join the First Lady. I'll stay there till FEMA Corps has things under control."

Unaware that FEMA Corps blue shirts were about to be wiped off the face of the earth, President Abomba reluctantly followed his protection detail across the White House lawn toward Marine One. He'd just reached the stairs to enter when the senior agent stopped him. "Wait, Mr. President,

I've just been informed there are several members of Congress in the Rose Garden who are asking to go with you to Andrews."

"*Damn!* Is there room?"

"Yes, Mr. President."

Just what I don't need, hangers-on, Abomba muttered under his breath, and then huffed, "Well, if there's room, okay. Tell the ingrates to get their lazy asses *onboard*. I have to get out of here," Abomba said over his shoulder as he climbed the stairs.

Seconds later the ingrates, Nellie Balogni, Harold Realdick, Betty Boxnutter, Charles Simmerman, and Dana Finkelstein all bolted up the stairs like Satan himself was chasing them, and Marine One lifted off.

Colonel Davidson led his flight of twelve A-10s toward the FEMA Corps positions. Each pilot had been assigned a target.

The Humvee with the yellow flag and three blue stars had last been seen at the Highway 50 interchange, and the colonel chose it as his target. Davidson was from Vermont and had a score to settle, and now it was the time to do so.

Lieutenant General (self promoted) Savage was standing by his Humvee parked on the I-495 overpass watching one of his Bradleys and two Humvees machine-gunning burning cars and trucks on U.S. Highway 50 below. Savage was elated, a man in his element. In fact he was so elated he totally forgot about the possibility of being attacked by aircraft.

Flying above I-495, Davidson and his wingman were approaching their target from the south. Both pilots saw the Bradleys and Humvees blocking the highway, and the burning cars and trucks littering the road. Davidson concentrated on the I-495 overpass where he saw a man standing beside a parked Humvee flying some kind of flag. A few seconds later, he was close enough to see the man's blue camo uniform. *Ten to one that's Savage. Yep, that's a flag all right and it has three stars ... Gotcha, you ass hole.* Keying his mike he told his wingman, "Farm Boy, take the targets on the highway. I've got the overpass."

"Click." Farm Boy acknowledged his order by clicking his mike and selected cluster bombs.

Davidson selected the 30mm cannon in the nose of his Warthog, the nickname for A-10s. Lining up on his target, Davidson placed his sight behind the Humvee and depressed the trigger button. A stream of 30mm high explosive shells impacted the road ten meters behind the Humvee and quickly walked over it.

Savage's peripheral vision had seen a flash in the sky. Turning and looking up in time to see the flame plume erupt from the nose of an aircraft, he instantly recognized it as a Warthog. It would be the last thing he'd ever see.

Marine One landed near Air Force One at Joint Base Andrews and everyone prepared to deplane. While the president and his lead secret service agent headed for Air Force One, Nellie and the other's waited for confirmation on the location of her plane. When told her airplane wasn't there, Nellie went into a tailspin.

"MR. PRESIDENT ... BARRY, *WAIT!*" she yelled at Abomba who was walking rapidly toward Air Force One. Running after him with her arms extended and waving with both hands, she screamed, "**MR. PRESIDENT! WAIT! PLEASE WAIT!**"

Catching up with him, as he was about to start up the stairs, she grabbed hold of his coattail and pleaded, "I don't have a plane. Can we go with you?"

"*WHAT?*" Abomba exclaimed, whirling around and swatting her hand away; so self absorbed, he'd hardly heard a word she'd said. "Why do you want to come with *me*? I'm going to Hawaii." *The last thing I want is to spend the next eleven hours listening to you whine. Damn ... I usually have time to practice my putting while we're flying—Oh my god! I'll bet they left my golf clubs back at the White House ... and I don't have time to send the helicopter back to get them. Damn!*

"*BARRY, WAIT FOR US,*" Finkelstein squalled, gasping as she stumbled to a stop behind Balogni. She and the others had seen Balogni closing in on the president near Air Force One and run after her.

"Oh my god," Abomba said, finally noticing the disheveled ingrates. "What the hell are *you* doing here ... and what's wrong with him?" he asked pointing at Realdick, who was doubled over panting, clutching his stomach with his hands.

"Barry," Finkelstein said, gasping, "Nellie's plane isn't here. We were going to fly with her but now ... we have no way to leave, and—we have to get out of Washington too. Can we go with you?"

"*What?* I'm going to Hawaii."

"Hawaii sounds good."

"Oh, hell," Abomba muttered, still fretting over his golf clubs. *I don't want to spend any more time with these ingrates than I have to. None of them will be of any use to me when I return. Once FEMA takes control of things, I won't need them anymore. I'll be running the show, and I don't want them anywhere near the White House. For that matter, why will I need Congress?*

Abomba looked at the bedraggled group and shook his head, *Just what I don't need on a long flight ... but on the other hand, they may still be useful until all the loose ends are tied up.* Frowning before turning and skipping up the stairs, he huffed, "All right, come on board, but don't bother me once we're in the air ... got a lotta stuff happening in Washington ... have to keep up with things. So don't get in my way."

After entering the aircraft, he stopped and waited for them to reach the top of the boarding stairs. When they did he said, "Oh, you'll have to make your own arrangements for accommodations when we arrive, and transportation back to the mainland. The First Lady won't want you hanging around our house, and I know she won't want you on board our plane when we return. She can't stand all the distractions."

It's bad enough she gripes about having to put up with the kid's roughhousing with that stinking pooch while we're vacationing—Oh my god! THE DOG ... I forgot about Beau. The First Lady told me to make arrangements to bring him—Oh, no, that Marine thing ... the thing with the tilt engines—it won't be able to fly to Hawaii, will it? Yeah, I'm going to catch hell for this, he groaned.

Looking for somebody to blame for his mistakes, he zeroed in on the senior Secret Service agent, "You did get my golf clubs—didn't you ... and the dog?"

"No, Mr. President. There wasn't time."

"Did any of you see the dog?" Abomba asked the ingrates.

"No, Mr. President, I don't think they got the dog," Nellie responded moving past the president to find a seat. "He was standing on the Rose Garden's portico wagging his tail when we left," she said over her shoulder.

"I don't give a rat's ass about the damn dog. He can fly out later. WHAT ABOUT MY CLUBS? Abomba stormed, glaring at the senior agent.

"Well sir ... there really wasn't time to—"

"Do something," the president snarled. "Get them on another plane and—"

"Excuse me Mr. President," the communication sergeant interrupted, hurrying up to the president. "Urgent message."

"What! What the hell do *you* want? Can't you see I'm busy?

"Sorry, Mr. President, but this is very important. We've just received a message that Air Force A-10s are bombing FEMA Corps roadblocks."

"WHAT? ... Who the hell told them to do that?"

"I don't know, Mr. President. The message didn't say," the sergeant said, cowering away from the president.

"Don't just stand there, you idiot ... find out—and ... and order them to stop!"

"Sir, I don't have the autho—"

"I'M ORDERING THEM TO STOP! Abomba raved his eyes bulging and shaking his finger in the sergeant's face.

"I'm going to have whoever gave that order PROSECU ... er, arrested ... er ... WHAT THE HELL DO YOU CALL IT?" he demanded, turning to the senior agent.

"Court-martialed, Mr. President," the bewildered sergeant muttered.

"Yeah, COURT-MARTIALED ... that's it," Abomba yelled, whipping his head around to look at the sergeant.

"Yeah ... that's what I'm gonna do," he mumbled, squinting and trying to remember what it was he was going to order the senior agent to do.

Take Back America marchers soon discovered that most of their targets had fled, however there are always those who didn't get the memo. Building security guards were quickly overpowered and the marchers stormed into their target buildings. The EPA Administrator, the Secretary of Energy, and the Secretary of Homeland Security were still in their offices, and the Secretary of Health and Human Services was found cowering in the underground garage. Three Supreme Court justices were also caught. All were restrained and taken to a nearby park to be dealt with later.

In the heat of the moment, many marchers argued for Incompentado and the Supreme Court Justices to be hung, and the EPA Administrator and Secretaries of Energy and HHS tied to trees and whipped with belts. Fortunately, cooler heads prevailed.

After several minutes of heated discussion, Take Back America's leaders decided that a court would be formed and a jury of twelve men and women selected. The trial would be held in the park across the street from the White House; thereby proving the American justice system was still revered even in the midst of the rebellion.

With the hated EPA administrator in their custody, the marchers set about destroying most of EPA's equipment and records. The Energy Department's Renewable Energy Division suffered a similar fate. Employees of HHS and the Veterans Administration all received harsh treatment, as did IRS employees. Several IRS employees responsible for healthcare—more accurately stated "non-healthcare"—and for releasing millions of personal records—including social security numbers—suffered the similar fate as the policeman in Temple, Texas. The world watched as they were paraded, with ropes around their necks, behind a truck circling the mall.

When the media broke the news President Abomba had fled Washington on Air Force One, Take Back America marchers went ballistic. As did the men and women in the military when they learned of the president's orders to fire on civilians. But their anger went off the chart when the media broadcast news of FEMA Corps firing on civilians with heavy machine guns. Next came news Abomba was issuing orders from Air Force One to arrest any military commander who'd refused or interfered with the commission of the president's orders to stop the rebels. In particular, Abomba had ordered the arrest of whoever ordered the Air Force A-10s to bomb FEMA Corps roadblocks. It seemed as though a civil war was inevitable. Conservatives and the military were rebelling against the president's dictatorial orders, while progressive-liberals rallied around him.

Brigadier General John Ulrich had been listening to the chatter on the command nets. When he learned the president had ordered the arrest of every officer at CENTCOM, he felt like a dark cloud had descended over him. *What has happened to my country?* he mourned, and without conscious thought climbed to 52,000 feet.

President Abomba was in his on-board office brooding. Everything was going wrong and it seemed as though everyone was against him. His Security agents had left his golf clubs, and he was sure to catch hell for leaving the dog. Worse still, he had no idea where Barrett was. *Of all times for her to disappear ... for all I know she's in cahoots with those bastards at CENTCOM. Yeah that's right, she's even sleeping with one of them. Oh, what the hell, she needs to go anyway. She's served her purpose. I don't need her anymore, however I do need a Cabinet. Maybe I'd better rethink getting rid of all the ingrates on board.* Abomba grinned. *Guess things do work out after all. Thanks to that bird-brained Nellie, I have her*

and Realdick—Boxnutter, Simmerman and Finkelstein too—on board.
Yeah, that's what I'll do. I'll have them prepare a list of new Cabinet
members. Washington's all torn up; so I'll move my capital and my stuff to
Honolulu for a while. First though, I'll have my security guys send my
stuff—my golf clubs and basketballs ... oh, yeah, and the damn dog too.

Brigadier General John Ulrich snapped out of his dark thoughts.
Turning to the west he accelerated to mach 1.5. *This has to end. If not,*
there will be a second civil war. A few minutes later he saw what must be a
large airplane with two smaller planes close to it on his display. Switching
off his radio, he concentrated on flying as his F22 rapidly streaked
westward. Thirty minutes later his display indicated the three planes were
ninety-five miles ahead at 36,000 feet.

Ulrich set his radio to the international emergency channel, and then
eased the F22's nose down. He'd made his decision. *As long as Abomba is*
alive, the civil war he's started will continue until it destroys America.
There's only one way to put an end to it.

Ten minutes later he turned on his targeting radar and armed his
weapons. Then, selecting four AIM 120D AMRAAM air-to-air missiles, he
locked them on the large aircraft and reduced speed.

When he was thirty miles behind his target, he keyed his mike, and
said, "This is Lone Eagle. What I am about to do, I do for God and country.
May God have mercy on my soul," and then pressed the firing button. The
center internal weapons bay opened and the launcher trapeze extended the
missiles into the air stream. In less than two seconds, four 3.6 meter-long
missiles with 18.5 kg warheads left the launcher and streaked toward Air
Force One.

As soon as the last AMRAAM left the launcher, the trapeze assembly
withdrew the bay closed, making the F22 stealthy again. Switching to AIM
9X Sidewinders, Ulrich pushed his throttles forward, rapidly accelerating to
mach 1.5.

Air Force One's onboard threat defense system detected the
missile launches and instantly fired chaff cartridges and IR flares. The pilot
saw the threat alarm and began defensive maneuvers. Traveling at mach
four, the first AMRAAM took the bait and detonated in a chaff cloud, as
did the second missile. The third AMRAAM detonated near the tail,
damaging the Boeing's hydraulics, and the fourth found the outboard port
engine.

Closing to eight miles, Ulrich launched two Sidewinder heat-seeking missiles from the starboard missile bay; and then, switching to guns, he pulled back on the throttles and followed the Sidewinders toward his target. One Sidewinder found the inboard port engine and detonated in the exhaust manifold. The second found the starboard outboard engine.

Placing his gun sight on Air Force One, Ulrich depressed the fire button, driving most of his 480 high explosive 20mm round into the aircraft's fuselage. Keeping his site on the burning aircraft, he pushed his throttles to the stop and drove his F22 into the wing root of Air Force One's mangled remains.

Chapter 69

Sky over West Virginia
Friday, May 24, 2016

The lead pilot of the two F-16 fighters escorting Air Force One had instantly reacted when his threat detector indicated inbound missiles. Since his radar didn't show any aircraft in the area, he initially thought it was a false alarm. Then Air Force One's countermeasure suite activated and ejected chaff and flare cartridges.

Keying his mike he said, "Execute Gamma," and pulled a maximum G 180° turn to face the yet unseen threat. As his F-16 completed its turn, he saw missile trails coming from a black speck, a speck that did not appear on his radar. The speck rapidly grew into an F-22 fighter launching two more missiles. As the F22 flashed past him the pilot saw a plume of flame coming out its right wing root.

The second F-16 had inverted and then dived, looking for a SAM. Completing a 360° loop, he came up behind Air Force One in time to see the F-22 impact the right wing root of the burning Boeing 747. Keying his mike, he reported on a scrambled frequency, "Air Force One attacked and destroyed by F-22. High probability Golfer is dead. Repeat, high probability Golfer is dead. Nobody on the plane could survive."

Air traffic control was tracking Air Force One and its two escorts when suddenly a voice broke into the net, "This is Lone Eagle. What I am about to do, I do for God and country. May God have mercy on my soul."

"Who the hell said that?" the controller exclaimed, looking around to see if someone had spoken near him.

A few seconds later he saw a blip indicating a small object appear on his screen, thirty miles east of Air Force One, quickly followed by four more small blips moving westward at an impossible speed. *"OH, NO!* he exclaimed, looking for his supervisor. When he looked back at his screen the first small blip was gone.

And then the two fighters escorting Air Force One suddenly broke off.

"Oh, my God ... Air Force One!" the controller gasped, quickly sounding the alarm as the four objects closed on the president's plane. "Where did they come from?"

Alerted by the controller's cry, his supervisor and other controllers watched in horror as two more missiles appeared. "Look, Air Force One must have been struck. It's turning south, losing altitude and breaking up into small objects," the controller said, raw emotion evident in his voice. "God help us, the President's plane exploded. No one could survive a crash from that altitude. Everyone on board is dead."

FOX News was the first to break the alert with a flashing banner, "President's plane explodes at high altitude over Ohio. No survivors are expected."

CBS was the first to obtain a copy of Lone Eagle's message, but it would be days before Lone Eagle was identified.

The tragic news put an end to the Take Back America marcher's activities. They, like the rest of the nation, began asking what does this mean? Who's in charge?

The Secret Service located Vice President John Blabberman, who was now POTUS, President of the United States, and announced, "Joker secured ... repeat, Joker secured."

President John Blabberman was sworn in at 6:14 p.m. by a district judge in the Green Room at the White House. America wondered if he was capable. Foreign governments wondered if any of their secrets would still be secret by the end of June.

Senator Crux took the spotlight, calling for calm. "It must now be obvious to the world that American patriots will not allow progressive-liberals to continue to trash our Constitution and impose their Socialist philosophy on our nation. We are experiencing a revolution ... and we are on the verge of a civil war.

"Blood has been spilt. If progressive-liberals don't admit their mistakes and quit trying to *change* America by fiat and judicial legislation, I fear a civil war will occur, and when it ends, only one side will survive.

"Our first civil war was brutal. This one will be worse."

Epilog

As we write the final chapter of this story, the Labor Day Weekend of 2013 has begun. Liberals are still calling for more gun control laws even though Congress has refused to pass most of their bills. Our president continues to issue Executive Orders that infringe on the Second Amendment and Congress' authority, with no pushback from the liberal Democrat controlled Senate.

Some events described in this story with specific dates are real. Others are products of our imagination. We meant this to be a serious work of fiction, but over time it morphed into more of a satire. As we labor through the editing process, more events are occurring that could be included in the story. The temptation to add more chapters is great, but if we do we will never finish.

The attack on the U.S. Embassy in Baghdad is a product of our imagination; however on September 6, 2013 *The Wall Street Journal* reported, " 'The U.S. has intercepted an order from Iran to militants in Iraq to attack the U.S. Embassy and other American interests in Baghdad in the event of a strike on Syria,' officials said, amid an expanding array of reprisal threats across the region."

Our purpose in telling this tale is to show one possible future, not a future we want, and certainly a future we hope can be a voided. It is our further hope that what we have imagined will cause the reader to consider that, though written as fiction, our story could become reality. We hope the scenarios we have created will spark discussions and debate.

The foundation of our great Republic is our Constitution, which can only be changed by amendment or by a Constitutional Convention. The Constitution cannot be changed by the president, or the Congress, or the courts—including the Supreme Court.

We purposely left our story with a "Lady or the Tiger" ending. There will be no sequel.

America's success is built entirely on the bedrock of our Constitution. It is what makes America unique among all the previous great nations. Move away from its bedrock, its Constitution, and America will become one more name on history's list of failed nations.

We have based some of the events in our story on real or similar events, and in some cases provided details of the real event in order to set the stage. Two examples are: (1) Army Master Sgt. Christopher Grisham, who was charged with misdemeanor interference with the duties of a police officer for "rudely displaying a weapon" in Temple, Texas* and the subsequent "Come and Take It" rally**; and (2) the Trayvon Martin - George Zimmerman trial. We wrote the "come and take it" story in Chapter 27 months before the real "Come and Take It San Antonio!" occurred on October 18, 2013.

New York City authorities have been sending out notices to residents who own guns, which now violate new ammunition capability laws, demanding they relinquish their weapons—and even though the notifications may just be standard police procedure, the text is a shocker.*** One such notice to a city resident, dated November 18, 2013 and posted on *The Blaze*, reads: "Immediately surrender your rifle and/or shotgun to your local police precinct, and notify this office of the invoice number. The firearm may be sold or permanently removed from the City of New York thereafter. Permanently remove your rifle and/or shotgun from New York City." This real event is similar to a story line begun at the end of Chapter 7.

The town of Mudford, Alabama exists only in the authors' minds and is meant to represent any patriotic American town or small city.

* http://www.youtube.com/watch?feature=player_embedded&v=A8r4MK3R4PI

** http://fishgame.com/gunnews/?p=2240

*** http://www.washingtontimes.com/news/2013/nov/28/nyc-alarms-notice-immediately-surrender-your-rifle/#ixzz2mPtBQz7A

About the Authors

 With his Nuclear Engineering Degree from North Carolina State, his three years service in the U.S. Army as an explosive ordnance disposal (EOD) officer, assigned to the Defense Atomic Support Agency (DASA), Sandia Base (now part of Kirkland AFB), Albuquerque New Mexico, and his ordnance design and development experience in the defense industry, Lee Boyland is well qualified to write about all types of weapons: nuclear, chemical, biological, and conventional. DASA controlled the development and stockpiling of all nuclear and thermonuclear weapons, providing Lieutenant Boyland access to the design details of every nuclear and thermonuclear warhead developed by the United States up to the Mark 63 warhead. His primary assignment was the DASA Nuclear Emergency Team, responsible for nuclear weapons accidents and incidents. Other duties included providing bomb disposal support to the local authorities, participating in tests at the Nevada Test Site, and teaching training courses provided by DASA.

After three years of active duty, Lee spent the next thirteen years designing conventional and special ordnance for the defense industry. During this time he participated in developing programs: to apply aerospace combustion technology to the incineration of Agent Orange for the Air Force; and to demilitarize chemical weapons at Rocky Mountain Arsenal and Tooele Army Depot for the Army. Later he transitioned into the hazardous waste industry and started the first full service medical waste management company in the Midwest. As a member of a U.S. technology exchange team on the management of biohazards, he traveled to Shanghai, Beijing, and Tianjin China in 2003 during the SARS outbreak.

Lee and his wife and co-author, Vista, live in Florida where he consults in waste management and writes. His published works include technical articles, a chapter in the *Biohazards Management Handbook*, and the *Occupational Exposure to Bloodborne Pathogens Training Series* marketed by Fisher Scientific.

Education and training:
North Carolina State University, BS Nuclear Engineering
Commissioned Second Lieutenant U.S. Army Ordnance Corps
U.S. Naval School, Explosive Ordnance Disposal
U.S. Naval School, Nuclear Weapons Disposal
Defense Atomic Support Agency, tri-service Nuclear Emergency Management
U.S. Army Ammunition and Explosive Safety Course
U.S. Army, Advanced Chemical Weapons, Dugway Proving Ground

A North Carolina native, Vista met and married Lee Boyland in Raleigh N.C. in 1961, while both were attending college: she majoring in classical vocal music performance at St. Mary's Jr. College, and he in nuclear engineering at N.C. State. After college, while Lee served as an Army EOD officer, Sandia Base Albuquerque, N.M., Vista performed with the Bel Canto Singers, a local coral ensemble, and kept busy managing their home and mothering their daughter Karen who was born in 1964.

While Lee began a career in the defense industry, Vista resumed her interest in solo performing: singing in recitals, chorales, and opera ensembles at prestigious venues such as Washington, DC's Constitution Hall, the Kennedy Center, and the National Cathedral; and acting in a variety of theatrical productions. While living in the DC area she returned to college to pursue a degree in applied fine arts at Northern Virginia Community College. Elected to Who's Who Among Students in American Jr. Colleges, she graduated Suma Cum Laude in 1974 with an AA in Applied Fine Arts.

While living in St. Louis, MO., Vista revived her interest in theater by founding *Theater West,* a drama school and community theater; and developed clientele as a freelance fine artist and author: rendering illustrations for the Missouri Conservation Commission, Washington University's, Tyson Research Center, St. Louis' Westport Playhouse; and writing feature articles for Missouri Life Magazine and Liguorian Press.

Moving to Florida in 1990, Vista joined the Space Coast Artist Association, where she taught mix-media drawing and won honors for her illustrations. In the aftermath of 9/11, Lee, long concerned about a nuclear attack on America, wrote his first award winning novel, *The Rings of Allah* with Vista editing. Realizing the book begged for a sequel, the Boyland's co-authored the award winning Clash of Civilizations trilogy, and the rest is history. By melding their mutual interests and varied life experiences—Lee's remarkable grasp of geo-political history and Vista's knowledge of script writing and stage craft—they have written five imaginative, informative novels filled humor, memorable characters and plots that are both entertaining and profoundly meaningful.

Coming in 2015

Triple Threat

We stopped writing *Triple Threat* and turned our efforts to writing this book, *Revolution 2016*, leaving Julian and Teresa in London. Now it is our intention to return to our series and see how much trouble we can get the OAS gang into. Yes, Erica and Melisa will be back too, and the three women are definitely triple trouble. We are providing the first chapter, picking up the story where *Pirates and Cartels* ended.

Chapter 1

Ciudad Juarez
3 p.m., Friday, September 29th

Vicente Carrillo Fuentes, kingpin of the Juàrez Cartel, had been pacing in circles on his patio for two hours. Stopping long enough to light his umpteenth cigarette, a Phillip Morris *Faro,* and fighting a rising tide of fury, Fuentes glared at his cell phone lying on a nearby table. For the last hour he'd battled the urge to snatch up the phone and call the general, while at the same time willing the damn thing to ring. *I should have heard from General Santillan—Raphael—as the idiot insists I call him. The assassination should have taken place by now. What the hell's he waiting for. I need confirmation,* Fuentes fumed, flinging his cigarette stub on the ground and reaching for his phone. His fingers were about to close on the phone when a new revelation struck him.

"Damn!" he exclaimed, jerking his hand back and sneering at the phone. *Yeah, that's it. The SOB's letting me squirm ... so he can hit me up for more money.* "Fuck that and fuck him!" he snorted, continuing to seethe as he lit another *Faro* and stomped away from the table. He'd just resumed pacing when the buzzing phone sent him rushing back to the table. Snatching up the instrument, he checked caller ID.

It was *El Teo. Damn ... now this idiot will want to know what's happened.* "*Buenos dias,* Teodoro," he answered through clinched teeth, stifling his annoyance.

"Is it done?" *El Teo* demanded.

Fuentes scowled, for he despised Teodoro Garcia, the sneaking traitor who'd been trying to take over the Sinaloa Cartel's leadership. Something Fuentes himself had been scheming to do, ever since the cartel's former kingpin, *El Chapo,* mysteriously disappeared following a shootout at the Monterey Holiday Inn. *I have to humor the SOB for a little while longer,* Fuentes sneered, *after all ... he did pay for President Wolf's assassination—though he doesn't know it.*

"No word yet, *Teo.* I'm sure everything is on schedule. I will let you know as soon as I get word. Keep listening to the news. The media is sure to cover the event," Fuentes snapped, breaking the connection before *El Teo* could say something he shouldn't. *Santillan is right about talking on the phone. You never know who might be listening to your calls.*

Still frustrated and growing increasingly panic-stricken, Fuentes snapped the damnable phone shut and growled in disgust. He was about to resume pacing, when, unable to stand the suspense, he threw caution to the wind and flipped the phone back open. "To hell with it," he muttered and punched Raphael's speed dial number. Then, holding his breath, he listened expectantly, hoping desperately to hear the general's voice answer, but instead hearing nothing but repetitious ringing—over and over and over. Finally, disgusted and resigned to the fact something was terribly wrong, he punched the END button and tossed the phone back on the table.

Lieutenant Commander Leroy Culberson and Captain Erica Borgg were riding in the rear passenger seat of a white SUV en route to Mexico City—an hour out from the site of their most recent mission at *Casa de las Estrellas,* a hacienda on a large estate near Oaxaca, in Southwestern Mexico. A leather case containing the personal belongings of General Jorge Heriberto Santillan, the recently deceased chief of staff of Mexico's Air Force, lay open on the seat between them.

Borgg had identified the case as belonging to the general while helping sanitize the *casa.* Additional personal items removed from the general's corpse, including a cell phone, had been hurriedly crammed in the case just before they left the hacienda. Now that she and Culberson had some down time, they'd decided to examine the contents of the case, in the event it might contain things pertinent to their mission. Other than agenda papers related to President Wolf's meeting, nothing of consequence drew their attention—that was, until Santillan's phone startled both of them by suddenly ringing. Reaching to pick it up, Culberson was about to answer when Borgg signaled him to stop. "Wait ... let it ring. It may be a co-conspirator calling. Check caller ID."

"The display says someone named José is calling," he said, turning the phone so Erica could see and giving her a look that asked—Do you know who he is?

"The call's from a José," Borgg replied loud enough for Second Lieutenant Melissa Adams, who was driving, and Navy Lieutenant Pete Duncan in the front passenger's seat to hear. "I never heard of him. Melissa, do you recognize the name?"

"No, but I'll bet Teresa would."

"Yeah, your probably right, but she's on the plane and out of touch," Borgg said, as the phone continued ringing. When it finally stopped, she turned to Culberson, "See if José's number is recorded in the Missed Call log," she suggested.

"Yeah, good idea," Culberson grunted as he checked the log. "Here it is," he said, showing her the number on the display.

Borgg studied the number for several seconds in silence. "Aha ... I just remembered something," she finally said, removing her secure AuthenTec cell phone from her bag. "Teresa gave me the number of a Sergeant Lucas at Fort Huachuca who's cleared for the operation. I'll bet he can help identify this guy. I'll call him and ask him to check out José," she added, as she began searching the directory for Lucas' number.

9th U.S. Army Signal Command
Fort Huachuca, AZ
Friday afternoon Friday, September 29th

Staff Sergeant Lee Lucas studied the caller ID on his ringing desk phone. The display read KATANA QUEEN and indicated the call originated from a secure AuthenTec cell phone similar to the ones being used by OAS personnel. *Hmmm, I wonder who this is?* Picking up the receiver he tentatively answered, "Sergeant Lucas here."

"Good afternoon, Sergeant. I'm Captain Erica Borgg, my partner and I are on our way from Oaxaca to Mexico City. Special Agent Teresa Lopez gave me your number. We are working for Major Taylor."

Lucas frowned. *Who the hell is Captain Erica Borgg?* "Yes, ma'am. What can I do for you?"

Borgg sensed the hesitancy in Lucas's voice. "I know you're aware of events related to the Oaxaca meeting. We were members of secret security detail there and things got rather dicey. The principals had to leave quickly and are currently out of contact flying to their home base. We are in possession of a cell phone belonging to *Raphael,* who just received a call from José. We need to know who José is. Grab a pencil and I'll give you both the generals' and José's numbers."

Lucus immediately recognized Raphael's. "Interesting ... Captain, how did *you* get possession of the *general's* cell phone?"

Borgg laughed, "Very good, Sergeant. To answer your question, he had a run-in with my partner and, uh ... no longer has any need for it."

Lucas sat back in his chair, putting the pieces together. *There were two women Deltas on the mission ... a couple of SEALS too. I'll bet they're the same ones who took part in the Casa Miedo raid to free that kidnapped American couple. That explains Katana Queen. I'll be damned.* "Captain, my niece is going to join Delta Phi sorority. Know anything about it?"

Borgg chuckled, "Oh yeah, it's a great sorority. We like to call ourselves Deltas. My *sister* and I are going scuba diving with a couple of guys we met at a lake party. Too bad you can't join us."

Now it was Lucas' turn to laugh. "Yes ma'am. I'd sure like that, but my current job is getting way too *intriguing* ... get to talk all kinds of *interesting* people. I'll get right on these numbers for you ... be in touch."

Fuentes gave up pacing, grabbed his phone, and hurried inside to his study to see if there was any news on TV. Flopping in his plush office chair he grabbed the remote, punched in the news channel's number and gasped. For flashing on the screen was a breaking-news alert, "*CONFERENCIA DE PRENSA DE LA PRESIDENCIA*," accompanied by the voice of an excited news anchor.

"*¡Atención! ¡Atención!* Stay tuned for a forthcoming presidential news conference at Mexico City's International Airport.

"*WHAT!*" Fuentes screamed, jumping to his feet.

"We have just received word from *Los Pinos* (The Mexican White House) that President Wolf will make an important announcement ..."

"The bastard's still alive," Fuentes hissed, gaping at the TV in disbelief, as the reporter prattled on, " ... after his plane lands later this afternoon..."

Vicente Fuentes' blood turned to ice.

Watch our Website for more details

www.LeeBoylandBooks.com

CPSIA information can be obtained at www.ICGtesting.com
Printed in the USA
LVOW06s1006280214

375537LV00001B/242/P